VINIUM
A Silver Ships Novel

S. H. JUCHA

Published by Hannon Books, Inc.
www.scottjucha.com

ISBN: 978-0-9994928-0-2 (e-book)
ISBN: 978-0-9994928-1-9 (softcover)

First Edition: November 2017

Cover design: Damon Za

Acknowledgments

Vinium is the tenth book in *The Silver Ships* series. I wish to extend a special thanks to my independent editor, Joni Wilson, whose efforts enabled the finished product. To my proofreaders, Abiola Streete, Dr. Jan Hamilton, David Melvin, Ron Critchfield, Pat Bailey, Mykola Dolgalov, and Lucy Kelleher, I offer my sincere thanks for their support. Despite the assistance I've received from others, all errors are mine.

Glossary

A glossary is located at the end of the book.

-1-
Negotiations

"The fleet is stationary. We're receiving the *Vivian*'s telemetry," Svetlana Valenko, the captain of the Trident warship, OS *Liberator*, announced.

The Omnian squadron had emerged outside the system that the SADEs, self-aware digital entities, had named Vinium. The Omnians were intent on rescuing one of their scout ships, the *Vivian*, which had been captured by a Vinian warship.

To be accurate, the two ships, Vinian and Omnian, had captured each other. The warship held the scout ship tightly tethered, and the scout ship, crewed by three SADEs, had shut down the flight control systems of the Vinian vessel. The pair were trapped together in a wide, circular orbit around the Vinian system.

Neither ship had done anything remotely aggressive after achieving the initial impasse. For nearly a month, the ships had been stuck together, while each side considered their options.

"Greetings, Alex," came the voice of Killian, the scout ship leader, over the *Liberator*'s bridge speakers. "We've been eagerly awaiting your arrival."

Alex Racine, leader of the Omnian forces, couldn't resist a smile at the calm announcement of the *Vivian*'s SADE.

"Have you been enjoying your tour of the Vinian system, Killian?" Alex asked.

"The early moments proved fascinating, Alex," Killian replied, "but it's the consensus of those aboard that we are ready to come home."

"We'll see what we can do about that, Killian," Alex replied.

Someone less familiar with SADEs might have urged Killian to be patient, but Alex, the human most intimately involved with the entities he helped to free from their boxes, felt no such compunction.

<Killian, your confidence that Alex Racine would come for us defied significant probabilities,> Bethley, the second-positioned SADE in the *Vivian* sent to him via private comm. <Yet, you've been proven correct.>

<There is logic, Bethley, and then there are humans,> Killian sent in reply.

<Alex, we're receiving the memory core dump from the *Vivian*,> Julien, Alex's crystal friend, signaled.

<Understood,> Alex replied via his implant. The tiny comm and data storage device within the human cerebrum allowed a multitude of capabilities, including private communications with other humans and the SADEs.

"Killian, Bethley, and Trium," Alex said, addressing the three SADEs wedged into the tiny scout craft, "please give us your assessment of what we face."

"Forgive my general characterization, Alex, but we face a most unusual situation," Killian replied. "These entities are definitely floral-based but with faunal characteristics. We have nothing in our historical data that enables a comparison."

"We can tell you, Alex, that our attempts at communications have yielded little information," Bethley added. "But we've gleaned some information on Vinian behaviors and the ship environment."

"Such as?" Alex queried.

"We're speaking, using arbitrary names for the aspects of these individuals, mind you, Dassata," Trium, the third-positioned SADE in the scout ship, added. He was using Alex's Dischnya name, which meant peacemaker. "The terminal pod of an individual acts as the head, and we refer to it as the bloom. It has no facial details, no eyes, nose, mouth, or ears."

"Their life processes must be plant-based," Julien surmised, having quickly perused the data accumulated on the warship by the *Vivian*, as every SADE aboard the flagship had done.

"Precisely, Ser," Trium agreed. "We managed to link with their vid system, without opening the warship's flight controls, and have been able to monitor much of their daily cycles."

"We discovered," Killian explained, "that when they converse, the blooms turn toward each other, but that might simply be a courtesy."

"But how are they communicating?" Admiral Tatia Tachenko asked.

"Unknown, Admiral," Killian replied.

"Best guess?" Alex asked, knowing full well that it took a SADE several years after release from confinement to be comfortable responding to that quintessential human expression. However, Alex had worked closely with Killian, while the SADE managed the buildout of the Sardi-Tallen Orbital Platform at Omnia.

"We believe, Alex, that they're using sonic waves or light frequencies outside the scope of human detection, but we've nothing to confirm that," Killian replied. "It would require a SADE to be in their presence to determine the Vinians' communications process."

"Wonderful," Tatia grumped. "We're supposed to negotiate with a plant species that doesn't communicate in any manner we can hear or see. What are you two grinning about?" she asked, looking between Alex and Julien.

"I'd imagine it's the challenge," Commodore Reiko Shimada posited. "After solving the dilemma of how to communicate with two alien species, these two are excited by a fresh opportunity."

"Sers, what else can you tell us about the Vinians' habits?" Alex asked, refusing to rise to Reiko's teasing.

"You get a sense of a Vinian's reactions by the opening and closing of the petals that ring the blooms and the generous-sized leaves along the stalks," Bethley said. "But we have no lexicon to translate any of these motions."

"A small but significant fact," Trium added, "is that the individuals remain inactive for extended periods of time in a space that's extremely bright. We estimate they're using the light for photosynthesis. Interestingly, they stand in a shallow liquid during this time."

Julien caught Alex's eye and sent a private message. <Alex, you'll recall that one of your suggestions on Sawa, as a means of decorating my new avatar, was that it could be covered in leaves. Where do those thoughts originate?>

<As if I knew that we'd find a species like this?> Alex shot back.

Because you're prescient, in some manner, and refuse to admit it, Julien thought.

Alex was dubious about the origins of the strange thoughts he occasionally had, which seemed to manifest themselves in future events. It did occur to him that the biotic-based minds of humans might have a capability that the crystal minds of SADEs would never possess.

While Alex continued to probe the SADEs for more information about the Vinians, Tatia communicated privately with Reiko, Z, and Miranda.

Z and Miranda, SADEs and close confidants of Alex, were busy plotting the course of the Vinian warship, and they shared their analysis with Tatia and Reiko.

<Fortune favors the expedition, Admiral,> Z sent. <The pair of locked ships are on approach to our position.>

<What's our exposure out here?> Reiko asked.

Tatia was paying close attention to her commodore's communications. Reiko was the only officer with experience commanding a squadron of warships in battle, having been a member of the United Earth naval forces. It had been Reiko's recommendation to wait outside the system, not only to buy time for Alex to assess the situation but to determine the Vinian warship's armament.

<An astute question, dear,> Miranda Leyton replied. <A review of the *Vivian*'s data indicates that the local warships responded quite slowly to the scout ship's initial entry. We surmise that this civilization is relegated to traveling within the system and handles communications and data transfer at the customary speed of electromagnetic frequency transmission.>

<Anticipating your next question, Commodore,> Z added, <the Vinian warship will detect our arrival in the next 5.45 hours.>

<If we wait to intercept the two ships until we have a minimal intrusion time into the system, when would that occur?> Tatia asked.

<Admiral, that opportunity would take place 0.5072 hours from now and require employing maximum acceleration of our gravity drives,> Z replied.

<Z,> Miranda sent privately, <as much as thoughts of you continually warm my kernel, it would have been sufficient to have told the admiral that she should launch the squadron in a half hour to meet her goal.>

<And, as much as your presence fulfills me, Miranda, precision will always be a part of my nature,> Z sent in reply.

Tatia refocused on Alex's bridge conversation in time to hear Trium hypothesize that the Vinians were relegated to traveling within the system, repeating what she learned, moments ago, from Z and Miranda.

"Alex, the ships are on approach now," Tatia said, interrupting the conversation. "According to Z and Miranda, if we launch within the next half hour, we can intercept the two ships as they pass in front of us."

"But would a fleet of Tridents rushing at the Vinian warship panic them?" Renée de Guirnon, Alex's partner, asked. "And if it did, what would they do?"

"Killian, what are your thoughts on the danger you might face if our ships approach the Vinian warship?"

"Alex, we believe the Vinians didn't perceive our scout ship as a threat, which is why we were captured. If they wished, they could have released us, at any time, and fired on us before we could have cleared their immediate space. Undoubtedly, our ship would have been either disabled or destroyed."

"Alex, there are small to moderate ports down the sides of the Vinian warship that hide what we believe to be armament," Bethley added. "We had a glimpse of them before we were captured, but we have been unable to deduce any meaningful analysis from our brief imagery."

Alex controlled the temptation to pace. Instead, he stared thoughtfully at his friend.

"The advantage of making the first move might soon be taken out of our hands, Alex," Julien said quietly. "In five hours, the Vinians will know we're here and might decide to make the first move."

Alex searched quickly through the data from the *Vivian* and pulled images of the Vinian warship taken from a variety of angles. He used the wide bridge monitors to display the critical angles he sought.

"What are you searching for, Alex?" Tatia asked.

"Angles of approach," Alex replied.

"Forward and aft," Z replied. "My analysis of the Vinian vessel predicts a 98.8 percent certainty that this particular warship lacks bow and stern directed armament. The portals that Killian mentioned are embedded in the hull and lay along the median lines of the ship. It's a most inefficient design."

"Like they haven't had any real practice at war," Reiko mused.

Alex regarded the commodore, and she added, "It's the response that you'd expect from a civilization that encountered an enemy or two and prepared for future conflicts by upgrading defenses, but the lack of in-depth experience means they'll make the basic mistakes of amateurs."

"And, if that's true," Alex said, "it means their reactions will be unpredictable." He accessed Z's analysis of the plotted intercept vectors that he had supplied Tatia and used the bridge holo-vid to project the Omnian fleet and the approaching warship. Steadily rotating the view, Alex continued to study his options.

"Admiral, I want you to assign one Trident to drop below the ecliptic, in an arc like this," Alex said, adding a curving line to the display. It ended far below the system's horizon and forward of the Vinian ship. "Be sure to use an OS ship," Alex added.

The squadron was composed of eight, tri-hulled warships. Five Omnian ships were designated by the prefix OS, and NT marked the three New Terran vessels.

"Time your final maneuver for all squadron ships like this, Admiral," Alex continued, adding three more lines. The first line marked the forward progress of the Vinian ship. The second line brought the remainder of the squadron close to the alien warship but stopped 10 million kilometers short of it. The final line showed the Trident emerging from below the ecliptic to intercept the warship.

"What are you proposing for the final disposition of the Trident that we're sending under?" Reiko asked, her eyes narrowing.

"You should be quite familiar with the maneuver, Commodore. You saw it executed frequently at Sol by your partner," Alex replied, grinning.

"You want a Trident to go bow to bow with that warship?" Reiko asked, incredulous at the proposal.

"I like it," Tatia said enthusiastically, her eyes alight with mischief. "We stand the squadron off in a tight formation to demonstrate our power, without attacking, and we give them a taste of the incredible capability of one of our ships. And, providing Z hasn't made an error in judgment, there's little risk to our Trident."

Miranda immediately jumped to Z's defense. "How can you doubt Z's judgment, Admiral? After all, he chose me." At which point, Miranda threw everything she had into her most alluring pose.

"She has you there, Admiral," Renée said, laughing.

"True enough," Tatia agreed. Turning serious, she addressed Reiko. "Commodore, your choice as to which Trident you wish to confront that warship."

"No choice there, Admiral," Reiko replied. "I'll assign Captain Thompson the task. With Ellie's experience as a low-altitude racer before she was judged an Independent and sent to Libre, she's the best choice. How close should she approach?" Reiko asked Tatia, who turned to Alex.

"As close as the captain is comfortable," Alex replied.

Reiko linked with Z to set up the maneuver, and the SADE laid out the ships' courses, launch times, and accelerations. When Reiko approved the details, Z copied the plan to the controllers of the other Tridents. Reiko linked with her captains to review the squadron's approach, assigning the frontal action to Ellie.

It was Svetlana who had to curb her disappointment at not being selected to confront the Vinian warship. During the years of squadron training at Omnia, Reiko and she had repeatedly clashed. At one point, Svetlana requested a transfer to a newly commissioned Trident so that she could be relieved as captain of the flagship. That evening, Reiko had asked Svetlana to sit with her at evening meal, and the pair took a small table to be alone.

"Your request for transfer is denied, Svetlana," Reiko said bluntly after they had sat down with their meal trays. Reiko was forced to hold up a hand to forestall Svetlana's response. "Now, I'm going to tell you why. It's simple. You're too good."

"Reiko that makes no sense," Svetlana replied with a significant amount of heat, which attracted the stares of a few diners nearby.

"And I can understand that, Svetlana, but you'll have to forgive me. I'm starting to think more like our fearless leader," Reiko replied.

"Now, that's dangerous," Svetlana shot back, but the light in her eyes said that it wasn't a bad thing either.

"I want you to think about the events that will call our squadron to action. We possess this immense amount of firepower. But, what if, and I say what if, it's not enough? What if we watch ship after ship be destroyed?"

"That's exactly why you need me at the forefront of the action, Ellie. I've proven my skills, and I can do the most good where the battle is greatest."

"That, Svetlana, is thinking like a captain. Now, I want you to think like a commodore, who has responsibility for the squadron. Most important, I want you to think about who will be aboard your flagship."

Svetlana furrowed her brows, working to understand Reiko's message. It was at that moment, that she heard the laughter of the front table, Alex's bass, Renée's treble, and Tatia's mellow contralto.

Reiko quirked an eyebrow at Svetlana, when her captain's eyes lit in understanding. "And that's why I need you as captain of the *Liberator*, Svetlana. One day, when we watch our best-laid plans crumble in our holo-vid display and the enemy comes for us, the last ship, I'll need your skills to get our leaders to safety. Our traveler pilots might be sacrificing themselves to buy you a narrow window of opportunity to escape destruction, and I'll be counting on you to take advantage of it."

Svetlana had reached a hand across the table, which Reiko took. "I'm your captain, Commodore," she said simply.

* * *

Ellie Thompson listened to Reiko's orders, while she eyed her ship's holo-vid display. Z had uploaded the maneuver into the controller, and she focused on the final sequence.

When Reiko finished her review of the squadron's maneuvers, Ellie linked to the commodore even as her ship, the OS *Redemption*, responded to the controller's demands and accelerated on the course that would take it under the ecliptic.

<Did Alex have a message for my final disposition, Commodore?> Ellie asked.

<He did, Captain, and I quote 'as close as the captain is comfortable.'>

<Understood,> Ellie said, closing the link.

Ellie studied the maneuver, trying to anticipate Alex's intentions. *One ship to intimidate the Vinians, or was that the wrong word?* she thought.

"Yumi, I want a change to our final maneuver," Ellie requested. "When we pop up in front of that Vinian warship, place us bow on at 10 kilometers out. Then decrease the distance at the rate of about a kilometer a minute."

"Until how close, Captain?"

"I think 25 meters should do it," Ellie replied nonchalantly.

"Yes, Captain," Yumi acknowledged, grinning.

Ellie regarded the slender young woman, who was about her age when she was sent into exile on Libre. She recalled the conversation with Alex and Julien when her new crew list was being reviewed a month before the launch of the *Redemption*.

"You've chosen an extremely junior lieutenant for a pilot," Alex had commented.

"True, Alex, she's young, but she distinguished herself in training at Haraken's naval academy, in three years of piloting a traveler, and I like her style."

There was a pause in the communication, and Ellie expected Alex to object. Instead, he said, "Yumi Tanaka … please tell me this isn't Miko's daughter."

Without the structure of Méridien Houses, Haraken parents, who were once declared Independents, had adopted the habit of gifting their sons with their fathers' surnames and their daughters with the mothers' names.

"If you prefer that I start lying to you, Alex, I will, if that's what you want," Ellie replied, struggling to keep a smile off her face.

"Has it been that long that those who fought with us at Libre are now supplying their children to continue the pursuit of our enemy?" Alex asked, his eyes reflecting pain.

The conversation had taken an unexpected turn for Ellie. She had thought of Yumi Tanaka as the daughter of Captain Miko Tanaka, not as the niece of Lieutenant Tanaka, who had sacrificed his life to save Alex. Ellie had been a junior pilot that day over New Terra and witnessed the lieutenant's efforts to absorb the missiles targeting Alex's ship.

"Your conversation about time passing, Alex, reminds me that I should investigate the newest avatars. Could be time for an upgrade," Julien interjected. "How about you, Alex? Oh, sorry!"

Ellie's mouth had fallen open at what she construed a cruel jibe.

Alex had squinted an eye at Julien and fired back, "One of these centuries, you'll miss me," and then he had laughed.

Ellie thought that was the end of it. She never knew Julien's reaction to Alex's comment. The SADE had imagined that terrible final day, thousands of times, and it had crushed him every time.

The ship's controller signaled the initiation of the squadron's final step, and it pulled Ellie out of her reverie. She enlarged the holo-vid's display of the *Redemption*'s telemetry to focus on the Vinian warship and her Trident, as the two ships closed.

"Approaching the ecliptic, Captain," Yumi intoned. She rattled off the steps the controller executed that converted the Trident's drives. "Main engines shutting down. Clamshell doors closing. Grav drives engaged."

Much later Yumi added, "On a reciprocal course to the Vinian warship, Captain."

The *Redemption*'s bridge crew tensed as the ships closed. The Trident decelerated and then reversed course until the distance from the Vinians held at 10 kilometers. Thereafter, Yumi signaled the controller to reduce the separation between the ships at the pace of a kilometer a minute.

Ellie had ordered the beam gunners to be at the ready. The outboard hulls of the Tridents were shaped in the traditional elongated gourd or seed, as was the central hull, enabling all three hull shapes capable of collecting the energy of gravitational waves to charge their enormous power crystals.

As opposed to a traveler's beam, which was aligned with a fighter's shell and necessitated turning the ship to direct the beam, the SADEs had cleverly set a crystal lens at the bow of each beam hull. This enabled the gunners to swing the beam in a limited but useful 8.5-degree angle from true center.

The gunners kept their eyes glued on their telemetry, anticipating the opening of undetected armament portals in the Vinian warship's bow. They were linked to their boards' controllers and adjusting their beam lenses to pin the warship, as they closed.

Trident's procedures for beam operation began with the captain, who was required to release the safety locks on the ship's controller before the gunners could respond to an order to fire. If Ellie was incapacitated, their young lieutenant, Yumi, would assume command.

Before the *Redemption* began its final run from below the ecliptic, Ellie had signaled the ship's controller to release the beam locks, and the gunners had seen their board's ready lights switch from red to white.

Anxiety on the bridge ratcheted up with every closing minute and spiked when Yumi announced, "Twenty-five meters distance, bow to bow, Captain."

"Well done, Yumi," Ellie replied calmly, despite feeling mortally frail.

"And we're still here," the young pilot murmured, which caught the attention of the gunner crew members seated left and right of her.

-2-
Seedling

Olive Tasker hurried to the recovery room as quick as stalks could move. Fronds along the ridgeline were tightly closed and vibrated gently. Poor Olive Tasker would have wished this errand on any other member of the ship. Scarlet Mandator had only recently retired to the recovery room to receive the benefit of the light. Unfortunately, it would be Olive Tasker's duty to interrupt the session and urge the mandator to return to the ship's operations center.

Olive Tasker cycled through the portal, which preserved the recovery room's moist atmosphere. Stalk pads adhered to the decking through the thin film of water, which contained life-sustaining minerals. Olive Tasker was momentarily excited. An opportunity to recover was less than an eighth of a cycle away.

Silently, Olive Tasker slipped past the others enjoying the brilliant light, their fronds fully displayed, and their stalks sipping at the shallow bath.

In front of Scarlet Mandator, Olive Tasker paused. The mandator's bloom was tilted upward, and the light had transported the leader into a somnolent state. At the end of a full-length recovery session, the lights directly above the bloom would blink to waken the mandator.

Reaching out a tentative stalk, Olive Tasker tripped the lights prematurely and scuttled back to wait. It would take some time for the leader to revive, especially after such a foreshortened period of recovery.

Finally, the mandator's brilliant scarlet bloom tilted down to regard Olive Tasker, who signaled the request. The mandator's bloom tilted up and down once, and Olive Tasker hurried from the recovery room.

Scarlet Mandator slowly followed the tasker out of the room, while stalks regained their equilibrium. Reluctantly, the mandator closed fronds when passing beyond the recovery room's portal and losing the bright light. By the time the leader reached the operations center, stalks were responding normally.

"Report," Scarlet Mandator requested of Golden Executor, who was responsible for directing the ship's bridge operations in the mandator's absence.

"Ships have appeared from beyond, Mandator," the executor replied, "They arrived, as did the great orb, as if from nothing."

"What of their shapes?" Scarlet Mandator asked.

"Similar to the seedling we hold in our grasp," the executor replied.

The mandator's stalks relaxed. The great orb, which came from beyond, had devastated many ships of the Worlds of Light and a multitude of the Life Givers' offsprings before it relinquished its quest to partake of their worlds.

"The progenitors have come to collect their wayward offshoot," the mandator surmised. "How many ships?"

"We saw eight, but only seven approach us now."

"Weapons ports?" the mandator asked.

"The ships are smooth like that of the seedling. Truly a superior design, Mandator."

"As only flora can create," Scarlet Mandator acknowledged.

Despite the many criticisms the mandator had received during the intervening cycles since first capturing the wayward seedling, the leader insisted that no force should be employed against it. The argument put forth by the mandator was that the essence of the captured ship, shaped as it was in the timeless and eternal design of a seedpod, indicated a superior flora was aboard, albeit a race's junior members, who had wandered far from its progenitors.

In support of the mandator's argument, the seedling never once fired a weapon at the ship. Grasping the pod as the mandator had ordered created anomalies in multiple operations systems, but that was to be expected when dealing with a superior floral species resisting treatment.

"Locate the eighth ship," the mandator ordered.

"We've searched, Mandator. The ship is nowhere on the horizon," Golden Executor replied, fronds trembling at the thought that the leader might be displeased by his response.

"The seven ships of the progenitors have ceased their approach, Executor," Teal Monitor, who oversaw the navigation board, announced. "They remain motionless at a great distance from us."

Teal Monitor's bloom hovered over a telemetry board that no human could read. A SADE would be required to detect the unusual wavelength of energy emanating from the board, but, even then, the SADE would be required to spend some time learning to decipher the output.

"The eighth ship has arrived, Executor," the monitor reported. "I believe it came from below the horizon."

"Distance?" the executor asked.

"Forty manels, but it's slowly closing on us, Executor. It's approaching us bloom first."

"Impossible," Golden Executor declared. "Coming at us from forty mantels, we would have passed each other before fronds could be folded."

Scarlet Mandator leaned a bloom over the monitor's board. "The readings are accurate, Executor. The ship before us faces us and is slowly closing the distance."

"Could these progenitors be seeking to ram us for capturing their seedling?" Golden Executor asked.

"Doubtful, but the better question might be asked as to how the progenitors knew their seedling was here and under duress," Scarlet Mandator replied.

"Do you think the seedling is capable of communicating to these ships even when they were in the beyond?" the executor asked.

"Undoubtedly, Executor, and they are communicating with it now but in some manner unknown to us," the mandator replied.

"Truly a superior floral species," the executor marveled.

"The eighth ship is no longer closing, Executor," the monitor reported.

The two leaders noted Teal Monitor's tightly closed fronds. The petals, which surrounded the circumference of the bloom, were tightly curled under. Both leaders leaned their blooms over the telemetry board, and their reactions were similar.

"How is that possible?" the executor asked. The board indicated that the progenitor ship was less than one-seventh of their vessel's length from their warship.

Scarlet Mandator turned a bloom toward the executor and then back to the telemetry board, unable to believe the evidence too. "Release the seedling," he ordered.

Golden Executor scurried to the right, and a stalk pad depressed a set of icons on a board, shutting down the ship's grasp on the seedling.

"And now?" Scarlet Mandator asked.

Teal Monitor rudely held up a stalk, requesting more time. "The seedling has fallen off to a position next to the progenitor ship." Moments later, the monitor added, "The two vessels are retreating."

With that announcement, petals uncurled and fronds opened.

"By the Light, I believe we might have escaped annihilation," Scarlet Mandator announced.

"Mandator, the Life Givers should be told of the truth of your reasoning," Golden Executor said. "I can't conceive of the enormity of destruction that might have befallen us if you hadn't argued for restraint in dealing with the seedling. If not for your communications, urging the preservation of the small vessel, the progenitors would have arrived at our worlds and discovered the loss of their seedling."

A shiver went through Scarlet Mandator's stalks and fronds at the foolish action the other mandators had urged. "Destroy it," they had said.

Golden Executor regarded Teal Monitor's bloom, which faced him. "Speak up," he ordered.

"Full control has been returned to our ship," the monitor replied.

"The Light is beneficent," the executor pronounced.

"What more?" Scarlet Mandator asked, noticing that Teal Monitor waited.

"The two vessels returned to the waiting group bloom first, and I was able to observe the stalk end of the progenitor ship. It too exhibits no flame, no gas output, no nothing. It's as if they moved by virtue of the Light," the monitor said in awe.

The mandator and the executor's blooms faced each other, but nothing was shared. Words failed them.

"Return us to the Life Givers. There is a message to share," Mandator ordered. "If the progenitor ships come dangerously close to us, disturb my recovery again. Under no circumstances are you to fire on them. If you were, it would probably mean the end of us all."

Golden Executor's bloom tipped, as the mandator left the operations center.

* * *

"You have our sincere appreciation, Dassata," Killian was heard to say over the *Liberator*'s bridge speakers.

"All part of the service, Killian," Alex replied, equally relieved to see the SADEs freed from the Vinian warship.

"What are your orders, Alex?" Killian asked.

"Take a station off this ship and link your controller to ours for flight control," Alex ordered. "I want you to stay close to us, in case I need more of your advice on this system."

"We're staying, Alex?" Tatia asked.

"It was my thought to further investigate this system," Alex replied.

"The presence of a multitude of Vinian warships doesn't deter your curiosity?" Tatia added.

"It never has, Admiral," Julien quipped. "I'm unsure as to why you think it would have changed."

"Wisdom cometh with age and all that," Tatia replied.

"True for most individuals," Julien replied.

Alex ignored the banter. He knew Julien was employing his unique skills to moderate the concerns of the admiral and her people.

<Z, where is that warship headed?> Alex sent.

<On its new course, I project that it will intersect the orbit of the fifth planet in the system.>

<Any calculation on its time to reach the planet?>

<If it continues at its present rate of velocity, I would estimate about eighteen days.>

<Shades of my time in a New Terran explorer tug,> Alex sent. His thoughts were colored with humor.

<I do believe you've become spoiled by advanced technology, dear,> Miranda sent, stepping into the conversation.

It was a habit of SADE partners to be constantly linked. Alex understood and accepted that if he was communicating with Miranda or Z, the other was undoubtedly listening. Likewise, a conversation with Hector or Trixie was likely shared, at that moment, if not later. Only Julien and Cordelia, the earliest of SADE partners, were careful to partition their conversations from him so that he rarely knew what or, better said, when a conversation was shared. More than likely, all of them were eventually known to one another.

"Killian, Bethley, and Trium, what data did you share with the *Liberator*'s controller?" Alex asked.

"All that we had on our interaction with the Vinian warship, Alex," Killian replied.

"I presume that you were recording telemetry data on this system until your capture," Alex said.

"And afterwards, up to this very moment, Alex," Bethley replied.

"I want that data," Alex requested. He wondered about Reiko's logic that the Vinian warship displayed a design iteration that announced early weaponry development after an initial encounter with a powerful enemy.

Tatia and Reiko had questions, as to what Alex was seeking, but both realized they were too late. Z, who was closest to Alex, had taken a position directly behind him. Z's broad Cedric Broussard avatar provided a convenient post for Alex to lean against. The other three SADEs, Julien, Z, and Miranda, had joined Alex in delving into the stream of data entering the Trident's controller from the scout ship.

Alex stayed on the periphery of the search, as the three SADEs sifted the telemetry for anomalies, using as a base the parts of the recording that evidenced little to no material.

<A great deal of residual organics, Alex,> Miranda sent, the first one to report findings.

<Refined metal too. Most likely stemming from the remains of ships,> Z added.

<The data appears to support Reiko's assumptions about prior enemy contact,> Julien surmised.

<And isn't that interesting?> Z sent.

Alex was immersed in his twin implants, and the bridge crew wondered what caused the slight smile that formed on his face. Z was universally known for his focus on mathematical calculations and their preciseness, and Alex was tickled to hear Z send something as vague as "isn't that interesting." Those SADEs closest to Alex were continually adopting subtle human characteristics.

The scout ship's telemetry data, which was taken during the trip through the system, consistently revealed similar chunks and bits of refined metals and organic material, except for one particular area. Z had discovered evidence of different types of metal.

Julien compared the analysis of the metals generally found against that of the anomalous materials. The discrepancy was too great to believe the same culture had created both compounds.

<Julien, Libre,> Alex sent.

Immediately, Julien accessed data from the *Liberator*'s private storage banks, historical data accumulated by Alex and the SADEs.

<The materials are too similar to be a coincidence,> Julien sent in reply.

Decades ago, the *Rêveur* had made a return trip to Libre to collect the Swei Swee hives, who would settle the Librans' new world, Haraken. Julien, who was ensconced in his box on the bridge of the luxury liner that Alex had rescued, had dutifully collected telemetry data on the system.

The Arnos system was the site of the massive fight to free the Swei Swee, the alien species enslaved by the Nua'll, who resided aboard their enormous sphere. The sphere and its bullet ships were completely destroyed by the avenging dark travelers of the Swei Swee, who lost many hives in the battle.

It was only later that Alex learned of the treasure trove of data that Julien had collected on the system, as part of his standing protocols.

<Similar, but not exact matches,> Z added.

<It wasn't our sphere,> Alex sent.

<You are a frightening human, dear man,> Miranda sent. <Against the odds, you predicted the possibility of another sphere, and you now possess confirmation of that conjecture.>

Rather than receiving a celebratory response from Alex, the comm was quiet.

<I believe Alex was hoping he was wrong,> Julien sent privately to the other SADEs.

<It's better to know the truth,> Z shared with his kind.

<Alex wouldn't disagree with you, Z. That doesn't stop him from imagining a future of more than two spheres,> Julien replied.

<That's an even scarier thought,> Miranda added.

The SADEs abandoned their private conversation when they noticed Alex drop off the link.

Alex gently shoved off from Z's Cedric suit. He wasn't concerned about disturbing the SADE. Locked in place, the avatar, modeled on the heavy-worlder body of a New Terran and massing more than twice Alex's substantial size, was similar to pushing off a granite wall.

"What did you discover?" Renée asked, having come to stand beside her partner. She made it her purpose to be present when Alex finished deep diving with the SADEs. Having spent years in space alone, tagging and shipping asteroids, and immersing himself in computational mathematics, Alex had developed a distinct preference for spending time communing with the SADEs through his implants. She was there to remind him that he was human and needed to stay connected to his kind.

"The *Vivian* collected evidence of metal compounds scattered in the system that are similar to the Nua'll sphere at Libre, but they aren't an exact match," Alex said perfunctorily.

<That would have been a critical piece of analysis to have run,> Bethley said to her comrades aboard the scout ship.

<That presumes that we had the data the SADEs with Alex accessed. I'm requesting the analysis from Z, at this moment,> Trium replied.

"A second sphere was here," Tatia said quietly, and Alex nodded his agreement.

"I say we get this out in the open right now," Reiko demanded, facing Alex, with her fists planted on her small hips.

The bridge, humans and SADEs, went silent at the appearance of a confrontation.

"You, Alex," Reiko said, pointing a finger at him, "need to close your eyes, go wherever you go, and count the number of spheres in our future so that we can do a better job of planning."

A grin split Alex's face, and the bridge broke out in laughter.

"It was worth a try," Reiko admitted, smiling and shrugging her shoulders in imitation of Alex's habitual gesture.

"I'm not sure I want to know the answer to that question, Commodore," Tatia admitted, which many present could understand.

"How much material was found?" Svetlana asked.

"Small amounts," Julien replied. "Enough to say for certain that a single ship, possibly a bullet ship, which accompanied the sphere was heavily damaged."

"Why not the sphere itself?" Reiko asked.

"Everyone and everything is sacrificed to ensure the sphere's survival," Renée explained.

"Nice aliens," Reiko said.

"You have no idea," Renée commented.

"Then there's information to be had from the Vinians, if we can find a means of communicating with them," Reiko said.

"Agreed," Alex said. "Besides, we can't leave this species wondering who we were. They could be an ally someday."

"Wonderful," Tatia grumped. "I want it on record that I refuse to start wearing a colorful, wraparound headdress with frills to imitate a bloom when we greet their leaders."

"Admiral, I think you would look adorable in the right ensemble, if you'd allow me to help," Miranda riposted.

Tatia narrowed her eyes at the SADE, who laughed at the expression. "Think on it, Admiral, I'm sure you'll warm to the idea," Miranda replied, refusing to be deterred.

"Orders?" Tatia asked Alex. She had insisted that she lead the expedition to rescue the captured scout ship. That action was successfully completed.

Now, the Omnians were playing in Alex's space, communicating with another strange, intelligent species in hopes of learning about humans' nemesis, the Nua'll. Having discovered evidence that the enemy had created two giant spheres, the nagging question became: How many more Nua'll vessels were out there ravaging the worlds of distant stars?

"Z said the Vinian warship is heading on an intercept with the fifth planet outward of the sun," Alex said. "Let's follow it. No closer than 250K kilometers, Admiral."

Mealtime approached, and the crews in every Trident broke to partake of an opportunity to be together over food and drink. But, as opposed to passenger liners with SADEs in control, Tatia was averse to allowing a warship's bridge to ever be unattended. Therefore, personnel were scheduled to relieve the bridge watch, during mealtime, every other day.

The New Terran Trident captains had adopted the same routines that Tatia authorized for her people, though they never had a choice. It had been a directive from New Terran President Harold Grumley. Unlike Grumley's predecessor, he paid close attention to Maria Gonzales, who had brokered the deal with Alex to have Omnia Ships build Tridents for her government. Maria had suggested to Harold that he instruct the Trident captains to imitate Tatia's command routines.

During a conversation with Grumley and Maria, the newly minted captains wondered why they should duplicate the Omnians' military protocols. Maria had tersely replied, "It's a simple historical observation, Captains. After twenty years of encountering more danger than any other group in this corner of the galaxy, they're still alive and prospering. You'd do well to remember that."

Throughout the decades, the head table, where once Alex and Renée had sat alone aboard the *Rêveur*, had steadily grown in size. On the OS *Liberator*, it now accommodated the couple, an admiral, a commodore, a captain, and three SADEs. Although the SADEs didn't consume a meal, they attended to demonstrate solidarity with humans.

When Alex was able to get a few servings under his belt to fuel his heavy-worlder body, he glanced at the SADEs and asked, "What do we know about this world where the Vinian warship is headed?"

"Telemetry indicates a warm, wet world, which exemplifies a dense coverage of foliage," Z replied.

"You could be misinterpreting the data, dear," Miranda replied politely. "We might land a traveler and discover that the dense foliage is merely a planet absolutely crowded with plant people."

The group's reply was a collection of half-hearted laughter.

"Perhaps my attempt at humor was mistimed," Miranda admitted.

"There is an absence of dense city structure that one would expect from a society that has the extent of warships and space exploration they exhibit," Julien reasoned.

The SADE comms and human implants received a comment from Bethley, and Alex wondered who at the table remained linked to the scout ship.

<In our leisurely tour of the system, courtesy of the Vinian warship, we spotted several moon bases with a high degree of industrialization, including ship construction,> Bethley sent.

"That would make sense," Renée replied. "Think about what the Vinians would honor."

"True," Tatia chimed in. "Certainly not a dense collection of buildings or heavy industrial complexes."

"Plants first; animals second; pollution last," Svetlana replied cryptically.

Alex pointed a utensil at Svetlana in approval, while he swallowed a bite of roll, which he'd used to wipe the juice of a serving dish. Even the only other heavy-worlder at the head table, Tatia, had finished eating, while Alex was busy cleaning up the serving dishes. "I agree," Alex finally said. "The Vinians would revere their greenery, especially immense tracts of forests. Therefore, as soon as possible, they would offload their heavy construction industries to moon bases to preserve their home world."

"I wonder what the plant people think of our ships," Svetlana said.

"Difficult to postulate," Z replied. "Obviously, they would have been confronted with our Tridents' superior capabilities, but that doesn't answer the question of what they think of our origins."

"It does bring up a more interesting question," Alex said, staring thoughtfully ahead. "We've demonstrated peaceful intentions, despite evincing superior technology. That should buy us an introduction, but we don't have a means of communicating with them. In fact, we're not even sure by what means they communicate. No, the real question is: Who would the Vinians be more willing to speak with ... flora or fauna?"

"Are you visualizing your headdress, Admiral?" Miranda asked and was redeemed by the table's solid round of laughter.

World of Light

Scarlet Mandator completed a round in the recovery room, when the booth's lights winked to signal the session's end. As opposed to the earlier, premature waking, the mandator's fronds were full of energy, which seeped throughout the stalks. The return to the bridge operations center found Plum Executor in charge.

"Status of the progenitor ships?" the mandator asked.

"They're following us at a respectable distance," the executor replied.

"It was as I thought," the mandator replied. "We aren't done with this species."

"Will they demand some sort of payment for what was done to their seedling?" Plum Executor asked.

"If they do, it will prove to be exorbitant. Imagine what a superior species, which can build ships such as these, will demand," the mandator replied.

Petals curling under the blooms of the executor, monitor, and several taskers caused the mandator to add, "Then again, they might wish to establish a relationship with us. In which case, we might benefit enormously from their patronage." Immediately, petals uncurled and blooms lifted.

"Messages have arrived for you, requesting advice, Mandator," Plum Executor said.

"Now the mandators request advice," Scarlet Mandator said in disgust. He shifted to a tasker's board to view the communications list. A stalk pad quickly opened each message and then moved on. The requests were the same. The mandators had witnessed the approach of the ships from beyond and the seedling's release, without a shot being exchanged. Seeing the foreign ships trail the mandator's warship, they were concerned for the World of Light.

"Take a message for all ships, Melon Tasker," Scarlet Mandator ordered. When the tasker was ready, the mandator dictated, "Under no circumstances approach my ship or the ships from beyond. We hope that this species wishes to speak with us in peace. If not, there is nothing you can do to prevent them taking what they want."

When Melon Tasker noted that the message was ready, the mandator said, "Send it."

During the many cycles it took to reach the home world, Scarlet Mandator kept a constant check on the progenitor ships and those of the Light. Nothing changed, and the mandator was grateful for that. Mesa Control had adopted the messages, going so far as to replicate the language in describing the ships from beyond as the progenitor ships and the captured vessel as the seedling. It repeated the mandator's message, requesting all ships to keep their distance.

Once Scarlet Mandator's warship was in orbit over Ollassa, the World of Light, the mandator took a shuttle to the surface. After touchdown, the mandator waited in the comfort of a gel enclosure, while the tail cooled from the hot exhaust and taskers rolled over a lift. When the executor communicated that all was ready, the mandator exited the craft and rode the lift to the ground.

A transport waited to carry the mandator to an elevator that rode from the mesa top to the lowest level, where tram lines exited the mesa onto the forest floor. Trams were the primary means of transport for the Ollassa. Narrow gauge tracks meant a minimal disturbance of the forest. The tram cars were covered in a clear bubble so that the passengers could enjoy the benefit of the Light.

"Destination, Scarlet Mandator?" a tasker asked, when the mandator exited the elevator car into the central switching station for the trams.

"Priority service to the Scarlet Life Giver," the mandator replied.

"At once, Mandator," the tasker replied, tipping a bloom toward the board and ordering the tram.

Scarlet Mandator locked stalks to wait. The pull of the World of Light was a reminder that the mandator was home, once again, and it would take a few cycles to become accustomed to the sensation.

"Your tram, Mandator," the tasker said, as a two-car transport slid to a stop in front of them. The first car held a tasker, who would drive the transport. The second car was for the mandator, and the station tasker hurried to open the bubble for the august passenger. It wasn't only that the mandator was an important figure, it was that the destination requested was to a Life Giver. Communication with a Life Giver was a rare thing and only held for the most critical of issues.

As the tram exited the mesa's tunnel, the mandator, who stood with stalks braced, opened fronds to the Light and trembled under the healing warmth. Soon, the tram entered the deep forest, and the Light was filtered. Undeterred, the mandator waited patiently for the openings to absorb the beneficence once again.

Meanwhile, Scarlet Mandator concentrated on composing a message. Conversations with Life Givers were brief. They were made so by the interpreters, who translated between the requester and the Life Giver. It was unknown by the mandators as to which of the pair, interpreter or Life Giver, required the communication be kept terse, or whether it was both.

After delineating the communication, the mandator dozed as the tram rolled through the forest. Occasionally, it was forced to slow to avoid striking the creatures of Ollassa that dotted the tracks. The fauna of the World of Light was considered a necessary nuisance that was required to maintain the environment's balance.

When the tram reached its destination, the tasker hurried from the car and opened the bubble for the mandator. The tasker reached out a stalk pad to wake the passenger, touching the mandator's stalk three times before the bloom rose.

"We're here, Mandator," the tasker said.

Beside the tram, a small, wheeled transport waited for the mandator, who climbed aboard. A pair of Ollassa walked ahead of the vehicle, as it followed a path through a thick portion of the forest. The overhead canopy was so dense that the Light struggled to penetrate, and the mandator and the taskers closed their fronds against the cool air.

Suddenly, the trees abruptly ended, opening to a luxuriant, grass meadow. The clearing was enormous, which allowed the Scarlet Life Giver complete access to the Light. *As it should be,* thought the mandator.

The transport stopped at the edge of the meadow, and the mandator descended and followed the narrow, worn path through the grasses to the base of the Life Giver. The immensity of the entity was awe-inspiring. Rooted firmly in the fertile ground of Ollassa, the Life Giver stretched its branches high and wide to the Light.

Pods of different sizes hung from the Life Giver's thick, upper limbs. The green ones were new buds; the larger, yellow ones were riper; and the scarlet ones were nearing maturity. Taskers, who maintained the Life Giver, carted nutrients, protected against intrusive fauna, and carefully, oh, so carefully, harvested the mature scarlet pods.

The taskers stopped work as the mandator approached the Life Giver. They tipped blooms and backed away to a respectful distance. At the base of the Life Giver, sat one of the rarest of Ollassa, who was wrapped against the massive trunk. The interpreter's fronds were withered, the Light failing to penetrate near the trunk base, but the interpreter's upper stalk pads penetrated the outer core of the Life Giver, who lent the interpreter its nutrients.

"Speak," Umber Interpreter said simply.

"A seedling ship was captured after entering the space of the Worlds of Light. Its progenitors came to collect it. Their ships followed us to Ollassa. They wait in orbit above."

Umber Interpreter translated for the Life Giver, stalks trembling to transmit the statements. All remained still for several moments before the great Life Giver quivered, its upper branches shaking with the effort.

"The Scarlet Life Giver asks, 'Losses'?"

"There were none," Scarlet Mandator replied. "The seedling was captured and released to its progenitors. No other action was taken by the Ollassa. The progenitors have taken none against us."

After the interpreter spoke to the Life Giver, the response came. "Peaceful, superior species."

"I believe so, Life Giver," the mandator replied.

"Speak to them," the Life Giver replied through Umber Interpreter. Afterwards, the interpreter's bloom turned away from the mandator, signaling the end of the conversation.

Scarlet Mandator reversed course, striding along the path, riding the transport, and taking the waiting tram to the mesa. *Talk to them,* Mandator thought. *How does one speak to entities not of the Light?*

Buried beneath the mesa top, where shuttles landed, sat the Ollassa space command center, known as Mesa Control. There, Scarlet Mandator found Indigo Executor in charge.

"A message to all mandators, Executor," Scarlet Mandator requested.

"Standby, Frosted Tasker," the executor ordered. When the tasker's bloom tipped, Indigo Executor said, "Ready when you are, Scarlet Mandator."

"The Scarlet Life Giver has spoken. I, Scarlet Mandator, am to speak with the progenitors. It's not known how this will be done. Opinions are welcome. If the progenitors land, they must not be accosted in any manner. If their shuttle were to land in the forest and burn the trees, it must be tolerated. Mesa Control will attempt to direct them to land on the mesa top, if at all possible."

Scarlet Mandator tipped a bloom at Indigo Executor and exited Mesa Control. The executor tipped a bloom over the tasker's board, read the message, and approved it to be sent.

Around the Worlds of Light, mandators read the message and were stunned. Many hoped that the Life Giver would require the destruction of the progenitor ships just as one of the Life Givers had ordered the great orb dispatched. To welcome these ships that came from beyond seemed to threaten the Ollassa way of life.

* * *

"Well, this is boring," Svetlana grumped to Reiko. "We've been sitting up here for four days and not even a hello."

"And how exactly are the Vinians supposed to do that?" Reiko replied.

"Knock on the hatch, how else?" Svetlana said, offhandedly.

"I'm so glad you're not in charge of this diplomatic mission, Captain," Reiko riposted.

"A diplomat, I'm not," Svetlana shot back, giving Reiko a fierce grin.

<Heads-up, Sers,> Julien sent to Reiko and Svetlana when he detected which officers were on the *Liberator*'s bridge, as he approached.

The two women jumped up from command chairs and came to attention, as Alex, Renée, Tatia, and the SADEs came through the bridge passageway.

"Z, planet topology," Alex requested.

Z used the bridge holo-vid, which could project a 3-meter wide display of the planet.

"Analysis?" Alex asked.

"We tracked the shuttle that departed the Vinian warship to this mesa top," Tatia said, signaling the display to rotate and expand to indicate the coordinates she'd stored in her implant.

The Trident squadron had orbited the planet, while the Omnians waited for contact. The ships had spread far apart to carefully record the surface, and the SADEs melded the various ships' data into a single complete sphere.

"Looks crowded," Alex commented, eyeing the mesa top with its shuttles and equipment.

"It would be difficult to judge the reception we would receive there," Z said. "None of our scans indicate weapons emplacements, but that doesn't mean that they're not there."

"Which means we need somewhere quieter. Somewhere where we can wait for the Vinians to come to us," Alex said, signaling the planet to rotate slowly, while he observed it. "That's a lot of forest," he said quietly.

"Rather what you would expect from plant people, as we surmised. They revere the greenery," Reiko added. "Around the entire planet, we found only the one shuttle landing site. One of the things to take away from that is the mesa is a geologically solid rock. If it grew anything before it was turned into a shuttle port, I would be surprised."

Alex nodded his agreement with Reiko, while he continued to rotate the display, but his control was interrupted. Renée shifted the display to zoom in to the mesa top and then rotated it to follow a small track that she had spotted. But, she lost it, when it disappeared into thick forest.

Z quickly shifted the telemetry to display thermal readings so that Renée could follow the metal rails, which, despite being partially hidden under the forest canopy, glowed thermally, warmed by the planet's local star.

"Thank you, Z," Renée commented. After following the tracks for nearly a hundred kilometers, she returned to the mesa top, whose bright thermal colors spoke of the tremendous amount of hot metal and gases released by the shuttles. Rotating the display slightly, Renée picked up another pair of tracks and followed them through the cool-colored thermal foliage for nearly the same distance. Twice more, Renée repeated the exercise.

"Quite astute of you, Ser," Julien said graciously.

"Thank you, Julien."

"What am I missing?" Reiko asked.

"Alex is looking for a quiet spot to land a traveler," Renée replied. "What we don't want to do is land in such an out-of-the-way place that no one comes to talk to us. If you follow these transport lines, each of them passes by an odd clearing. Renée rotated the display to showcase one of the clearings and enlarged the view.

"A huge circular meadow with one tree in it?" Reiko asked in confusion. "Why this one tree out of a whole forest of them?"

Quickly, Miranda filled the warship's bridge vid screens with closeups of many of the clearings. She placed a detail in each of the images' corners. "As a feminine entity, I'm always fascinated by the use of color," Miranda said. "What I noticed about these particular trees, which Renée has identified, are the pods. You'll observe that every small pod on each tree is green, but, as they ripen, they turn to one particular color for each tree."

"Trees, flowers, they all have identifying colors. Why are these pod colors useful to us?" Tatia asked.

"How big would you say those pods are when they're ripe?" Alex asked, peering at several of Miranda's inserts.

"Approximately 2 meters," Z replied.

"The Vinians," Alex and Julien announced together.

"Synchronicity achieved," Miranda commented wryly.

"Wait, Alex, you think these trees are producing the Vinians?" Reiko asked.

"Unless you believe in coincidences that defy the probabilities, Commodore," Z replied. "It would appear so."

"Alex, if you wanted to get the Vinians' attention, landing at one of Renée's trees would do it," Tatia said.

"What's your color preference, Renée?" Alex asked, slipping an arm around her waist.

"Not so fast. I've another thought," Renée replied. "Let me ask our crystal friends if it can be determined whether they can discover a correlation between the shuttle that left the Vinian warship and a transport that went to one of these trees."

"Doesn't that presume that the leader of the ship would want to visit a tree upon landing?" Svetlana asked.

"It's not so much a presumption as a curiosity," Renée replied. "The leader might have stayed on the mesa, and a messenger sent. I have no idea. I was just wondering."

Immediately, the SADEs dug into the Tridents' scan data. The time of the shuttle landing was locked in, and the data streams divided among them. A template, outlining the mesa, with all transport lines defined, was shared by Z.

Finally, the stored data streams of the area surrounding the mesa, as the warships passed overhead, were converted to thermal reads to detect the transports exiting the base of the mesa.

"We have three transports leaving the mesa in a period within one hour, following the landing of the shuttle," Julien said.

"One transport stops at a small area that appears to be a population center, if we can judge this type of thing," Z said.

"What do you mean?" Tatia asked.

"The suspected gathering area is indicated by a clearing, to some degree, of small shrubbery and grasses. Within the clearing are bubble-like structures. I would surmise the Vinians can rest inside these structures, recharge during the daylight, and not be bothered."

"Bothered?" Reiko asked.

"Herbivores, insects, and vermin," Alex replied.

"Wow. You know, I never gave a thought to what might chew on a plant," Reiko said, her brow furrowing, as she considered the new perspective.

"To continue," Z said. "This first transport stops at the clearing and returns to the mesa. It never passes by one of these great trees."

"I located a second transport," Miranda added. "It left the mesa and was tracked by three of our ships, as it continued on a long journey. It did pass by two great trees, but it never stopped at either of them. Unless the Vinians are inclined to leave their transports, as the Dischnya are fond of doing, I would have expected the transport to halt for a passenger to disembark."

The group snickered at the reference to the Dischnya's preferred method of catching their open air grav transports, which the Omnians had supplied. The powerful, hock-legged, canine-like Dischnya would race after a passing transport and, at the last moment, as their energy flagged, leap aboard to grasp a handhold. It was a dangerous sport that their warrior nature loved.

"A low probability I would suspect," Alex commented.

"The third transport," Julien said, "left the mesa within 0.44 hours after the shuttle touched down. As opposed to the other two transports, which had six and twelve cars, respectively, this transport had only two cars. It halted at a great tree, stayed there for only a half hour, and then returned to the mesa."

"Sounds like an important person visited the tree," Alex surmised.

"But for what purpose?" Reiko asked. "What's the warship leader going to do? Talk to a tree?" Reiko grinned at the absurdity of the notion, but, looking around, she found no one else shared in her humor. "Oh, no," she added, shaking her head.

"These are aliens, who resemble plants, dear," Miranda said gently, in commiseration. "Who else would the Vinians seek advice from in times of great stress?"

"I can't wait to see how you achieve this one," Tatia said, directing her comment at Alex. "I have an image of you shinning up this giant tree because you have to speak to some orifice at the top of it. You *can* climb a tree, can't you, Alex?"

Alex grinned and pointed the index fingers of both hands at his torso, which Renée patted.

"This oversized body is capable of many wonderful things," Renée said, winking at the female officers, "but it isn't built for climbing trees."

"Personally, I tend to shout to be heard," Alex replied.

"In what language or, should I ask, on what spectrum?" Julien teased.

"Well, my friend," Alex replied, slapping Julien on the shoulder with a resounding thwack, "you and your crystal comrades have until tomorrow morning to figure that out before we undertake a journey to a great and wonderful tree for a delightful conversation."

Instead of Julien projecting a bit of haberdashery from his head via his holo-capable synth-skin, he displayed a delicate crown of flowers and greenery.

"That's so becoming," Miranda quipped. "I need one of these types of avatars, dear," she added, sidling provocatively next to Z.

Alex offered his arm to Renée, and they strolled off the bridge. Tatia and Reiko followed them.

"Good fortune," Tatia said to Julien as she passed him.

Z and Miranda regarded Julien, who said, "This might be a good time for all of us to shrug our shoulders."

-4-
Planetfall

Alex and Tatia had an extensive discussion about the circumstances of his impending visit to the Vinian home world. In the end, as usual, it was a compromise. Alex got his way — only one traveler would make planetfall; and Tatia got what she wanted — a squadron of travelers would station themselves above Alex's traveler on overwatch duty.

As to who would accompany Alex aboard the traveler, it was simple — Renée, three SADEs, the twins, and a pilot.

Tatia spread the other seven Tridents around her flagship, which held stationary positions in high orbit above the great tree with the scarlet pods.

Julien signaled Alex and Renée when all was ready. The pair left their cramped cabin, one requested by Alex so as not to interfere with the workings of Svetlana's crew, and met Julien in the corridor. The threesome made their way to an airlock, cycled through, and were met by their escorts, twins Étienne and Alain de Long; Z; and Miranda.

The twins, Z, and Miranda were outfitted in their Sawa gear. Before journeying to the Dischnya home world, Z rolled out an idea for extra protection, and the twins had enthusiastically adopted it. The twins and the SADEs were wearing a combination vest and harness. Crystal power packs nested on their backs and supplied the twin shoulder-mounted stun guns, which could be controlled by implants and comms.

Z wore his Cedric Broussard avatar. His shoulder-mounted weapons were even more intimidating than that of the twins. But the standout of the group was Miranda in her new avatar, which she first wore on Sawa. It was an imitation of a New Terran body type, as was Z's. She appeared as an exaggerated model of Tatia Tachenko, except she was a brunette, and the SADE carried the same powerful stun weapons as Z.

Alex had frowned at the immense armament when he first saw the group. Later, he'd apologized to them when they managed to successfully defend themselves against a Dischnya nest. The aliens were angry at the Omnians for defiling their learning center by entering it.

The escorts and the SADEs stood erect in their armament, expecting some sort of argument from Alex, again. Instead, as Alex passed the group, he asked, "Are you sure that stun guns will work on the Vinians?"

Alex grinned to himself, as he helped Renée board the traveler. He could imagine the immense amount of comm and implant communication the foursome was maintaining. They would be postulating about the physiology of plant people and whether they would have nerves similar to humans that might be affected by stun charges.

<You couldn't have asked that question of them earlier?> Julien sent to Alex. <I'm sure the thought occurred to you before now.>

<It's good to keep security on their toes,> Alex sent in reply, and his humor bubbled through his thought.

A quick scan of the pilot's bio ID surprised Alex, and he stepped forward to chat.

"We rate a group leader?" Alex asked Franz Cohen, who was Reiko Shimada's partner.

"I don't think anyone was worried about you, Alex, but there was a great deal of concern for Ser's safety," Franz replied, making a reference to Renée.

When Alex's brow furrowed, Franz quickly replied, "The admiral's orders, Alex, and I can direct the overwatch squadron just as effectively from on planet as up above, probably better."

Alex relented, patted Franz on the shoulder, and returned to the main cabin. Z and Miranda stood in the aisles, rearward of the hatch, and locked their avatars. None of the shuttle's seats would accommodate their huge bodies and half-meter deep power packs that supplied their stun weapons.

Taking a seat next to Renée and across from Julien, Alex settled in for the ride. Viewing the heavy, tail-down landing of the Vinians' shuttles had Alex's mind drifting over memories of the early days aboard his explorer-tug. There were lengthy periods of gut-wrenching acceleration and deceleration, while he was strapped in his pilot's chair. During these times, his suit managed his wastes and fed him water.

As opposed to then, Alex saw the main cabin lights dim, and all was quiet. The traveler lifted from the deck, smoothly exited the bay, and made its way down to the planet without sensations reaching the passengers. The hull of the fighter-shuttle was made from a material invented by Emile Billings, with some help from others. It imitated the Swei Swee building material, their spit, as Mickey Brandon, a senior engineer, called it.

The squadron's fighter complement stood by to accompany Franz's traveler, and he communicated with the pilots by way of his ship's controller. There were no windows in the Omnians' fighter-shuttles. The hull was a single, integrated structure. Even hatches and landing gear were carefully designed so as to seal into the shell and not impede its ability to intercept gravitational waves with its harmonic resonance.

All visuals and telemetry for a traveler pilot came through the helmet. The ship's controller collected data and presented it in the helmet's heads-up display. However, pilots could communicate directly with the controller through their implants.

<We're coming in over the great tree, using the coordinates supplied by Julien, Alex,> Franz sent. <The atmosphere is suitable for Omnians, but the daylight is considerably stronger. Overall, I wouldn't recommend an extended stay. Does your request to hover at the far edge of the meadow still stand?>

<It does,> Alex sent in reply. He hadn't opened his eyes to respond. There was no way of knowing when and how they would receive a welcoming committee. Soon afterwards, Alex was fast asleep, and Renée curled up next to him and closed her eyes.

* * *

Scarlet Mandator itched to be gone from the mesa top, not understanding how Ollassa put up with the noise, stench, and intermittent light. The mandator longed to be resting in the airy, bright bubble considered to be home.

Growing impatient of the wait for the progenitors to instigate contact, Scarlet Mandator decided to enjoy a trip on a tram. The tram wouldn't journey too far from the mesa, but it would present the mandator with an opportunity to absorb the brightness and relish the quiet. No sooner had the mandator reached the tram station than the Ollassa heard the hail of a tasker.

"Mandator, the progenitors are landing," the tasker said.

"On the mesa top?" the mandator asked.

"Unknown, Mandator. A group of vessels, much in appearance to the seedling, have left the progenitor ships. They're organized and descending."

"Back to Mesa Control," the mandator ordered, having recognized the tasker as working there.

The two Ollassa hurried to the elevator and rode it up to the command center, which was set deep under the mesa top to protect it from a shuttle accident, which had been known to happen, although not recently. Mesa Control's main corridor was alive with the movement of monitors and taskers, who stepped aside when they spotted Scarlet Mandator.

"Mandator," Indigo Executor said, greeting the center's guest.

"What more is there to report?" Scarlet Mandator asked.

"A group of small ships descended from the progenitors' ships. They took up positions high above and remain there. Only one descended."

"Remain there? Explain?" the mandator questioned.

"That's all that one can express, Mandator. The ships spread into a circular pattern, appearing like petals on a giant bloom."

"What of exhausts or gases from their rear?" the mandator asked, recalling the words of his ship's monitor.

"None, Mandator. The ships hover in place effortlessly with no sense of fuels being consumed."

"Extraordinary," Scarlet Mandator commented. "By the Light, we should possess these capabilities if the progenitors would share. What of the last ship ... the one that left the group?"

"We believe it waits for you, Mandator. It floats at treetop level at the meadow's edge at the site of the Scarlet Life Giver."

Mandator's bloom faced the executor, and Indigo Executor tipped a bloom in commiseration.

"Order an express tram," Mandator requested, hurrying from Mesa Control, making way to the elevator, and descending to the tram station level. Scarlet Mandator was disappointed to see three other mandators standing in two of the tram's cars and a third car's bubble open and waiting. When Scarlet Mandator's bubble was closed, a tasker slid the tram out of the station and, soon, bright light shone through the clear sky.

The thought occurred to Scarlet Mandator that hurrying to meet an alien species with whom no conversation could take place was a fruitless venture. Equally troubling was the presence of the three mandators who traveled in the trailing cars. Reviewing the Life Giver's sparse words, Scarlet Mandator was unsure whether the conversation to take place with the progenitors was meant to be exclusive or could include others. Either way, Scarlet Mandator was determined to ensure hierarchy among the mandators, for the event was clearly understood.

Hours later, the tram slowed to a stop, and the tasker hurried to open the three passenger cars. When the mandators were assembled, Scarlet Mandator addressed the other three.

"The words of the Life Giver are unclear to me as to whether the greeting of the progenitors should be mine exclusively or whether you should accompany me. It must be noted that I visited this very Life Giver on the cycle that I landed on the mesa top. Now, the progenitors are above this spot, awaiting a greeting. Is this a momentous coincidence? I don't believe so. Consider that their seedling ships float in the sky without effort. We are dealing with a species far advanced above us. In the name of peace, I will not object to your accompanying me, but I will speak for us until it's time to bring the progenitors to the Life Giver. Do you agree?"

Scarlet Mandator received the assent of the others, and the mandators made their way from the tram tracks through the path to the clearing. The small transport was bypassed. It was designed to carry a single Ollassa.

When the mandators reached the meadow, three of them stopped, and Scarlet Mandator stepped gingerly farther along the path, keeping the bloom tilted upward toward the seedling ship.

* * *

<We have movement, Alex,> Julien sent to his friend, waking him from a nap.

Snapping awake, Alex accessed the controller's output. His movement disturbed Renée, who woke and did the same thing.

"That's something you don't see every day," Renée quipped. "The flower is rather pretty … like a big, beautiful scarlet sunflower. Did anyone notice that the face, if that's what it is, matches the color of the pods on this great tree?"

"But not the three waiting at the tree line," Miranda said.

Alex and Renée shifted their viewpoint to observe the three aliens they had missed.

"They appear to be similar except for the color of their flowers or faces or whatever," Alex said. "I wonder if the colors represent a hierarchy."

"Doubtful, Alex," Julien said. "The great trees that we observed during our searches displayed a range of pod colors. It would be logical that the face colors are a distinction of subspecies. I would surmise that capabilities that we can't yet observe define their societal structure."

"Well, first things first," Alex said, rising and stretching, popping out heavy muscles in his shoulders and back. "We need a vocabulary, and that will take an intermediary … namely you, Julien."

"Where are Cordelia and Mutter when you need them?" Julien commented.

"Nonsense, Julien," Renée shot back. "You needed Alex and three SADEs the first time because the Swei Swee represented your first alien language challenge. But Willem, Ginny, and Keira cracked the Dischnya language based on their work with the aliens, and that was one SADE and two humans."

"However, Julien isn't going to get far stepping off this traveler and looking like that," Alex said. "We need a disguise."

"Oh, how fun," Miranda enthused. She supplied a model of Julien's avatar and began decorating it, and Renée joined her, playing with an assortment of leaves, branches, and flowers.

Renée would glance at Alex, who was observing the progress in his implant and who often frowned at their efforts. She would laugh and remove the most recent additions.

Finally, Alex said, "Stop. This is going in the wrong direction. I don't want Julien to look like the Vinians. He should appear as a superior individual that, in some manner, would be acceptable to this species."

Miranda stripped the avatar's image, and Renée and she started over again. It was Renée's great store of vids that she had collected, especially the fantasies, which enabled the avatar's final version. Julien's body was clothed in small, dark, pointed leaves but laid in a reptilian pattern that resembled scales.

The SADE was crowned with a pair of antlers that were textured like branches. That was Miranda's idea, who thought Julien should have some sort of adornment above his head to signify a lofty position. Julien completed the body by texturing his hands and feet the same as the antlers, but he chose to leave his face unadorned.

"You can't leave your face flesh-colored, Julien," Alex argued.

Immediately, the face of the avatar's image became a deep blue, which morphed to green and continued to shift through a human's visible spectrum of light.

"That, I like," Renée said.

"I borrowed it from Cordelia's presentation, as the Haraken queen on meeting the Dischnya queen, Nyslara," Julien admitted.

"Who got the idea from Trixie," Alex added.

Julien rose and made his way to the back of the shuttle. As he walked, he communed with the other two SADEs to help him program his kernel's display application, which was capable of projecting the image they had created. Only Julien and Cordelia had designed avatars that could project clothing, not that they always did. Julien's special synth-skin enabled his favorite manner of expressing his emotion by projecting some sort of hat or adornment on his head.

Miranda and Z rose and blocked the view of Julien from the human passengers, not that they had any intention of turning around. It's not that SADEs were modest, quite the contrary; it's that SADEs worked to preserve a similarity to human appearance. Few humans knew their entire secrets, as did Alex.

Julien stripped out of his clothes and, as the programs were completed, he added them to his application and projected the pieces from his synth-skin. When he was ready, he signaled Miranda and Z, who eased aside to allow him to pass.

"May I present your Vinian envoy, Sers?" Julien announced.

Renée stood and applauded.

Alex took in the measure of his friend, and said, "Now, I would be humbled before that image, if I were a Vinian."

"Let's hope so," Julien said.

"No security?" Alain asked.

"We can't disguise the two of you," Alex said, addressing the twins, "and those bubbles that the SADEs identified make me think that fauna, or, more precisely said, animals, aren't appreciated."

"Ready, Julien?" Alex asked.

The SADE reached into a small equipment bag and pulled out a portable holo-vid. He strapped on a power supply to his forearm and plugged it into the holo-vid. Then he let his eyes take on a faraway look, turned on his face colors, and said in a warm, rich tone, "I am prepared to greet the aliens."

Alex laughed and said, "Go forth and project or whatever, my friend. Good fortune." He signaled Franz, <I want a mysterious, superior alien sort of landing for our envoy.> Alex added an image of Julien, and he could hear Franz's laughter from the pilot's cabin.

Franz linked with Julien to convey his idea for the landing and received Julien's assent. The SADEs cleared the hatchway so that the Vinians would only observe Julien exiting the craft.

Franz swiftly dropped the traveler. As he did, Julien signaled the hatch open. When the traveler halted its descent, gently touching the tips of the meadow grass, the SADE stepped through the hatch and dropped 2 meters to the ground. With the avatar's power, Julien landed so lightly as to appear to have taken a single step forward.

Immediately, Franz lifted the traveler to the treetops, closing the hatch as he ascended. Everyone aboard was linked to the controller to watch the proceedings on the ground.

Julien allowed the Vinians time to absorb him. They appeared frozen in place. The individual with the bright red face was closer than the group, which waited at the meadow's edge, and Julien singled out that individual. The SADE turned toward the alien, raised the holo-vid, and switched it on. With his free hand, Julien gestured the Vinian forward.

* * *

Scarlet Mandator watched in awe as the seedling ship descended but failed to complete its landing before the alien stepped from the floating vessel. *Do these entities ignore the pull of the worlds in everything they do?* the mandator wondered.

The mandator wanted to look at the other Ollassa, who waited at the meadow's fringe, and seek their advice, but the opportunity was stolen when the progenitor beckoned. Frightened to move forward and yet frightened to disobey the Life Giver, the mandator finally persuaded the stalks to move.

Edging slowly closer to the progenitor, the mandator stopped two lengths away. If it wasn't for the progenitor's leafy covering and the texture of bark, Scarlet Mandator might have suspected the progenitor was an animal, which sent a shiver through the fronds. But, the cascade of color across the face of the entity announced a superior species. The mandator found the rich kaleidoscope of color mesmerizing.

When the mandator approached the progenitor no closer, the alien held up a stalk that ended in five pads, but only one was extended. The confusion as to what the alien was requesting was quickly dispelled when the stalk displayed two pads and then three pads.

Responding to the request, Scarlet Mandator counted one, two, and three, hoping it met the alien's need. When the progenitor continued extending pads, the mandator joined in and kept counting for the alien, overjoyed to have understood the process so quickly. It was unknown how the progenitor would communicate to Scarlet Mandator, but the first part was obvious. The mandator realized the alien must be taught the Ollassa language.

While the red-bloomed Vinian counted out numbers, Julien detected the ultrasonic waves the alien used to communicate. Every signal frequency the alien sent was linked to a human word or phrase, which built the lexicon the SADEs could use for translations.

When Julien was ready, he held up a hand to the mandator, who unsure of the meaning of the gesture, nonetheless, stopped counting. Julien pointed to the holo-vid.

Unexpectedly, the mandator saw a light emanate from the progenitor's device, and it displayed a simple image. Scarlet Mandator responded by naming it. The alien continued to show more and more images. Eventually, the images became more complex, and Scarlet Mandator struggled to name them with a single word. Rather than be daunted by the challenge, the mandator chose to trust in the progenitor's abilities and decided to discourse on the subjects.

Eventually, the images displayed motion of one sort or the other, and the mandator proceeded to explain the subjects in depth. Eventually, the mandator forgot that this was a teaching session and jabbered away, as a new seedling was wont to do.

It was the soft chill of shade from the trees and the fading of the Light that abruptly ended the mandator in mid-sentence. Fronds shivered, and Scarlet Mandator grew apprehensive of the dark. The mandator was unaware of how to explain to the progenitor the imperative to return to the safety of the tram for the night and was concerned about irritating the alien.

However, the progenitor's light from the device winked off, and a single pad was extended from the other stalk, which pointed down the path toward the tram. The mandator tipped a bloom in acknowledgment and hurried after the others, who had already deserted the meadow to seek shelter aboard the tram.

<Well done, envoy,> Alex sent to Julien.

<Credit must be given to Scarlet Mandator,> Julien sent in reply. <He, she, or it ... I'm still not sure on that point ... was a superb communicator.>

<Alex, I think your analysis of the Ollassa aversion to animals was intuitive,> Miranda sent, using the term by which Scarlet Mandator had referred to the Vinians. <I observed the mandator's fronds and petals throughout the session with Julien. You can read emotions in them.>

<What did you detect?> Julien asked.

<In retrospect, I believe Scarlet Mandator was in awe of you, Julien, but, soon afterwards, there was a moment before you began that I detected fear. That same response was repeated when shadows fell over the Ollassa.>

<Miranda, do you surmise that Scarlet Mandator was afraid of Julien for an instant because our disguise combined both faunal and floral elements?> Renée sent.

<Yes. And it was Scarlet Mandator's same display, fearing the night, fearing predators, that signaled the desire to scramble for the safety of the transport,> Miranda finished.

<Predators?> Alex sent, questioning Miranda's characterization.

<Possibly herbivores, but, to a plant, it would amount to the same thing,> Miranda replied.

<Julien, do you want to come aboard?> Alex asked.

<I imagine Scarlet Mandator and companions will return when light falls on the meadow. If I'm standing in the same spot and the traveler is in the same position —>

<It will be more awe-inspiring,> Alex finished.

<Precisely,> Julien replied.

<We will keep watch for anything untoward, Julien,> Z sent. <As it is, we have hours of work to parse today's lessons. We should be able to formulate more complex displays for tomorrow.>

<Franz, lock the controller on this spot and join us. It's mealtime,> Alex sent.

Aboard the traveler, Z and Miranda joined Julien in cataloguing the language he'd recorded.

5

Life Giver

Scarlet Mandator struggled awake when the beneficence of the Light seeped through the trees to stroke fronds. There was a desire to sip from a mineral bath, but there was none available. Deciding not to wait for the waking of the others, whose tram cars remained in deep shade, the mandator slipped quietly from the car. The tasker tipped a bloom, as the mandator passed.

Stalks responded sluggishly as the mandator entered the shaded path that led to the meadow beyond. Fronds closed tightly awaiting the return of the Light. Breaking through the trees to enter the meadow, which was bathed in the Light of the morning, the mandator paused, while fronds opened and stalks limbered.

Refreshed, Scarlet Mandator swung a bloom to look for the progenitor, surprised to find the alien standing in the same spot and gesturing as it did the cycle before. The mandator hurried to do as bidden, gazing eagerly at the device for the next image.

Instead, Scarlet Mandator was frozen by the image of the giant orb that had attacked the Worlds of Light. To add to the shock, the mandator heard the progenitor speak, saying, "We seek this ship."

Julien had opened his mouth and left it open, as he generated the ultrasonic frequencies to communicate with the Ollassa.

Glancing from the device to the progenitor's face and back, the mandator was unsure how to reply and fought to order conflicting thoughts. "Predator of progenitors?" Scarlet Mandator asked.

"Yes," Julien replied. "I am Julien, Scarlet Mandator," the SADE added, pointing to himself.

The mandator politely waited for the full name, but that was all the progenitor said. The Ollassa repeated the single word, in case he misunderstood, but the progenitor's confirmation indicated he hadn't. The conundrum for the mandator was that sharing information about the orb would fall under the Life Giver's purview. The mandator didn't have permission to discuss this well-protected subject with Julien.

"More images?" Mandator asked, pointing to the device on Julien's arm.

<What level is Scarlet Mandator in Ollassa society, Julien?> Alex sent. The traveler's passengers had been woken by Julien, when the SADE saw the Ollassa enter the meadow.

"Scarlet Mandator is leader?" Julien asked. The SADEs had discovered the particular frequency shift that the Ollassa used to indicate a question versus a declarative statement.

"Ship leader," Mandator replied, a bloom tilting up.

"Ollassa leader?" Julien asked.

<Did Scarlet Mandator turn a bloom toward the great tree?> Renée asked. Like Alex, she had her eyes closed to concentrate on Julien's feed, which included the SADE's visuals.

<Affirmative, Ser,> Julien sent. He loaded an image of the scarlet-pod tree into the holo-vid and displayed it for the mandator.

<What did you make of that, Julien?> Alex asked, after the mandator replied to the holo-vid visual.

<Difficult to say, Alex. Definitely something about life,> Julien replied, working to understand the mandator's response.

<The probabilities are that Scarlet Mandator is indicating the tree is a life creator,> Z sent.

Julien hoisted his holo-vid, which displayed the tree, and rephrased his question.

It dawned on Scarlet Mandator that the progenitors must have some other method of creation and couldn't understand the life cycle of the Ollassa. Picking up a small stone, the mandator spoke the word for life and, with a stalk, offered the pebble to the alien.

"Life giver," Julien said to the mandator.

"Scarlet Life Giver," Mandator agreed, turning a bloom to regard the Ollassa's creator.

It clicked for humans and SADEs alike.

<The pods, Alex, as you thought,> Renée shared on the comm.

<Precisely, Ser,> Z agreed, <and one life giver for each Ollassa subspecies.>

<Our primary question is not being pursued, Sers,> Alex sent. <We've established that the Ollassa venerate these unusual trees since they produce the species. However, Scarlet Mandator appears reluctant to discuss the subject of a Nua'll sphere with Julien. Instead of responding to the question, the life giver is indicated as the Ollassa leader. But how are we supposed to talk to a tree to tell us what we want to know? In lieu of that, how do we get permission for Scarlet Mandator to talk to us?>

Alex waited for a clever idea to be proposed, but none was offered.

<Oh, dear,> Miranda added, after the silence extended.

<Julien, time to provoke a response,> Alex sent.

<I believe provocation is your forte, Alex, and I await your suggestion,> Julien retorted.

<Speak the name of the great tree, Julien; turn and walk toward it,> Alex sent.

<Julien, use the well-worn path to the tree. That should mitigate some of the aggressiveness of your action,> Renée added.

<The voice of moderation, Ser,> Julien replied. The SADE did as Alex suggested, but he took only a few steps toward the pathway when the other three mandators, who had been observing from a distance, hurried forward to take up stances on the path to block Julien's route to the tree unless he was to push past them.

<Diplomacy appears to have met a stalk wall,> Julien quipped.

Alex debated his options. It was an easy choice to abandon the attempt to communicate with the Ollassa, pack up, and return to Omnia. Except, the purpose of everything he'd done at Omnia was to nurture the quest for the Nua'll home world and stop the creation of the spheres at their source. Having discovered traces of the Nua'll metals in the Vinian system, Alex was loath to leave without any information of the sphere, which had visited these worlds. He felt obligated to push the situation with the Ollassa.

<Franz, grass-top descent,> Alex ordered tersely. <Julien return to the shuttle.>

When Julien turned away from the path, Scarlet Mandator hoped they would resume their communication. Instead the alien, Julien, walked past and boarded his seedling ship, which had descended to hover above the grasses.

<Normal attire, Julien,> Alex sent on open comm. <Sers, prepare to disembark. Franz, when I give the word, land this ship.>

Julien quickly turned off his projection and slipped on his clothes behind Z and Miranda.

<Julien, take first position,> Alex sent. <Hold out your holo-vid, as you did before. Twins follow and spread out. Renée, you and I are next. Z and Miranda stay in the background and try not to look intimidating.>

<Well, why did I wear this outfit if you didn't want me to look as if I could defeat an army?> Miranda shot back.

<I think you look indomitable,> Z replied privately, which garnered him a host of wonderful images and sentiments from Miranda.

<Now, Franz,> Alex sent.

Scarlet Mandator watched small pedestals extend from the bottom of the seedling ship. Then, it touched down softly on the grass. To Scarlet Mandator's shock, aliens of all shapes sprang forth from the vessel and arranged themselves in a half circle behind one of them, who strode forward. The alien held Julien's device.

Julien held up his holo-vid to Scarlet Mandator, announced his name, and ran the synth-skin application to project the face and antlers he had displayed before he switched it off.

"Animals," Citron Mandator said, and Scarlet Mandator twisted a bloom, to observe the others, who had crowded close. Fronds were closed and quivering.

"Some of us are fauna; some of us are not, Scarlet Mandator," Julien replied. "We seek our enemy. This predator," he added, displaying the Nua'll sphere once again.

"Ollassa are forbidden to speak of the orb, without permission," Scarlet Mandator replied, belatedly realizing the mistake.

"We know an orb has been here. Our data tells us this," Julien retorted.

"But how?" Citron Mandator asked. "It was many revolutions in the past."

Alex stepped forward, and the mandators shrank away, frightened by his monstrous size.

"This is our leader, Alex Racine," Julien said, by way of introduction. "He's been known by many titles, but I prefer to think of him as companion." Julien had used a word that Scarlet Mandator had offered to describe the other Ollassa, who came with him to the meadow.

"Our data says the debris was minimal," Alex said to Julien, who relayed the message. "That means you probably didn't destroy the orb, which we know to be a Nua'll sphere."

"You know who inhabits the orb?" Citron Mandator asked, forgetting the prohibition to discuss the event.

"We do," Alex replied through Julien. "More important, we can tell you that this is not the only sphere. My people destroyed a different sphere."

Alex mentally asked for forgiveness from the Swei Swee, who were the responsible party for the sphere's destruction, but it wouldn't have served his purpose to explain that, at this time.

Citron Mandator would have asked another question, but Scarlet Mandator spun around to face the other mandators. A discussion ensued, and the Omnians watched blooms swing to and fro, as the mandators addressed one another.

<Change of this magnitude always takes time, oh, impatient one,> Julien sent to Alex, when he noticed his friend shifting his weight from foot to foot.

"Julien, we must ask the Life Giver for permission to speak further of the orb," Scarlet Mandator said, when the discussion with the other mandators ended, gesturing toward the great tree in the center of the meadow.

When the Omnians took a step in the tree's direction, front stalks were raised in protest.

"Not all the creatures," Citron Mandator said.

"How many?" Julien asked.

"One," Citron Mandator replied.

"No," Julien retorted, which resulted in another discussion among the mandators.

"My colleagues say those four resemble predators," Scarlet Mandator said, pointing to Z, Miranda, and the twins, "and the size of your leader is intimidating. The mandators have agreed to allow two of you to approach the Life Giver. You and the small one." A stalk was pointing toward Renée.

Julien was relaying the translations of the mandator's words on the fly, and the comms erupted with objections before Alex silenced the lot.

<Who knew my slender self would finally be the preferred choice of aliens?> Renée quipped to the group.

<Alex, Ser should have at least one escort,> Alain objected.

<Has anyone seen a weapon?> Alex asked. The comms were silent. <Recall that the Ollassa retreat in the evening to hide in bubbles until daylight. Does that strike you as an offensive habit?>

<Don't worry, Alain,> Julien sent privately to the escort. <I will ensure that Ser is returned unharmed.>

<Accept the terms, Julien,> Alex sent, ending the discussion.

"Two," Julien agreed, holding up the same number of fingers to Scarlet Mandator, who tipped a bloom in acceptance.

"Ser?" Julien asked, proffering his arm.

"Such a gentleman," Renée replied, smiling and slipping her hand into the crook of Julien's arm. She knew it was more than politeness that had prompted Julien's offer. The SADE wanted her close. A slight shiver ran up her spine, as she left her friends behind.

Rarely, throughout her entire life, had Renée been without the protection of her people, escorts, or Alex. She had no doubt Julien would do everything possible to keep her safe, but the SADE was unarmed, except for his avatar's exceptional strength and speed.

Julien and Renée followed Scarlet Mandator up the path toward the Life Giver. The other mandators stayed behind.

Alex kept a link open with Julien and Renée. His implant, employing an application via his eyes, calculated the distance to the Life Giver. His implant would remain within range. Otherwise, he was prepared to bounce his implant signal through Z or Miranda.

<Renée,> Alex sent privately. <Do not consider yourself to be a part of Julien's negotiations to gain the information. Consider yourself a prosecutor for the truth of what transpired here.>

<Understood, my love,> Renée sent back.

<Now, that's something you don't see every day,> Miranda sent over the comm, when Julien reached the base of the Life Giver. The Omnians were sharing Julien's visual transmission, and he was gazing at a deformed Ollassa, wrapped against the enormous trunk, stalk tips buried in the tree's bark-like outer covering.

"Umber Interpreter, this is Julien, who seeks permission from the Life Giver for the Ollassa to discuss the orb," Scarlet Mandator said.

"Creatures do not talk to the Life Giver," Umber Interpreter replied.

"I'm not flora or fauna," Julien said. "We believe the Ollassa drove an orb away, but we're here to tell you that there is more than one. We seek to stop these dangerous predators."

"All living entities are either animal or plant. You don't speak the truth," the interpreter replied.

"Umber Interpreter, Julien's request is most important for the well-being of the Ollassa," Scarlet Mandator said. "If you don't speak to the Scarlet Life Giver for him, I'll travel to every other Life Giver, until an interpreter heeds my plea. If you force me to do that, I promise you that I will inform all Scarlets that their interpreter is not worthy of consideration. When that happens, you'll receive no visitors. You will sit alone, attached to the Life Giver until you pass."

Renée, who received Julien's transmission of the conversation, as did the other Omnians, watched the faded scarlet bloom of the interpreter swing first toward Julien and then her way.

"I will ask," Umber Interpreter said, relenting.

The Omnians watched the shivers of the Life Giver, when the request was put to it. Unfortunately, whatever the interpreter asked, it wasn't an answer about the orb. Instead, the Life Giver was curious as to what classification Julien considered himself if he wasn't flora or fauna.

Julien fielded the questions from the Life Giver, thinking it important to satisfy the entity's curiosity. Eventually, the interpreter's bloom tilted down in the middle of one of Julien's replies.

"Umber Interpreter rests," Scarlet Mandator said, enigmatically.

"For how long?" Julien asked.

"Until Umber Interpreter wakes," the mandator replied.

<I get an opportunity to be at the forefront of an alien first contact, and I can't get an interpreter who lasts longer than a half hour,> Renée grumped over the comm.

<Julien, ask if the interpreter will revive before the day ends,> Alex sent.

<The mandator says that it is a certainty,> Julien replied, after questioning their host.

Julien locked his avatar. The mandator stiffened stalks, and Renée sat on the short grass that circled the base of the Life Giver and leaned against the back of Julien's legs.

Meanwhile, Alex took up a perch on the traveler's steps so that he could keep an eye on Renée, while Z, Miranda, and the twins kept a vigil over the surroundings.

Hours later, Julien sent a quick message to the Omnians, when he saw the interpreter stir, saying, <Sers.>

Renée struggled upright. <Julien,> she sent, ensuring that the group at the traveler was included on the comm, <we know we have a limited window of opportunity. Tighten the parameters on your requests.>

Julien tried to do that, but the interpreter's translation of the Life Giver produced short statements about the superiority of flora over fauna, and Renée lost her patience.

"Life Giver, you do know there is a fallacy in your argument," she declared, her hands balled on her hips.

Julien translated for the mandator and the interpreter, as, "Renée de Guirnon, partner to our leader, dismisses the Life Giver's statements."

Umber Interpreter was aghast at the creature's presumption. Flummoxed, the interpreter repeated the words and inadvertently transmitted them to the Life Giver.

"Enlighten us," the interpreter said, repeating the Life Giver's response, after the tree shook.

"I'm human," Renée declared, and Julien translated. "You classify me as animal. But before you, and by our ship, stand SADEs, who are neither plant nor animal. They possess great honor and loyalty to their kind, humans, and all manner of life. You stand rooted in your soil, requiring the light of your star to survive, but these SADEs draw energy from stars, planets, and dead moons, where no life is found."

"Inconceivable," was the Life Giver's reply.

"And that demonstrates the fallacy of your limited knowledge. Humans and SADEs travel to the stars, building worlds where intelligent species live in peace, respecting one another. Life is not perfect, but they persevere. Can you claim as much, when the Ollassa have never left the Worlds of Light?"

"You spoke of a fallacy," the Life Giver said through the interpreter.

"Yes, it's this. You argue for the superiority of plants over animals. That you believe in superiority demonstrates an inferior view of intelligent life. Inherent in those who believe they are superior is a will to dominate. The orb that you chased away is just such a species that believes they are superior to all forms of life, and they destroy other living things with impunity. You would argue for which form of life deserves the loftier role in the universe. Therefore, I ask you, whose view of life has the greater truth ... yours, which argues for tiers, requiring intelligent species to accept their roles ... or ours, which says that there are no tiers, only those who will live in peace and those who won't?"

<Brilliant logic, my love,> Alex sent, his thought wrapped in a heady mix of admiration and desire.

<My bladder has been full for a while, and I wanted to bring this silly discussion to an end,> Renée shot back, and the comm was filled with laughter.

<Necessity, a powerful motivator,> Julien sent.

The interpreter completed the lengthy translation from Julien to the Life Giver. However, unlike previous exchanges, the great tree didn't respond immediately, and the Omnians were forced to wait.

The soft rustle of leaves had Renée glancing upward, but it was only the freshening of a breeze. <Let's just hope our interpreter doesn't pass out on us again. Otherwise, I'm going to need a break,> Renée sent privately to Julien.

The interpreter stirred, as the Life Giver shook briefly. "Ask, creature," the interpreter said, and Julien politely edited the message for the Omnians.

It was Scarlet Mandator, who had doubts about the translation. He had visited the Life Giver many times and was attuned to the length of quivering compared to the delivered reply. In the mandator's mind, the Life Giver had communicated one word. He was suspicious of Umber Interpreter, who must have supplied the second. The ramifications of that thought shocked Scarlet Mandator.

"We request that you give permission to your Ollassa to share what they know of the orb," Renée said.

After the translation reached the Life Giver, the branches shook ever so briefly.

"Given, animal," the interpreter said.

Scarlet Mandator tilted the bloom to study Umber Interpreter. However, the gaze was lost on the Ollassa, who had entered, once again, into a torpid state.

The mandator indicated the path to Julien and Renée, with a single stalk. As the threesome proceeded down the meadow, the waiting mandators were surprised to see Scarlet Mandator striding beside the small alien creature, the bloom held high.

6

The Orb

When Renée stepped off the path, she abandoned decorum and ran for the traveler, and Alex hoisted her neatly through the hatch.

Scarlet Mandator stopped to share the Life Giver's words with the other mandators. There was no argument. The Life Giver had spoken. The group of Ollassa approached Julien, who stood beside Alex.

"Please explain to your leader, Julien, the records that you seek are kept at Mesa Control. We have a rocky outcrop that manages our shuttle base," Scarlet Mandator said.

"We're aware of your shuttle site," Julien replied.

"I had assumed you were but believed it polite to explain," the mandator said, tipping a bloom. "The control center is buried beneath the mesa top. Access is by an elevator either from the top of the mesa or from deep below where our trams enter and leave. The only means of transport we might offer you is by way of our trams, and we must wait until a larger tram arrives to carry you and your people."

"Ask the Scarlet Mandator if the Ollassa would like to travel aboard our shuttle to the mesa top," Alex said, having received Julien's translation, as did every Omnian.

When Julien relayed the offer, the mandators surrounding Scarlet Mandator shrank back. After a brief discussion, Scarlet Mandator announced to Julien that the other mandators had declined Julien's offer.

"And you, Scarlet Mandator? What do you choose to do?" Julien asked.

Scarlet Mandator was torn. On the one hand, intrigued at the prospect of riding in an alien vessel, and, on the other hand, fearful at the prospect of being trapped in a vessel, which might be unprepared to supply the beneficent Light. However, the occasion was too momentous to ignore the gesture, and anxiety was curbed.

"I will travel with you," Scarlet Mandator said.

Immediately, Z and Miranda boarded so they could occupy the rearward portion of the traveler's central aisle. Alex, Julien, and Étienne easily followed, and Alain waited for the mandator to board.

Scarlet Mandator approached the shuttle and tipped a bloom to regard the steep steps. The bright interior calmed the Ollassa. Slowly, stalks navigated the incline. Inside the shuttle, the mandator swung a bloom right and left, first taking in the massive progenitors at the shuttle's rear and then Julien, at the front, who beckoned the mandator forward.

<I believe our travelers might need a redesign,> Julien sent to the Omnians. <Some sort of nanites-triggered seats that reform when the species is detected.>

<Expensive accommodations,> Alain replied.

<Especially at the rate that Alex collects aliens,> Étienne added. <We would need to upgrade once every few years.>

Scarlet Mandator's bloom swung rearward, realizing the last progenitor had boarded, shut the hatch, and the ship had darkened. Regarding the seats designed to hold the aliens' forms, the mandator realized there was no gel enclosures, which sent stalks and fronds trembling.

Alex signaled the traveler's controller to bring the main cabin's lights full up.

<Julien, the holo-vid,> Renée sent, with urgency. <Show the mandator the ground view.>

Julien linked to the controller's telemetry and held up the holo-vid toward the mandator's bloom.

"This is the view outside of our shuttle, Scarlet Mandator," Julien said.

The mandator was slow to understand the progenitor's words. But, as Julien continued to explain what was presented, the meaning penetrated. Fronds and stalks ceased their trembling. The return of the seedling ship's bright lights had helped.

"We have lifted?" Scarlet Mandator questioned.

"Yes," Julien replied.

The mandator's bloom swung to examine the alien seats more closely. They weren't gel enclosures, merely an arrangement to recline upon. Eagerly, the mandator returned to the view from Julien's device, listening to the running commentary the progenitor offered. Quicker than Scarlet Mandator could have believed, the ship was above the mesa top and settling down on an outcrop, away from Ollassa shuttle activity.

"We will exit now," Julien said to the mandator, turning off the holo-vid, and gesturing toward the shuttle's rear.

Scarlet Mandator turned a bloom in time to see the hatch open without the aid of one of the aliens. Stalks carefully managed the difficult task of turning around in the aisle.

Alex sympathized with the Ollassa and kept to himself an offer to hoist the alien and reverse the mandator's orientation.

Scarlet Mandator realized the momentous offer that had been made to him by the progenitors. An Ollassa would be the first to descend from an alien ship atop the mesa, the center of the planet's space effort. Stalks navigated the narrow aisle, and the mandator paused in the open hatch, bloom held high, while surveying the Ollassa, who had gathered. After a few generous moments, Scarlet Mandator carefully descended the steep steps.

<I believe we made the dear alien's day,> Miranda commented on the comm, after the mandator was on the ground.

The Omnians piled off the traveler, and Alex ordered Franz to lift.

<Apologies, Ser, but no can do. Admiral's orders,> Franz sent back.

<Well, we wouldn't want Tatia angry with you, would we?> Alex sent, his humor evident. His relaxed mood stemmed from his expectations. He was hoping to receive an enormous payoff for his dubious gamble to follow the Ollassa warship and confront the plant entities on their home world.

<Is it my imagination or is the mandator walking a little funny?> Renée asked over the comm.

<Odd as it appears, I believe the dear one is strutting,> Miranda replied.

Instead of keeping the stalks flexed, facilitating an easy stride, the mandator was walking with them fully extended, as if on stilts.

<Well, Sers, let's make like a parade and follow the leader,> Alex added, and the Omnians fell in behind Scarlet Mandator.

At a massive elevator housing, probably overbuilt to protect it from shuttle or fuel accidents, a number of Ollassa scuttled aside to allow the mandator and aliens unfettered access to the car. When it arrived, three taskers exited the elevator, hurrying past the Omnians, their blooms twisting behind them for second looks even after they passed.

Scarlet Mandator strode onto the elevator car and relaxed the stalks after the car doors closed. Sympathetic expressions passed between the Omnians. It appeared as if the mandator's performance had cost the Ollassa some precious energy.

Descending to a lower level, the car stopped and the mandator led the Omnians down a wide corridor. Mandators, monitors, taskers, and other Ollassa castes squeezed aside to give the aliens a wide berth.

Scarlet Mandator signaled the progenitors to wait and entered the primary center for Mesa Control.

"Flame Executor," the mandator announced, "on the words of the Scarlet Life Giver, the aliens are to view the records of the events surrounding the giant orb."

Activity in the command center halted, as blooms swung the mandator's way, but a rebuke from the executor returned them to their tasks.

"Mist Monitor, provide the mandator with access to the alternate command center and set up the records list. You're to remain with the mandator until the aliens are satisfied with the viewing. Understood?" the executor ordered.

"Yes, Flame Executor," Mist Monitor acknowledged and followed the mandator out of the primary command center.

"This way, Scarlet Mandator," Mist Monitor said, hurrying to the forefront of the group and freezing when confronted by a broad, powerful alien. Stalks and fronds were close to collapsing.

Miranda stepped aside and swept an arm in the direction that the Ollassa, with the muted blue bloom, was headed. "Recognize, Ollassa, that you appear odd to us too," Miranda said, as the monitor passed. The SADE had generated the ultrasonic wavelengths through her mouth, as Julien had done.

Briefly, Mist Monitor considered the progenitor's words. Could the aliens find the Ollassa as intimidating or as repulsive as they did them, the monitor wondered.

Farther along the main corridor, Mist Monitor tipped a bloom toward a small glass plate set beside a pair of doors. Signaled, the doors opened. Inside, the monitor set about activating the backup command center. When up and running, Mist Monitor accessed a panel and searched the Mesa Control's archives for the requested events. The mandator was required to unlock the carefully protected files for viewing.

The twins took up posts when they entered the command center. Étienne positioned himself in a corner where he could watch the entire room, and Alain stood slightly to the left of the twin doors' seam, prepared to intercept anyone coming through them.

"Ready, Scarlet Mandator," the monitor announced.

"Julien, what does your leader wish to see?" the mandator asked.

<A closeup of the orb, first, Julien,> Alex sent, when he received the question.

"He requests a view of the orb in its entirety, Mandator," Julien repeated.

The blooms of the Ollassa tipped briefly toward each other, before the mandator asked, "Julien, you say your leader requested this of you now?"

"Yes."

"But the formations on the head that produce words, as was seen at the site of the Life Giver, did not move," the mandator said.

"True, Scarlet Mandator, my leader speaks to me with his mind," Julien replied, tapping his temple.

"And you hear this and can reply to him in this manner?" the mandator asked.

"Yes, my leader is an exceptional form of fauna, but I'm much more," Julien replied, knowing Alex and the other Omnians were linked to him.

Julien received an image from Alex of his head growing larger, like a balloon expanding, until it burst, sending miniature Juliens scampering everywhere. The image war ended abruptly, when the mandator directed Julien's attention toward a panel.

"Can you see what is displayed here, Julien?" Scarlet Mandator asked.

Julien examined the panel, and Z got as close as his Cedric Broussard avatar would allow. The SADEs ran spectral scans on the panel's output until Z identified the frequency spectrum. Julien tweaked the display in his kernel until the image represented something that was manageable by human sight. Then, Julien broadcast his view of the panel to the Omnians.

"This is further proof that the Ollassa orb is not the Libran sphere," Z commented. "This one has a different ring configuration."

Miranda was quickly assimilating the conversation and data. She possessed Z's general knowledge but not the data trove Z had accumulated when he was aboard the city-ship, *Our People.* That hefty bit of data had been transferred to Haraken's Central Exchange vault and later copied to the *Freedom,* the other city-ship stationed at Omnia.

"What's the date of incursion, Julien?" Alex asked. It seemed politer and less confusing for the Ollassa if he spoke his questions.

In response to the progenitor's request, Mist Monitor politely pointed to the file date at the corner of the imagery, but it meant nothing to the Omnians.

Z was able to link to Franz's traveler, although the connection through the massive layers of heavy rock was weak. He culled through the telemetry data collected by the *Vivian*'s SADEs to obtain the orbital speeds of the home world, by which it was assumed the Ollassa would mark their annual cycle.

While the SADEs worked, Alex and Renée leaned against the wall opposite from the bank of panels and work stations.

Scarlet Mandator eyed the pair of leaders. "Stalks don't lock?" he asked Julien.

"Fauna," Julien replied, and the mandator tipped the bloom in understanding.

The SADEs were able to calculate the Omnian equivalent of the Ollassa annual cycle. Then, they questioned Mist Monitor and obtained today's date.

"By our calculations, Alex, this event took place 58.65 years ago," Julien said.

"Julien, have the monitor play any vids they have of events surrounding the orb after its incursion," Alex requested. He never left his post against the wall, knowing it would take the SADEs more time to assimilate the disparate imagery.

Mist Monitor began by playing a collection of image sequences, most of them taken from the ships that encountered the orb, at normal speed. When Z asked if the sequences could be played at a higher rate, the monitor pointed to a small slider to the left of the panel.

Julien, who was closest to the slider, moved it up farther and farther until it reached its apex. After that, the SADEs viewed the recorded image files at twenty times the normal rate.

Mist Monitor spared a moment to regard the mandator, who replied to the Ollassa's unasked question, with, "Aliens."

Julien and Z collected more than two hundred imagery files. While they recorded the data, Miranda stitched the imagery into a coherent record of what had taken place.

"We're ready, Alex," Miranda said, when her process was complete.

"Play it," Alex said.

Julien quickly informed the Ollassa that they would be busy, for a few moments, and he pointed to his temple. The mandator's bloom tipped slightly in acknowledgment.

Miranda projected the stitched imagery to the Omnians. The Nua'll sphere had moved into the Ollassa system on a tangent that would have it intercepting the home world. Nearly sixty small ships left the planet's orbit to engage the sphere. At the same time, many more Ollassa vessels left orbits around other planets and moons, where bases were established, to join in the fight.

As the Ollassa ships neared the sphere, it rotated its upper and lower halves in opposite direction, as the Nua'll vessel did at Libre. Two bullet-shaped ships emerged from two different ports, 180 degrees apart, located around the sphere's midline, which the separating halves of the sphere had revealed. The Omnians knew these were the sphere's primary defense.

<Only two?> Alex sent. <I wonder if this sphere lost some of its bullet ships in prior conflicts.>

<We don't have imagery that encompasses the entire sphere,> Miranda sent in reply. <However, we have enough visuals to identify three of the large ports. During the upcoming fight, only these two bullet ships, which you witnessed exiting, were ever seen.>

<Odd warships from these worlds,> Étienne commented, taking in the shapes of the Ollassa vessels, as they closed in on the bullet ships.

The ugly truth behind Étienne's comment became clear, as Miranda continued spooling out the compiled vid. The bullet ships began firing their beams, and the Ollassa ships were destroyed two and three at a time. Soon, the mass of defenders scattered, seeking to swarm the interlopers from all directions.

<Julien, ask the mandator what sort of weapons the Ollassa ships carried. I'm not discerning their offensive actions,> Alex requested.

Julien knew the answer to Alex's question, but he considered that it was best that Scarlet Mandator becomes aware that the Omnians knew of the Ollassa's sacrifice.

"At the time of the great orb's arrival, our ships had no means of repelling invaders," the mandator replied. "We weren't even aware of the possibility that there would be ships from beyond the Worlds of Light. We foolishly believed the Light was reserved only for us."

Julien relayed the mandator's words, and a short exhale of sympathy escaped Renée's lips before she covered her mouth. Alex frowned and his jaw tightened, popping out the muscles along the sides.

The Omnians watched in horror, as ship after ship of the Ollassa dove at the two bullet ships, only to end up as space debris. Finally, the strategy of swarming one of the sphere's bullet ships paid off. Two small Ollassa ships, approaching from opposite sides of the enemy ship, managed to get through the deadly beam strikes and impact the Nua'll protector. The three vessels burst into an expanding ball of tortured metal, hot gases, and organic debris.

Afterwards, the remaining bullet ship immediately retreated toward the Nua'll sphere. Once it was recovered, the sphere accelerated out of the system. The small Ollassa craft valiantly attempted to catch the fleeing sphere, but they quickly fell behind.

<May the stars protect the Ollassa,> Renée sent in the hush that followed the ending of Miranda's vid.

<The poor dear ones died by the thousands to defend their system,> Miranda added.

<Julien, send my condolences to the mandator and the monitor on the loss of so many brave Ollassa to chase the sphere from their Worlds of Light,> Alex sent.

When Julien relayed the message, the Ollassa tipped their blooms deeply, and Mist Monitor wondered if perhaps, alien or not, the visitors might not be so different from the Ollassa.

<Well, now we know why these early space explorers were able to succeed against the sphere,> Alex sent. <The Nua'll had already lost two of their four bullet ships in some other system or systems. Then, when the Ollassa refused to retreat and attacked with every ship they had, the sphere lost a third bullet ship. With only one remaining defender, the Nua'll ran for it.>

"We wish to determine the path the great orb took when it left the system," Julien said to the mandator.

Mist Monitor accessed charts of the Ollassa system and the surrounding stars, presenting it as a view from across the ecliptic. Then the monitor added the last position of the orb before it recovered its last defender and headed out of the system. A line was added that extended from that position to the last sighting of the orb by the Ollassa. The SADEs immediately recorded that piece of valuable information.

"Do you have any more questions for the mandator, Alex?" Julien asked.

Alex ruminated on the information they'd received. It appeared he had everything the SADEs and he needed. Alex's impression of the Ollassa was that they were an insular species. They would focus on developing their system's resources, but Alex thought they would never travel beyond the limit of their precious Light. As such, the Ollassa would probably never become Omnian allies in the fight against the Nua'll.

<Problem, Alex?> Julien asked privately, noticing the frown on his friend's forehead.

<I don't like the idea of leaving the Ollassa to the mercy of the next sphere, especially if it has a full complement of defending ships or even more powerful offensive armament,> Alex sent in reply.

<We have the option of doing the same thing we did for the Swei Swee at Libre,> Julien sent.

<Ask the mandator if the Ollassa would want it,> Alex replied.

"Scarlet Mandator, we have gathered the information on our enemy that we required. Before we leave, we have an offer for you," Julien said.

"Any offer must be received by a group of, at a minimum, five mandators, and four of the five must approve. I will arrange it," Scarlet Mandator replied and hurried from the backup center.

Mist Monitor stepped away from the panels. Required to stay, the Ollassa was unsure of whether to engage the aliens in conversation.

"Mist Monitor, Renée de Guirnon, one of our leaders, requests a favor of you," Julien said. "She would like to approach you and touch the petals of your bloom. Is this allowed?"

The monitor glanced at the small alien. Of any of the progenitors, it seemed safest to interact with this one. Curiosity drove the monitor's thoughts. The Life Givers created all Ollassa, who lived until stalks and fronds failed. Ollassa lives were highly communal. However, in many respects, their lives differed greatly from animals, who produced and nurtured young. Thus, Ollassa lives were characterized by an element of isolation.

"The petals only, Julien. The bloom is sensitive," Mist Monitor replied.

On receiving Julien's translation, Renée slowly approached the monitor. She couldn't resist the temptation to touch one of the aliens, who resembled the beautiful flowers of the worlds she had visited. While facing the monitor, she carefully lifted an arm to the side. The monitor's bloom tipped toward her hand, but then turned to face her.

Delicately, Renée touched the top of a single petal. She expected it to be soft and give under her touch, but, while the petal's surface gently tickled her finger, it had a degree of tension. She touched other petals, relishing the feel and elasticity. Soon, the monitor's bloom tilted down to allow Renée more access.

At one point, Renée slipped a finger under a petal, and it curled momentarily around her finger, which made her smile.

<You had best be careful, Alex,> Miranda sent privately. <The Ollassa might decide to keep us animals here to be their massage therapists and groomers.>

<Mist Monitor does seem to be enjoying it,> Alex replied, noticing Renée was using both hands to stroke the underside of the monitor's petals, which fluttered and curled under the touch of her fingers.

On the hiss of the doors sliding open, Renée stepped back, and Mist Monitor broke from reverie. The Ollassa was saddened by the curtailment of the wonderful sensations.

"We're ready, Julien," the mandator announced. The senior Ollassa led the group to a meeting room farther down the main corridor. Typical for the species, the room was bare of furniture. Four mandators stood with stiffened stalks at the far end of the room, and the Omnians occupied the other end, which left Scarlet Mandator standing in the center.

Mist Monitor chose to attend the meeting, despite not being invited. Then again, the mandator hadn't said that attendance was forbidden.

There were a few humorous comments sent between the Omnians when they noticed Mist Monitor was standing next to Renée.

"Julien," the mandator said, indicating with a stalk a nearby position to the alien.

"Mandators, thank you for hearing our offer," Julien began congenially. "We will soon depart your Worlds of Light, but we would like to offer you a gift before we leave. We're concerned for your safety if a sphere returns. Our analysis of the imagery of your conflict with the great orb indicates that the Nua'll ship had only half the usual defenders. The next orb might be better protected."

"What do you offer?" Citron Mandator asked. The Ollassa had recently arrived on the tram, with the other mandators, from the site of the Scarlet Life Giver.

"We have a means of allowing you to communicate with us anywhere among the stars, far beyond that of the Light. If another great orb arrives here, you only need to push a single button, and we will come to help you repulse your enemy."

"Why would you offer this?" another mandator asked.

"Why shouldn't all intelligent species assist one another?" Julien asked in reply.

"It's an animal trick," Citron Mandator challenged.

"The progenitors came from beyond the Light to rescue their seedling," Scarlet Mandator replied. "How did they know to come here?"

"I've no doubt the progenitors have the capability," Citron Mandator retorted, "but I say it's a trick. The device isn't designed to contact them. It's probably designed to watch us, or worse, to poison us."

"All of you know the progenitors travel between the stars, and you've witnessed their ships' advanced technology, which can maneuver in ways we can't even comprehend. Do you doubt they could eliminate all Ollassa life, if they so choose? Why would they need to trick us?" Scarlet Mandator said, rising on stalks, and the Omnians took that as a sign of the Ollassa's passion.

The four mandators began conducting a private conversation, and Scarlet Mandator joined them. For the Omnians, it was surprising that

Ollassa discussions required such an extensive amount of time to conclude. It was close to two hours later when Scarlet Mandator approached Julien.

"I offer my regrets, Julien. Only three mandators approved of your offer," the mandator said.

Julien relayed the message, thanked the mandators for their time, and led the Omnians out of the room.

Scarlet Mandator and Mist Monitor followed the progenitors down the main corridor. At Mesa Control's primary command center, the monitor halted. It was time to return to duty.

Belatedly, Renée noticed that Mist Monitor had stopped. The bloom focused on her, and she hurried back to the monitor.

<Halt,> Alex sent to Alain, when the escort meant to follow Renée.

Renée used both hands to stroke the petals on the sides of the monitor's bloom. She laid a finger of each hand under a single petal, which curled tightly around them before releasing her fingers. Then, Renée quickly hurried to join the Omnians, a huge smile on her face.

<How to win alien friends,> Miranda commented over the comm.

Scarlet Mandator's bloom had swung between the monitor and the little alien, during their interaction. The mandator was unsure of what had taken place, but the Ollassa had every intention of discovering it later.

Exiting the elevator at the mesa top, Scarlet Mandator said farewell to the progenitors.

Julien relayed their appreciation for the Ollassa's help. Then the Omnians boarded their traveler.

"Julien, seed this system. I want a comm station, with observation capability, tucked somewhere on the system's outer limits ... where the station is unlikely to be discovered. Then send three more observations drones around the system's periphery."

"We will support the Ollassa whether they wish it or not. Is that the case?" Julien replied.

"Not sure, Julien," Alex replied, as he closed his eyes and leaned back in his seat. "Maybe it's not to protect the entire species. Maybe it's to protect Mist Monitor. If something happens to that particular Ollassa, my partner might never forgive me," Alex added, reaching a hand out for Renée's.

-7-
Omnia

While the squadron and the *Vivian* returned to Omnia, the SADEs used the information provided by the Ollassa, to overlay their extensive star charts. They worked to narrow the field of potential next destinations for the Nua'll sphere.

Alex had been brooding since the Omnians left the Ollassa system, and Renée and Julien decided an intervention was necessary.

In a small meeting room aboard the OS *Liberator*, Julien asked a key question, "We have vectors for the sphere's entry into and exit from the Ollassa system, Alex. Do you intend to see where it came from, in case we can trace the sphere back to its home world, or do you wish to pursue the great orb?"

Julien thought injecting a tiny bit of humor would get a rise from Alex, but he sat with arms folded and staring into space.

<It's polite to answer your friend, my love,> Renée sent privately.

"Hmm, sorry, Julien," Alex said, and replayed Julien's question from his implant. "We could be centuries backtracking along the sphere's previous stops. We've no idea how long the Nua'll have been gone from their home world. Sometimes, I wonder if their home world exists anymore."

"So, we pursue our quarry," Julien said.

"It's a possibility," Alex replied, but he didn't put much conviction behind his words.

Julien and Renée exchanged concerned looks. Julien was intent on analyzing Alex's words, but Renée intuited the problem and arrived first at the answer.

"My love, I wish you'd admit what you've already decided," Renée said.

"But, I haven't decided anything yet," Alex objected.

"But, you have, Alex," Julien added, recognizing that Renée had accurately identified the reason for Alex's somber mood.

"Will you two stop ganging up on me?" Alex complained.

"You want to chase the Ollassa sphere, correct?" Renée said, intent on having Alex confront what was bothering him.

"Yes," Alex quietly admitted. He leaned on the table, steepling his hands, and fingertips touching his chin.

"But you're concerned for what that decision will mean for Omnia, which is in a nascent state," Julien added.

"Yes, that too," Alex replied.

"What happened to Haraken?" Renée asked.

"What do you mean?" Alex asked.

"Did it collapse when you stepped down as president or when we left?" Renée challenged.

"That's not a fair comparison, Renée. Haraken was well-established before any of those events occurred." Alex pushed away from the table and began to pace.

Renée and Julien exchanged brief smiles. Alex's pacing was a good sign. It meant he was engaged.

"Alex, I believe what will ensure Omnia's future is solid financial growth potential, much as what Haraken possessed," Julien hinted.

Alex stopped pacing and focused on Julien.

When Alex and Julien stilled, Renée slipped out of the meeting room. As she entered the corridor, she muttered, "Finally."

* * *

The Omnian warship squadron and the *Vivian* exited space into the Celus system. Alex stayed off the comm, allowing the SADEs to communicate. A great deal more information could be passed more accurately and much quicker through them.

<Welcome home, Alex,> Senior Captain Cordelia of the city-ship *Freedom* sent.

<Thank you, Captain,> Alex sent in reply.

<We see you've recovered our wayward scout ship. Well done, Alex. Julien tells me that you were unable to adopt the new aliens.>

<The Ollassa are probably generations away from wishing to join the worlds of humans, who they think of as animals, and SADEs, who they don't comprehend.>

<It's probably just as well, Alex. Lately, life is getting complex enough. You have guests who arrived five days ago.>

<That sounds cryptic, Captain.>

<You will be pleased to see Envoy Maria Gonzalez again. You might not be pleased to be introduced to the man who accompanies her. The New Terran Assembly has elected an admiral to command its Trident squadron.>

<That definitely doesn't sound good,> Alex replied. <I'll meet the Ser soon enough. But, let me pass you to Renée. She's been anxious to speak with you.>

<Greetings, Ser,> Cordelia sent, when Alex's bio ID was replaced by Renée's on the comm.

<Greetings, Cordelia, I want to celebrate the recovery of our three SADEs. Let's have a fête aboard the *Freedom* the next evening after we make orbit.>

<If I might make a suggestion, Ser. Captain Hector has been anxious to have an opportunity to display the *Our People*'s reconditioned status.>

<That's a wonderful idea, Cordelia. We'll hold the fête on his city-ship. Please relay my request to him.> There was a brief silence, much too long for a SADE. <Cordelia, speak up. We've known each other too long, at least in human years, not to be direct.>

<Ser, Hector is quite proud of what he's accomplished after Alex appointed him captain.>

<I see. It would mean a great deal to Hector if the request came from Alex,> Renée replied.

<You understand the situation clearly, Ser.>

<Consider it done, Cordelia.>

* * *

After reaching Omnia's orbit, Renée was able to return to her considerably more expansive staterooms aboard the *Freedom*. The suite was designed and built, courtesy of the SADEs, during the reconditioning of the city-ship.

Alex requested Franz to transport him from the OS *Liberator* to the Sardi-Tallen Orbital Platform.

The design of the scout ships necessitated that the three SADEs be loaded aboard, one at a time, down the length of the slender hull. Then they were required to lock their avatars for the entire journey. Due to the scout ship's overall length, the vessel couldn't be recovered by one of the Tridents. It was the orbital platform that was a convenient location to disembark the SADEs from their scout ship.

Julien signaled Killian that Alex was coming to meet them. The *Vivian's* SADE delayed his landing at the station until he detected Alex exiting a traveler in a platform's bay near to where the scout ship would dock.

Alex had no need to hurry. He knew when he told Julien that he wanted to greet the SADEs that his friend would arrange everything. Alex was aware he could never compete with much of what the SADEs could achieve computationally, but he could demonstrate to the digital entities, his friends, what it meant to be human.

A little smile crossed Alex's face, when he arrived at the docking bay in time to witness the *Vivian* slide into place. He watched the SADEs exit their ship and enter the airlock, looking the same as they did the day they crawled backward into the scout ship, except for the odd creases in their wardrobes.

Killian broke into a huge smile at the sight of Alex when he gained the corridor. The hug from Alex was expected and appreciated.

Bethley extended her hand in greeting to Alex, but she received the same treatment as Killian.

<You should enjoy it,> Killian sent to Bethley, when he saw her blank expression over Alex's shoulder.

<It seems an unnecessary gesture,> Bethley replied.

<Much about human practices seem unnecessary, even frivolous, Bethley, until you understand the reason for these demonstrations.>

Bethley stepped aside, and Trium happily accepted his hug. <While I can't say I comprehend why Dassata employs this particular gesture, I, for one, am delighted that it means I was valued, missed, and now welcomed home,> Trium sent.

"Get your wardrobes in order for a fête tomorrow night aboard the *Our People*, Sers. You'll be the guests of honor," Alex said, and promptly left the SADEs to return to his traveler and join Renée aboard the *Freedom*.

<Why should we be honored for being captured and requiring every Trident warship to come to our aid?> Bethley sent to her companions.

<Come, and I'll explain,> Killian sent in reply.

In a quick flight from the orbital platform, Alex and Franz landed aboard the *Freedom*. They'd missed evening meal and decided to enjoy some food together before retiring to their cabins. There were no intimate dining facilities aboard the enormous vessel, which was constructed to house an eighth of a million people for decades.

As the two Omnians reached a meal room's double doors, Alex said, "We have company," and he grinned at Franz. The twin doors slid apart, and the noise of hundreds of fellow diners reached them.

<I forgot the Trident crews would be late to mealtime too,> Franz sent to Alex.

Reiko hurried to hug Franz, and the couple walked to a seat she'd saved for him.

Alex glanced around and saw many of his friends paired up — Reiko and Franz, Alain and Tatia, Étienne and Ellie, Ben and Simone, Julien and Cordelia, and Z and Miranda. Of course, the SADEs weren't dining, but they were joining in the lively conversation. Presumably, the premier subjects were the Ollassa and the Omnians' adventures on the Ollassa home world.

And you'd risk their lives to chase entities that might never come this way. If only I could be sure of that, Alex thought.

A slender arm slipped though Alex's, while he'd been musing.

"I heard that stomach grumbling, while you were out in the corridor, my love," Renée whispered in Alex's ear. "Let's feed that enormous belly of yours."

Alex patted his stomach. Twenty-three years after meeting the love of his life, it was still flat.

"And keep it that way," Renée chided.

A host of server attendants populated the meal room. They'd extended their shifts, knowing the fleet would make orbit late. The crews would be hungry, but, more than that, they'd be anxious for a taste of life aboard the city-ship.

For the Omnian crews, the vessel, with its enormous gardens of trees, flowering shrubbery, and bubbling brooks, was a heartwarming place they thought of as home. Lining the parks was a collection of shops — eateries, goods, and entertainment — that could fill an evening and afford an opportunity to relax and mix.

"Didn't you eat?" Alex asked, as he chose an intimate table for the two of them, and the nanites-active, narrow seat under him adjusted to accommodate his width.

"Of course, I did. Only one of us is a foolish heavy-worlder, who ignores his needs," Renée replied tartly.

Alex's eyes narrowed at Renée, and she returned his stare with a warm smile. "Ah," Alex said softly, realizing that Renée was intent on shifting his mood. "It was only there for a moment," he protested.

"And who knows how long you'd have stood there brooding, when you should be eating, before I interrupted you," Renée shot back.

Servers headed the couple's way, interrupting their discussion. Renée had signaled she'd eaten, which meant the pile of food dishes, warm buns, and pitcher of hot thé were intended entirely for Alex. Every New Terran heavy-worlder tended to absorb two to three times more food than their companions of Méridien origin, and Alex was one of the largest heavy-worlders. The only Omnian greater in size than Alex was Benjamin "Little Ben" Diaz, who was sitting with his tiny Méridien partner, Simone, and shoveling food, as if it would disappear before he could consume it.

Alex nodded his thanks to the servers, who smiled at the sound of his gurgling stomach, as he took in the rich, delectable scents. As had become his habit, Alex ate directly from the serving dishes, which had been designed to accommodate the appetites of slender Méridiens.

Tatia waited until Alex had a good start on his meal, before she stood, quieting the audience. There was a moment when Simone had to gain Ben's attention. A brief tittering from the others at his table accompanied his belated action to put down his utensil and a roll.

"We've no guests from whom to request a story," Tatia announced. "Nonetheless, most of us were aboard our ships when momentous events took place on the Ollassa planet. We, the crew, request a story from Ser."

Clapping and stomping accompanied Tatia's statements, and Renée rose, hushing the crowd with upraised hands.

"I don't want to delay your enjoyment of these meals," Renée said. "Therefore, I'll tell you a short story of your choice."

The crews took up a chant of "Mist Monitor."

Renée smiled at their choice. "Well, my story might have been much longer and more exciting, if my partner hadn't hustled us off the planet so quickly," Renée said, with a grin.

"Alex was afraid of the competition," a crew member yelled from deep in the room.

"The possibilities of that are strong, Ser," Renée replied, and Alex grinned at the supposition.

Renée related the story of her encounter with the Ollassa, enthralling her audience with her desire to touch Mist Monitor's entrancing petals and the entity's reactions to her fingers. When she finished and sat down, the crews were quiet, absorbing the concept of intimately interacting with an alien, who resembled a walking plant.

<An adventuresome woman, my partner,> Alex broadcast to the room, which broke the diners into laughter and polite applause.

Plates were cleaned of every scrap by the hungry crews of the squadron and the city-ship. Thé and aigre, a favorite Méridien drink, were consumed. Eventually, the room quieted, except for the sounds of Alex and Ben finishing their meals.

Tatia waited respectfully for the two huge New Terrans to drain the last of their thé. When their service was removed from their tables, she stood again. "We have one more request for a story. We would hear from Julien about his contact with Scarlet Mandator."

Alex was one of the first to lead the applause and stamping, doing both. Over the noise could be heard an assortment of unusual, but entrancing, sounds issued by the SADEs. Over the course of time on Haraken and Omnia, no one could remember when the courtesy of a story had been requested of a SADE.

Julien rose and projected from his synth-skin an ancient, pointed felt cap, with a long feather that swept rearward. Crew members trapped images in their implants. Immediately after their meal, they could compete to see who could discover first the historical source of Julien's choice of haberdashery.

"The Ollassa see the creatures of their Worlds of Light as falling into the categories of either flora or fauna," Julien began. "Humans, to them, appear as the latter group. Animals, they called our biological friends. I must admit that after conversing with Scarlet Mandator for a period of time and discovering the Ollassa's superb sensitivities on many subjects, I was torn between keeping this human-style clothing or wearing a covering of leaves."

Much of the audience was stunned by Julien's opening, but those humans who knew the SADEs best howled and whistled at his jest. Other crew members applauded timidly.

<Too much?> Julien sent privately to Alex.

<I love it,> Alex replied, <but you might be scaring our newest Omnians.>

"However," Julien continued, "the latter direction appeared to be fraught with a number of challenges. For instance, if one was to be true to the Ollassa's example, should my foliage be real, or could it be faux?"

The audience chuckled and tittered at the idea of Julien wearing dirt and leaves, which would require diligent maintenance, and Julien warmed to his subject.

"Then, there was the question of accommodation. Surely, if I was to produce a live garden for my covering, then it would most likely attract an assortment of birds and insects. And, I wondered if that would make me their host. Was I now responsible for their well-bring?"

By now, the audience was roaring with laughter, and Julien hung his head, as if the weight of the decision was too much for him.

"In the end, I admit the choice was beyond my limited capabilities to decide. I realized that I must relent. I was neither plant nor animal. I'm just a SADE."

The crews rose from their seats, applauding and stomping. Alex's whistle pierced the noise and joined with the cacophony of tones produced by the SADEs.

Cordelia sent Julien an algorithm snippet for Julien's synth-skin to display, and, in a single tick, he installed it.

As Julien bowed from the waist, he reached for his feathered cap, transferring the projection from his crown to his hand. It appeared as if he swept the virtual cap from his head in a broad flourish.

Whistles and renewed shouts demonstrated the crews' hearty approval of the trick, and Julien extended a hand toward Cordelia, who rose and accepted the audience's appreciation.

<Well done, Julien,> Alex sent. <I loved the lesson. However we're born, we must make the most of who and what we are.>

* * *

Renée woke in the early hours of the morning and stretched an arm across Alex's chest only to discover he wasn't beside her. "I know I had a man when I went to bed," she muttered. A quick check of Alex's location by her implant app located him on the city-ship's bridge in the company of Tatia and the SADEs.

"As if the calculations couldn't have waited until a decent hour," she said, annoyed with her partner, and snuggled deeper into the welcoming bedclothes.

On the bridge, Alex examined the SADEs' projection of the Ollassa system in the holo-vid. Overlaying the star and planets were the vectors of the Nua'll sphere.

"The vessel entered the system's space on one trajectory and immediately changed course to intercept the Ollassa home world," Tatia said, eyeing the display.

"Executing an 83.5-degree port turn on the horizon and a 23.7-degree swing upward toward the ecliptic," Z added.

"Which gives us no idea of their prior destination," Alex said. "I'm more interested in their final moments in the Ollassa system."

"From the time the sphere collected the remaining bullet ship, its course never varied, as it left the system and continued on," Julien said.

"What is a notable point, Alex," Miranda added, "is that the sphere didn't take the shortest route to exit the system or evade the Ollassa ships. The Nua'll might have chosen a course directly above or below the ecliptic. They could effect a transition much quicker and more safely that way."

"Instead, they selected this course," Tatia said, highlighting the display, "which did require them to outrun the swarm of small Ollassa ships."

"Which means, the Nua'll had selected their next destination and wanted to proceed in that direction despite the present danger," Alex surmised. "Now, isn't that odd?"

"It's certainly not smart," Tatia commented.

"It does, however, indicate a presumption of superiority over other species, which is consistent with the actions of the Nua'll," Julien replied.

"I wonder how they're targeting the systems," Alex said quietly. "Do these spheres have the telemetric capability to accumulate data on the planet environments they need across great expanses of space, or have they been selecting these destinations over time by some other method, such as probes?"

Immediately, the SADEs dove into the accumulated Ollassa telemetry data collected by the squadron and the scout ship. They sifted through exabytes of data, searching for anomalies among the debris readings, trying to determine if they could detect the remains of a foreign probe.

A lieutenant had relinquished her command chair when Alex and Tatia had entered the bridge. The two individuals were resting comfortably, while the SADEs continued their search.

<Alex, Admiral,> Julien sent to notify the humans, who had dozed off. Once they were alert, Julien said, "Unfortunately, we have no conclusive evidence concerning the existence of an alien probe, Sers. The perusal of the Ollassa system by the squadron and the scout ship could best be described as cursory. We lack the in-depth survey necessary to make a definitive declaration."

"There is another means of ascertaining your conjecture, Alex," Z said. "It will require a request from you, Ser, to Council Leader Gino Diamanté. The Confederation will have stored, on Méridien, the telemetry data files that the Confederation ships collected at their colonies during the attacks of the Nua'll sphere. The data will be extensive and will require the shipment of memory crystals from the Council."

"Captain Cordelia, please make the request of Gino in my name. Ask him to expedite the transfer. Omnia Ships will cover the cost of delivery and return of a passenger liner."

"What's the advantage to us of learning whether the sphere is able to use telemetry to locate the next destination or probe signals?" Tatia asked.

"Probes must communicate, Admiral," Miranda explained. "If we knew they existed, we would know what to look for when we examine our own data, such as that collected by our scout ships."

"And because probes communicate," Z added, "if the Confederation ships inadvertently collected that data, it might help us with directionality, even if we can't understand the messages."

"Now that would be a language to decode, wouldn't it, Julien?" Alex asked his friend, adding a big grin, and Julien smiled in return.

"We'll probably wind up discovering that the alien probes exist, and they point to a galaxy location occupied by a vast civilization that's home to the Nua'll," Tatia groused.

"In which case, Admiral, it might be prudent to relocate our civilization before the Nua'll come here in force," Julien replied.

-8-
Fête

The SADE, Captain Hector, eagerly awaited the arrival of his special guests. He faced the city-ship's central lift, which would deliver them from the landing bay level to the magnificent central garden. Hector wore the dark-blue uniform originally designed for Alex and company, later adopted by the Harakens, and ultimately imitated by the Omnians.

Subtle gold insignias on the jacket's short stand-up collars identified Hector as a ship's captain. A patch on one shoulder identified his ship, the *Our People*, and on the other shoulder was the Omnians' adopted emblem.

Trixie, Hector's partner, stood beside him. She had commissioned an outfit to wear that complemented her bright-blue skin and delicately pointed ears. She was as eager as Hector for the start of the evening.

Hector had kept to himself the years of suffering at the hands of the demented ex-Council Leader Mahima Ganesh, who had descended into depression and, later, into insanity, unable to cope with events she couldn't control. A source of outlet for Mahima's wild mood swings was her House SADE, Hector, whom she threatened relentlessly. Imprisoned in his box, deep below the Ganesh mansion, Hector was at the mercy of the sadistic, raving woman. He constantly feared that one night Mahima would fulfill her threat to open his casing and pour cold water over his crystals.

Alex knew of Mahima's hatred for him. In the momentous agreement that freed the Confederation SADEs, he specified that Hector should be one of the first SADEs to be liberated. Sadly, Alex's remembrance of that occasion was marred by his failure to emancipate the young SADE, Allora, who had fomented events.

Over time, Hector shared his story with Trixie, who had endured a different sort of privation. She had been left to control a moon's mining robots and ore shipments with only occasional human contact. The two SADEs had formed a tight bond that sought to put their early lives behind them and create new ones with the Omnians.

Standing beside Hector, Trixie was excited for him — on the occasion of the first fête aboard the city-ship, which had finished its lengthy refit only months ago.

It fell to Cordelia to ensure the success of the evening, having crafted many of the successful fêtes aboard the *Freedom*. Cordelia's background was steeped in artistic pursuits, including creating digital realities that viewers could immerse themselves in with the aid of their implants. Cordelia supported Hector's efforts by assisting in lighting the grand park, programming the evening's music, and directing the many personnel who swarmed the park and prepared the venues surrounding it.

Officers and crew from the Tridents and thousands of Omnians from all walks of life on the nascent planet were already in attendance and enjoying themselves. Cordelia had coordinated with Hector the late arrival of Alex and Renée, who were accompanying the three SADEs who the fête honored.

The lift doors opened, and Alex and Renée exited first, but quickly stepped aside. Killian, Bethley, and Trium walked into the thunderous applause and whistles of thousands of well-wishers, who welcomed their safe return home.

<And how do you interpret this reception?> Killian sent to Bethley.

<I believe I prefer Dassata's embrace,> Bethley replied.

Trium had no such reservations. He raised his arms high in a victory salute that he'd seen in a New Terran vid, courtesy of Renée's extensive library, which had been installed on the scout ship's controller. His actions generated an even greater level of noise from the assembled crowd. Eagerly, he waded into the audience, accepting hugs and slaps on the back.

"Welcome to your celebration," Hector said, addressing the other two SADEs. "Bethley, your demeanor indicates you're not pleased by the event."

"You're generous to have made the effort, Captain Hector, but it was quite unnecessary."

"Oh, I agree with you, Bethley, it was absolutely unnecessary," Hector replied smiling, and Bethley was forced to consider the ramifications of that odd statement. "While unnecessary, Bethley, it's a true pleasure. In time, you might learn that lesson," Hector replied. "Please enjoy," he added with a sweep of his arm.

Hector and Killian exchanged knowing smiles, as they passed each other. Then, Hector turned his attention to Alex and Renée.

"Greetings, Alex," Hector said. His right hand covered Trixie's, which rested in the crook of his left arm. It was a custom that the SADEs had copied after witnessing Alex extend the courtesy to Renée, many years ago.

"An attractive couple," Alex said, complimenting the pair.

"And a happy one, Dassata," Trixie replied.

"That's most important," Alex agreed.

"I love the outfit, Trixie," Renée said.

"I wanted to be prepared for the evening," Trixie replied, displaying her infectious grin. "Word has spread that Ser has been teaching Dassata to waltz."

"And he has only begun to learn the steps," Alex warned.

"Then this is a perfect evening to practice, and, as the hostess of the evening's function, I reserve the honor of the first dance, providing Ser approves."

"Oh, she does," Renée replied, adding her own grin.

"I see our New Terran envoy is anxious to speak to me," Alex said, hastily extricating himself from the group.

"Was it something I said?" Trixie asked mischievously, which caused both females to break into laughter.

Renée felt no urgent need to follow Alex and greet a woman she considered a family member. Not waiting for this evening's formal occasion, she'd taken the opportunity to visit with Maria aboard her liner, the *Rover*, where the two women spent most of the afternoon catching up on current events. It was for that reason that Renée knew Alex would need time to talk privately with Maria on a sticky political issue. She watched Alex and Maria hug warmly.

"Shall we dispense with the pleasantries, Alex, and get to business?" Maria asked.

"As we usually do, you mean?" Alex replied, grinning.

"Seems to be our style," Maria agreed.

"I think we should have Tatia join us," Alex said, and sent a request.

Tatia homed in on Alex's location, and the threesome navigated toward one another through the park.

"Envoy Gonzalez," Tatia said, greeting Maria formally.

"Admiral Tachenko," Maria replied, adding, "Does that dispense with the formalities?"

"I believe so," Tatia replied, and the two women embraced.

"Shall we deal with the news?" Maria asked.

"Speaking of which, where is your new admiral?" Tatia asked.

"Our Trident captains are keeping him occupied. I wanted an opportunity to speak to the two of you first," Maria replied.

"This doesn't sound good," Tatia replied, locking her hands behind her back, as if her ex-Terran Security Forces general were about to deliver bad news to her ex-TSF major.

"Our new admiral, Anthony W. Tripping, is a political appointee," Maria explained. "Originally, he was a fighter pilot, trained on the old Daggers and retrained as a traveler pilot."

"Maria, this doesn't make much military sense," Tatia objected. "We've invested a great deal of time and effort, training as a cohesive attack squadron. If New Terra wanted a senior captain or a commodore, why not promote one of the captains who has been part of the squadron? All three have done well, but I'd recommend Captain Alphons Jagielski of the NT *Arthur McMorris*.

"It's a done deal, Tatia," Maria replied.

"I presume the three New Terran Tridents will be returning home with you," Alex said, disappointed at losing three of the squadron's eight Tridents.

"Well, that's where it gets a little sticky," Maria replied, wincing at what she was about to say. "President Grumley has asked me to request that Admiral Tripping have an opportunity to train with your squadron and provide additional command support on your foray to find the Nua'll home world."

"Harold Grumley surely has to know that we have no idea how long that might take, Maria," Alex replied, disturbed at this turn in the conversation. "And I can tell you that it won't be a foray. It will be a hunt … a lengthy, arduous hunt."

"And a dangerous one at that," Tatia added.

Alex and Tatia turned to regard each other, and Maria could imagine the private conversation taking place between two of her favorite people.

"I'm willing to see if Admiral Tripping can develop his skills, as a commander, sufficiently. Under those conditions, I believe he can be allowed to operate as a second in command," Tatia finally said. "Oh, no," Tatia added in disbelief, when she saw Maria's face screw up in a sour expression.

"Yes, I'm afraid the admiral is insisting on joint command, and President Grumley has given him leave to determine his own command structure."

Alex stared briefly at Maria before he broke into laughter so loud that he attracted the attention of several hundred fête attendees.

"Maria, the president can't be serious," Alex replied. "Tripping has no experience captaining a warship, much less a squadron of warships. And, to be blunt, we're not searching for some privateer in a single, unarmed vessel. One Nua'll sphere is incredibly difficult to handle. What if we encounter more than one at the Nua'll home world?"

Alex regarded Tatia, reading her reluctance. "No, absolutely not, Maria," Alex said with finality. "Take your three Tridents and head for home."

"Thank you," Maria replied, hugging Alex briefly. "I was hoping you'd say that. I'll take your response to Tripping. It'll frighten him to no end. He knows he can't go home untrained, and your response will force him to see reason."

"I'm firm on this, Maria," Alex replied. "Squadron command lies with Tatia, and if she doesn't think Tripping measures up to her standards, at any time, then he and your Tridents are headed for home."

"Agreed," Maria replied. "I should tell you that Tripping wishes to get to know the NT Trident captains. He says he wants to drill with them, exclusively ... watch them in operation."

"You mean the admiral wants to learn what his captains know, so that he doesn't appear completely useless in formation," Tatia replied.

"It's a good thing that the warship controllers manage much of the squadron's navigation," Alex said.

"Hopefully, you can disabuse our new admiral of another notion," Maria said. "I explained to him how the warships are coordinated. His response was that New Terran warship movements should be directly under his command."

"As I said, Maria, any and all of these ideas of Tripping are nonstarters. Either he does it Tatia's way or —"

"Its home for us," Maria finished. "I have the message, Alex, and I'll do my best to deliver it." Maria left to find her admiral. She considered it her responsibility to guide Tripping through the delicate process of suborning himself to Omnian command. After all, she knew there was no one else who had defeated foreign warships and an alien sphere — only the Harakens, who Alex and Tatia had led, and they were now leading the Omnians.

"Uh-oh, incoming," Tatia said, with a grin.

Alex turned around, expecting to find Tripping headed toward him. Belatedly, he noticed the sweep of the music to begin the familiar tune that Killian first danced to with the little Daelon girl, Vivian. Trixie was on a collision course with him, and, amid the electric blue face, her eyes gleamed.

"Cordelia is playing our tune, Alex," Trixie announced.

"This is some sort of revenge for something I've done, isn't it, Trixie?"

"On the contrary, Dassata, this is an excellent opportunity for us, and you have Julien to thank for it."

"Julien?" Alex queried.

"Yes, Dassata. He reminded us all that we must be who we are. We're SADEs, and Omnians will see tonight that you're merely human."

"I've never pretended to be anything else, Trixie," Alex replied.

"And those who know you understand this, but not everyone does. Come, Dassata, have courage."

Alex glanced at Tatia. He was looking for help, but her hand covered her mouth to hide her grin, and a lift of her eyebrows said she was unavailable to render assistance. Alex scowled at her and politely, if reluctantly, offered his arm to Trixie.

Leading Trixie to an open space reserved for dancers, Alex focused on the dance practice sessions he'd had with Renée. He was intent on not embarrassing Renée, as his teacher, or himself. Searching through his implant recordings, an answer to his dilemma occurred to him.

On the open deck, Trixie turned to welcome Alex's embrace. She expected to find a degree of consternation on his face. Instead, Alex wore a huge grin. On tempo, Alex strode forward, and Trixie was whisked away.

It had occurred to Alex that he hadn't recorded the steps he was taught as a simple list of where and how to move. Instead, he'd recorded his body's muscle movements, as Renée danced with him, during her many sessions. Originally, he intended to practice the steps later. Of course, *later* in his life rarely happened.

Walking toward the dance space, Alex had hurriedly recalled his last dance practice, which had been one of the most complex, and he spooled it from his implant on cue with the music. In a highly unorthodox manner, Alex let his implant recording drive his own muscular coordination.

As Alex danced Trixie around the floor, he felt as if someone else was in the pilot's seat, certainly not him. For a moment, he'd wondered what other Méridien individuals throughout the centuries had done the same thing.

Alex wasn't a graceful dancer, far from it, but he was energetic. It was the movement of that much mass with that much energy that made it a sight to behold. Alex was stepping lively across the deck and occasionally twirling Trixie.

When the music stopped, Alex gratefully bowed to Trixie. She regarded the relief in his face and compared it to the mischievous grin he displayed before the dance started.

"Your implants," Trixie guessed, and, when Alex nodded, she burst out laughing. "Dassata, perhaps you're not entirely human, and that's the lesson for Omnians," Trixie said.

Alex would have led Trixie off the dance floor, but Renée stood in their way.

"I didn't put in those hours of practice with you, my love, to relinquish this moment," Renée declared.

"Ser," Trixie said, slipping her hand out of Alex's arm, "your partner is a wily one."

"Don't I know it," Renée said. "And truth be told, Trixie, we're better off for it."

Alex was about to lead Renée away, when Killian spun by with Vivian. She was old enough to dance as the SADE's partner, rather than resting on his arm, as she had first enjoyed. Killian was smiling, and young Vivian was ecstatic.

* * *

At evening's end, Alex and Renée said their thanks to Hector and Trixie before retiring to their suite aboard the other city-ship, the *Freedom*. Relaxed in their shuttle seats, Alex reached out to Tatia.

<Any final thoughts on our conversation about Tripping?> Alex sent.

<There hasn't been much else on my mind since our conversation with Maria,> Tatia sent in reply. <I think my partner is miffed by my

inattentiveness this evening. But, not to worry, I'll make it up to him when we get to our stateroom.>

Alex could hear the mirth in Tatia's thoughts.

<About Tripping,> Tatia continued, <I would hate to lose three Tridents. Much of my strategies have been built on the concept of surrounding a sphere, if we could catch it in system. Tough as that scenario might be to execute, it would be a great deal harder to do with five warships instead of eight.>

<But the inclusion of three Tridents in the squadron, which are commanded by a pretender, would also seriously hamper our fighting potential and possibly cost the lives of our own people.>

<I think the best course of action, Alex, is to let the man play admiral, and see what happens. It might not be too bad.>

The long pause in the conversation seemed to indicate to the two Omnians that there was little hope for Anthony W. Tripping.

<Tatia, record every conversation your captains, the SADEs, or you have with our new admiral.>

<Every one of them, Alex?>

<Every one of them, Tatia. I want them stored aboard the *Liberator*, and I want backup copies on the *Freedom*.>

<It's conversations like this that make me more nervous than chasing down a sphere. You know that Alex, right?>

<Good evening, Tatia.>

Unfortunately for Alain, he didn't receive the attentions from Tatia that she'd told Alex he would get. Instead, the couple talked for hours about Alex's request. Afterwards, Alain fell promptly asleep, as was his habit, and Tatia lay awake for a while longer, wondering if Alex was just being careful or if he'd had another premonition.

9

New Arrivals

During the course of the next month, Tatia put the squadron through intensive exercises. She used the Celus system as the squadron's target. The Tridents exited the system, transited away, and then reentered the system on different tangents. The purpose of the exercises was to surround their quarry on, above, and below the ecliptic.

It was presumed from the SADEs' analysis of the sphere's movements that it would attempt to use the gravitational forces of the planets and star to accelerate along the ecliptic. But Tatia didn't believe in fortune protecting her battle plans. Six Tridents were assigned to divide up the ecliptic, and a single Trident each would be above and below the system's horizon.

Naturally, Admiral Tripping objected vociferously to the assignment of two of his Tridents to what he considered to be ancillary positions.

"Based on your digital bodies own analysis of this sphere's movement, Admiral Tachenko, my ships are likely to see little, if any action," Tripping had declared during a post-action analysis meeting. "I insist that you rotate us equally within the squadron assignments for your scenarios."

"I can accommodate that, Admiral," Tatia had replied evenly. She'd quietly ordered her commodore, captains, and SADEs to record every conversation with Tripping, as Alex requested. The more she dealt with the admiral, the more she could understand the value of Alex's directive. Although Tripping was a quick learner, he had an agenda, which was to prove his mettle in combat. A hero complex, Julien had termed it.

Tatia thought she had mollified Tripping, but she was soon disabused of that notion.

"To revisit a point that I've mentioned before, Admiral," Tripping had said. "There might come a time when it will be necessary for a New Terran captain to take command of his ship, independent of the squadron. It could be a loss of maneuvering power, damage to the ship during an encounter, or crystal power vacillations in the beam hulls. Then again, there might come a time when I decide my ships must abandon the search and return to New Terra."

"The controllers are coupled only during actions, Admiral Tripping," Ellie had explained.

"That is understood and unnecessary for you to state, Captain," Tripping replied.

"I'll take your point under advisement, Admiral," Tatia quickly replied, before Ellie could react to Tripping's condescending comment.

However, Tripping was only briefly placated by Tatia's answer. During the course of the next month, he continued to pursue the subject, until Tatia eventually relented to shut Tripping up.

Z designed a pair of override keys for the admiral that nested in a small control device. If, during the action, Tripping was incapacitated, his captain or senior lieutenant could take control of the tool and use it to exit the three NT warships from squadron control.

None of the Omnians understood the reason for Tripping's insistence on this subject. Every warship's controller was programmed by the SADEs and constantly upgraded after each exercise. While the ship was a weapon of war, each controller had, as its priority, the survivability of the ship and crew. Working in concert, the controllers could maximize the possibility of every Trident surviving an encounter with a sphere through innumerable scenarios.

One thing was clear to the Omnians, their new admiral played favorites. During the exercises, it was evident that Tripping had quickly placed his captains into three categories — supporter, undecided, and nonsupporter — the latter captain being Alphons Jagielski. Alphons was the captain who Tatia had recommended to Maria that New Terra promote.

After deciding who he favored, Tripping appointed his supporter's Trident, the NT *Geoffrey Orlan*, as his flagship, making Captain Jonathan Morney a happy man, who saw his star rising under Admiral Tripping.

* * *

<Alex, we have guests,> Cordelia sent.

<Round or oblong shaped?> Alex asked.

<I imagine, even though I'm a SADE, I would be hard-pressed to remain calm if the guests arrived in a sphere, Alex. Obviously, you don't have enough to occupy you these days, if you can be so flippant,> Cordelia admonished.

<You were saying about guests, Captain?>

Cordelia heard the humor in Alex's thought. He was unrepentant about his jest, and she smiled to herself. *There will come a time, soon enough, when all is desperate again,* she thought.

<It's the *Il Piacere*, Alex. Council Leader Gino Diamanté and Leader Katrina Pasko are aboard.>

<Direct them to the *Freedom*, Captain, and send a message to Admiral Tachenko. Tell her not to scare the Méridiens with her war games.>

<You're much too relaxed,> Cordelia scolded, but Alex received the tinkling of her silver bells, indicating her laughter, before she cut the comm.

When the *Il Piacere* took up station near the *Freedom*, Alex and Renée chose to meet the Méridien Leaders as they landed aboard the city-ship. Standing in the airlock, they waited for the bay to pressurize and the Confederation's premier couple to exit their traveler.

After a round of handshakes and hugs, Omnian style, the Leaders gazed around the enormous bay.

"You know, Alex, I've never had the opportunity to visit one of these city-ships. It takes your breath away, and we're only standing in a bay," Gino said.

"After evening meal, I'll take you to our grand central park. You'll love the experience," Renée suggested.

Both Méridiens murmured their agreement, and Katrina said, "I must thank you again for the travelers that are being delivered to the Confederation, Alex. I've never ridden in shuttles that are so incredibly quiet and comfortable."

"You're welcome, Katrina. Is that a Haraken shell or an Omnian shell?" Alex asked.

"How do you tell the difference?" Gino asked.

Alex linked to the traveler's controller, which identified itself, providing Alex with the relevant data. "That's an Omnian shell," he said.

"How is it that this controller responds to your query?" Katrina asked in surprise. As the Leader of the Confederation House that created Méridien implants, of which Alex had two, she was constantly fascinated by what he could do with his.

"Didn't you know?" Renée asked Katrina, linking arms and guiding the House Leader toward the bay's airlock. "Everything responds to Alex."

Katrina stared at Renée briefly, before she erupted in a delightful laugh at the absurdity of the idea.

<Nice deflection, my love,> Alex sent.

<Who's deflecting? I can't help it if our Méridien cousins don't recognize the truth,> Renée sent in reply.

In the suite, the Leaders gazed at the open space and sumptuous furnishings. Gino turned an awed expression on Alex, who held up his hands.

"Don't look at me or my partner," Alex said in protest. "The SADEs were in charge of the refit. I had my hands full with other projects."

"Impressive," Katrina said in a hushed voice.

The Omnians didn't know if she was praising the suite or the SADE's determination to make Alex and Renée comfortable.

Alex directed the Méridiens to a couch. Renée served thé and, shortly thereafter, Julien and Cordelia joined them.

"We've brought you the telemetry data that you requested, Alex," Gino said.

"And it was such a precious cargo that two Méridien Leaders were required to accompany it?" Alex asked.

"We had other items that we wished to speak with you about, Alex," Katrina added.

"Well, I'll have Julien support the transfer of the data, and the SADEs can get started on the analysis right away," Alex said.

"I don't believe that will be necessary, Alex," Cordelia said.

"Captain Cordelia … I love saying her name with that title, by the way," Gino replied. "Cordelia included in her message the reason that you were requesting the data. I believe she wanted to ensure that we understand the importance of the request and that every piece of telemetry data, whether we thought it was relevant or not, was transported to you. Realizing the critical nature of your request, I hired more than a hundred of the best analytical specialists I could procure on short notice."

When Gino smiled, Alex said, "You hired SADEs."

"Yes," Gino replied. <Theodore,> he sent.

Alex accepted a link request and heard, <Greetings, Alex. I'm Theodore.>

<Welcome to Omnia, Theodore,> Alex replied.

<I'm pleased to have been of service, Ser. I have tidings for you concerning your request.>

Alex instantly linked Renée, Tatia, Julien, Cordelia, Z, and Miranda into the comm call with Gino, Katrina, and Theodore.

<Julien, the preeminent SADE,> Theodore said in a hush, when he detected Julien's ID.

<We are all equal, my brother,> Julien replied.

<Some are more equal than others,> Theodore riposted.

<What did you find in your review of the telemetry data, Theodore?> Alex asked, putting the conversation back on track.

<To answer your query, Ser, we discovered the Nua'll did seed our systems with probes. It required an extensive amount of analysis to

identify the initial device. It was a small object and hidden near a moon circling Méridien's outer planet.>

<And what are the statuses of these probes now?> Alex asked.

<We destroyed every one of them that we found,> Gino replied. <I've ordered all Confederation systems to be searched.>

<What was the operational statuses of the probes before you destroyed them?> Tatia asked.

<We recorded every probe's transmissions for several hours before it was destroyed,> Katrina replied. <The transmission data is included with the telemetry data you requested.>

<Have you learned anything, Theodore, from the transmissions?> Z asked.

<Regrettably no, Z,> Theodore replied.

<After Confederation ships located the first probe, Alex,> Gino said, picking up the thread, <it took some time to detect the probe's broadcast.>

<It's an unusual form of transmission,> Cordelia added. <I imagine it's similar to the one I recorded at Libre, moments before the Nua'll sphere exploded.>

<Just so,> Gino agreed. <Once we detected the probe's output, it became extremely simple to sweep our systems and detect the presence of the other Nua'll devices.>

<Have all the Confederation systems been searched, at this time, and did every one of them have a probe?> Miranda asked.

<Miranda,> Theodore said, with the same reverent hush he'd exuded when addressing Julien.

There was a pause in the conversation, which led each participant to believe that Theodore was desperate to say more, but particular individuals on the comm prevented him from speaking bluntly. And every Omnian knew who they were — Gino and Katrina.

The Confederation SADEs had long calculated that their heroine, Allora, who had disappeared in a supposed accident, was somehow linked to the miraculous propagation of a SADE, Miranda Leyton, that none of them had ever known of before. It was too great a coincidence to ignore.

<Kind of you to think so much of me, dear,> Miranda replied, graciously. <And the answer to my question?>

<Seven more reports have reached us from governors who were still searching their systems when we left Méridien. All acknowledged finding probes,> Theodore replied.

<And your nearby uninhabited systems?> Miranda asked.

There was another pause in the conversation, in which Miranda interjected, <Come, come, dears, you don't suppose that our enemy, who exhibits a high degree of anality in their processes, would restrict their seeding of probes to our settled systems. One can surmise from this brief conversation that the Nua'll have probably seeded tens of thousands of stars in this area of the galaxy.>

The pause was much longer this time.

<Perhaps I should have broached this subject a little more gently,> Miranda sent to the Omnians.

<That would have worked for me,> Alex sent privately to Miranda.

The enormity of what had been discovered was sinking into everyone's minds, human and SADE. The Méridien and Haraken societies had been incredibly lax by failing to investigate the possible means by which the Nua'll might have targeted their worlds.

<The spheres are following a line of probes that are reporting the conditions they seek, Alex,> Julien sent.

<Which explains why the Ollassa sphere headed off on the unexplained vector. It was headed toward another probe's signal,> Alex commented.

<I beg your pardon, Alex. Did you just say you encountered another sphere?> Gino asked anxiously.

Alex was about to reply when Cordelia held up a finger, signaling for his attention.

<We have another guest, arriving in an oblong vessel,> Cordelia sent privately to Alex. <Haraken's new president, Terese Lechaux, is aboard.>

* * *

Alex tabled further discussions with the Méridiens to await the arrival of Terese, but Renée wasn't prepared to wait that long to speak to her close friend before she got the answers to her burning questions.

<Terese, please,> Renée sent to Cordelia, when she found a moment of spare time.

<Ser Renée de Guirnon,> Terese replied formally, when she accepted the comm call.

<Madam President,> Renée replied, and the two women erupted in laughter. <How did this happen?> Renée asked.

<Tomas finished his term, and, for a while, no one announced their candidacy. Then, Jason Haraken stepped forward,> Terese sent.

Renée groaned. Any number of the famous Haraken clan might have served the people well. However, the one individual, Jason Haraken, who wouldn't have done the populace any good was the clan member who had run for the presidency.

<Precisely,> Terese replied, after hearing Renée's simple utterance.

<So you ran to ensure that Jason couldn't achieve the presidency,> Renée said.

<At the time, my thought was that if I joined the election process, others would too. Then I could withdraw and support one of the other candidates.>

<Did others stand up?> Renée asked.

<As fortune would have it, they didn't. It came to a contest between Jason and me.>

<And you won.>

<By a six-to-one margin. Would you believe it?>

<According to my calendar app, you've been president for about a third of a year. What have you been doing with your presidency?>

<That's why I'm out here, Renée. I have business to discuss with Alex.>

<Your timing is excellent, Terese. Alex has critical information to share with you, but I'll let him do that.>

<My captain has identified two passenger liners, in addition to the *Rêveur*. Who was aboard them?>

<Gino and Katrina arrived on the *Il Piacere*, and Maria came on the *Rover*. She brought an admiral with her to command the three New Terran Tridents.>

<I bet Alex and Tatia loved that.>

<I warn you, Terese. Don't tease them about it. Admiral Tripping is a sore subject.>

<Consider me fairly warned, Renée.>

Terese closed the comm call and returned to the bridge holo-vid view, which she had been observing.

"Notice the two Tridents above and below the ecliptic," Tomas Monti, Terese's partner, said.

"I'm not sure I understand what Tatia is trying to achieve. It appears she's trying to surround a planet," Terese replied.

"There's the possibility the planet is standing in for a sphere," Tomas suggested.

"Renée said Alex had important news. I sincerely hope it isn't bad tidings about another sphere."

"You know, Terese, Alex has been hunting for them. Why would you think he wouldn't find them?"

"Because I've been hoping there was only one," Terese admitted, her shoulders drooping desultorily.

* * *

Renée had whiled away the afternoon touring their guests, Gino and Katrina, through the enormous city-ship. The Méridiens were intrigued by the delightful elements that were incorporated into the vessel, particularly the central park, smaller gardens, venues lining these green spaces, and Cordelia's vid reality display. The couple spent several hours in it the first time they saw it, and they visited the entertainment site several times afterwards.

On their latest tour, Renée introduced the Méridiens to Captain Hector, who had planned an evening aboard the *Freedom* with Trixie.

"Captain, I never had the opportunity to offer you my condolences for what you suffered at the hands of Mahima Ganesh," Gino said.

"I was fortunate to be guided by Winston through those dark times and the decision to prosecute Leader Ganesh," Hector replied. He was referring to the Council's former SADE, who was freed at the same time he had been. Inherent in his words was the accusation that no Confederation human had come to his rescue.

Renée sought to rebalance the brief meeting, saying, "It was probably fortunate that one human's concern was paramount."

"Yes, Ser. May the stars protect him," Hector replied. He dipped his head slightly, saying, "Excuse me, Sers. Duty calls."

"He carries a great deal of animosity," Katrina said, after Hector left.

"Yes, it's difficult to tell whether that was from his more than a century of incarceration or whether it was due to his last years of mental torture by Mahima," Renée replied.

Gina drew breath to speak, but Renée held up a hand. "President Lechaux of Haraken has arrived. It's too late to make the bay and welcome her. We should proceed to the conference room."

10

Conference

Renée and the Méridien Leaders were the last to arrive at the conference meeting.

Terese, who was speaking to Alex, abandoned her conversation in mid-sentence, when she detected Renée's approach. She hurried to the door and intercepted her friend, as Renée came through it. The tearful reunion occupied some time before Terese and Renée untangled themselves.

After everyone was seated, Alex opened the meeting by saying, "If I'm not mistaken, everyone here has met everyone else, at one time or another."

Faces gazed around the table and every head nodded in agreement.

"Fine. Then we can get right to business," Alex announced. "One of our scout ships, the *Vivian*, was captured. Our squadron went to the rescue, and we encountered a race called the Ollassa. They're a derivative of flora with capabilities of thought and animation."

"Plants?" Katrina asked.

"Of a sort," Alex replied. "During the *Vivian*'s capture by the Ollassa warship, the SADEs aboard the scout ship collected an abundance of telemetry data on the Ollassa system. In that data was evidence of a great deal of debris. Most of it was from the host system, but some of it was similar to the Nua'll sphere."

"You say similar?" Gino pressed.

"According to Omnian SADEs, the material was similar enough to be positively identified as Nua'll, but it was not a match to the sphere at Libre. It was during negotiations with one of the Ollassa Life Givers, a tree that produces one of the species' sects, that Renée managed to convince the giant tree to grant us access to their records."

"Does anyone else find this story tearing you in two different directions?" Tomas interjected. "I would love to hear more about the Ollassa, but I'm desperate to know about the sphere."

"Darryl Jaya, the Minister of Space Exploration, will be upset that he missed out on the discovery of another intelligent species," Maria added.

"In reviewing the Ollassa data," Alex continued, "which incidentally only the SADEs can see because it's outside human's visual spectrum, we watched a SADE-converted vid as the Ollassa threw unarmed ships, by the handfuls, at two bullet ships, which had exited the sphere."

"Why only two?" Maria asked. "Aren't there supposed to be four?"

"The Ollassa sphere had the large bays around its circumference, separated at 90 degrees, as did the Libran sphere," Z explained. "That indicated it should have had the four defensive vessels, but only two engaged the Ollassa. When two Ollassa ships rammed one of the bullet ships, exploding it, the other one retreated into the sphere, and the Nua'll ship left in a hurry."

"Alex, you say that the Ollassa ships rammed the bullet ship. How could they get close enough to do that?" Katrina asked.

"That's because, my dear Leader," Miranda remarked, "the Ollassa, who had no armament at the time, threw themselves against the Nua'll defenders by the hundreds. They literally overran the bullet ships in an effort to drive the invaders from the system. Quite a contrast to the Confederation's reaction against the first sphere over the course of decades, wouldn't you say?"

Gino and Katrina gritted their teeth and bit back their remarks. It was true. The Confederation watched colony after colony get turned to dust, while they did nothing but flee to safety — those who could.

"The woman who led the Council during that time is no longer in power," Alex said sternly, and the individuals around the table could feel the power radiating from his implants. "Recriminations about the past don't help, and, yes, the Ollassa exhibited unimaginable courage and self-sacrifice to save their home world. But, let's remember, they had only the one. Their fronds, so to speak, were against the wall."

"Apologies," Miranda said to the Méridiens.

"Accepted," Gino said quietly.

"The point of my story," Alex continued, "is that we couldn't understand why the sphere chose an exit vector that didn't immediately remove it from harm's way. Up or down from the ecliptic would have been a faster escape course. It did outrun the Ollassa ships, but that got us wondering how and why the Nua'll chose that tangent. Obviously, there was a reason for that choice, which made us ask how the sphere collected the information about the potential destinations."

"Alex requested telemetry data from the Confederation detailing what our ships monitored during the sphere's incursion into the Confederation," Gino said, stepping into the story. "He requested all our telemetry data. The message stated that he wanted his SADEs to search for evidence of probes."

"Probes?" Maria, Terese, and Tomas echoed, at the same time.

"We immediately investigated the data for ourselves and discovered the presence of Nua'll probes in our systems. I can report that you have rarely seen our Council in such turmoil as when the existence of the devices was announced to the public," Gino said, with a grin, recalling the Leaders' furor.

Renée chuckled, which drew attention her way. "I believe I can imagine the Leaders' consternation, having personally witnessed that sort of reaction, once or twice." She smiled at Alex, who was seated across the table. She was referring to the occasions when Alex had confronted the powerful Confederation Council.

Human eyes swiveled momentarily to Alex, and the SADEs shared comments among themselves, far different than the thoughts of the humans.

"Maria, Terese, you'll be receiving the data on the probes," Alex said. "It will allow you to identify their signals and locate them. My advice is to sweep your systems clean and continue to do so. I would love to have you record as much of their broadcasts as you can before their destruction, but that would be selfish on my part. My recommendation: Destroy them as soon as they're found."

"Putting this together," Terese mused out loud. "You've found evidence of the existence of a second sphere, which means, odds are, there are probably more." She was regarding Alex, as she spoke, and watched for his agreement, as she worked her way toward the reason she came to Omnia. "In addition, the Nua'll have probably been planning their expansion across this part of the galaxy for a while, as evidenced by the use of probes at who knows how many stars."

When Alex acknowledged her reasoning, Terese turned to Tatia. "Which brings me to my question about your battle strategy, Admiral. Obviously, this slip of a man and you, along with this foolhardy outfit, will be charging after this sphere, with the aid of your trusty computationally capable, digital friends."

Many at the table were grinning at the personality surfacing of the woman they had known for nearly a quarter century, who was often referred to as the fiery redhead.

"Why, thank you for asking, Madam President," Tatia replied, rising to the occasion. "We'll be trying to trap the sphere in system by surrounding it. With fortune, the Nua'll might surrender once we defeat its remaining bullet ship."

"And is that your estimation of the expected outcome?" Terese asked.

"That would be a negative, Madam President. I expect the sphere to sacrifice its remaining defender and make a run for it. At which time, I intend to have the Trident squadron cut it to pieces," Tatia replied, displaying her patent wolfish grin.

Maria politely covered her broad smile. In many ways, the TSF major she knew hadn't changed one bit.

"And that brings me to my reason for coming here, Admiral," Terese replied. "Wouldn't your strategy have a much greater opportunity for success if you had more Tridents? Space is huge, and the sphere is fast. More ships mean less chance for the sphere to slip past you." When Terese finished, she turned in her seat to eye Alex.

"I'm listening, Madam President. What are you proposing?" Alex asked.

"I've come here to understand Omnia's intentions, concerning warships. It looks like I've arrived just in time to learn how far behind humans and SADEs are in defending our worlds from the Nua'll. Therefore, I've decided that Haraken must get in on the construction of faux-shell ships, and we're willing to commit a portion of our Trident force, with travelers, to assist in your search."

"What portion?" Alex asked.

<This should be good,> Z sent to Julien.

"Say a quarter," Terese replied.

"Say a half."

"Say a third."

"Say half."

After a moment's consideration, Terese replied, "Half is acceptable."

"Omnia Ships will give you the specifications for the Tridents, the scout ships, and the faux-shell technique, but it will require a license fee for each ship produced. Furthermore, you can't use the faux-shell technique for any other type of vessel, except Tridents, fighters, and scout ships."

Terese started to object, but she caught Renée's subtle shake of her head. Her friend was warning her off from pushing Alex on this subject. "How many credits for the licensing of each type of ship?" Terese asked instead.

"Speak to my bankers," Alex replied.

Terese would have asked for more information, but she spotted the four SADEs, each holding up a finger, which they were gently waving in the air. "I should have guessed," Terese said, chuckling.

Alex turned to Gino, who demurred, saying, "I believe the New Terran envoy should go next."

"That's where you're uninformed, Council Leader Diamanté," Maria replied with a grin. "New Terra already has a deal with Omnia Ships. Three of those eight Tridents out there are ours. Although New Terra would be interested in amending our agreement to get the same type of deal that Haraken is being offered."

When Alex's eyes narrowed at her, Maria added. "More production capability means more Tridents, fighters, and scout ships sooner, which means we find the spheres faster than they find us." Alex nodded grudgingly, and Maria felt like she had won a major concession. *Now, if I can just keep Admiral Tripping from screwing up our relationship with the Omnians, we might be able to defend ourselves, in the future,* Maria thought.

"Then I believe I *am* next," Gino acknowledged. "As odd as this might sound, coming from the Confederation's Council Leader, we want Tridents, fighters, and scout ships too."

Conversation, both vocal and comm, came to a halt. The Confederation had resisted the idea of offensive capabilities throughout the invasions of the alien sphere and Earther warships.

"Is this you talking, Gino, or the will of the Council?" Alex asked.

"Having located a probe in every system that we've searched has scared the Leaders out of their lethargy on the question of adopting offensive ships. They aren't sure where it might lead, and they've even discussed hiring the New Terrans or Harakens or both governments to protect the Confederation."

"We're too small, even if we combined forces to defend your worlds," Maria noted. "We could sit for generations in our ships waiting for a sphere to appear, while you expanded the reach of the Confederation. That's not a feasible idea."

"Excuse me," Alex said, holding up a finger.

Those at the table watched Alex, Tatia, and the SADEs quiet.

"They've located our system's probe," Renée said into the silence.

While the Omnian guests waited with Renée, Gino said, "Maria and Terese, we had considered sending ships to your systems to assist you locating your probes, but it was decided that would be politically insensitive."

"Smart decision, Gino," Maria commented.

"Agreed," Terese added. "The subject of a Nua'll probe monitoring the system will be disquieting in and of itself. A Confederation ship arriving to announce the message would only make it worse for our leadership."

Silence once more enveloped the table, while individuals wondered at the communication taking place with Alex.

<Status, Commodore?> Tatia asked Reiko.

<Approaching the probe now, Admiral,> Reiko replied. <We didn't locate the object by its broadcast as detailed by the Confederation data. The SADEs located it by sifting through a huge mound of telemetry data collected during the past three years by ships entering and leaving the system. It was the *Sojourn*, an explorer ship, which had done a thorough job of researching the space, which recorded the probe, although it never realized it.>

<Visually located, Alex,> Z noted.

<Details, Z?> Alex asked.

<A round sphere approximately 2 meters across with a matte black finish,> Z replied.

<Makes it easy to spot,> Tatia commented sarcastically.

<Telemetry is resolving details,> Reiko said, narrating what she was seeing on the OS *Liberator*'s holo-vid display. <Captain, let's circle the sphere and collect more data before we close.>

Julien linked to the Trident's controller and relayed the display to Alex, Tatia, and the other SADEs at the table.

<It's been holed, Alex,> Julien said, analyzing the visuals.

<In and out the other side,> Miranda added. <Most likely created by a piece of high-velocity space dust.>

Alex's expletives were heard across the link. <Why do we have to get a broken one?> he asked rhetorically, which caused Reiko and Svetlana to share quick grins.

<Orders?> Reiko asked. Deliberately, she didn't direct her question to either Alex or Tatia.

<Thoughts?> Alex asked.

<Tamper and boom,> Z replied.

<There is that possibility,> Julien agreed. <The question is: Do we ever intend to examine a sphere, and, if so, under what conditions would it be optimal?>

<If we follow where Julien is leading, Alex, it would be smarter, certainly safer, to examine a defunct sphere under controlled conditions,> Tatia commented, and the SADEs agreed.

<Mickey,> Alex sent.

<Here, Alex,> Mickey Brandon, the engineer responded.

<Mickey, you get to investigate a Nua'll probe that we located in our system. It's not broadcasting due to a meteorite holing it, but I want you to devise a method of capturing and transporting it to a mining base. All initial operations designed to recover and investigate it are to be conducted remotely. I want the risk of detonation and subsequent injuries to our people reduced to an absolute minimum.>

<What sort of distance do you think needs to be maintained?> Mickey asked.

The SADEs quickly calculated a dangerous energy radius based on the size of the sphere and the potential to carry a nuclear drive or some other highly volatile energy source.

<Ten million kilometers appears to be a safe distance, Mickey,> Z replied.

<Commodore, coordinate with Mickey to assist in the retrieval. This is a priority,> Alex replied. <And, Mickey, while you play it safe, I want to know everything about this sphere ... how it was assembled, the energy source, how its transmission was created, what the circuitry is based on ... I want to understand as much about the civilization that created it, as how and what the probe might be possible of communicating.>

<Understood, Alex,> Mickey replied and dropped off the comm, as did Reiko.

"Our probe has been hit by some space dust," Alex said, returning to the table. "It appears to be inoperable, but we're taking all precautions, while we collect and investigate it."

Renée, Maria, and Terese looked at the stricken faces of Gino and Katrina and either smiled or chuckled.

"You didn't expect him to destroy it outright?" Renée asked, surprised at the Méridiens' reactions.

"Will you bring the probe here, Alex?" Katrina asked.

"Sure. Mickey has his engineering labs on board the *Freedom*, best place to examine it," Alex replied with a deadpan expression.

"Alex," Terese admonished, narrowing one eye at him.

"Apologies, Sers, I was joking. We'll collect the probe remotely and examine it at a distant mining site," Alex replied. "You were saying about the Council's new attitude toward armed ships, Gino."

"I always thought, given enough time, that someday I would become as agile-minded as you, Alex. Now, I think I won't live that long," Gino replied, shaking his head. "Yes, I want the Haraken deal to present to the Council."

"That's only half the challenge, Gino," Maria said, leaning on the table with her forearms. "Once you have the ships, you need crew, and, most important, you need well-trained senior officers, captains, commodores, and admirals, who have the knowledge and expertise to sail and coordinate your ships in a fight."

Gino looked at Alex for guidance.

"If I were in your boots, Gino, I'd make good use of what's at hand. There's an extensive naval training base at Haraken, where individuals are trained to pilot and service travelers and sting ships. Both are examples of the technology employed in Tridents. Train your people there."

"We can offer you the expertise of our senior commanders to teach your best naval personnel how to operate squadrons in combat situations," Terese said.

"And, one more critical point, Gino, never stop the training and testing of your squadrons for readiness," Alex added, staring hard into the Leader's eyes. "You'll probably not have advance warning of a sphere entering one of your systems, and the odds are against you having stationed a squadron there. That means you'll arrive too late to save the colony that resides there. But if your squadron attacks a sphere, carrying bullet ships, without proper readiness, you can say goodbye to your warships and their crews."

-11-
Nua'll Device

The Omnians' guests, Gino, Katrina, Terese, Tomas, and Maria, continued negotiations, while their hosts took on the task of capturing the Celus probe. None of the guests were in a hurry to complete the contractual agreements. They were determined to wait and see what the Omnians discovered during their investigation.

Mickey prided himself on his hands-on engineering approach, but manipulating the capture and investigation of a probe at a distance of 10 million kilometers needed thinking far outside his normal box. It required Mickey to broadcast an appeal for ideas.

<Not a problem, Mickey,> Claude Dupuis responded immediately. <Z has a collection of avatars and remotes in a *Freedom* bay. I'm sure we can prepare some of them to operate remotely for the probe's investigation. Don't know about collection and transport though. You'll have to solve that one.>

<Tell me how you can help with the examination of the device, Claude,> Mickey sent.

<We've a collection of shadows that you can use,> Claude sent in reply. <Their energy beads are too small to last for the length of time you'll need, but you can configure some of the larger specimens with grav shells for their energy supply and then outfit them with a set of tools.>

That was easy, Mickey thought, smiling at the collection of individuals Alex had amassed, who came with a plethora of experience, skills, and, oh, yes, toys!

The mechanics of capture, transport, and dissection weren't the only issues requiring resolution. Mickey also needed a means of collecting the minute observations that Alex required, which meant data collection.

<Miriam, I need your help,> Mickey sent to the SADE.

<With the probe?> Miriam replied. Every Omnian SADE was aware of Alex's request, concerning the probe and its subsequent investigation.

<Yes. It's Alex's priority. We'll need a team to work with Claude on reconfiguring Z's shadows to investigate the probe. They'll have to be controlled remotely. I still need a concept for remote collection and transport though.>

<I will enlist Glenn to help with the method of transport,> Miriam sent. <We can use Killian, Bethley, and Trium for the team. Alex has ordered the scout ship to remain in system.>

<Are the SADEs upset about being restricted to the system?> Mickey asked. Only humans who had lived in close association with the freed SADEs, understood that even though they were digital entities they had emotional algorithms that required satisfaction.

<Alex told the *Vivian*'s crew that he would be ordering every returning scout ship to remain in system. He said, "We have a target. When we're ready to sail to find the sphere that left the Ollassa system, the scout ships will accompany us.">

Glenn chose to co-opt the *Vivian* to use as the sphere's collection and transport vehicle. The enormous bays of the city-ship accommodated the scout ship for its augmentation, although it did require an empty bay.

Mickey's engineering team took Glenn's concept and turned it into reality. A small trap box was built and attached to the scout ship's hatch with programmable extension rods to reduce interference in the shell's collection capability.

When all was ready, the *Vivian* and OS *Prosecutor*, captained by Darius Gaumata, left orbit and headed for the outer rim of Celus. Killian would control the *Vivian* remotely from the bridge of the Trident warship. The SADEs had estimated that 10 million kilometers should be a safe distance, but it was unknown what sort of alien technology and power lurked inside the device.

When the *Prosecutor* came to a stationary position, the controller identified the distance to the probe at 16.43 million kilometers, and Killian glanced at Darius.

"Insurance," Darius replied, which Killian translated as that was as near to the probe as the captain was going to get.

The scout ship's telemetry was streamed to the warship's controller, which Killian monitored. The SADE eased the *Vivian* beside the probe. Glenn's design required Mickey's team to mount four vid cams at the corners of the box, which allowed Killian to center the probe in the box's opening.

The grav-capable scout ship enabled Killian to delicately maneuver the vessel. Mickey had wondered if a tethering process might have been the better way to go, but the SADEs had vetoed that idea, saying that the beam's energy might disturb the probe enough to have it execute a fail-safe routine, even though it was incapable of transmitting.

Glenn had chosen the trap approach based on Killian's assurance that he could easily slide the sphere into the box. And that was what Killian did. The sphere entered the enclosure without touching a side or the far end of the box. Killian signaled the twin doors of the box to close, trapping the sphere, and the walls of the nanites-coated box closed on the sphere, anchoring it in place.

"Well done, Killian," Darius remarked. His warship's controller was transmitting everything — telemetry data, vid cam views, comms, and bridge conversation — to the *Freedom*, where the action was being closely monitored.

Killian slaved the scout ship's controller to that of the *Prosecutor's*, allowing Darius to carefully back the warship away, towing the scout ship behind it, and maintaining a safe distance.

It took two anxious days before the Trident was positioned near a moon, which held a recently abandoned mining site. Killian released the controller link between the two vessels and guided the scout ship to an area that had been cleared and flattened for the upcoming operation. Once the *Vivian* was on the surface, the hatch was triggered and slowly lowered. The extension rods that supported the box were capable of cantilevering. This allowed the box to be kept level and prevent the probe from rotating.

The box gently touched the moon's surface. The rods released it, and the box was detached from the scout ship's hatch.

The SADEs aboard the warship began the next stage of the operation. Miriam, Killian, Bethley, and Trium were each linked to separate shadows via the scout ship's controller.

The small devices, called shadows, that Z had first created to penetrate an Earther warship, which had masqueraded as an explorer, had a limited comm range. This meant the scout ship must remain on the moon's surface during the investigation of the probe to facilitate communication. This aspect of the operation, exposing the scout ship to possible obliteration, didn't settle well with the *Vivian*'s crew, but they kept their thoughts to themselves.

Killian activated the doors of the box. Then the SADEs initiated control of the four spider-like shadows. The devices crawled from the vessel, across the hatch, and dropped to the moon's surface. Ever so carefully, the small but powerful creations hauled the probe from the box. The vid cams mounted on the box were repositioned to maintain a visual for the individuals monitoring the proceedings.

The first task was a minute examination of the probe's surface, which every shadow was capable of transmitting.

Mickey was hosting a small gathering in his engineering bay, where everyone was focused on an incredibly large holo-vid display.

"Looks like a miniature sphere," Tatia commented.

"Typical of any intelligent species," Mickey replied. "If a design works, why not keep using it until something better comes along?"

"Okay, Mickey, does that mean we can grasp it by the top and bottom, twist the two halves, and get it to open up like the sphere does to disgorge its bullet ships?" Ellie asked.

"Not a bad idea," Mickey quipped, giving Ellie a quick grin, before his face took on a flat expression, and he added, "But I don't suggest it."

<Council Leader Gino Diamanté,> Miriam sent, while her shadow continued its closeup scanning, <I am unable to find details in my recording of your communication with Alex as to how you destroyed the probes that you found and what the results of your actions were.>

Suddenly, more than one Omnian was berating themselves for not having asked the same question but much earlier.

<I'm embarrassed to say, Miriam, that without defensive weapons we resorted to primitive methods,> Gino sent.

<Which were?> Alex coaxed.

<We used mining excavators accompanied by ore loaders to launch rocks at the probes until we demolished them. It was a slow and laborious process. Many times, I wished for a single, beam-capable fighter or warship,> Gino lamented.

<And, specifically, Ser, what happened to the probes?> Miriam prompted.

<There was no active reaction from the probes,> Theodore interjected, after quickly reviewing the pertinent data. <In every case, the impacts continued to dent and then break the probe into pieces.>

<But you never collected the pieces?> Alex asked, wanting to ensure he understood what Gino had said during the conference.

<Ser,> Theodore replied, <the excavators launched continuously. By the time it was observed that the probes were breaking up, there were many more metric tons of rock and pebble headed the probes' way. Eventually, the entire stream of device debris and rubble sailed out of the system. We always located the probes at systems' peripheries, and the Méridiens were careful to direct the streams of ore outward.>

<Pardon my desire to ensure accuracy in our communication, Theodore,> Miriam sent, choosing to ignore discussing the fine details with a human. <How did the probes break apart?>

Theodore pulled the detailed vids recorded from the observing vessels and sent the imagery to Miriam, who studied the probes' demolishment.

<Sers, the cases of the probes dented, cracked, and sections broke off, exposing the internal systems. In every case, the probe revealed a glow from some unidentified source. The opportunity to study the inside of each probe is limited to a few ticks of time before the next onslaught of rocks demolished more pieces of the probe and extinguished the light source,> Miriam summarized.

There were audible sighs of relief from the humans, who shared the comm link. Having missed the opportunity to delve deeper into the Méridiens' method of removing the probes, it appeared that there had been nothing more to glean.

Belatedly, it occurred to Alex that if a warning about a probe's demolishment had been needed, Theodore would have sounded the alarm, which made him wonder why Miriam was questioning Gino and Theodore so closely.

<Miriam,> Alex sent in a private comm. <What are you concerned about?>

<A thought has occurred to me, Ser. Our enemy is a technologically sophisticated species, much more so than us. Therefore, I asked myself: If I could design a probe to do anything I wanted, what would it be capable of doing?>

<And the answer was?> Alex asked.

<First and foremost, I would have designed my probe to tell the difference between common space events and investigations by intelligent life forms.>

<Meaning, when the Méridiens resorted to the simplistic approach of rock throwing, your probe would have acquiesced to being demolished rather than give up its secret,> Alex replied.

<Precisely, Ser. However, if my probe were discovered by a spacefaring life form, one probably originating from the system under observation, then —>

<You would detonate your power source, eliminating all trace of your surreptitious observation of the system and those arriving to observe you,> Alex finished. <We've already captured and moved the probe, Miriam. Doesn't that negate your theory?>

<Unfortunately, Ser, I'm unable to model the Nua'll psyche. I can't predict exactly what they might do, but the probability is high that our investigation of the probe will be terminated sooner than later.>

Alex trusted and accepted the advice of SADEs, especially those who were free and had lived side by side with humans for years. They shared the priority to protect their comrades, humans and SADEs, while pursuing the enemy.

<Abandon the probe's investigation,> Alex ordered, the power of his thought striking hard at implants and comms alike. <SADEs, freeze the shadows where they are. Killian, lift the *Vivian* without closing the hatch. Captain Gaumata, fast exit.>

The four SADEs cut their links to the shadows. Killian eased the scout ship clear of the probe. He waited to close the hatch after he'd launched the vessel from the moon's surface.

Darius applied maximum acceleration with his grav engines in an effort to get his Trident as fast and as far away from the device as possible.

The blinding light of the probe's detonation speared out and was faithfully recorded by the OS *Prosecutor*'s controller.

Killian lost his telemetry view from the *Vivian*, as the expanding wave of energy shredded the scout ship.

Miriam selected a view of the moon for her broadcast to Mickey's engineering suite or, rather, she selected a view of what was left of the moon. A wave of rock and dust expanded outward, taking a quarter of the dense moon with it. The mining site had been situated on the far side from the enormous planet, protecting it from the force of the blast.

As the rocky debris expanded outward, Tatia ordered the Trident captains to employ their warships and travelers to pulverize the moon debris to prevent them from becoming navigation hazards.

<Well done, Miriam,> Alex sent on open comm.

<Congratulations aren't in order, Alex, I failed to deliver my thoughts in time to protect the *Vivian* or Z's shadows.>

<Those are things, Miriam. There was no loss of life. What you did was think as our enemy might and make observations from that viewpoint. As I said, well done.>

"Alex, what happened when you went off our common link?" Mickey asked.

"Miriam postulated that the Nua'll might have designed their probes to differentiate between natural accidents and intelligent investigations. It dawned on me that if the probe's monitoring system were that sophisticated, it might be trying to determine the optimum time to detonate. When we were operating remotely, the probe might have perceived the unmanned scout ship as an insignificant target. So, it decided to wait. However, when we deserted our investigation, it chose to detonate to take out the observation craft."

"Just how are we supposed to compete with that level of paranoia?" Katrina asked.

"Stand back and destroy the probes and spheres at a distance. Simple!" Tatia announced.

"Like she said," Alex said, tossing a hand in Tatia's direction.

Julien contacted the warship's controller. He wanted the telemetry data, which would identify the extent of the expanding energy wave. It was greater than projected, but Julien compensated for the effect of the moon's mass directing the forces outward, away from the gas giant. He transferred the data and calculations to Theodore and various repositories on board the Omnian, New Terran, and Haraken ships.

After a moment of reflection, Alex sent, <Mickey, Julien, and Tatia, I need a means of destroying the probes at a distance without us having to throw rocks. The method must be simple, foolproof, and disposable. Make me ten of them.>

An hour after the spectators in the engineering bay had dispersed, Alex received a comm from Bethley.

<Dassata, before we seek advice from Trixie about how we might help planetside, is there anything that you need done for the ships or station?> Bethley sent.

<Proceed to query Trixie, Bethley, but keep your assignment temporary,> Alex sent in reply. <Another scout ship will be released from its construction bay in thirteen days. It will be yours, and it will need testing before you accompany the Trident squadron on the hunt.>

It didn't surprise Alex when Killian, who he suspected was listening to the exchange, said, <Dassata, the *Vivian* might be an unfortunate name for a vessel. Should we choose another?>

<Why do you consider it unfortunate, Killian?> Alex asked. <You, your crew, and your ship led us to a system inhabited by a race who

fought a second sphere and shared with us the direction it took when it fled. But, I take your meaning. You might consider something that keeps the original intent but with a slight variation, such as *Vivian's Deuce*,> Alex offered and closed the comm.

Killian immediately contacted Julien, the ultimate translator of oblique comments made by Alex.

<Killian, deuce is an anachronistic name given the number two card in Alex's ancient game,> Julien replied.

-12-
Probes

Once Admiral Tripping was made aware of the Nua'll tendency to seed a probe in every system, he insisted that his flagship, the NT *Geoffrey Orlan*, be released from duty. He was determined to be the one to locate the probe in the New Terra system, if it existed.

"Are you demanding to be relieved of duty, Admiral, or are you asking permission? By your tone, Admiral, I'm unsure of the nature of your words," Tatia replied with her ex-major's parade-command voice. She would have preferred a private conversation with Tripping via her implant, but New Terrans had yet to adopt the technology. To make matters worse, Tripping started the conversation over the *Freedom*'s bridge speakers.

The bridge crew attempted to appear busy at their consoles, but all ears were focused on Tripping's response. Both Tatia and Cordelia were carefully recording the conversation.

"Naturally, this is a request, Admiral. If I sounded a little strident, it's only that I'm worried for my home world and the thought of an alien probe circling the outer system," Tripping replied, in a conciliatory tone.

<This human is erratic. That makes him dangerous to his people and ours,> Cordelia sent to Tatia.

Tatia decided it was better not to respond to Cordelia's comment, not that she disagreed with the SADE. "Admiral, you and your flagship are temporarily relieved from the agreement. If and when a probe is located and destroyed, you're expected to return your ship to formation."

"Thank you, Admiral," Tripping replied. He never considered sending one of the other NT Tridents to New Terra. Now that he possessed the means of identifying a probe's signal, he intended to be the one to locate it. To his way of thinking, whoever uncovered the alien device would be a hero in the eyes of the planet's populace, and Tripping fully intended to be that man.

"Admiral Tripping, this is Envoy Maria Gonzalez," Maria said, stressing her title. She had been in Alex's suite working with Alex, Julien, Terese, and Gino on the agreement. Alex had set up a call for her in his work study where she could converse privately with the admiral.

"Good day, Maria," Tripping replied casually.

"Just so you and I have an understanding, Admiral," Maria said forcefully. "Your controller will soon receive a coded message for President Grumley from me. It will be released the moment you enter New Terran space. It will detail the possible existence of an alien probe in the system, the means to locate it, and the danger of approaching it. It will also inform the president that the Omnians are working on a solution to safely eliminate the probe. If a probe is found, I'm advising the president to wait for the arrival of the Omnian remedy."

"That's quite unnecessary, Maria. If I didn't know better, I would think that you didn't trust me to be forthright with our president."

Maria didn't reply, and Tripping cleared his throat, before he said, "We'll be breaking formation immediately. If you're intending to send a message, you'd better hurry."

Maria ended the comm and smiled. "Idiot," she murmured. Tripping had tried to pressure her, as if she wasn't aware that the NT *Geoffrey Orlan* would cross about two-thirds of the Omnian system before it exited and transited to New Terra. She had days to compose her message and have Julien program the ship's controller to broadcast it when the Trident arrived.

"Maria," Julien said, stepping into the work study. "The *Geoffrey Orlan* is diving below the ecliptic. Admiral Tripping intends to exit our space within 2.35 hours. Cordelia took the liberty of sharing your communications with me. Considering the admiral's intention, I've composed a message that you would probably wish to send. You have a copy on your reader, if you would like to approve it first."

"Send it, Julien," Maria said. As she walked past the SADE to rejoin the discussion in the salon, she gently patted Julien's cheek, and said,

"Don't think that because you did me this favor that I'm going to let you get the best of me in these negotiations."

"The probability scored so low that it wasn't worthy of consideration," Julien replied with a smile.

"Yes, but you calculated it anyway," Maria replied.

"I did have the time," Julien replied, and he sprouted his infamous negotiations cap, the one he wore at Alex's card games, the open cap with the translucent green visor.

Maria's hearty laugh echoed from the study, and the heads of those in the salon turned her way. "That's a good one, Julien," Maria remarked. "You had the time," she repeated and laughed again.

As opposed to Tripping's choice, Terese accepted the loan of an Omnian Trident to search the Haraken system. The message that Captain Darius Gaumata would deliver to the planet's Assembly Speaker was that he had made the journey at the request of the president. To wit, he was authorized to conduct a survey of the system's periphery in support of the president's negotiation with Alex Racine of Omnia Ships. It was anticipated that President Lechaux would be returning to Haraken with a favorable and valuable contract.

It was hoped the latter part of the message would keep the Harakens focused on future prosperity instead of worrying why an Omnian warship was cruising their system.

* * *

Weeks later, Alex, Julien, and Tatia headed for the *Freedom*'s engineering bay, at Mickey's request. They discovered the engineer observing his oversized holo-vid display, surrounded by some of his team, including Miriam.

"Mickey, why is this holo-vid constantly getting larger than the one on the bridge?" Tatia asked.

"Always upgrading it, Admiral, and we do have much more space in this bay than on the bridge," Mickey explained.

"And engineers need to see details," Alex allowed, although his expression didn't show that he believed that.

"See, Alex understands," Mickey said, feeling exonerated.

"What do you have for us, Mickey?" Alex asked.

"As you requested, Alex, it's your probe destroyer or, as we call it, the banisher," Mickey replied with a grin.

"Appropriate, Mickey," Tatia said, chuckling. "We are trying to divest ourselves of alien vermin."

Revolving in the holo-vid display was an odd-looking craft. It was obviously a shell-type vessel, but it appeared to have a small bulb on one end and a larger protrusion on the other.

"Okay, Mickey, which is the bow, and which is the stern?" Tatia asked.

"This is the stern, Admiral," Mickey replied, pointing to the end with the greater deformation. This little vessel is only 5.5-meters long, and it's grav-driven as you can see by its smooth hull."

"Only a grav drive?" Alex queried.

"We didn't see the value of both types of engines," Miriam replied. "Based on the data supplied by Theodore, which is similar to the circumstances of our own probe, the Nua'll devices inhabit the orbits of the outer planets or asteroid belts. Once our banisher captures a probe, it can accelerate sufficiently to carry the probe safely beyond the system before the power crystals are drained."

Alex nodded his understanding and acceptance of the logic.

"And just how are you supposed to capture this probe?" Tatia asked.

Mickey's face split into another huge grin, and Miriam signaled the holo-vid display. The bow of the tiny vessel split into an imitation of the clamshell rear ends of the sting ships and Tridents. In this case, there were no engines.

"We approach the probe from a system inward position, close slowly on it, and grasp it," Mickey explained, like the proud father introducing his newborn.

"What if the probe detonates on contact?" Tatia asked.

Mickey glanced at Alex, wondering if he hadn't understood the requirements of Alex's request.

"We ensure the probe is never within ... what, Julien?"

"The original estimate of 10 million kilometers is satisfactory, as long as the probe is not backed by a significant celestial body. In that case, Captain Guamata's *insurance* distance of 16.5 million kilometers is preferred."

"In other words, we wait until the probe is out in the open," Alex finished.

"What would be your preference, Alex, if the probe is orbiting a gas giant?" Miriam asked.

"When we picked up our probe with the *Vivian*, it didn't detonate," Alex replied. "I'm hoping we can count on that reaction if we scoop up the probe gently with Mickey's banisher. Speaking of that, Mickey, what if the probe determines that being enclosed is an alien investigation?"

"That's the beauty of this design, Alex. We don't enclose the probe. The SADEs postulated that there was a high probability our probe didn't explode when we captured it because we constructed the *Vivian*'s external box out of plex-crystal."

"That's a stretch, Mickey, to say the clear box didn't allow the probe to reach a decision between a natural event and an artificial one," Alex commented.

"If we examine the following events, Alex," Julien said. "Our probe was damaged, which meant it couldn't broadcast its data, but obviously it could run its monitoring program. We believe it wasn't until the shadows' interventions that the probe's decision tree was triggered to conclude the event was artificial. After that, it merely waited until an opportune moment. When the *Vivian* deserted its immediate vicinity, I would imagine the probe's self-protection program calculated a decreasing opportunity to cause damage, and it detonated."

"You're making these probes sound almost as sinister as the sphere," Tatia commented.

"I would imagine they're similar in nature, Admiral," Julien replied. "Miriam's theories about the probes being a product of a ruthless and technologically superior enemy civilization have done much to reorient the SADEs' thinking about the Nua'll, their vessels, and any of their devices."

Miriam tipped her head in Julien's direction, appreciating the recognition. <Freedom does wonders for opening up the thought processes to new ideas,> Miriam sent to Julien.

"Back to your concept, Mickey, that we don't enclose the sphere," Alex requested.

"Miriam, if you would, please?" Mickey asked. "Everyone, this is a simulation. It's to scale for the two devices, mind you, of how the process would work."

<The Confederation probes were the same size?> Alex asked Julien privately.

<Identical, Alex,> Julien sent in reply.

The group watched the presentation. The banisher approached the probe. Then it slowed, and the bow's clamshell doors opened. Gently, the doors closed on the probe, the tips of the doors barely reaching past the point of its circumference. Then the banisher accelerated out past the system's periphery, disappearing into the dark.

"All well and good, Mickey, but what if the probe never figures out that this is an artificial intervention?" Tatia asked. "I can't believe I'm talking as if these probes are sentient," she muttered.

"Admiral, the probes must have some form of artificial intelligence, what is more properly connoted as machine intelligence. It's calculating probabilities based on input and programming, but sentient it's not," Julien said with determination.

"To answer your question, Admiral, look here," Mickey replied.

Miriam reset the holo-vid display to the moment when the banisher captured the probe in its clamshell doors. Then the view of the banisher was transformed to an internal view, the shell disappearing. Inside the slender hull could be seen a shaft with a long, thin drill at its tip.

"We wait until the energy from the power crystals falls to 25 percent, as the banisher speeds out beyond the system. If the probe hasn't detonated, and we'll be far outside the system by then, we start drilling the probe," Mickey said, clapping his hands in delight.

"That'll guarantee to wake up its programming," Tatia replied.

"And what if its programming is defunct due to the probe's inoperable state?" Alex asked.

"We keep drilling holes until we hit a power core," Mickey replied. "Our machine is set to punch through the probe, pull back, move 7 centimeters over, and drill another hole. The SADEs calculate that within a maximum of twenty drill points we'll rupture the energy source, if it's still active, which they assure me it probably will be, even if the probe appears inactive for every other condition."

"Talk to me about our ship's end of the operation," Tatia said.

"The banisher is a vessel like any other," Mickey replied. "It has a small controller, which a SADE or a ship's officer can direct through the Trident's controller. Once the banisher is directed toward a probe, which is when you have a safe opening, its programming takes over. You don't have to do anything else."

"And transport?" Tatia asked.

"It can land and launch from a bay," Mickey replied. "The banisher's controller will follow a simple navigation procedure once the command is given. It's really self-contained in many ways. Alex said to keep it simple."

"I like it, Mickey," Alex said, slapping the engineer heartily on the back.

"The team," Mickey replied, pointing to Miriam, the engineers, and the techs, "deserves the credit."

A slender Méridien-built tech, who stood next to Alex, held up his hands in protest when Alex eyed him, "I'm good, Ser," he said, hoping not to receive the same indication of praise as had Mickey.

"We need a few to test, Mickey. How soon?" Alex asked.

Some engineers and techs grinned, when Mickey nodded to them. They ran to structures, resting on the deck, and yanked back the covers.

"Three banishers ready to test," Mickey announced with a flourish.

"I can see I don't keep you busy enough," Alex said, chuckling.

"Julien, target?" Alex asked.

"The first test should be conducted at Haraken, Alex. Based on Theodore's telemetry analysis and the Confederation's discoveries, a probe will be located in the Hellébore system."

To the SADEs and others, logic indicated the probe must have been in place for a century or more, before even the Méridiens founded the Cetus colony on the planet the Harakens now called home. The Nua'll sphere had destroyed the colony, ships, stations, and sites within the Hellébore system, when the Méridiens inhabited it, before moving on. The thought that the Haraken's home system had continued to be spied on by an alien probe for more than two decades after it was resettled gave the humans a chill.

Alex signaled Tatia and Julien and left the bay in a hurry, the celebratory noise of the engineering team dying out only after the airlock's hatch closed behind them.

<President Lechaux and Envoy Gonzalez, would you please meet me on the *Freedom*'s bridge?> Alex sent, while Tatia requested Reiko and her Trident captains to link to Cordelia.

Terese slid out of the arms of her partner, Tomas Monti. "President Lechaux is requested on the bridge," she said.

"Uh-oh," Tomas replied.

"Yes, Alex's sending is accompanied by a little extra implant power. I think I liked it better when he used to call me Terese or his fiery redhead."

"Should I attend?" Tomas asked.

"It wouldn't hurt."

In contrast to Terese's subdued reaction, Maria wore a fierce grin. "It's about time," she muttered, as she hurried to catch a lift about to close that would take her to the city-ship's bridge level. She'd been trying to enjoy a relaxing moment in the grand park and failing miserably. She was anxious for the Omnians to produce whatever they would use to remove the probes. She had a sinking feeling if she didn't return to New Terra soon, with a viable solution, the admiral might do something foolish.

"The commodore and Trident captains are on the bridge comm line," Cordelia stated, as Alex, Tatia, and Julien came through the bridge accessway. "I've taken the liberty of cuing the imagery from the engineering bay, which you were recently viewing. Miriam believed that was the reason for your hasty exit and anticipated that you'd wish to communicate to the other world leaders."

<One of these days, I will simply change my facial expression to indicate my need, and the SADEs will take care of everything for me,> Alex joked privately to Julien.

<Or we will worry that you've developed a nervous facial tic and your medical nanites have failed,> Julien replied.

"Well done, Captain," Alex said, approaching the holo-vid, which displayed engineering's banisher.

Soon afterwards Maria, Terese, and Tomas arrived together.

Terese and Tomas were slightly breathless. "This ship is an exercise in itself," Terese quipped.

"What do you have for us, Alex?" Maria asked, anxious to hear about any progress that Mickey might have made.

"The engineering team's answer to the probes," Alex replied, waving at the holo-vid display. "They call it a banisher. Alex played the animation for the audience. Then he walked them through the same questions and answers exchanged only moments ago with Mickey and his associates.

"When can we have one?" Maria asked.

"Apologies, Maria, but you won't be carrying one to New Terra to deliver to Admiral Tripping," Alex replied, and held up a hand to forestall Maria's retort, which seemed to be on the edge of her lips. "I need detailed telemetry on how well a banisher works, and I need a captain who I can count on to follow my instructions."

Maria's lips tightened. She knew Alex was right not to trust Admiral Tripping to follow his orders, especially when they came from an Omnian, who carried no military rank.

"Admiral, announce your choices for deployment," Alex requested.

"Captain Thompson, you'll accompany Envoy Gonzalez to New Terra. Locate the probe, and deploy the banisher. You'll take your launch order from President Grumley," Tatia ordered.

"And need we add, Captain, there's to be no one else involved in your operation?" Alex requested, glancing at Maria, who tipped her head in agreement.

"Your message is clear, Alex," Ellie replied.

"You'll need a SADE, Captain. I'll request Killian go with you," Alex added.

Alex had no sooner said that than Killian was updated by Julien. He bid his comrades farewell and hurried to catch a traveler soon to lift from the planet, which could transfer him to the OS *Redemption*.

"Captain Gaumata, you've already been to the Hellébore system and located its probe," Tatia said. "Therefore, you'll pick up a banisher and accompany President Lechaux to Haraken."

"Captain Gaumata," Alex said, "once you've determined the safest window of opportunity to deploy your banisher, you'll communicate to the president. She will approve its release. This is to ensure that she's had time to properly inform the Haraken Assembly."

Julien sent a quick message to Alex, who agreed to add Miriam to the conference. "Miriam, I'm requesting that you accompany Captain Gaumata to the Haraken system to coordinate the release of the banisher. Captain, Miriam was instrumental in the design and construction of this tool."

"Subject experts are always welcome," Darius replied, "especially when they come in the shape of a SADE."

"Flatterer," Miriam laughed, her SADE sound for laughter imitated a pair of songbirds.

-13-
Home Worlds I

The OS *Prosecutor*'s controller held the telemetry of the Hellébore probe's orbital track from its earlier survey, which enabled Miriam to quickly calculate the optimum point of intersection for the Trident the moment it transited into the system's space.

President Lechaux's ship and the Trident had immediately parted ways. Her captain charted a course for Haraken, and the Trident cut across the ecliptic to intercept the probe, which was crossing behind Hellébore's outermost planet.

Terese wasted no time scheduling an extended Assembly session. She left her message vague. While she had good news regarding the agreement with Omnia Ships, news of the probe and a sharing of the warships to aid in Alex's hunt of the spheres would come as a shock.

With Haraken in a near orbit, Terese made the planet days ahead of the Trident's passage across the system. Landing at Espero's primary traveler port, Tomas and she took a grav car to the Assembly building. She had only made three addresses to the body of representatives before now, and they had been mundane.

"Members of the Assembly," Terese said, opening her address. "I will begin with startling news, which might frighten you, but, rest assured, I will end with good news. The Omnians have discovered a second sphere. It's not coming our way, and the Omnians intend to hunt it down. During these past months, it was questioned how the Nua'll located their target systems, and we discovered the answer. Each of our systems appears to have a Nua'll probe monitoring it. The Méridiens have taken drastic steps to destroy theirs, but they were fortunate in their primitive technique of throwing rocks at the devices. When the Omnians attempted to investigate theirs, it detonated. The explosion was massive, but, fortunately, no one was harmed."

"What is being done to locate our probe?" an Assemblyman asked.

"It's already been found," Terese supplied. "An Omnian warship, a Trident, captained by Darius Gaumata, is making its way across the system to intercept it." The mention of the Libran, who had fought with Alex since the beginning, gave the representatives a reason to relax.

"Does that mean the Trident will use a beam to destroy it?" an Assemblywoman asked.

"Negative," Terese replied. "When the Omnian probe detonated, it was being remotely investigated at a preexisting mining site. The explosion destroyed more than a quarter of a medium-sized moon and created a danger radius of 13.8 million kilometers."

"What are the Omnians going to do?" Terese was asked.

"Well, Alex put Mickey Brandon, his engineering team, and the SADEs on the job to come up with an answer. Mickey calls his solution the banisher." As Terese hoped, speaking of the irrepressible engineer was guaranteed to produce a high level of confidence in the Omnian invention. Terese activated the Assembly's primary holo-vid and ran the animation for the representatives.

"The Omnians' approach will be to catch the probe in the open and snare it, then take it where a detonation can do little harm," Terese said.

"When will that happen?" a second Assemblywoman asked.

"The Omnians will notify me when they're ready, and I will give the order," Terese replied. "In the meantime, I have an agreement for this body to review and ratify. It underpins the dire realization that the Nua'll have seeded thousands, perhaps tens of thousands, of systems with their probes. It's come to our realization that the Nua'll didn't come from some lone home world, with an intent to expand via a single sphere, which was destroyed. They appear to be a significant civilization, with designs on expanding across the galaxy."

"There's no proof of that," Jason Haraken shouted.

Ah, the willful, rancorous one raises its ugly head, Terese thought.

"Wasn't it you, Ser Haraken, who claimed for years that we shouldn't be spending money on military power?"

On Terese's signal, Tomas sent an implant recording of Jason railing, during an Assembly session, on just that subject. It was heard by the entire Assembly via their implants, facilitated by Elizabeth, one of the SADEs first freed by Alex.

"This is fearmongering," Jason was heard shouting. "There was one sphere, and that was more than twenty years ago. No one has seen another since and probably never will."

"Well, Ser Haraken, the Omnians have proven you wrong," Terese said, after the recording played. "We're finding a Nua'll probe in every system the sphere attacked and in every system that it didn't. Now, a second sphere has been discovered."

"President Lechaux, may we proceed with your overview of the agreement?" another Assemblyman asked.

"It's quite simple, Sers. Omnia Ships is willing to lease the technology and plans to allow us to construct our own faux-shell Tridents, fighters, and scout ships." Terese was unable to continue, while the majority of representatives broke out in applause. A small contingent, led by Jason, sat with sullen expressions on their faces.

"At what cost?" Jason shouted.

"I'm glad you asked that question, Ser Haraken, although you might try to modify your volume. I'm only 10 meters from you." The tittering that followed Terese's rebuke had Jason's face competing for color and brightness with her hair. "We pay, what I consider, a modest licensing fee for each ship that we construct. The primary codicil is that we must supply half of these ships with crew to support the Omnians in their effort to locate and destroy the spheres."

"For how long?" Jason yelled, but he did make an effort to lower his voice a little.

"Twenty years," Terese replied. "Afterwards, all the ships we construct are ours to deploy as we see fit."

"Can we still produce the Tridents and the scout ships with the faux shells?" a third Assemblyman asked.

"Negative, Ser, after the twenty years, the rights to use the faux-shell technique reverts to Omnia Ships. Although, there is always the possibility that a new agreement with the Omnians can be negotiated by your president, at that time, if she's clever." Terese couldn't resist a broad smile to punctuate her vision of the future. She spotted Bibi Haraken, the matriarch of the Haraken clan, who grinned at her from the gallery.

"I will leave this Assembly to review the agreement in detail, but I urge you to make a quick decision," Terese continued. "Events are moving quickly, whether we want them to or not, and Haraken needs to prepare for the dangers that threaten us."

Terese turned to leave, but stopped. "Before I go, I would leave you with one thought. We did a poor job of welcoming the Confederation SADEs to our planet, and, because of that, they isolated themselves in an enclave. I was reminded, watching the SADEs at Omnia, how effective they are when they're welcomed by humans. Our society needs to take a fresh approach to communicating with the Confederation SADEs. They're invaluable if Haraken wants to have a strong, competitive, economic future."

Three days later, Terese received a comm from Captain Gaumata. The OS *Prosecutor* was in position. Terese and Tomas were sharing a quiet evening with Alex's parents, Duggan and Katie, and Alex's sister, Christie.

"It looks like I'll require some broadcast time tomorrow, Christie. It will be a president's message," Terese said.

During most of Alex's time on Haraken, a single city, Espero, had dominated the planet's landscape. Little Ben, affectionately known as Rainmaker, had pummeled the skies and oceans with ice asteroids to rehydrate the thirsty planet after the plundering of resources by the Nua'll sphere.

The increase in the planet's rain cycles and storms led to the replenishment of grasses and shrubbery. Then the Harakens planted wide swaths of trees, whose seeds were slowly spreading the forests. The return of streams and, eventually, rivers allowed the population to spread out into hundreds of new enclaves.

To reach the present population required a media broadcast, and the largest media company with the greatest reach was owned by Christie Racine. What began as a small news channel had steadily grown in size and scope. Now, its multichannel format linked the population for news, entertainment, financial data, and interviews. It was the primary tool employed by Haraken presidents to communicate critical announcements to not only the planet, but also systemwide and to Haraken ships sailing the deep dark.

"Darius was quick to locate our probe," Katie commented. "Perhaps a little too quick?" she added, narrowing her eyes at Terese.

"Confession time, is it?" Terese said, draining her drink and leaning back in the comfortable couch next to Tomas. The nanites underneath her, distributed their positions to accommodate her slender stature.

"It's okay, Terese," Christie replied. "We know the *Prosecutor's* first visit wasn't to survey the system for a new agreement, as you hinted, but to locate the alien probe."

"That obvious?" Terese asked. "I thought it was rather subtle, using the potential contract with Omnia Ships to obfuscate the *Trident's* real purpose."

"It was a smart idea, Terese," Duggan replied, laughing, "until anyone with a brain realized that the *Trident* is an Omnian ship, probably with one or more SADEs aboard, and would have access to every scrap of telemetry data on the Hellébore system. The Omnians would have no more need of a survey than I would have need to look down and count my toes to see if I had ten."

"Which means that the *Prosecutor* was searching for something that was small and could easily hide ... something designed to be hidden," Christie said.

"They have been well hidden," Terese said. "Alex and his people had to do a blind search to locate the Omnian probe. It had been damaged, but they have the SADE power to conduct that type of investigation. The Confederation and we have been fortunate, or maybe not, if you think about it."

"How so?" Duggan prompted.

"Apologies, Duggan, lost my train of thought there. After the Méridiens located the initial probe, they were able to identify the signature broadcast. This allows us to find the probes much more easily, providing the device is transmitting. Ours is still broadcasting ... still inviting the Nua'll here."

Katie's hand flew to her mouth. Lowering it, she said, "I was about to say that the Nua'll have already been here so what value is a probe in our system, but then I realized the naiveté of that thought."

The group nodded in commiseration.

"Yes," Tomas said, dispirited. "I imagine that piece of alien technology is happily reporting the revival of this planet, saying, "Look it's green and prospering again. Time to plunder!"

"Exactly where is the probe, Terese?" Christie asked.

"It's been circling in the outer asteroid belt hidden amid millions and millions of metric tons of space rock and ice," Terese replied.

* * *

"You have my permission to launch your device, Captain Gaumata," Terese sent over her comm link. "The populace has been informed."

"I'm acknowledging your permission to launch our banisher at the Nua'll probe, Madam President," Darius replied formally and closed the link.

"You heard the president, Miriam," Darius said to the SADE, who stood next to him on the bridge. "You may launch when ready."

Miriam quirked an eye at Darius, the controller's telemetry registered a distance of 20 million kilometers to the probe.

"Extra insurance," Darius explained.

Miriam signaled the crew chief that she was prepared to launch, and she received the crew chief's response acknowledging that he'd cleared the bay. That Miriam could determine that by locating bio IDs was immaterial. She enjoyed adopting human protocols. They added a bit of uncertainty to her life, which was filled with ordered thought.

When the bay doors opened, Miriam slipped the banisher out and pointed it at the probe. She had already transferred the probe's coordinates and trajectory to the device. Then, she triggered the banisher's programming, and the tiny vessel launched itself forward.

From the bridge, the course of the banisher was tracked, and its telemetry recorded. Soon the little ship decelerated and came to a stop, mere meters from the probe. Slowly its jaws opened, and it closed the intervening distance. The moment the four leaves of the clamshell closed on the probe, the banisher's telemetry went dead.

On board the Trident, the captain, crew, and SADE witnessed the blinding light of the probe's detonation.

"It appears, Captain, that Nua'll technology detects our style of intervention as artificial," Miriam said.

"So long as we keep our distance when these things go off, I don't care what they detect," Darius replied. He'd been nervous about this experiment, having just survived a similar affair with the Omnian probe.

"Danger zone for our ships, Miriam?" Darius asked.

"Twelve point eight million kilometers, Captain," Miriam replied. She wanted to tease him about his desire for *extra insurance*, but her senses had registered his heightened biorhythm levels, indicating anxiety. Instead, she asked, "Omnia, Captain?"

"Indeed, Miriam," Darius replied.

* * *

Killian transited the OS *Redemption* into Oistos space. The Trident sailed alongside the *Rover*, a mere 35 kilometers separating them. "Too close for your preferences, Captain?" Killian asked Ellie, when he noticed her frown.

"What if the *Rover*'s controller had erred in its settings or the captain had chosen a different exit point?" Ellie asked.

"Your pardon, Captain, I eliminated potential errors by linking our ship's controller with the *Rover*'s. The New Terran captain might have thought he was responsible for the exit from Celus and the entry into Oistos, but he wasn't."

Ellie laughed at Killian's response. "It's easy to see who you've spent too much time with, Killian. The man is a bad influence on you."

"I do enjoy the manner in which Dassata eliminates many of the superfluous discussions and bureaucratic processes around him," Killian replied, proud to be recognized as a close associate of Alex.

"Superfluous discussions. I must remember that one," Ellie replied. "Contact Admiral Tripping, please, Killian."

"Captain Thompson," Morney replied cordially, "we're ready to take possession of whatever solution you're delivering to eliminate the probe."

<Killian, add Maria to this conference,> Ellie sent.

"Envoy Gonzalez," Ellie said, giving Maria a heads-up, as to the formal nature of the conversation. "There seems to be some confusion as to who will manage the elimination of the probe. Captain Morney believes they will handle the operation."

"Hardly," Maria replied gruffly. She was one of the few individuals who didn't handle transit in and out of systems well, and she was in no mood to cater to a Tripping sycophant. "Get me the admiral, Captain," Maria ordered.

"The admiral is indisposed, at the moment, Envoy Gonzalez. I can tell you that Admiral Tripping has had extensive conversations with President Grumley and has cleared this exercise with him."

"Exercise?" Maria ground out. "You call ridding our system of a dangerous alien probe that when detonated spreads a powerful energy wave that can destroy ships within 10 million kilometers or more an exercise?"

"Perhaps that was an unfortunate choice of words, Envoy Gonzalez, but I can assure you that we have the capabilities to manage any process. We're merely requesting the Omnians to hand over their solution with whatever instructions that accompany it."

"Do you want their SADE too, Captain?" Maria asked.

"I beg your pardon, Ma'am?"

"You said you wanted the instructions, Captain. Who do you think will handle the *exercise* for the Omnians?"

"Perhaps you had best speak to Admiral Tripping, Ma'am. I'll have him contact you, when he wakes."

"Don't bother, Captain," Maria said, cutting her comm link.

Immediately, Maria placed a comm call to Government House, New Terra's residence for the president, located in the heart of the New Terra capital, Prima.

"Envoy Gonzalez, its 4.85 hours in the morning. The president is asleep," the Government House comm operator replied.

"And I'm awake. Harold can join me," Maria growled.

"I'll contact security, Ma'am. Please wait," the comm operator replied.

Maria fumed for nearly a quarter hour. She thought better of her desire to straighten out the admiral at this hour of the morning, but it was too late now.

"Maria, what's happening?" the president asked, his voice nervous and slurred.

"My apologies, Harold, I should have waited until later. You know I don't handle transit too well."

"My sympathies, Maria; what's got you riled?"

"I thought I was clear in my message, Harold. Why does Captain Morney, quoting Admiral Tripping, believe they should handle the operation to remove the probe?"

"Ah, well, after Tripping located the probe, the fear level of the populace ratcheted incredibly. Tripping made the pronouncement over and over again that he and his crew would remove the probe. He said they were only waiting for some simple item from the Omnians, who were late in delivering it."

"Late? Why that trumped-up little excuse for an officer," Maria fumed.

"I know, Maria," Harold replied, trying to clear his mind and think of a way to mollify her. "I've been under pressure from some Assembly members, who want more separation between Harakens and Omnians, but the majority have been in favor of closer ties.

"Well, Harold, I tell you what. Maybe you should hear the Omnians' side of the story. I'll connect you with Captain Thompson of the Trident warship, OS *Redemption*. She's the amenable sort."

"That's fine, Maria. I'm sure the captain and I can come to some agreement."

Before Harold Grumley could think through the implications of Maria's offer, the *Rover*'s controller linked him to Captain Thompson.

"Apologies for disturbing you so early in the morning, President Grumley," Ellie said graciously.

"These things happen, Captain ... the price of leadership. What would it take to transfer your technology to our Trident, Captain?"

"Actually, it could be accomplished fairly easily, Mr. President."

"Fine, Captain. When can you begin this process?"

"My apologies, Mr. President, you asked what it would take. You didn't ask whether I would do it."

Maria bit a finger to keep from laughing. If Grumley were more awake, he would have considered the possibility that any Omnian Trident captain would be someone who had been with Alex from the early days. Odds were good that they would be a Libran, who were fierce supporters of Alex Racine and not easily dissuaded from following his directives.

"What's stopping you, Captain?" Harold asked.

"I've been ordered to remove the probe, Mr. President ... my ship and no one else. This was supposedly made clear to you in your envoy's message."

"This is the Oistos system, Captain. As president, I have the right to overrule your admiral's orders, concerning any action you might take here."

"To be clear, President Grumley, it was Alex Racine, who gave me these specific orders. Now, if you don't wish me to remove your nasty alien probe, that's your right. Killian, turn this ship about. We're headed home," Ellie ordered in a clear voice, winking at the SADE, who grinned at her.

"There's no need to be hasty, Captain. I'm sure that we can resolve this matter amicably, with a little effort on both our parts. Give me a moment, if you will, Captain."

Maria was close to biting through the skin on her knuckle. Even good politicians like Grumley were used to considering everything negotiable. Every one of them were required to learn, at one point or another, that Alex Racine and Admiral Tachenko weren't politicians.

Grumley was wrapped in his dressing gown and seated behind his study's desk. He indicated to his comm operator, who was seated at a small console to the left of his desk, to silence the connection with the ships.

"Get me Admiral Tripping," Grumley ordered.

The comm operator located the controller code for the *Geoffrey Orlan* and sent the request.

"President Grumley, this is Captain Morney," came the response over the president's desk unit.

"Captain, I believe the request was for your admiral," Grumley replied.

"Yes, Mr. President, it was, but the admiral is asleep."

"So was I, Captain."

There was a pause before Morney caught on. "I'll wake him, Sir. Shall I comm you back?"

"I'll wait, but only briefly, Captain."

Morney turned to a second lieutenant and said, "Wake the admiral. Tell him the president is on the comm."

The lieutenant hurried off, as directed, loathing the captain's decision not to call the admiral on his reader. Whoever woke the admiral would receive a negative mark in his book.

"This is Admiral Tripping, Mr. President. Is there an emergency?" Tripping was seated at his cabin's desk to take the call. He had been startled awake by a pounding at his door and wondered why he didn't receive the contact via his reader. A muffled voice spoke a message about the president on the comm, and, in Tripping's hurry to answer the call, he forgot to ask the crew member to identify himself. *Odd that he didn't,* Tripping thought.

"Of a sort, Admiral," Grumley replied. "You made a point of saying to one and all that Envoy Gonzalez's message was her opinion and not to be taken as a directive from the Omnians. Captain Thompson has entered our system aboard the OS *Redemption.* She's stating unequivocally that you were directed to locate the probe and then stand aside. Your Captain Morney has stated otherwise to her."

"With all due respect to the Omnians, Mr. President, they continually overstate the importance of their role in matters."

"Do they, Admiral?"

"Continually, Sir. It's frustrating at times."

"I take it you'd like to press for being the one to destroy the probe. Is that it, Admiral?" Grumley asked, beginning to realize what Maria was up against in attempting to guide the senior officer.

"It's a New Terran probe; it should be a New Terran ship that eliminates it," Tripping replied, congratulating himself on the pithy summary, considering that he'd just been woken from a deep sleep.

"And here I thought it was an alien probe. Silly me," Grumley replied.

Tripping swallowed with difficulty. His mouth had suddenly gone dry. Grumley was noted for resorting to humor when his patience was exhausted.

"Here's what you're going to do, Admiral. You contact Captain Thompson and give her the coordinates of the probe ... never mind that. Her SADE probably already has them off your controller, if he or she hasn't found it by some other means. You be a good naval officer. Apologize for the confusion and stand aside. Do I make myself clear, Admiral, or do you wish me to address the Assembly Leaders when they convene today and request that they rescind your appointment?"

Tripping drew breath to object, but his comm light winked off. The president had cut the connection. Instead, the admiral called the bridge. "We've been ordered to stand down, Captain. Relay that message to

Captain Thompson, and follow her directions concerning where you should station our ship."

Tripping didn't give Morney an opportunity to reply. He cut the call and returned to bed, angry that a golden opportunity to promote his career had slipped through his hands.

When Ellie received Captain Morney's brief message of acquiescence, she frowned. "That was unexpected," she commented to Killian.

"Perhaps it was due to the admiral's conversation with the president," Killian replied.

"And how would you know about that, my nosy friend?"

"I thought it expedient to gather the probe's location from the *Geoffrey Orlan*'s controller and begin my calculations, as to when would be the opportune time to intercept the probe. I might have lingered long enough to overhear the conversation of the president with the captain and then with the admiral."

"Imagine that," Ellie said, in mock surprise. "The SADE, who is to conduct this critical operation to destroy an alien probe is so slow, regarding communication, that it takes him the length of two conversations to capture a tiny piece of data from a ship's controller."

"My excuse does seem farfetched," Killian replied with a grin.

"That's your role model at work again, Killian," Ellie admonished. "Store those conversations with mine for the admiral's review."

"Already done, Captain."

"Fine. Let's go kill an alien probe."

-14-
Decision Time

After the OS *Redemption* returned to Celus, Ellie transferred her files to the *Freedom* and sent a link to Tatia. Immediately, she received a comm request.

<I didn't expect to find you up this late in the evening, Admiral,> Ellie sent. She detected Tatia's rapid breathing and could guess at her choice of exercise. It made her ache for Étienne's embrace.

<Good timing, Captain,> Tatia sent. Her thoughts were flushed with excitement.

<I can imagine, Admiral,> Ellie replied, and the two women laughed.

<Success, Captain?> Tatia asked.

<One alien probe destroyed ... on contact by the banisher, I might add,> Ellie replied. <No harm to ships or stations. It was a clean job by Killian.>

<It was the same for Darius ... detonation on contact, I mean. Any issues, Captain?>

<I uploaded some conversations that you should listen to, Admiral. Two of them were collected privately by Killian.>

<Privately? That's a term that I would expect to hear from Alex.>

<Now you know the source of the influence, Admiral.>

<Where's our New Terran admiral? I would have expected him to be with you.>

<He chose to give his crew an additional week to visit family and friends, Admiral.>

<When you make orbit, Captain, I want you and your crew to take two weeks of rest. I'll have a watch crew for your ship to free everyone.>

<And after that?> Ellie asked.

<It will be Alex's decision, but you and I can probably guess what that will be.>

Tatia briefly joined Alain in the refresher before she went to her study and listened to Ellie's recordings.

<Revealing, aren't they?> Tatia heard in her implant, when she finished the last one.

<This is getting creepy, Alex. How do I know you're not listening to me anytime you want?> She heard the sound of Alex and Renée's laughter. <Now I'm group entertainment?>

<Tatia, be at ease,> Renée sent. <Julien cued us of Ellie's upload, and Alex and I listened to the conversations at the same time you did. We finished, and, moments later, Julien said you had closed the last file.>

<The only thing I did differently, Tatia,> Alex said, <was to send you my thought without pinging you.>

<You're a little unsettled, Tatia. Were you involved in something that you hoped to keep private? Something personal ... something intimate?> Renée asked.

Tatia could hear Renée's snickers.

<The two of you are going to have to seek your fun elsewhere,> Tatia growled, and she heard Alex and Renée break into laughter.

<Okay, to business, Tatia,> Alex sent, and Tatia could feel the power under his thought. <Two probes that were still broadcasting exploded on contact.>

<I think that's the reaction we should expect as the norm, going forward,> Tatia replied.

<I'm in agreement, although I would have loved to capture one.>

<That might never happen, Alex. These probes underline Miriam's surmises about the Nua'll civilization, and let me admit that it's frightening to say that.>

<Agreed. I always thought of the Nua'll as tightly confined to a small home world and desperate to get off by building a sphere. Thinking of them that way made it easier to cope with the threat. Now, considering they might be a civilization that has been expanding for tens of thousands of years, if we can extrapolate from the probe saturation, scares me too.>

<Does it change your mind about hunting the second sphere?> Tatia asked

<Would it change your mind, Tatia?> Alex riposted.

<No,> Tatia answered simply. <The more you know about your opponents, the quicker you can defeat them,> she sent, falling back on a phrase she used repeatedly, while training her TSF troopers.

<That's the way I feel. Hiding from the threat would mean certain ruination of every intelligent species in our corner of the galaxy, as the Nua'll discovered their expanding technological power.>

<On to a more pleasant subject, Alex ... you reviewed the communication between Ellie and Morney and between Grumley and Tripping.>

<Unfortunately, I did.>

<He's dangerous, Alex.>

<Agreed, Tatia, but he hasn't crossed the line yet.>

<I'm afraid when he does, Alex, he'll take a great many people with him.>

<Mitigate his role, Tatia. After we locate and destroy or capture the second sphere. I think we'll disband our liaison with the NT Tridents.>

<Let's revisit one of the words you just used, Alex.>

<Which one?> Alex asked.

<Capture,> Tatia replied.

<Well, what do you suggest we do, Tatia, if the sphere surrenders?>

<My first thought is that I hope that doesn't happen. My second thought is that I wonder how we're supposed to recognize when it does. Is it going to hoist a giant, stiff, white flag?>

<I guess we'll discover that if and when it happens. I'll let you return to your ... uh, activities,> Alex said. He discovered that Tatia's reply to his final comment was an abrupt ending of the comm link. He chuckled, slipped deeper into the bedclothes, and Renée wrapped around him.

* * *

"Theodore informs me the tests of the banishers were successful at Haraken and New Terra, although the probes blew up on contact," Gino said, as he took a seat at the head table with Alex and many others.

Alex eyed Gino, while he picked up his mug and took a deep swallow of his thé. Then he resumed his morning meal.

<There will be a brief interruption in your conversation, Council Leader Gino Diamanté, while food is consumed to a satisfactory level. Do remember the caloric needs of New Terrans,> Julien sent privately to Gino.

Before Gino could send a response to Julien, Katrina took a seat next to him and said, "Did you ask yet?"

"We eat first," Gino replied.

Katrina was about to object, but Gino's private message stopped her. <I already made the mistake of interrupting Alex's meal. It didn't go over too well.>

Servers surrounded the new individuals at the table and took their orders, and the only sounds to be heard, for a while, were the clinks of utensils, dishes, cups, and pitchers.

When Alex's dishes, the last on the table, were removed, he said, "Yes, Gino, the tests were successful. No damage to life or property, in either case. As far as we're concerned, the banishers have proven themselves ready to deploy. You'll find they'll be a great deal easier, more efficient, and portable than rocks," Alex added, smiling.

"Yes, well, you use what you have at hand. How many of these can I order, Alex?"

Alex glanced at Julien, who immediately recovered the list of parts and construction time to produce a single banisher. He was getting quite accomplished at this process, having done it for a variety of ships now. This one was easy. After estimating the total cost, Julien added a surcharge for profit and a codicil that the Méridiens were responsible for transport.

Alex received Julien's summary, shared it with Gino, and said, "That's my accountant's proposal for the purchase of a banisher. Concerning the quantity, you can order as many as you would like."

Gino glanced at Julien. During the brief moment he had regarded Alex, he discovered the SADE had adorned his head with a fedora.

"A more than fair figure, Alex. My appreciation to your accountant," Gino replied, winking at Julien. "How about one hundred banishers?"

"One hundred it is, Gino," Alex replied, reaching across the table and gently shaking the Méridien's slender hand. "The orbital platform will begin construction on your order, and you'll be notified when you can pick up the first shipment."

"In which case, we'll be leaving this morning, Alex. I have my work cut out for me to convene the Council and present our agreement for ratification. And you? What will you be doing in the meantime?"

"Why, Gino, I thought you knew," Renée said, cheerfully. "We're going sphere hunting. Would you like to join us?"

Gino and Katrina stared aghast at Renée, who wore an expectant expression.

"All of you are beginning to sound more and more like Alex every time we see you," Katrina said, shaking her head in disbelief at the offer.

"It's a requirement of our offices," Julien explained. "You have to be a little disturbed to follow Alex."

"But you should know, Katrina, that, in reality, I'm the sane one," Alex added. However, the odd grin and wide-eyed expression he extended her conveyed something entirely different.

Gino and Katrina burst out laughing. "Come, my partner," Gino said, standing and offering a hand to Katrina. I think it's best we leave soonest. This mental aberration might be catching."

The Méridiens said their goodbyes and left for the *Freedom*'s bay levels.

"Are they serious about chasing that second sphere?" Katrina asked, as they walked a long corridor to a lift.

"Oh, yes. Alex and his people might sound as if it's a jest, but they're deadly serious."

"And when they catch it?" Katrina asked.

"They'll destroy it, or it will destroy them."

"You make the possible outcomes sound so simple."

"They *are* simple, but one of them would be a great tragedy."

* * *

Olawale Wombo, an Earther refugee, who was now governing the Dischnya's new school, caught a transport from the planet and lifted for the *Freedom*. He had an urgent appointment with Alex, who met him as he exited his traveler.

"Everything okay with the Dischnya?" Alex asked, as they entered the corridor from the bay's airlock.

"Oh, yes, the Dischnya are fine," Olawale replied, as Alex guided him toward a lift. "I wanted to talk to you about Sol."

"Sol?" Alex asked, perplexed by the choice of subject.

"Alex, my people have no concept of the Nua'll sphere, especially of its insidious nature. They're as likely to welcome it, as attack it, and we're responsible for that."

"I don't follow you, Olawale," Alex replied. The lift took them to the city-ship's grand park, and the two men strolled through its pleasant gardens.

"Prior to our arrival, my people had no extensive contact with anyone outside the Sol system. Yes, the Tribunal and a few select others heard the stories that were told by Captain Lumley and his crew, who returned on the explorer ship from our space, but our arrival was proof of the existence of others beyond Sol. And look what we did."

"I thought we helped them and United Earth's crumbling society," Alex replied.

"We did, and that's my point, Alex."

"Ah, I see what you mean. Because of our visit, their experience with outsiders was a positive one. So, if a sphere were to arrive, they would think that the proper approach would be to act as gracious hosts."

"Exactly, and how devastating would that be?"

"I take it that you want to make a trip to Sol?" Alex asked.

"Yes," Olawale replied.

"Okay, Olawale, but I can't spare a warship. At this rate, I might be short one and a New Terran admiral. You'll have to take the *Rêveur*. In which case, Captain Lumley, as a fellow Earther, will be a good man to have at the helm. I'll load the liner with travelers and two banishers. You'll need a SADE. Do you have a preference?"

"I don't suppose I could take Julien?" Olawale asked.

When Alex stared at him with flat, hard eyes, Olawale chuckled. "Apologies, Alex, perhaps my jest wasn't as humorous as I thought. Please choose one for me."

"How about any of your Earther scientists? Will they be traveling with you?" Alex asked.

"In fact, Alex, they aren't interested in making the trip. As a group, we thought Sol should be warned, but that takes only one of us. Besides, it's important to keep the Dischnya's school open. The SADEs and an engineering team are building a new addition, and we're adding new courses. Two of the Confederation SADEs are now acting as educators."

"What type of courses?" Alex asked, curious as to the direction of the Dischnya's interests.

"They're courses for the younger Dischnya. They're fascinated by our technology ... power crystals, comm systems, implants, nanites ... all of it."

"What do the queens think of that?" Alex asked.

"The usual responses. The older ones snuff and snort their disapproval; the younger ones cheer them on."

"How are Edmas and Jodlyne doing?" Alex asked.

Alex was referring to a pair of Earther orphans that Z had adopted from Idona Station. Edmas had studied engineering at Espero's university after having worked for years, as a teenager, with Z and Claude, creating the SADEs' raft of avatars. He was a brilliant engineer in his own right and helped to discover the faux-shell process. Jodlyne, also an engineer, was Edmas' partner, and the levelheaded one of the pair.

"I understand their new business is doing exceedingly well, Alex. With their income from Omnia Ships, they started a flit business. The little machines are quite a success for the growing city."

"Have there been any issues?" Alex asked, with concern for the use of the sporty, single or tandem, rider grav units.

"You're speaking of possible overflights of the green. Z constructed the algorithms for the controller's mapping. The flits are restricted to the plains within the Omnia city's continent. Flights over the green or oceans are impossible, unless someone figures out how to break through the controller's encryption."

Alex grinned. "If they could, every Omnian SADE would know it in an instant."

"There's that," Olawale laughed, his bright white teeth shining in his dark face.

More than anything, Alex was worried that human curiosity might lead the foolish to investigate the deadly swaths of forests north and south of the midland plains. Z had ventured into the green to investigate the possibility of it harboring an intelligent species. What he found was a vicious environment of flora and fauna that competed for survival every moment of every day. And the most dangerous species was the Nascosto, a troop of chameleon-capable, venomous, tree dwellers. Z's Cedric Broussard suit was the only reason he survived his time in the green.

"I'll speak to Edmas and Jodlyne," Alex said. "I think they should accompany you."

"As you wish, Alex. I'll get started on the preparations."

"Before you go, Olawale, hear me well. You travel to Sol, communicate to whoever is in charge, and gain permission to search the system for a probe. If you find one, destroy it, and then sail back here immediately. No extended visit. Am I clear?"

"Absolutely, Alex. It wasn't my intention to sit down and have some long-winded chats."

"Be safe, Olawale."

"We'll be careful," Olawale said, rising from the bench where the two men had sat to talk. "And thank you, Alex," Olawale added, grabbing

Alex in a bear hug. He was one of the few individuals who could manage that. Though not as heavy as Alex, Olawale was taller and a big man.

"Say hello to Nikki and Patrice, if you get the opportunity," Alex called out as Olawale walked away, referring to Nikki Fowler and Patrice Morris, two antagonists, a rebel leader and a militia lieutenant, who chose to bury their animosities and work to rebuild Sol's Idona Station.

Olawale waved his acknowledgment, a smile lighting his face.

"And may the stars watch over you," Alex said, with quiet intensity. He watched Olawale disappear along a path and waited for passing impressions of the Earther's impending return to Sol. Alex might deny the insinuations of others about his premonitions, but he had lived with them too long to ignore them. The reason he refused to own up to having the unlikely impressions was that he felt the admittance would separate him even further from his fellow humans.

<Julien, I need a recommendation for a SADE,> Alex sent. <Olawale will be taking the *Rêveur* to Sol and searching for a probe.>

<Who will be accompanying him, besides Captain Lumley?> Julien sent in reply.

<None of the other Earther scientists. I'll be asking Edmas and Jodlyne to travel with him, if they can get away from their flit business.>

<The pair have been working closely with a Confederation SADE named Esteban. They've made him a partner in their business, GravMania. You might suggest he accompany them, and I can prepare Esteban to handle the probe search and manage the deployment of the banisher. There are several engineers and SADEs, the company's parts suppliers, who would be willing to oversee the final assembly and delivery of the flit orders, while the threesome is gone.>

<Thank you, Julien,> Alex said, switching his comm link to Cordelia.

<Greetings, Alex. I'll inform Francis of his mission. What do you wish to have his ship carry?>

Alex smiled, always impressed at the speed of SADE communication.

<Francis will need travelers and two banishers. I'll request Edmas, Jodlyne, and Esteban travel with Olawale. Get Tatia's recommendations for traveler pilots. Francis will need good fighter pilots with cool heads.>

<Understood, Alex. Anything else?>

<Edmas and Jodlyne, Cordelia, please.>

<What's this about you two selling flits to the Dischnya?> Alex demanded, when Cordelia connected him to the pair.

There was dead silence on the call, while the two young people tried to figure out how to respond.

<Apologies, you two, I was kidding,> Alex said.

<Don't do that, Alex,> Jodlyne hotly replied. <I'm too young to have a stroke or something.>

<Good one, Alex,> Edmas said, chuckling. <I was trying to figure out who was buying and reselling our flits across the waters. Then it dawned on me that the Dischnya don't have any credits. They're still on the barter system.>

<Quick thinking, Edmas,> Alex replied.

<Now that you two foolish men are done congratulating yourselves, what was it you wanted, Alex?>

<Olawale wants to warn Sol about the Nua'll spheres and check the system for a probe.>

<Does he intend to stay for a while?> Jodlyne asked.

Alex could hear the trepidation in Jodlyne's thoughts. <Negative, Jodlyne. He has my directive to take care of business and return.>

<Is he traveling aboard a Trident?> Edmas asked.

<No, the *Rêveur*.>

<And the reason for your comm, Alex?> Jodlyne sent.

<I'm asking the two of you to accompany him. In addition, the ship needs a SADE to help with the probe's location and the banisher's deployment. I was told that Esteban might be a good choice.>

Alex waited. Obviously, the two partners were in a deep discussion, which probably included Esteban.

<We're worried about our business, Alex,> Edmas said, after resuming the connection. <A competitor is starting a flit business, and we don't want to lose our customers.>

<And if I arrange to have some of your suppliers manage the final assembly, delivery, and sales for you, while you're gone?>

<I don't see them doing that for free, Alex,> Jodlyne replied. <They might require some incentive.>

Alex chuckled to himself. Jodlyne was not only the levelheaded one of the pair, she was also the business-minded one. <Omnia Ships will ensure the individuals, who manage your affairs while you're gone, are adequately compensated.>

<In that case, we're happy to help Olawale, Alex,> Jodlyne replied joyfully. <We'll coordinate with Francis for launch.>

<And Esteban?> Alex asked.

<He's aboard,> Edmas replied.

After Alex ended the comm, Jodlyne yipped in pleasure and threw herself into Edmas' arms. "This is going to be a fantastic trip to see what's become of Sol," she said.

"Well negotiated, Ser," Esteban said. The Confederation SADE's synth-skin was patterned in a subtle flow of what appeared to be waves of water, with blues, greens, and occasional white peaks. Some humans, who stared too long at him, could feel a little nauseous, something akin to seasickness.

Jodlyne released Edmas and narrowed her eyes at Esteban.

"Apologies … that was well negotiated, Jodlyne," Esteban replied, correcting her address in his comment.

"That's better," Jodlyne replied, hugging Esteban.

The SADE had received many such attentions from the pair of engineers, who had hired him and soon afterward given him a minority share in their business. The initial handshakes of Edmas and hugs from Jodlyne were confusing, but the more he understood the genuine warmth that the two humans exhibited, the more he coveted their attentions to him. If the pair were going to Sol, he intended to accompany them to ensure their well-being.

"Do you think we finally got the better of Alex?" Jodlyne asked. She looked at Edmas' flat expression before she added, "Probably not."

"But you held up our end," Edmas said, throwing an arm around her shoulders.

Farewells

<I'm not waiting any longer for Admiral Tripping, Tatia,> Alex sent one morning. He had awakened, enjoyed a stint in the refresher, and checked the dispositions of Tridents through the *Freedom*'s controller. The squadron was still one ship short.

<When do we leave, Alex, and do we take the other two New Terran Tridents or send them home?> Tatia sent in reply.

<How do you feel about the two remaining captains, Tatia?>

<Both are solid. If we took them, I'd make Jagielski the senior captain.>

<Then we take them. We leave at 8.5 hours, two days from now.>

<We'll be ready, Alex.>

As it was, the NT *Geoffrey Orlan* arrived in system late that afternoon, and Tatia reached out to the warship.

"Captain Morney," Tatia said, speaking to him via the *Freedom*'s bridge comm system, "please connect me to Admiral Tripping."

"I'm here, Admiral Tachenko," Tripping replied.

"I'd like a private conversation, Admiral," Tatia said.

"I'm comfortable speaking in front of my captain and officers. As New Terrans, we exhibit solidarity, or have you forgotten that?" Tripping replied, with his usual condescending tone.

Tatia took a deep breath, blew it out, and relaxed her clenched fists. Alex's words surfaced — let Tripping trap himself. "I understood you would be returning to Omnia within a week, Admiral. It has been nearly two weeks. Did you experience difficulties with your ship?"

"Quite the contrary, Admiral. My crew and I enjoyed a longer period of relaxation on our home planet. However, we're here and ready to join your practice deployments."

"Maneuvers are over, Admiral. The squadron is deploying at 8.5 hours in another day and a half."

Tatia could detect a whispered conversation between Tripping and one other person.

"I'm informed, Admiral, that we can't reach Omnia in that time. Perhaps, you can delay your departure for two more days?"

Tripping's voice had undergone a noticeable shift. Gone was the hauteur, replaced by a tentativeness.

"That's a shame, Admiral. It looks as if I'll be taking the other two New Terran Tridents with me on the hunt. You might as well turn around and report to President Grumley that your extended vacation caused you to miss our sailing date."

Around Tatia, Cordelia and her crew grinned at her, and Tatia had to admit, she enjoyed twisting Tripping's tail.

"I'll remind you that I'm the New Terran senior officer," Tripping declared hotly. "Those ships are mine. You can either wait for me, or I'll forbid the captains to sail with you."

Tatia had been waiting for this moment. Tripping had neatly stepped into a trap of his own making.

"Let me clear up a few misconceptions you have, Admiral. The three NT Tridents aren't yours. They belong to your government, which signed an agreement, obligating you and your captains to follow my commands. If you order the New Terran captains to disregard my lawful commands you're abrogating the agreement, outright, and that means that I can remove you from command of the NT Tridents."

Again, Tatia picked up the muted sounds of whispers. She suspected it was Tripping and Morney discussing the validity of her argument.

"We seem to be at an impasse, Admiral. Do you have a suggestion as how to proceed?"

"Your controller will have received coordinates from Captain Cordelia. She's marked an interception point. Proceed there immediately, and you'll catch the squadron before we exit the system."

"That works for me, Admiral."

"One more thing, Admiral Tripping. Don't ever challenge my authority again or threaten to divert your captains from following their duties. I won't give you a second chance."

Tripping was considering his reply, when Captain Morney cued him that the comm link had been cut by Admiral Tachenko.

* * *

The day before the fleet's launch to hunt the Ollassa sphere, Alex and Renée took the opportunity to visit many of Omnia's sites. In four years, the planet's plains had changed in extraordinary ways.

With the fighter squadron enjoying time off, it was Franz Cohen who snatched the opportunity to pilot Alex and Renée around for the day and view the planet up close. He set the traveler down on the bluff overlooking the hive of Wave Skimmer. The Swei Swee was chosen as the First of several hives, which had combined to construct an enormous enclave against the face of a cliff.

After exiting the shuttle, Alex let loose an ear-splitting whistle. Renée, Franz, and he heard a resounding reply from hundreds of Swei Swee voices along the beach, out in the waters, and from the cliff-clinging domiciles. The response had Alex laughing delightedly, and Renée and Franz smiled at his antics.

The threesome worked their way down the cliff path, which the Swei Swee had cut and fastidiously maintained, mostly for their human visitors. As they stepped onto the beach, Wave Skimmer, who had been called to shore by other males and was dripping seawater from his search, whistled his greeting to Alex.

Alex thumped the huge claws of the First, who returned the greeting.

Despite Renée's love of the Haraken Swei Swee, she found the Omnian Swei Swee intimidating. Wave Skimmer's massive claws were each as great as Alex's chest, and, on extended legs, the adult male stood a full meter taller than Alex. There was nothing in Wave Skimmer's demeanor that indicated he was anything but an intelligent, gentle giant. *But he's so big,* she thought, grappling with her anxiety.

On the other hand, Alex either had no concerns or he hid them well. After Alex's greeting with Wave Skimmer, the two began walking or scuttling, as in the case of the Swei Swee, down the beach. They whistled their chat, like two old friends.

At one point, Wave Skimmer abruptly halted and turned to face Alex, who communicated to the Swei Swee for several moments. When the First's sudden pause was noticed, the action along the beach froze. The hives stood still to hear what the Star Hunter First was saying.

"We've found a second world traveler," Alex whistled, using the Swei Swee term for the Nua'll sphere. "We will search for it."

"Dangerous," Wave Skimmer warbled. He feared for the Star Hunter First and his people.

"The world traveler is wounded. It will be an easy hunt," Alex whistled, tweeting his derision of the sphere's ability to defend itself.

"When?" Wave Skimmer asked.

"When the sky lightens tomorrow, my ships will sail and start the search," Alex replied.

"The hives will think of you on the search. Come, Star Hunter First. I will show you our hive's pride."

Wave Skimmer led Alex along a long stretch of sand to where several youngsters were splashing in the shallow waves. He whistled lightly, and a young female broke away from the group and raced up to the First. She slid to a halt, tweeting a greeting to the First.

"Greet the Star Hunter First, young one," Wave Skimmer invited.

The youngster issued a brief tweet, which Alex gracefully accepted. However, Wave Skimmer's four eyestalks bent down to examine the young female, and hers drooped in concern.

"That is the best you can do for the human who has brought us peace? Greet and celebrate him, as it should be. On the following day, he goes to search for the hives' greatest enemy and, if he fails, he might never be seen again."

The two-year-old Swei Swee gathered her courage and lifted her torso on spindly legs. From deep in her genetic memory came the desire to celebrate the Swei Swee's friend and protector. She sang in her high, clear voice, with purpose, composing her little verses on the fly. At the end of her song, her voice turned sweet and soft, as she wished Star Hunter First a long life.

Renée whistled her amazement, "Wave Hunter, the People have a Hive Singer."

The First rose on his legs and whistled loudly in celebration, the hive joining in.

Alex chuckled and reached down to pick up the youngster. The two warbled softly to each other, before the young female tweeted, "Slide me." She folded her legs tightly under her, and Alex obliged by walking to the water's edge. With a tremendous heave, he threw the youngster, spinning across the shallow waters. Her high-pitched scream of pleasure waved in and out, as she spun in a dizzying pattern.

"Congratulations," Alex said to Wave Skimmer, smacking the giant Swei Swee's claws.

Alex, Renée, and Franz turned around and headed for the cliff trail, while the hive continued to celebrate the sharing of their wonderful discovery. It was Wave Skimmer who was silent, his four eyestalks focused on the humans. *Successful search, Star Hunter First,* the Swei Swee thought.

Alex, Renée, and Franz gained the traveler, and she said to Franz, "I want to see Omnia city next."

Franz piloted the traveler across the ocean to Omnia's second continent, where humans and SADEs had created their first city, which bore the planet's name. When they landed, blue synth-skinned Trixie was there to greet them. She stood beside the city's first, four-seat, grav car.

"These are similar to what we enjoyed on Haraken," Renée marveled.

"GravMania's newest product. I've been chosen to test drive this initial version," Trixie replied.

"And promote Edmas, Jodlyne, and Esteban's business as you flit around the city," Alex added.

"Promotion and commerce. They go hand and hand, do they not, Dassata?"

"That's true, Trixie," Alex replied.

The SADE and the three humans loaded into the grav car. Alex sat in the back with Franz so that Renée could enjoy the better view. As they lifted, Renée twisted around to eye the rear seat. "I do have a minor suggestion for GravMania," she said.

Trixie glanced behind her. "Yes, Ser, I see what you mean. Either GravMania makes a larger vehicle, or we can't allow two New Terrans to ride together in the back seat."

Alex and Franz grinned at each other. Their shoulders were tightly compressed together.

Trixie dropped elevation, slowed the grav car, and retracted the clear canopy. It allowed the men to extend an arm outside the vehicle and gain some room. As she flew, she gave the humans a running commentary.

"The city is growing so fast," Renée said.

"The faux-shell technology is at the center of it all, Ser. Investment in support industries is growing rapidly. Despite that, demand is outpacing supply. It has the positive aspect of bringing humans and SADEs alike to Omnia. Even the Nua'll are contributing to growth."

"The Nua'll?" Renée exclaimed.

"Now that Dassata's query has led to the discovery of probes in every system that has been searched, there are new industries providing the means of destroying them. We're fabricating parts for more than a hundred banishers, even now. And, we expect to receive orders from other systems to support the manufacture of some of the more esoteric parts of Tridents, travelers, and scout ships. This industrial growth is in addition to traveler manufacture, which is ongoing."

"What of the Dischnya, Trixie?" Alex asked.

"An interesting query, Alex. I visited with some of the queens, six days ago. There are subtle schisms growing between the nests. The eldest queens want little change, but are grateful for their structures, which provide them much comfort. The younger queens are anxious for their young soma to embrace the new technologies. Those young attend school and fervently wish to become part of the spacefaring opportunity."

"When do you think they'll be ready, Trixie?"

"Not surprising you ask when and not if, Dassata. I would expect to see the desire of the young ones manifest in some form of demand to their queens within the next three to five years."

"What about introducing them to aspects of this city?" Alex asked.

"This has been proposed and discussed, Dassata. What we do not envision is how to integrate them into our world. We are certain that if they visit the city, they will want to stay, and we're concerned for the creation of something similar to Sadesville."

At the mention of the tiny, poorly outfitted enclave of SADEs, who were the first to immigrate to Haraken from the Confederation, Alex winced.

"Let me think on it, Trixie. I'll see if I can't come up with a means of eliminating that problem, when the Dischnya are ready to join Omnian society."

<Well said, Trixie,> Hector sent. <I'll inform the others that Alex is working on a solution.>

"By the way, Trixie, say hello to Hector for me."

The electric-blue face turned to Alex, and her mouth split into a wide smile. "Dassata, you know us too well."

When Alex, Renée, and Franz finished their aerial tour of the city, they said goodbye to Trixie, who hugged each of them.

"May the stars protect you," Trixie whispered in Alex's ear.

"Last stop, Nyslara's compound," Alex said to Franz, as they boarded the traveler.

After a short flight over the waters to the Dischnya continent, Franz announced, <Alex, you have a welcoming committee.>

Alex and Renée picked up the controller's view of the ground.

"Imagine that," Renée commented. "Looks like the entire Dischnya soma turned out."

Alex eyed Renée, who maintained an indifferent expression on her face.

<Set us down where you can, Franz,> Alex requested.

The trappings of the waiting queens were evident at the rim of the vast body of Dischnya. Franz headed there and chose a spot 20 meters in front of them.

Alex, Renée, and Franz stepped from the traveler, and Nyslara's young heir, Neffess, broke from the crowd and raced forward on her long, slender legs. Despite her small, 1-meter stature, she covered the ground quickly and jumped into Renée's waiting arms. Hoisting the young heir up, Renée received a wet tongue in the ear for her efforts. It was a sentiment of pups, who had yet to learn the manners of adult Dischnya.

"You're growing so quickly, Neffess," Renée complimented her.

"You go?" Neffess asked, as Renée sat her on the ground. It was a sign of the changes in Dischnya society that the pups were bilingual.

"Yes, Neffess. I have told you this," Nyslara said, as she approached the humans. Her command of the human tongue was limited, but she kept working at it.

"Stay," Neffess pleaded, but a soft growl from Nyslara had the youngster backing behind her matriarch.

The queens of the Dischnya nests stepped forward to array themselves beside Nyslara.

"Dassata, Ené, and Fanz," Nyslara said, greeting the humans. Her snout, sharp rows of teeth, and long tongue managed the last two names as best they could.

"We understand you leave on the sky's new light to hunt your enemy," Nyslara said in her native language, which the Omnians could translate with their implant software, and Alex nodded his agreement.

"You take warriors?" Homsaff asked. One of the rare young queens, Homsaff trained with many of the battle-scarred wasats and senior warriors under Myron McTavish, commandant of the Dischnya military training academy.

"No, Homsaff. We hunt the enemy in our ships. We land on no worlds. Someday, Dischnya warriors fight with Omnians, and, someday, Dischnya will crew starships, but not today," Alex replied in the Dischnya tongue.

It always surprised other humans how fast Alex adopted an alien language, not only their words but their speech pattern and mannerisms. In this case, Alex started with his hand, palm up but low, before he swung it gently to the side, a Dischnya sign of negation.

"Dassata promises this?" Homsaff asked.

"It's not in my power to promise this, but I see it happening," Alex replied.

Homsaff dipped her muzzle in acceptance, though she was disappointed. She felt her warriors were ready to fight with Dassata and his kind, despite being unable to envision the circumstances under which that would happen.

"No warrior," Neffess huffed from behind Nyslara's powerful legs.

"What would Neffess be when she is queen?" Renée asked.

"Neffess fly starship," the heir replied, stepping into the open and pointing at the sky.

Alex was struck by the accuracy of Trixie's analysis. The Dischnya young had received a taste of a better life, having crawled out of their dim tunnels to inhabit Omnian-designed and built structures. Now, they wanted more than a communal existence of bartering on the dusty plains. They wanted what the Omnians had.

Alex raised a hand high in the air, saluting the Dischnya, and the soma tilted their muzzles to the sky and howled as one. The harmony of thousands of voices dominated the plains.

When the Dischnya salute died, Nyslara stepped close to Alex. Long gone were the admonitions of wasats that it was dangerous for queens to close on one not of the nest.

"There are no words, Dassata," Nyslara said, her muzzle mere centimeters from Alex's face, her eyes boring into his. "You and your people have fulfilled my dreams for the Dischnya beyond what I could have imagined. Know that the entire body of Sawa Messa soma send their wishes for your safe return." On a final note, Nyslara slipped her muzzle to the side of Alex's head, and a long tongue curled around his ear. When she pulled away, she barked her laughter, as Alex grinned at her.

Alex raised his hand once more as the three humans turned to board the traveler. When the hatch closed, it silenced the tremendous howls of the Dischnya.

"Everyone is entirely too sentimental today," Franz said, as the threesome made their way forward. "You'd think they believed we can't handle a nearly unarmed sphere. It's like they aren't expecting us to return."

Renée had taken a seat, but Alex noticed that Franz had stopped and was waiting for a response from him. It was the specter of Alex's premonitions. He realized that the emotional farewells had unsettled his fighter group leader, which wasn't good. But Alex didn't have an image beyond the one he had shared that he sensed there had been other spheres than the one at Libre, which had proven to be true.

"We will take the necessary steps to trap and confront the Nua'll without unduly risking our people, Franz. Be assured of that," Alex said.

Franz accepted the answer and hustled to the pilot's cabin.

When Alex sat beside Renée, she took his hand in both of hers, squeezed tightly, and then leaned back into her seat to be alone with her thoughts.

-16-
Return to Ollassa

The Trident squadron and scout ships rendezvoused with Tripping's ship before exiting the system, and the NT *Geoffrey Orlan* assumed its place in formation. The five Omnians ships formed a wedge, and Tripping chafed that his Tridents were relegated to positions behind the wedge.

Killian and his companions had received their new scout ship, *Vivian's Mirror*, in time to test the vessel and announce it ready for service. The other five scout ships had completed their assigned search patterns and returned in time to accompany the squadron on the hunt.

After a long transit, the fleet exited into the Ollassa system. The SADEs initiated the search for a probe, focusing on the broadcast signal. Immediately, they detected a strong signal and others that ranged from faint to barely detectable.

Having determined there was a probe monitoring the Worlds of Light, Alex ordered the *Vivian's Mirror* forward.

<Killian, locate Scarlet Mandator. My thought is that the mandator will be aboard a ship instead of on the Ollassa home world. Take up a station abreast of the mandator's ship so that we can have quick communication.>

<Affirmative, Dassata,> Killian sent in reply, and the scout ship closed its clamshell rear to enclose its drive engines and convert to grav power.

The fleet was required to traverse about one-third of the Ollassa system to close on the probe. In the meantime, the scout ship came abreast of the nearest Ollassa warship. Trium linked to the ship's comm systems, and Bethley, utilizing Julien's Ollassa lexicon and ultrasonic frequencies sent, <We request the Scarlet Mandator.>

"It's one of the progenitors' seedling ships," the tasker said, who managed the ship's comms, the bloom turning toward the executor. "It's requesting to speak with Scarlet Mandator."

"Tasker, respond to its query," the executor ordered.

"How?" the tasker asked. "The aliens won't comprehend our coordinate system."

"It was said that Julien used images to first converse with Scarlet Mandator. Monitor, try sending an image to the seedling ship," the executor ordered.

The monitor thought, wondering how to communicate the information to the aliens. Staring at the navigation board, the monitor had an epiphany. First, the monitor annotated a display of the Worlds of Lights with a small circle and placed next to it the shape of the seedling ship. Then a small plus sign located the Scarlet Mandator's ship position. Finally, a line connected the two positions.

"You believe the aliens will understand that?" the executor said, the bloom hovering over the monitor's position.

"Any navigator would understand this, Executor," the monitor replied. "And the progenitors, who travel between the Lights of the dark, will certainly understand it."

"Then send it," the executor replied.

The monitor's bloom swung toward the tasker, seeking help, and the tasker captured the image on the monitor's board and sent it to the seedling ship.

"A progenitor, who goes by the name Bethley, offered thanks to those aboard this ship," the comm tasker said.

"The seedling vessel has left," the monitor noted, the pad of a stalk pointing to the line on the panel. A bright dot traced its path, and the monitor's stalks proudly straightened.

<We have Scarlet Mandator's location, Dassata. The mandator is indeed aboard a ship. Unfortunately, you're approaching the mandator's position and so is the probe,> Killian sent.

<We have the mandator's location, Killian,> Alex replied. <Nice work, the three of you. Continue with your assignment, Killian.>

Two days later, the *Vivian's Mirror* sidled next to Scarlet Mandator's ship.

"Scarlet Mandator welcomes your return," Melon Tasker sent over the comm. "We query if you're the seedling vessel that was originally entwined with this ship."

"The alien, Bethley, assures you, Scarlet Mandator, that this is so," Melon Tasker announced, relaying the response.

<Bethley, Julien will translate for me, and you will relay to Scarlet Mandator,> Alex sent.

<Affirmative, Dassata,> Bethley sent.

<Julien, the mandator must head inward immediately,> Alex sent. <Our common enemy has left a dangerous piece of equipment orbiting the Worlds of Light, and we must destroy it.>

Julien's first thought was this was Cordelia's forte, creating images that portrayed complicated statements. He decided to rely on simplistic images that built on one another.

"By some means, Scarlet Mandator, we're receiving images on the navigation board," Golden Executor said, indicating Teal Monitor's panel. "Aliens," the executor added.

Scarlet Mandator's stalks moved to place the bloom over the panel. A representation of the Worlds of Light had appeared first. A dot indicated what the mandator considered the mandator's ship's position. The dot grew to encompass the panel and morphed into an image of a scarlet bloom, then shrank again to the dot. Then the dot moved toward the home world. Finally, as the dot cleared the second outermost planet's orbit, a massive bright light blanked much of the edge of the display.

"Turn the ship inward, now," Scarlet Mandator ordered. "The progenitors are warning us."

Golden Executor ordered the course change, without understanding the reason, but it was known that the mandator knew the aliens best.

"More images, Mandator," Teal Monitor announced.

The blooms of both the mandator and executor bent over the panel to watch. The image of the Worlds of Light appeared again. A tiny dot came from outside the system and took up an orbit around the outermost planet. The dot grew to display a small round object, and the blooms of the mandator and executor swung toward each other. Concentric waves emanated from the object, pulsing in all directions.

"The device from beyond is communicating," Teal Monitor said, which answered the senior Ollassa's questions.

Julien had the probe's image slide off to the left, and he focused on the representation of the communication waves. Extending them on past stars for enough time to represent a long distance. Then, from the right, entered the sphere's image where the transmission ended.

<Clever, Julien,> Killian commented.

Bethley continued to repeat Julien's visual messages. When the first ship had sent the image from the navigation board via the comm, Bethley was able to trace the path and reverse it to display Julien's imagery for Scarlet Mandator.

On the Ollassa's bridge, the four entities, who were watching the image display, froze. Stalks and fronds trembled.

"The great orb came to the Worlds of Light, following the transmission of that object," Scarlet Mandator said, understanding dawning.

"Golden Executor, warn all ships. They are to proceed immediately away from the progenitor ships. Tell them that the Omnians have found a dangerous device belonging to the great orb."

The executor complied with the orders and asked, "What will the aliens do with the device?"

"Recall the images," the mandator said.

"The bright light at the far-world's orbit," the executor surmised.

"Yes," Scarlet Mandator answered simply.

"Was the representation inaccurate? The light covered a great amount of distance," Golden Executor asked.

"Or is the great orb's device that dangerous?" the mandator posited.

Several days later and by the Omnian fleet's ship time, it was the middle of the night. Leaders and senior officers were asleep, and junior officers manned the bridges of the Tridents.

<Julien, the Ollassa ships are clear of the danger zone, and the probe is entering a safe area for detonation,> Z sent. <Should we wait for Alex to rise and give the order?>

<The window of opportunity will close in four hours when the probe enters that massive asteroid section,> Julien replied. <Launch the banisher, Z. I will inform the squadron's bridge officers.> It was unnecessary to mention communicating to the scout ship SADEs. As had become common, they were maintaining constant links with Julien, Z, and Miranda.

Z checked the status of the bay, ensuring there were no humans present. With the bay clear, he signaled its depressurization, after which he opened the doors. As soon as there was clearance, Z selected one of the banishers and activated its program. Guiding the device out of the bay, Z pointed it toward the probe, and transferred the device's location coordinates and its trajectory path to the banisher's controller.

Programmed and armed, the banisher accelerated toward its target. As the Omnian tool had operated at the Oistos and Hellébore systems, the banisher slowed when it approached the probe and gingerly gripped the alien device with its clamshell claws. Instantly, the probe detonated, blanking the Omnian vid telemetry.

<The Nua'll toys just don't like being handled,> Miranda sent. <Poor dears, something must be amiss in their upbringing.>

<It does make you wonder what we'll discover when we come face-to-face with the Nua'll,> Killian sent.

<I, for one, have spent too much time and crystal energy assimilating the collected data on the Nua'll and trying to envision them,> Z said.

<It is a subject that Cordelia and I have discussed interminably, and we are no closer to a conclusion than when we first encountered the Libran sphere,> Julien said.

<Julien and Z, is it possible that the problem is that the two of you are trying to resolve your data into an image of a single species, when there might be more than one operating in cooperation?> Miranda asked.

<Considered frequently,> Z answered

<Considered interminably,> Julien replied.

<Well, then it looks like we shall have to capture this second sphere so that we can knock on a hatch and ask for a vid,> Miranda quipped.

The SADEs shared their creative versions of laughter with Miranda.

<After that suggestion, I believe I will borrow a concept from Alex,> Z sent.

<Which is?> Miranda inquired.

<That females should be given the privilege of proceeding first,> Z replied, which resulted in a second round of laughter.

<You, my dear, may be cut off from my charms if you're not careful,> Miranda replied. The only one laughing in response to Miranda's retort was Z, but then he was the only one allowed.

<What now, Julien?> Killian asked.

<I'm directing the fleet toward the sphere's position where it picked up its last bullet ship after the conflict. Within several hours, Alex will awake and join us, and then we can discuss how we wish to proceed. With many options open to us, it might be difficult to identify which probe signal the sphere focused on.>

<There will be celestial drift, in its many forms,> Z reminded Julien.

<We have an approximate time displacement. We will need our combined processing power to compute the drifts and accurately correct the vector, or we'll be chasing signals without results,> Julien advised.

Scarlet Mandator and Golden Executor had received the data on the explosion. The detonation's magnitude had the petals on both blooms curling under in trepidation.

"The device was so small as not to be found during the annuals that it sat out there," the executor said. "Yet, its destruction engulfed more space than one could believe."

"Thanks should be given to you, Scarlet Mandator, when you withheld your pad from the seedling vessel," Teal Monitor said.

"The praise belongs to the Omnians," Scarlet Mandator. "They retrieved their seedling ship and worked to communicate with us, learning of the existence of the great orb's passing. I wonder at the reason for their return. Was it to benefit them in their pursuit of the predator, or did they wish to rid us of the orb's device? We might never know their motivation."

"The progenitors' methods indicate that they're experienced with these dangerous devices," Teal Monitor reasoned. When blooms of the mandator and executor swiveled toward the monitor, the Ollassa added, "The aliens cleared a wide swath of dark around the tiny device, much more space than one would consider reasonable. They must know of these devices' destructive capabilities when they're approached."

"Teal Monitor, where are the Omnians headed?" Scarlet Mandator asked.

"Not on any vector that will intersect one of our Worlds of Light, Mandator," the monitor replied.

"I will be retiring to the recovery room," the mandator said. "There will be time later, much later, to attempt to identify the progenitors' purpose."

* * *

Alex woke in the morning, following the probe's destruction. After a meal, Alex, the senior officers, and the SADEs stood on the bridge to review events.

"Congratulations, Julien, on a successful execution of the probe," Alex said, ensuring that the bridge officers heard that he had no problem with Julien's decision to proceed, while the leaders and senior officers slept.

"Yes, well, I know how much humans need their beauty sleep, so I was loath to interrupt yours," Julien replied, with a sly smile. He was immediately bombarded by imagery, portraying him in a variety of negative ways, by every human on the bridge, especially from the women, Renée, Tatia, Reiko, and Svetlana.

"Was it something I said?" Julien asked innocently, and Alex, laughing, slapped him on the back.

"So where are we headed, Julien?" Alex asked.

"To the starting point, Alex, where we believe the sphere was before it took up the vector that sent it chasing the next probe's signal."

Tatia stared at Julien, Z, and then Miranda. She asked, "How in the stars are you going to determine the start point and the vector with all the factors that complicate those determinations after the decades that have passed?

"With great difficulty, Admiral," Z replied.

"The SADEs have been at work on the subject since we destroyed the probe, Admiral," Julien added. "Regrettably, we've yet to finish our calculations."

"The SADEs have been working through the night and haven't come to a conclusion. How is that possible?" Reiko asked.

"The data we received from the Ollassa didn't have the specificity of our telemetry parameters, Commodore," Z replied.

"In addition, we've been challenged by multiple suggestions, which halted the calculations, and required us to rerun them once each new idea was researched," Julien explained.

"In the past hour, no more suggestions have been made, so we believe we're close to a final estimation," Z added.

"What is the expected accuracy?" Alex asked.

"With regret, Alex," Z replied. "We calculate 36.7 percent for the starting point, and 22.4 percent for the correct vector."

"Wow," Svetlana said, eyeing the SADEs.

"Unfortunately, too true, dear," Miranda said.

"On another subject, how many probe signals have you detected?" Alex asked, looking from SADE to SADE.

"More than you would believe, dear man ... now that we know what we're seeking," Miranda said.

"Which leaves us considering what ... signal strength?" Reiko asked.

"That was our primary assumption, Commodore," Julien replied, nodding to Reiko. "We've ranked the probes by that parameter," he added, sharing a link to the file with every human.

"You're kidding, Julien," Reiko said, when she reviewed her copy, amazed at the number of entries.

"The Nua'll appear to have been at work, investigating this part of the galaxy long before humans arrived here," Julien said.

"It makes one reconsider the viewpoint of our enemy, who undoubtedly see us as interlopers," Z commented.

"They could have asked us nicely to leave," Miranda replied tartly. "Not that we would have obliged them, but it would have been polite of them to have made the effort."

"If I understand the plan, it's to set up on the spot where we estimate the sphere was last stationary. Estimate the vector it took, factoring in drift we don't have accurate data on. Then we check the strength of probe signals and hope one of the stronger ones is close to our intended trajectory. Is that about right?" Tatia asked, incredulous at the proposal's feebleness.

"Precisely, Admiral," Julien replied, with a charming smile. "At least in regard to your accurate description of our somewhat feeble plan."

That comment ended the morning's discussion. Alex and his officers had left the fleet's sailing in the hands of the SADEs until Alex received a short comm from Julien in the evening, which said, <We're here, Alex.>

Alex left his desk, kissed Renée quickly, and strode to the bridge. He was joined by the senior officers and the SADEs.

"What do our options look like?" Alex asked.

Julien triggered the holo-vid and displayed a representation of their ship's position, a line detailing the proposed vector, and a set of tiny lights in the distance, which varied in brilliance.

"Those are the probes out there and their relative strength?" Reiko asked.

"Precisely, Commodore," Julien replied.

"None appear to line up with the calculated trajectory," Svetlana observed, staring closely at the holo-vid's display.

"Also true, Captain," Julien replied.

"Perhaps the sphere is choosing a new destination, not on the strength of the signal, but by what information a probe is broadcasting," Alex surmised.

"That would be helpful if we could decode the broadcast and understand the language," Tatia grumped.

Alex was undeterred and stood staring at the holo-vid.

"What's the plan then?" Reiko asked. "Which probe signal do we chase?"

The SADEs glanced at one another.

"Forgive them, Commodore," Miranda groused. "They don't wish to admit that they have no suggestion and are hoping our dear leader has some sort of intuition as to which way we should go."

"Do you, Alex?" Tatia asked.

"Not a clue," Alex replied. "Julien, display the map cones that correspond to every scenario that you ran. Include any proposal that received a probability above 10 percent," Alex requested.

The SADEs pulled up their various analyses and mapped them into the display. Julien color-coded them as Alex preferred. The cones were semitransparent, which allowed colors to combine in an additive process.

"That's bewildering," Reiko commented, but she said no more, when Tatia signaled her for quiet.

Alex drew close to the display and enlarged it, focusing on the point of the cones, which lay at the ship's present position. "I like this trajectory," he said, pointing to an extremely thin segment that was nearly as black as the dark of space.

"The overlap of our scenarios' probabilities," Z said. "A mathematician's delight."

Julien eliminated the cones and added a dotted line that represented the overlap of their many calculations. It became their tentative new vector. In the far distance lay a probe with moderate signal strength.

"Who would have thought of that?" Reiko whispered in a hush.

"Only a human," Julien replied, grinning at his friend.

* * *

"The Omnian ships are moving," Teal Monitor reported to Golden Executor, who, in turn, hailed the mandator to come to bridge control.

Scarlet Mandator arrived on the bridge and immediately entered a code into the navigation panel. A line popped up in the display. It didn't quite match the trajectory of the Omnian ship.

"What is the plot you added, Mandator?" the executor asked.

"It's the vector that the great orb used when it left the Worlds of Light."

"The aliens are off target. Should they be warned?" the executor asked.

"Are the Worlds of Light fixed? Do the Lights beyond not subtly shift their positions over the course of time? If any species understands this, the Omnians surely do," the mandator explained.

"What does the action of the progenitors mean, Mandator?" Melon Tasker asked.

"The Omnians came to the Worlds of Light to eliminate the device left behind by the great orb. That task is complete. Now they go to find the great orb itself and destroy it. Courageous animals," the mandator said, "and others," adding absently and thinking of Julien.

17

The Hunt

Tatia ordered the fleet to transit to a destination millions of kilometers outside their target system, and she sent the scout ships forward to look for evidence of the Nua'll vessel.

<The sphere has been here,> Linn reported from his scout ship. <Telemetry indicates a water planet, with incongruent areas of missing greenery and what could be thought of as significant areas of strip mining, but there are no indications of a civilization.>

"The ashes would reveal that," Tatia commented to Alex.

"Your deduction was decisive, Alex," Z said. "As one who embraces the world of numbers and probabilities, I must appreciate your abstract reasoning."

Alex craned his neck to stare at the SADE.

"I'm practicing," Z replied, his expression one of apology. "Miranda said I was to be more in touch with my emotional algorithms, elevating them in my hierarchy."

"That was creepy, Z," Reiko commented, and several individuals on the bridge nodded their agreement.

Alex replied, "I deeply appreciate the sentiment, Z," which drew a smile from the SADE before Alex added, "But your technique needs work, a lot of work."

Z's frown was juxtaposed to the laughter around the bridge, but Alex brought everyone quickly back to business, when he sent to the scout ships, <Locate the probe.>

<We have, Dassata,> Trium replied.

Alex was linking to the controller for the data, but Julien anticipated his needs. "Captain Bellardo's Trident, the *Judgment*, is closest, Alex."

Tatia had chosen to spread the Trident squadron wide, encompassing nearly a quarter of the outer planet's orbit. She didn't expect to catch the sphere in this first system, but she was being careful.

The Libran Nua'll sphere, which had devastated half of the Confederation's colonies, never stayed longer than twelve years in any one system. In some cases, the sphere moved on within seven years. According to the Ollassa data, the sphere had been gone for nearly six decades.

<Captain Bellardo, eliminate that probe,> Tatia ordered.

<With pleasure,> Lucia replied.

Lucia Bellardo signaled her controller to take the warship on a course that arced in system. Using the scout ship's data, Lucia directed the controller to focus on the probe's present position. The telemetry data revealed it would be a while before she could launch a banisher. At present, the probe was moving through a heavy asteroid field.

<I want a closer look at the planet that the Nua'll hit,> Alex said, and Tatia ordered the remainder of the squadron to proceed in system. She left the scout ships on the system's periphery to facilitate an early warning.

Several days later, the squadron surrounded the sphere's targeted world.

"Did you want to land, Alex?" Tatia asked, but he shook his head.

"No reason to, Tatia," Alex said. "I wanted to get close enough to see if we could detect anything about the civilization that might have been lost. But, as usual, there's nothing left to give us an indication of that."

"Alex, there is little evidence of a civilization," Julien said, attempting to mollify his friend. "We can't identify any significant deposits of ash. It looks like the Nua'll might have taken an opportunity to collect resources from a planet inhabited only by nonsentient species."

"I don't understand why the Nua'll don't settle one of these planets. This one seems perfect," Reiko said.

"The Nua'll appear to harvest just enough resources to allow the planet to recover in decades or a century," Svetlana added.

"Perhaps what the Nua'll require isn't available to them out here but only from their civilization," Z reasoned.

"So why come out here like a bunch of prospectors, take what they need to keep going, and move onto the next world?" Reiko asked, continuing to press for an explanation that made sense to her.

"The spheres might be tools of colonization, but not in a manner that we would be comfortable understanding," Alex said. The bridge crew quieted, waiting. "What if the spheres are like farmers, tilling the land for future habitation? In some systems, like this one, they take what they need for resources to enable them to keep moving. Then, in other systems, like the Confederation colonies, they clear the competing civilizations."

"This means the Nua'll are taking the long view. The same as they've done with their probes," Tatia said thoughtfully. "That's more evidence of an extraordinarily extensive and ancient race."

"I'd agree," Alex replied.

Silence lay over the bridge. Hunting the second sphere had seemed like an exercise in the squadron's favor. They could easily remove an enemy vessel hampered by limited protection. Suddenly, that encounter appeared to be a minor event in what well could become their civilization's single focus, survival against a great and powerful enemy.

"Considering space is three-dimensional, one can only conclude that the Nua'll are expanding in every direction. It makes one reconsider the number of spheres and probes that they have launched," Z said.

"The longer this discussion continues, the scarier it gets," Renée said. "I'd say let's pack our bags and move, but it would probably only delay the inevitable. Someday, somewhere, the Nua'll will come for our worlds."

"Well said," Alex replied. "Better we find out who and what we're dealing with now."

"In hindsight, the proposals to the other governments to lease our technology so that they might build Tridents, fighters, and scout ships, seems most timely," Svetlana commented.

"What now, Alex?" Tatia asked.

Alex looked at Julien, who said, "As expected, Alex, we have a significant number of choices."

Miranda commented, "It was our thought that the prime factor was probe strength, but our dear man has disabused us of that notion with his choice of a moderate-strength signal, which against all probability, turned out to be accurate. Now, we are left to do what my partner loves most ..."

"Guessing," Z said, as if he had a disgusting taste in his mouth.

There were polite chuckles, but no one suggested an alternative.

"We can't afford to separate the squadron to chase the possibilities," Reiko insisted. She had her hands on her hips to accentuate her opinion.

"Wouldn't think of it, Commodore," Alex replied, chuckling.

"Then narrowing the systems to our next target falls to the scout ships," Tatia stated.

"Julien, have the SADEs make their six best ..." Alex glanced over at Z, as he finished, "guesses. Then get them on their way."

"Commodore, move the squadron far outside this system in the direction we'll most likely be heading. I don't want to sit here," Tatia ordered. "Z, please transfer the squadron's destination coordinates to the scout ships that might return before we move again."

This became the fleet's routine. Mind-numbing tedium was the order of the day, week after week. The scout ships would search until they found the next system where the Nua'll had visited. Communication would fly between the squadron and the scout ships, and the fleet would converge on the new location. Then the process would start over again.

At one evening's meal, after the fleet had started the process again, having arrived at the most recently attacked system, which indicated evidence of a rudimentary civilization burned to ash, the conversation became despondent.

"Another society that we were too late to save," Reiko lamented.

"I understand that seeing these planets ravaged, as they are, is depressing," Renée said, sipping on the remains of her aigre, "but I recommend a different view. We are expending weeks to locate the next system and then using that same amount of time again to travel to it, but the Nua'll spent an average of seven to twelve years in these systems. With every step, we're closing on our target. Eventually, we will find it. Focus on that."

Alex stared at his partner, as if she had sprouted a senior officer's cap on her head. When Renée glanced at him, he grinned, and she smiled in return.

* * *

"I want order on my ships," Admiral Tripping railed. He was on the bridge of the NT *Geoffrey Orlan*, with Captain Jonathan Morney at his side and Captains Alphons Jagielski and Bart Fillister on the comm. "My officers are to discipline any conduct unbefitting New Terran naval service. Am I understood?"

When the captains signaled their affirmatives, Tripping continued his rant. "There is to be zero tolerance for any infractions. I don't want to hear that a fight started but was quickly broken up without also hearing the individuals were charged and punished. Lock them up if you have to."

"Admiral, excuse me, these are Omnian-designed ships. They have no means of incarcerating crew," Jagielski said.

"Impossible," Tripping replied, his voice rising.

When Morney nodded his head in agreement with Jagielski, Tripping ground out, "Are you telling me that the Omnians don't have fights?"

"It's their implants, Admiral," Jagielski shared. "I've spoken to Commodore Shimada and Captain Thompson several times on this subject. The implants allow them to share their thoughts quickly and simply. It makes it nearly impossible to lie or hide behind a false mask, as it were. The troubles between our crew members are created because individuals are hiding behind lies and sly actions meant to get the better of others. The problem is that when the true intent of their words or deeds are exposed, angry reactions develop, and fights break out."

"What are you suggesting, Captain, that New Terrans should get these Méridien devices installed in their heads? Then we'd play nice with one another?"

"No, Sir," Jagielski replied. He regretted trying to educate Tripping. It had failed so many times, and he wondered why he kept trying.

"Well, we need to find a way to lock up these regulation breakers, so they understand that there will be discipline on my ships," Tripping replied, moderating his voice, since he felt he'd made his point.

"We could always keelhaul them, Sir," Fillister suggested.

"Excellent suggestion, Captain, implement that immediately," Tripping said and ended the conference.

Immediately, Alphons commed Bart Fillister. "Well, Captain Fillister, I'm ready to introduce your punishment of keelhauling, but I'm having some problems with the details. First, I don't have any rope to stretch around the midline circumference of my ship, and, second, how do we keep the crew members alive after we throw them out of the airlock and drag them around the ship. Finally, it was my understanding that we were supposed to have some sort of growth on our hull, something about mollusks that were supposed to scrape the hide from those we're punishing. Where do we get those?"

Alphons was trying hard to keep from laughing. He wanted to hear how his affable friend would reply.

"I thought surely that Admiral Tripping would help me with the details," Bart replied, trying desperately to contain the mirth that threatened to bubble out of him.

"Well, there's your first mistake, Bart. You know you're going to be in hot water with the admiral when he finds out you were toying with him."

"Probably not," Bart replied, finally chuckling at the exchange. "I'll tell him that I read the expression in an ancient naval manual, but I didn't know what it meant. Claiming ignorance allows our admiral the opportunity to lecture me, which does wonders for his ego."

"That's too true," Jagielski agreed. "About the admiral's point ... are you having many problems on board your ship?"

"Nothing like those on Morney's, Alphons," Bart replied. "The rumor mill has it that the chiefs aboard his ship have had to deal with an assortment of issues, including three knife fights, an attempted sexual assault, and an assortment of fistfights that involved five or more crew members, most of them over gambling arguments. How about you?"

"Nothing like that either. Some one-on-one scuffles that the chiefs or crew broke up and some vocal arguments that involved name calling. What're you doing for punishment besides keelhauling, Bart?"

"Basically, I keep my officers in line, and I let the chiefs handle the issues with the crew. If they write someone up, then they suggest the punishment length, which, in most cases, I've approved. Then the crew member spends time in some spare cabins that are aft of the ship near the drive engines. They're fairly utilitarian."

"How is their time spent?" Alphons asked.

"They're told to stay in the cabin, and food and water are brought to them. They have no access to vids, and no one is allowed to talk to them. Isolation seems to do the job. It shows them that absolute boredom can be an ugly thing."

"I know we're getting closer to this sphere with every transit," Alphons replied, "but I don't think any us, by that I mean New Terrans, thought it would take this long to track it down. The Omnians are a patient lot. I wonder how they're passing the time."

* * *

At the time of Alphons' musing, there was a raucous celebration among a fair bunch of the OS *Prosecutor*'s crew, who had won a round against the crew of the OS *Liberator*. There was nothing at stake but the pride of winning.

After the squadron had completed its transit to a stationary point far outside the Ollassa system, Tatia could visualize the long and tedious effort that tracking the sphere would require. Immediately, she recruited Renée, who would understand her intentions.

"We need to start the games, Renée," Tatia had said that evening in Renée's cabin.

"The old games for implant training?" Renée asked.

"Yes, I'll devise a schedule that will maximize off-duty time for the crews, while we wait for a scout ship to notify us of our next location. But, I can't afford them to sit idle, watching vids from your collection … fabulous as they might be," Tatia said, quickly adding the last phrase.

Renée chuckled. She knew Tatia wasn't a fan and probably never would be. More than likely, the admiral, in her off time, could be found participating in hand-to-hand combat exercises with the twins, which they hosted for the more aggressive crew members. Short of Étienne and Alain, there were few that could best her. Tatia often thought one or two of the larger, more agile New Terrans let her win, but the twins assured her that the crew members would consider it a coup if they could defeat the admiral.

"Most of our crews haven't played the games since they were at the naval academy on Haraken, Tatia. It won't be like signaling an old algorithm to run."

"That's why I'm asking for your thoughts, Renée."

"Well, if we borrow from Alex's methods, he wouldn't try to jump-start the process across the squadron. Instead, he'd do something like get a couple of small groups together and start the game. Once those crew members started having fun, it would spread quickly."

"What about the officers?" Tatia asked.

"Good point. Tatia, you should start a second game, exclusive to the officers, but make it ship against ship. When the crews on the other ships hear about the games being played on this ship, and that the officers are competing across ships, they'll want to do the same thing."

"Should we set up a reward or prize?"

"If I was thinking like Alex, I would say no, Tatia. Winners will have bragging rights. When do you intend to start the games?"

"Who me? I'm the admiral. I have to stay out of things like officer and crew competitions and that sort of rivalry."

"Ah … now I understand why you wanted to chat."

"I knew you would," Tatia replied, grinning, as she exited Renée's cabin.

The games grew, as Renée predicted. It wasn't long before Alex and the SADEs thought it was full-scale war between ships.

Teams formed ad hoc during duty time, in preparation for the next contest. The teams had to be equal in number, and the SADEs were kept busy setting up the games and monitoring them.

Franz and his commanding officers constituted a sixth Omnian officer group that competed against the other ships, and his pilots formed their own groups and competed against one another.

As the squadron's commodore, Reiko was embarrassed to admit that her team frequently lost, and she was often the weak link. Initially, she had been trained to use the implants with the aid of the games. But, her time at Haraken's naval academy had been demanding, and, soon after graduation she was tasked to be the captain of the Haraken's first sting ship, the *Tanaka*. She did note that by participating in these games, she learned more about her implant's capabilities than she had in many years.

The twins, Étienne and Alain, did their part to relieve the boredom. Their demonstrations, which usually consisted of the twins sharpening their escort skills, often drew admirers from the crew, and they had expanded their efforts to include the onlookers.

Now, the twins took advantage of the time the fleet sat stationary, waiting for a report, to jump from ship to ship to put on their demonstrations and start small classes. Their training techniques caught on, and soon the twins were kept extraordinarily busy.

Alex ordered vid cams mounted in all of the Omnian ships' training areas. Julien programmed them so that only Étienne or Alain could activate them. It allowed the twins to monitor the classes across the Omnian ships, and offer real-time critiques.

18

Home Worlds II

The ratification of the Omnian agreement was a fait accompli for Presidents Lechaux and Grumley. Their governments, having only the one system, had allowed each populace to witness the immense explosion of the relatively diminutive probe.

Previous to these events, the fight against the Libran sphere, which was viewed by many New Terrans, at the time, courtesy of Julien's vids, was more than two decades ago. There was little to suggest that there was anything more to fear from whoever had created the mysterious sphere. However, the announcement that the Nua'll had been monitoring systems throughout the galaxy, including theirs, and the detonation of the probes changed all that for New Terra and Haraken.

In a flood of concern for their populaces' safety, the agreements were ratified by New Terra and Haraken and sent to Captain Cordelia, who had been authorized by Alex to accept them. Her approval, once received by the respective presidents, provided the means to unlock the data vaults that Terese and Maria had carried with them from Omnia.

While Alex and the fleet chased the second sphere, Haraken and New Terra began construction of the enclosed bays they would need to spray the faux shells on the manufactured frames and bulkheads of their first Tridents. Neither government saw a need to hurry and build scout ships. The tiny ships required SADE crews, and the Harakens and New Terrans thought the long-range searches were best left to the Omnians, who had a knack for it.

On the other hand, it wasn't smooth sailing for Gino with the Confederation Council, but he didn't expect it to be. Rather than present the agreement directly to the body of Leaders, Gino gathered his strongest supporters, Bartosz Rolek, Emilio Torres, Shannon Brixton, and, of course, Katrina Pasko.

"You want to convince the Council to build warships?" Bartosz asked in surprise, unable to let Gino finish his presentation.

"Add the Omnians, Harakens, and New Terrans together, Bartosz. How many worlds do you have?" Gino asked rhetorically. "We can't expect them to protect the entire Confederation."

"Look how many probes have already been discovered," Katrina added. It was obvious to the small group whose side she favored. "And what have we been doing about them? Throwing rocks at them. Once, we were the technological leaders of humankind in this small part of the galaxy, and we prided ourselves on that. But we aren't anymore."

"Sers, how many times must danger visit our worlds, before we decide to take up the defense of our systems in our own hands?" Gino asked, rising from his chair to address his friends. Unknowingly, he was imitating an approach often used by Alex and Omnian senior officers.

"But you aren't only asking us to build warships," Emilio said. "You're also asking us to provide military-trained personnel to crew them."

"Alex Racine has offered an idea for that," Gino argued. "We can train our personnel at the Haraken naval academy. What better place could there be?"

"I don't see Méridiens volunteering for service," Shannon Brixton said.

"Perhaps, Ser, that's because you don't view the Independents as Méridiens," Katrina replied.

Gino's friends glanced from Katrina to him and back. Gino wore a grin and cocked an eyebrow.

"You'd force the Independents to serve in the military?" Emilio asked. He was incredulous and then taken aback when Gino and Katrina burst into laughter.

"My friends, I love you dearly, but I must admit that sometimes I'm confused by your thinking!" Gino said.

"It's our thinking that has remained consistent, Gino." Shannon accused. "You and Katrina have spent a great deal of time throughout the years with Alex and Renée."

"That's true, Shannon, but do you know who else was in their company, in addition to New Terrans? Méridiens ... Independents," Gino replied. "They're Alex's fiercest supporters, and, with the SADEs, they're the leaders in the fight against the Nua'll."

"What's your point, Gino?" Shannon asked.

"It's this, Shannon. We won't force the military on the Independents. In fact, I'd like to suspend the process of branding our people as Independents. I believe the Méridiens who display a displeasure with our societal strictures, might be the individuals who would embrace naval service. And, if they don't, we should find another means of keeping them within our society rather than shipping them off to some forsaken colony."

"Especially since Alex Racine continues to liberate them and make them a valuable part of his worlds," Katrina interjected. "If nothing else, that should prove the insanity of what we do ... discarding our citizens for what we believe are errant behaviors, while another individual, who has twice protected our worlds, collects them for their value to his societies."

Quiet followed Katrina's words. This particular group of Leaders hadn't been in favor of the harsh environment of Daelon, the dead moon that served as the last Independent colony. In contrast, many Council Leaders had been incensed at Alex's efforts to support the evacuation of the first colony at Libre and, more so, when he liberated Daelon.

"Are you intent on tying all this together in your presentation to the Council, Gino?" Bartosz asked, dubious about the success of that possibility.

"How can we accomplish the goal of protecting the Confederation if we don't line up every element ... the agreement's approval, warship construction, cease branding the Independents, raising a military force, and requesting training at Haraken?"

Gino's three friends looked from one to another, and the Council Leader shared a glance with his partner, Katrina. When no one had much to say, Gino thanked them for coming and showed them to the door of his luxurious sky tower suite.

"That went well," Katrina joked, but when she noticed Gino's crestfallen expression, she hugged him. "Apologies, Gino. That was insensitive of me."

"I'd hoped for a sign of support, at the least from this group. In manner of thought, they're closest to us. If I can't convince them to see the way forward, how am I going to convince the Council, with the likes of Darse Lemoyne and Lawrence Teressi in attendance?"

Gino walked to the slate of windows that encompassed one entire side of the salon. Clouds had moved in far below the sky tower's uppermost level, where Gino's suite of rooms occupied the entire floor. The lights of the Méridien capital were obscured.

Katrina came up behind Gino and encircled his waist with her arms. "I don't have an answer for you, my partner," she said. Then she laughed softly.

Gino turned around within her grasp and pulled her to him, nuzzling her ear. "Why do you laugh?"

Katrina chuckled and said, "Of all things to think, I was wondering what Alex would do." She could feel Gino's soft laughter through her chest and she hugged him tighter. Then his laughter halted, and she pulled her head back to study his face. Gino was staring into space.

"Yes, what Alex would do," Gino repeated in a whisper. Then he smiled, a huge, broad smile, and kissed Katrina's forehead.

* * *

In an unprecedented move for a Council Leader, Gino Diamanté waited for his guests in Confederation Hall's ornate and awe-inspiring main entrance corridor. Translucent panels along one side of the corridor splayed the light of Méridien's star in mesmerizing colors.

"Sers, thank you for coming at short notice," Gino said, by way of greeting the four SADEs who advanced quickly toward him.

"Generous of you to say, Council Leader Diamanté," Domino replied, "but we serve the Confederation and a request by your personage, as polite as it was couched, isn't something we would ignore.

Gino nodded in appreciation, and asked, "Were you able to complete your tables and come to a conclusion?"

"For something as considerable as what you've asked, Leader Diamanté," Serge replied, "we would have preferred considerably more time to research the data. However, we're prepared to offer the Council a preliminary summary."

"Excellent," Gino replied. "This way, Sers."

Those seated in the Supplicants Hall, which preceded Council Chambers, rose and nodded at Gino as he passed. The attendant at the Council's massive doors was shocked to see the Council Leader using this manner of entrance to the exalted Chambers. He hurriedly signaled the doors aside, and his mouth was slightly ajar, as Gino and his guests marched inside.

"To business, fellow Leaders," Gino said, as he ascended his centrally located podium, which allowed him to meet the rows of Leaders at eye level. The four SADEs stood patiently beside the raised dais, waiting for their cues.

Gino spent the best part of an hour outlining his plan, but his presentation wasn't without interruption. He'd decided to divulge his entire concept in one go, and, as certain Leaders heard various elements that they found incredible, they vocalized their objections.

In the case of each interruption, Gino halted and waited, while the Council's controller called the Leaders to order, indicating to them that the Council Leader held the floor and hadn't opened the meeting to discussion.

When Gino finished and requested comments from the Leaders, Darse Lemoyne jumped to his feet. "This is a preposterous assembly of fiction meant to frighten us into tearing apart the fabric of Méridien society."

"Which part do you consider fictional, Leader Lemoyne?" Gino asked. "The second sphere the Omnians have located? The probes that have been found in every human system and that we are still finding in nearby systems? The Nua'll aren't a single event that we're fortunate to have survived with the aid of others. They're being considered an extensive and ancient civilization with an age-old habit of expanding their territory."

"The Confederation is wealthy," Lawrence Teressi called out. "Even if we were to require protection from these aliens, we have the credits to hire others, who have a taste for killing."

"And how would you go about that, Leader Teressi?" Gino asked. "I have it on good authority from President Lechaux of Haraken, Envoy Gonzalez of New Terra, and Alex Racine of Omnia that they will be constructing warships to protect their systems and hunt the Nua'll sphere. After that, they intend to find the aliens' home world or worlds, as it might be. Do you think they'll be eager to accept our credits, so they might protect us, while they leave their own people vulnerable?"

"At this point, I must admit I'm undecided about the Council Leader's proposal," Shannon Brixton said, standing to make her statement. "But I must point out the fallacies in Leader Teressi's consideration that we might pay for protection. The governments enumerated by our Council Leader have responsibility for a total of three worlds. They haven't the time or resources, even if they had the will or desire, to provide the forces for the number of Confederation systems we presently occupy. And consider these additional two points: Are we to sit idle and cease expansion so that we don't strain a military shield, if we could hire one? And how long would these employed forces be required to patrol our systems? It might be generations before the Nua'll come our way. Then, when the incursion finally came, Leader Teressi has every expectation that these hired individuals would happily expend their lives defending worlds that aren't inhabited by their people."

Shannon's observations were scaring the Leaders, who, for the most part, wanted no part of Gino's proposal. On the other hand, they disagreed with Darse Lemoyne that the threat wasn't real.

"I took the liberty of providing assistance to help you reach a decision on what I'm proposing," Gino said. "All of you know the fours SADEs beside me, but you might not recognize them in their present guise since they were freed." Gino had used a word unwelcomed by the Council Leaders. They preferred to refer to the SADEs as released, not freed. Gino's term, although accurate, connoted the distasteful image of imprisonment.

"May I introduce Domino, Serge, Linton, and Pierce?" Gino said.

The four SADEs gave a Leader's salutation to the Council, as they were introduced.

Murmurs, whispers, and thoughts ran through the rows of Leaders. The four SADEs had never sailed a starship, managed a station or a sky tower, or run a House. The Confederation had installed these four SADEs independent of any such tasks. They were created specifically to offer risk assessment to any Leader, regarding business proposals.

Across the Confederation, there were few SADEs respected more than these four, except for Winston, the ex-Council SADE, who now headed the SADEs' Strategic Investment Fund, referred to as SIF.

Compared to the flamboyant synth-skins adopted by many of the SADEs, who had immigrated to Haraken and Omnia, these four SADEs appeared normal, bland even. In most respects, they adopted common human characteristics, except for their avatars' stature, which was neither the slender Méridien nor the robust New Terran.

Domino took a step forward. "I have been asked to present our findings on the risk assessment of whether the Confederation should provide military protection for its colonies or not. We aren't commenting on how a force might be procured if the Council chooses that direction. Despite the complex nature of Council Leader Diamanté's query, we examined the financial risks of this choice, based on actuary data and standard risk management practices."

Domino outlined what data the SADEs had used to create their actuary tables. She enumerated the evidence collected about the Nua'll spheres and probes. Carefully and succinctly, she built toward her conclusion.

"In summary, Leaders, it's evident that the threat is of such magnitude that it would be foolish not to provide some sort of insurance to mitigate a potential disaster," Domino said.

"My colleague is careful with her words, Leaders," Linton said, stepping beside Domino. "In simpler terms, we believe the Nua'll threat is severe enough that there is every possibility the Confederation could be wiped from its systems. Our advice is: Spend your credits and protect yourselves and us."

"While I appreciate the service of these four individuals, who have been of great value to all of us," Lemoyne said. "I might point out that these are conjectures ... what ifs that we can't depend on to require us to make extensive changes in our society."

"Leader Lemoyne, I must correct your statement," Pierce said, "Your House and you, personally, have relied on our recommendations for more than a hundred years. In every case, our advice was in response to your *what ifs*, as you refer to them. This is no different. It's merely pondering a much more frightening scenario."

Gino was about to accept another question from the Leaders when Domino signaled him, and he offered her the opportunity to speak.

"Leaders, the Council Leader asked a single question, which we've tried to answer," Domino said. "However, due to the serious nature of the subject, we took it upon ourselves to investigate further and see if we could model the risk-assessment dynamics as events unfolded over time."

"We tried an experiment, in a manner of speaking," Pierce said. He was the one who had suggested to the other SADEs that they delve deeper into the possibility of a potential crisis. "We formed our tables at three different points within the Confederation's timeline ... before the attack on the *Rêveur*, immediately after the destruction of the first sphere, and in the present circumstances.

A Leader stood to speak, but Gino signaled for restraint, while Pierce continued. "At the first point in time, we saw little risk to the Confederation from any substantial outside interference ... foolish as that conclusion now appears to be in hindsight. At the second point, we saw the elimination of the Nua'll vessel as heralding an enormous future risk that this Council has seen fit to deny on many occasions. It wasn't logical to us that Leaders would depend on our services for so many of their decisions, but, on this particular subject of possible outside interference in Méridien society, you would fail to heed our advice."

"Considering the present circumstances," Linton said, picking up Pierce's thread, "we've concluded the future is not one of measuring the extent of the risk, which would indicate the potential of the interference returning. It has become a matter of assuming a 100 percent probability of that happening. The only variable remaining becomes postulating when that might happen."

The Leaders spent hours questioning the SADEs before the Council broke for midday meal, and Gino thanked the SADEs for their efforts.

"We're concerned, Ser," Serge said. "While I'm not astute at reading the body languages and facial expressions of humans in regard to this stressful situation, it appears the Council members are unconvinced by our presentation. We would appreciate an explanation."

Gino thought of some of the statements made by Alex about working with the first group of SADEs he'd freed at Haraken. Honesty and bluntness were what he advised.

"Many of the Leaders are scared," Gino explained. "They're frightened by the difficult choice and of making the wrong decision. They worry that if they choose a military option and nothing happens, then they would have perverted our society, as they see it, for no reason at all. In the other case, they're afraid of not choosing the military option and risk being responsible for the elimination of every human and SADE in the Confederation."

"But fear should not be part of the equation in making a decision of this magnitude," Domino argued. "The more critical the subject, the more important to decide logically on weighted risks."

"That's a SADE thing to do, Domino, and one that rational, calm humans can make."

"But frightened ones might not," Pierce supplied, understanding what Gino was driving at.

"And the fate of all of us is in the hands of scared humans?" Linton asked, shaking his head in disbelief.

"A decision hasn't been made yet, my friends," Gino replied. "Have faith that the Leaders will find the courage to do what needs to be done."

The SADEs paid their respects to Gino with a salute and left the Chambers.

Gino had invited his partner and close friends to his sumptuous offices and ordered midday meal served there. Now, he hurried to join them.

"The SADEs did well," Katrina commented, when the servers had left.

"Yes, they did," Gino agreed.

"I find I'm leaning toward your proposal, Gino," Shannon commented. "Our House has profited immensely from Serge's advice. It seems idiotic not to heed it now because the question before us requires a significant shift in our future's path."

"What about you two?" Gino asked Bartosz and Emilio, and he was disappointed to hear they were still undecided.

"And if these are the opinions of my friends, I can imagine what the majority of the Leaders are thinking," Gino said. Silence descended on the group, and the Leaders consumed their meal without another word.

When the Council resumed, Gino was undecided how to proceed. He was loath to call for a vote, knowing his proposal would probably be defeated.

<Council Leader Diamanté, you have a petitioner in the Supplicants Hall, who wishes to be heard. It's Winston,> Gino received from the attendant.

<Admit him,> Gino sent in reply. He had no idea what Winston was prepared to say, but everything he had learned from Alex taught him to trust the SADEs to speak what they believed. In this case, it would mean giving Winston an opportunity to address the Council, whether he supported Gino's proposal or not.

"I offer the floor to Winston," Gino said, when the SADE took up a position beside the elevated podium.

"Sers," Winston said, without a gesture of respect to the Council. "You'll pardon my uninvited presence among you, but I was only recently made aware of Council Leader Diamanté's intentions. I'm here representing the Confederation SADEs. Only a relatively small number could be polled in the short time available, but the response was overwhelmingly singular. The SIF Directors believe this poll is representative of the opinion of their entire membership. As such, I'm required to make you aware of their demand."

Winston's words created an angry rumble through the rows, and Katrina smiled at Gino, anticipating what was to come.

"I see that you don't appreciate that word *demand*, Sers. I don't use it lightly. As you are aware, every SADE is a member and contributor to the SIF. Therefore, when the SADEs, who could respond to the poll in time, demanded the Council take action to protect the Confederation, we, as the directorate, must heed the membership, not that we disagree with their uniform opinion."

Lemoyne and Teressi simultaneously jumped up, but, before they could speak, Winston held up his hands and thundered, "You will hear me out, Sers, or regret that you didn't."

Despite their outrage, Lemoyne and Teressi were forced to sit by an outpouring of cries from other Leaders, who shouted for them to sit down and be still.

"Our demand is simple." Winston continued. "Take action to protect Méridiens across the Confederation. Fund a military force, and disabuse yourself of the idea that you can hire others to do it for you. The majority of SADEs want a future in the Confederation, but not at the risk of watching Nua'll spheres descend on our colonies and decimate everything we've worked to build. If you don't heed our demand, the SIF directorship will recommend to its members that they seek safety with some other society that will be enacting the necessary steps to protect its populace against the possibility of invasion."

Several Leaders jumped up to ask Winston questions, but they were faced with a view of his retreating back. Winston triggered the doors to the Supplicants Hall and strode briskly through them.

Confused and dazed by the turn of events, Gino was unsure what to do next.

<Ask for the vote on your proposal, Gino,> Katrina sent urgently. <The Leaders are frightened of your concept, but they're more frightened of losing the SADEs. This is the same difficult decision they faced with Alex that forced them to free the SADEs in the first place. Do it now,> she urged.

Gino called for order and waited while the Leaders quieted. "I have no more information to present on this subject. You have received the agreement with Omnia Ships, and you've received my proposal. I'm not prepared to separate these into individual parts for you to pick and choose between. That would make no sense. I call for a vote on the agreement and my proposal as a package. Roll call, please," Gino finished, cueing the controller.

The process took a while. The controller continued to ping the Leaders, during the course of the afternoon, for their votes. They, in turn, were busy discussing the subject with their close associates.

Gino retired to his office to await the outcome. He wasn't permitted to query the controller, while a vote was being taken. Instead, he sent, <Winston, you made me nervous for a moment. I wasn't sure what you were going to say.>

<Ser, I wish you to understand that what I told the Council wasn't an idle threat. The Confederation would lose its independent SADEs immediately, and, as others were freed and finished their one-year indentures, they would undoubtedly leave too. There's the distinct possibility that other human worlds wouldn't accept so many of us, but we're prepared to make our own way, find a new world, and the SIF has the credits to do just that.>

<I hope it doesn't come to that, Winston. The Confederation needs you and your kind; the peoples of our worlds need you.>

<Understood, Leader Diamanté, but what good is standing by Confederation humans only to perish with them for lack of an effort to protect ourselves?>

<I can't disagree with those sentiments, Winston,> Gino said, ending the comm. He'd refused the servers' offers to bring him a small repast. Instead, he sat at his desk. The thought running through his head was, *Katrina, I tried to do what Alex might have done, but I don't know if I'm as practiced or as effective as him.*

The controller notified Gino that voting was completed. He stood from his desk, straightened his jacket, and assumed a confident air, although he felt no such thing. He marched with sure steps across the Chamber's floor to climb the steps of the dais and grasp the podium's curved rail.

"Announce the vote," Gino ordered the controller.

"The Council votes in the majority to accept the agreement with Omnia Ships and the Council Leader's proposal to construct warships and raise a military contingent of Méridien volunteers, who might be trained at Haraken to command and crew the ships," the controller replied.

Gino's legs threatened to collapse at the announcement. The Confederation's future safety had ridden on the Council's vote to accept dramatic changes in Méridien culture, and he couldn't believe it had happened. <Success, Winston,> Gino sent.

<As we intended it,> Winston replied enigmatically.

The *Rêveur* completed the long transit to Sol's space. Per Captain Lumley's request, Esteban had exited the passenger ship outside the system's dense, outer asteroid belt. The first thing the SADE did was send a code to access the comm probes left behind by Alex and the Harakens, which would enable the Omnians to quickly communicate across the system.

"Esteban, please proceed to locate Patrice Morris and Nikki Fowler for us," Olawale requested.

Olawale and Francis had decided to get an update from the friends that the Harakens had made at Idona Station, namely Patrice and Nikki, before they attempted to contact Sol's leadership. Originally enemies, Patrice, a militia lieutenant, and Nikki, a rebel leader, formed a working partnership and, later, a tight bond, as they proved that antagonists can work together, and old wounds can be healed.

"Please repeat," the Idona Station communications operator said. "Did you ask for Lieutenant Morris? How long have you been out in the belt? It's Colonel Morris now."

"Then might I speak with your colonel?" Esteban asked.

"The colonel is presently in the belt. I don't have her schedule, but I can refer you to her adjutant, who can give you that information. By the way, you didn't identify yourself, and your access code didn't show."

"Please connect me to the colonel's adjutant," Esteban requested. "To answer your questions, we're old friends of Ser Fowler, and we haven't a need for your access codes."

The operator's jaw dropped. "Ser," he whispered, and the operators left and right of him, jerked their heads to stare at him. Immediately, the operator called the colonel's adjutant, explained what he heard, and connected her to the mysterious caller."

"This is Adjutant Dormer, kindly identify yourself," Mel said, after tapping her earpiece to accept the call.

Esteban switched the comm to the *Rêveur*'s bridge speakers and audio pickup.

"This is Envoy Wombo," Olawale said. He grinned, as he glanced around him, at Francis, Edmas, and Jodlyne. All four of them were, in one way or another, outcasts of United Earth, the overarching political, military, and judicial system of Sol society. That they were returning to their native system, as vibrant contributors to Omnian society, tickled them.

"Envoy? We don't have envoys," Mel replied, beginning to think the call was a joke.

<Help our adjutant, Esteban,> Olawale sent.

Mel, who was seated at her desk and keeping her call on audio only, found she was looking at the dark face of Olawale on her monitor.

"Oh, you've changed your militia uniforms," Olawale said, congenially. "I much prefer the new ones. The old ones were too severe. I think they were designed to provoke fear in the hearts of everyone, especially the rebels."

"Rebels?" Mel managed to whisper.

"While I'd like to chat, Adjutant Dormer, I prefer to be talking to Colonel Morris. I have an urgent message from Alex Racine. Kindly inform me of her location."

Olawale could barely contain himself. When Alex pronounced him an Omnian envoy, Olawale had objected, thinking the title too lofty. But, during the trip to Sol, he considered its advantages. The mention of an envoy from Alex Racine would open doors, and this was his first test of its weight.

An expletive slipped quietly from Mel's lips, before her brain could kick in gear. "One moment, Sir, I mean, Ser," Mel managed to spit out. She tapped a code into her console and placed a call to one of the mining hubs in the far belt. The comm lag would be evident, but she didn't know what else to do.

Esteban traced the focused comm signal and determined its terminal point, signaling Olawale that he was placing the next call.

"Thank you for your assistance, Adjutant Dormer, we can handle it from here," Olawale said, and Esteban smoothly switched the comm from Idona Station through the mining hub's comm station to the colonel's reader.

"Colonel Morris here," Patrice replied. She'd finished lunch with a collection of mining bosses. Piracy wasn't dead in the belt, and probably never would be, but the militia, with the help of a coalition of captains, station commanders, and citizens, had severely curtailed the activity.

"Hello, Patrice," Olawale said.

A tiny pulse in Patrice's earpiece told her that her audio call had switched to vid, and she held up her reader. The face of the ex-Earther administrator smiled at her. "Olawale," Patrice replied, her heart warmed by the sight of an old friend she thought she would never see again. "And here I was wondering why you don't call anymore," she added, laughing.

"I understand that it's Colonel Morris now. Congratulations," Olawale replied.

"That's your leader's fault, Olawale. He reset how this place works. Now it's merit-based promotion. I keep making the mistake of working hard and trying to do a good job."

"As you always did, Patrice."

"By the way, Olawale, is this some sort of Haraken long-distance call, or are you nearby? And, most important, is Alex with you?" Patrice watched the smile slip from her friend's face.

"Colonel Morris, I'm Omnian Envoy Wombo, and I'm requesting your assistance on an urgent matter for your government," Olawale stated formally and severely.

With part of her brain, Patrice was trying to parse Olawale's request, including the new terms, while another portion reverted to her training, and she was calculating how to deal with the situation.

"We're 3.5 hours out from your position, Patrice," Olawale said, shifting to a softer voice. "We'll land a traveler for you. This might go much quicker if we can talk face-to-face."

"Sure, Olawale. I'll wrap up things here and meet your ship in the landing bay." Patrice didn't bother to give Olawale more details. Her experience with the Harakens had taught her many things about those who possessed advanced technology, one of which was that those types of individuals rarely needed directions.

"Colonel," Patrice's militia aide called, running up to her. "The outpost has one of those Haraken ships on approach. I think they're back."

"Omnians," Patrice corrected. "Now, they're Omnians … I think," she added, holding up her reader to indicate her call.

"Wow," the aide murmured.

"I'll be riding back to Idona with them. Collect the reports that I've requested from the mining bosses and have the captain return our ship to the station," Patrice ordered. She left her thunderstruck aide standing in the corridor. With time to kill, she located a lounge where she could get a cup of caf. She found a seat, took a sip, and stared at her reader, as if it would provide some answers. And, in a strange way, it did. At the top of her contact list was her best friend, Nikki Fowler. With a grin, she tapped Nikki's contact.

"How's my favorite colonel?" Nikki replied cheerfully, after a time lag for the distance.

"Out chasing privateers and trying to keep the peace," Patrice replied. "Where are you?"

"I'm about an hour out from Idona. I only have a day layover before I'm sailing again. Too bad we can't have dinner. I'd have loved to catch up."

"Get out your best outfit, Nikki. We'll be dining out."

"I thought you were in the belt, Patrice. What changed?"

"I *am* in the belt. I'll be catching an Omnian transport back to Idona."

Nikki frowned at her reader, wondering if something had happened to her friend's mental capabilities. "Okay, Patrice, could you tell me about this Omnian transport?" Nikki asked. She felt like a psychiatrist, who was questioning a slightly imbalanced patient.

Patrice bit her lip to keep from laughing and replied in a laconic voice, "I don't know. It must be some sort of name change. I mean, when they left, they were called Harakens, and now they're back calling themselves Omnians."

"Oh, you rat," Nikki called out, and Patrice burst out laughing. "Where, who?" Nikki asked excitedly.

"All I know is that Olawale Wombo is aboard a single ship. I took a look at the mining post's scans, and the ship looks similar to the passenger liner that was here, the *Rêveur*. But, here's the important thing, Nikki, Olawale called himself an Omnian envoy with a critical message for our government."

"Oh, that can't be good," Nikki replied. "I mean if it makes the Harakens ... I mean Omnians ... nervous, it'll scare the wits out of the representatives."

"Nikki, I just realized why we're Olawale's first contact," Patrice said.

"You mean, why you were his first contact," Nikki retorted.

"I would have called you next, Nikki," Olawale said, his voice coming through on both women's readers, "but we thought it easier to let Patrice locate you for us."

Both women noted that with Olawale's communication, the comm lag time had disappeared between them.

Nikki laughed, enjoying the moment. "I should be angry at you, you aging excuse for a scientist, eavesdropping on us like this," Nikki said. "You should be more respectful of a rim governor," she added proudly.

"Congratulations, Nikki," Olawale rejoiced. "It's much deserved, I'm sure."

"Thank you, Olawale. And how are we addressing you?" Nikki asked.

"For the purpose of this visit, it's Envoy Wombo. I'm here with a message from Alex that your government must hear."

"There's no one chasing you, is there, Olawale?" Patrice asked, suddenly concerned about the possibility of a military confrontation.

"The issue is not of that nature, Patrice, but I must speak to the Tribunal," Olawale replied.

It occurred to Nikki what Patrice had started to say about why Olawale reached out to them. He needed orientation. His information was long out of date. Since Olawale was last at Sol, the Tribunal had expanded into the Council, and, with the ratification of a system-wide constitution, that body was replaced by elected representatives, regional governors, a president, and a cabinet.

"From what Patrice tells me, we'll be meeting this evening at Idona," Nikki said.

"Yes, and, if you don't mind, we'll dine aboard the *Rêveur*."

"Yes," the women shouted and laughed at their similar reactions, which reminded Olawale that they had never been aboard a Méridien-built ship.

After Olawale ended his comm, Patrice and Nikki chatted and theorized about what brought Olawale back to Sol. At one point, Nikki's concerns were getting the best of her, and Patrice calmed her, by saying, "Nikki, don't let your imagination run away with you. Olawale came aboard a passenger liner. There are no Omnian warships, and there is no Alex. If it was a big problem, we'd see one or the other or both."

Soon afterwards, Nikki cited calls she had to make to Idona and ended the comm, and Patrice spent the next hours musing about the days before and after the Harakens arrived. Before she knew it, her reader chimed with a message that the Omnian shuttle was on approach. Shaking her head to clear her reverie, Patrice hurried to recycle her cup, descend to the mining hub's bay level, and passed through the tunnel to the landing bay.

"Coming in now, Colonel," the crew chief announced, when Patrice stepped into bay control. Behind the blast glass, Patrice watched the huge bay doors open to the dark of space. A rim of lights outlined the bay opening.

"What kind of a shuttle is that?" the crew chief asked in a muttered breath. "It's not even got windows for the pilot. And where in blazes are its engines or attitude jets?"

Patrice grinned at the chief, slapping him lightly on the back. "That, my dear chief, is what you call advanced technology, which yours truly gets to ride in today. And, by the way, chief, that's not only a shuttle it's a hellaciously powerful, beam-capable fighter."

"No," the chief replied in disbelief.

"Yes," Patrice said, smiling.

The bay lights highlighted the blues, greens, and creams that swirled through the hull's shell. The outer doors were closing, and Patrice left the chief to chew on what she'd said. Her aide met her outside bay control with her bag. She thanked him, snatched it, and hustled to the airlock.

Patrice was as nervous and giddy as a schoolgirl about riding in one of Omnia's incredible fighters. When the airlock telltale, reporting bay pressure, flashed green, she smacked the hatch release and stepped through.

For a second, Patrice faltered. She couldn't detect where the hatch would appear, but a slender outline soon cut the smooth shell and then the hatch lowered. Patrice crossed the bay's deck in quick steps and pounded up the steps. The pilot, Jerry, stepped quickly out of her way.

"Welcome aboard, Colonel. Sit anywhere you like," Jerry said, gesturing toward the rows of empty seats.

"Is their room upfront?"

"Absolutely, Colonel."

Jerry led the way forward, took one seat, and offered the other to Patrice. He handed her a helmet and signaled the controller to provide a forward view in the helmet faceplate. Usually, an Omnian would take the controller's views through the implant where data apps could more quickly respond compared to a human's visual system.

"Ready, Colonel?" Jerry asked.

"Absolutely," Patrice replied, echoing Jerry. Her faceplate displayed a crystal sharp image of the bay. Rather than the high-contrast visual usually seen in person, due to the bay's harsh lighting, she received a beautifully moderated image that made the bay look better than it ever had.

Patrice waited with impatience for the enhanced thrum of the engines, as they readied for takeoff, and the powerful thrust that must surely accompany the fighter's launch into open space. Instead, the ship lifted, turned into the opening, and exited the bay in a silent, smooth rush.

Patrice glanced at Jerry. Their launch was the eeriest thing she'd ever felt, and her pilot was adding to the weirdness of it all. He sat with his hands folded together, quiet, no movement, as the traveler twisted this way and that way around asteroids, accelerating at a tremendous rate, judging by the enormous rocks that sped past.

"Who's flying this machine?" Patrice asked, not without a little trepidation.

"I'm in charge, Colonel, but the controller is flying the shuttle. I requested coordinates for Idona, confirmed them against my telemetry data, and requested the controller deliver us there."

"How did the controller know the coordinates, if this ship has never been there?"

"Oh, I see what you're asking. Anywhere that Alex, Julien, and the Méridiens have ever been is embedded in this controller's memory."

"Everywhere?" Patrice asked, seeking confirmation.

"As you know, memory crystal banks can hold an enormous amount of data." Silence followed Jerry's statement, and he thought that perhaps he'd made a faux pas. "Doesn't your civilization employ crystal for memory and power?" he asked.

"No," Patrice replied flatly. The expectation of seeing Olawale again and experiencing the world of the Omnians was blunted. She was reminded of the huge technological gulf between their societies and lamented the time lost by Earth and its satellites, during the long period of stagnation and the hard-governing hand of United Earth's Tribunal.

"My apologies, Colonel, I meant nothing by my question."

"No problem, Jerry," Patrice replied. But that exchange effectively ended their conversation. Much sooner than Patrice expected, the image of the *Rêveur* appeared in her faceplate.

"We're headed to your ship," Patrice remarked.

"Yes, Colonel. Those were my orders. Do you need to speak with Envoy Olawale to discuss alternative arrangements?"

"No, but I must inform Rim Governor Fowler of the change."

"The governor is aboard the *Rêveur* now, Colonel."

"Very efficient of the envoy," Patrice remarked.

Jerry wisely chose not to reply to the comment. He had the feeling that he'd mishandled the conversation with the colonel and failed to develop a rapport. But, Jerry needn't have worried. If anything, Patrice Morris had an irrepressible personality. When she exited the traveler, and saw Olawale waiting to greet her, she cried out in joy and gave him a fierce hug.

"The man who started it all," Patrice said in Olawale's ear.

"I wasn't alone," Olawale reminded her.

"You led," Patrice reminded him. She glanced at Olawale's left and exclaimed, "Captain Lumley," giving him a hug too. "Why don't you two look like you're aging?" Patrice challenged them.

"That's what I asked," Nikki said, stepping from the rear of the group. "I think it's more technological magic. Remember how the Harakens helped our people recover. But, putting that aside, Colonel, here are two people who I've been wanting you to meet."

Nikki's arm gesture directed Patrice to focus on the tall, young man and the young woman leaning on his arm, both of them smiling at her.

When a frown formed on Patrice's face, Edmas, using the tone and slang of an Idona teenage rebel, asked, "You still a milt, Colonel?"

"Edmas?" Patrice asked, and the young man beamed at her. "Jodlyne?" she asked, looking at the woman, who nodded. "Incredible," Patrice replied in a hush. "You two look wonderful." She threw her arms around the young couple who she last knew as scrawny rebel rats that crawled through air vents to attack the militia and steal their equipment.

"And may I present our SADE?" Olawale said, stepping aside.

"Greetings, Ser. I'm Esteban."

"Is that face paint, Esteban?" Patrice asked. She stared at the subtle blues, greens, and occasional white peaks. It reminded her of waves approaching the beaches of Sol.

"It's a pattern embedded in my synth-kin, Colonel. There's a long story behind what you see. Perhaps it's a discussion best saved for later," Esteban replied, diplomatically.

Olawale had been careful to impress on the Omnians the culture shock Patrice and Nikki would experience, saying, "They briefly knew the Harakens, and, while time crawled for the people of Sol, it leapt for the Omnians. We have to focus on the mission Alex sent us out to accomplish. Our goal is to communicate with the government about the probe and get permission to destroy it."

After the greetings were finished, Olawale said, "It's mealtime, Sers. If you'll follow me?"

Patrice and Nikki expected the usual Earther treatment aboard ship of a private dinner served in the captain's quarters. Instead, they walked into a dining room, busy with people taking trays to seats, already eating, and everyone chatting. However, the moment the Earthers entered, everyone stopped, and nodded heads, with hands to heart, in a coordinated motion.

"I forgot about those ... the implants," Nikki said, as Patrice and she returned the greeting.

When they sat at the head table, servers brought food and drink. Patrice looked at the dishes in front of her. Tears clouded her eyes. They were the favorite foods that she'd enjoyed from the meal dispensers the Harakens had installed on board Idona to help the rebels recover their health, and that later everyone enjoyed until the Harakens left.

Patrice stood up and looked around the dining room. She located Jerry, who was staring at her. *Yes, implants,* she thought, recognizing the message had been passed silently through the diners that she was seeking someone. Patrice crooked a finger at him, and the pilot quickly crossed the room to her.

"I'm sorry, Jerry. Crystal does hold a tremendous amount of data. Even minutiae, such as the food a foolish militia officer enjoyed. My apologies for my attitude," Patrice said, laying a comradely hand on the pilot's shoulder.

"None needed, Colonel. We're pleased to be of service," Jerry replied, and returned to his seat.

"Nanites chair," Nikki said, smiling, having felt the chair adjust to her bottom. "I still have mine."

"Yes, and you take it to whatever new quarters that you're assigned. I hear there's a pool that's betting on who might get that chair someday. Word is that amount is getting enormous."

"I'm taking it with me when I die," Nikki remarked, and the table enjoyed the joke.

"Oh, how I remember this food," Patrice said around a mouthful. "Pardon my manners, everyone, but I'm going to wallow."

Olawale smiled genially and let his guests enjoy their food. The crew was hoping for a story, but Olawale warned them off with the excuse that the Earthers had experienced a long day and crossed into another world's technology.

After meal, the group retired to Olawale's cabin, which was used by Alex and Renée when they were aboard. Olawale had tried to relocate his bags when he found them deposited there by the crew, but Francis had ended that attempt when he said, "Renée's orders."

"Sers, we need your help," Olawale said, settling into his chair. People were enjoying a cup of thé or a cup of caf, which had been hastily programmed by Esteban. "We can discuss the events that have taken place throughout the years that have brought us to the reason for this trip to Sol, during the next few days —"

"Days?" Nikki asked with concern.

"This will take days, Governor, but the safety of your entire system depends on you helping us, immediately. More than two decades ago, Alex helped an alien species called the Swei Swee escape their prison and destroy it. It was a giant sphere operated by a race known as the Nua'll. It was thought, by most, to be the end of things, but not for Alex. He sensed there was always more, and it turns out he was right. A second sphere has been located, and a squadron of Tridents are chasing it."

"Tridents?" Patrice asked. When Olawale held up his hand, Patrice replied, "Right, later."

"During the preparations for this operation, it was questioned as to how the spheres were locating potential targets," Olawale continued. "We discovered that the alien race has been sending a probe to every system to monitor it and report back as to the nature of the system, civilizations, ship movement, and potential resources."

"How many probes have you found?" Nikki asked, setting her cup of caf on the small table beside her.

"One in every system investigated to date," Olawale replied. "Based on the social progress that you've made here, Alex has authorized me to tell you that, where we come from, humans have settled more than fifteen worlds and are regaining other worlds that the Nua'll sphere devastated.

"Does this mean that you think you'll find one of these probes here?" Patrice asked.

"The apt word, Colonel, is found. We located your probe soon after transiting into your space. The signal is quite distinctive," Esteban said.

"Why all the hush-hush, Olawale?" Patrice asked. "Give us the coordinates, and an admiral will order a destroyer to take it out."

"The probe has a ship destruction radius of 10 million kilometers or more, depending on the circumstances, Colonel," Esteban explained.

The Earthers stared at Esteban and then Olawale.

"I'm not the expert on these things," Olawale apologized, "which is why Esteban is along. He carries the data about the probe and will manage the launch of a special tool, our inimitable engineer, Mickey Brandon, calls a banisher."

Nikki glanced over at Edmas and Jodlyne. "Why are you two here?" she asked.

"Esteban is our business partner," Edmas replied, which didn't really answer Nikki's question, and it showed on her face.

"And we wanted to see the two of you," Jodlyne added brightly, which caused both Earthers to frown.

"And Alex requested it," Edmas confessed, which cleared up the confusion.

"Essentially, you made this trip back to Sol," Patrice said, focusing on Olawale, "to check on us, and it turns out you were right to be concerned.

We do have one of these dangerous probes, and you know how to remove it. Is that about right?"

"Yes," Olawale replied.

"You're a good man, Olawale," Patrice said.

"Echo that," Nikki added.

"Now we need to inform your government and ask permission to proceed," Olawale said. "Which leads me to ask who and where?"

"President Elbert Munford, who is located on Earth," Nikki replied.

"And do you know him personally?" Olawale asked Nikki.

"A good friend, yes," Nikki replied.

"Excellent," Olawale said, clapping his hands. "Esteban, the president, please."

"A call would be more appropriate in about nine hours, Ser," Esteban replied.

"Then let's turn in and get some sleep, while we can," Olawale suggested.

Francis lowered his head and his eyebrows furrowed, as he focused on Olawale.

"Yes, well, Francis reminds me that I should inform you that we're on our way to the probe's location. We should be there within another day and a half," Olawale said, wincing slightly.

"Now you tell us this?" Nikki asked. "If it wasn't for the fact that you're doing us a huge favor, Olawale, you'd be in deep trouble with me. We call this kidnapping in our system. But, as it is, big man, I'm going to sit back, enjoy the ride, consume your food, and take great pleasure in twisting your tail every chance I get," Nikki replied.

"Echo that," Patrice replied, adding her fierce grin to that of Nikki's.

-20-
New Model

Nikki and Patrice shared a cabin, enjoying a night of deep sleep in the nanites beds, which adjusted so nicely under them. Jodlyne had shown them how to work the refresher, and Esteban had installed a brewing device to make them caf in the morning.

"If you need anything at all, use your readers. Esteban has added a link for you that connects directly to him," Jodlyne had said.

"Yes, our secure and impenetrable readers," Nikki had replied, eyeing Patrice.

"SADEs," Jodlyne had replied offhand, shrugging a shoulder before she let herself out.

"SADEs," Patrice had repeated to Nikki after the cabin door closed behind Jodlyne, as if Nikki hadn't understood Jodlyne's response. Nikki had swatted Patrice's shoulder, as she said, "Impudent colonel."

On waking in the morning, the women spent a luxurious amount of time in the refresher. Now, they were seated in the cabin's main salon, cups of caf in their hands, and their bare feet resting on small padded stools.

"These are what pass for Omnian robes?" Patrice asked.

"We do look a little ridiculous with our underwear showing through these sheer things," Nikki agreed.

"I think Jodlyne said they were donated from Renée's wardrobe."

"Quite the adventuresome woman," Nikki commented.

"You'd have to be if you were Alex Racine's partner."

A knock at the cabin door interrupted their banter, and Nikki called out, "We're indecent. Come back tomorrow."

"Is that an actual command, Ser, or is it meant to twist my tail?" Esteban asked.

"Oops," Patrice whispered, grinning.

"Sorry, Esteban. I thought you were Olawale," Nikki replied.

"I believe the envoy might have lacked the courage to face you first thing, Sers, but he wishes your attendance in his quarters for the call to the president."

"Okay, Esteban. Give us five," Patrice called out.

"I'm at your disposal, Sers," Esteban replied, taking up a post outside the cabin door to wait for the women. He accessed Patrice's readers and checked its chronometer timing against that of the ship's. He presumed Patrice had referred to five minutes instead of the next increment, which would be five hours.

Within minutes, the women joined Esteban, who led them to the ship's owner suite.

"I was thinking about this suite last night," Patrice commented, gazing around the well-decorated salon. "It's luxurious, don't you think, Governor?"

"Probably much too nice for an envoy," Nikki added.

"Truce," Olawale pleaded. "At least, until after the call to your president."

Nikki and Patrice eyed each other, as if deciding Olawale's fate. When Patrice nodded, Nikki said, "Truce … for the length of the call."

Olawale groaned and Edmas and Jodlyne snickered.

"Esteban, if you'll begin," Francis requested, while Olawale fetched another cup of thé for himself.

"Do you need our assistance?" Nikki asked, moments before the speaker on the central table's console issued a woman's voice, saying, "President Munford's offices, how may I direct your call?"

Olawale locked eyes with Nikki and gestured at the comm console.

"Hello, Selena, this Nikki Fowler. I need a moment of Elbert's time," Nikki said, taking a seat at the table.

"Let me check his schedule, Governor," Selena replied.

"No, Selena, this is a comm call from the rim."

The cabin's occupants heard nothing from the president's aide, which led Nikki to prompt, "You still there, Selena?"

"Pardon, Governor, had to take a sip of water. I thought I was hearing things for a moment."

"You aren't, Selena. Our faraway friends are back, and their comm system is active."

"Oh, I see," Selena said, excitedly. "Let me get you the president."

Elbert Munford was listening patiently to his guests explain their problem, when his aide rushed into the office.

"Sorry, Mr. President, but you have an urgent call from Rim Governor Fowler," Selena announced.

"Thank you, Selena," Elbert said, rising from behind his desk. "Everyone, I'm sorry to cut our time short, but I promise to look into your issue." He nodded at Selena, who knew she had been cued to add this committee's report to his agenda to study.

When Elbert's guests left, he said, "Nicely done, Selena. Send Nikki's message to my queue."

"Begging your pardon, President Munford, but Governor Fowler is on the comm."

"Oh," Elbert replied, leaping behind his desk and tapping the call button, without waiting for Selena to explain. "Nikki, how are you? When did you get back to Earth?" he asked, waving his fingers at Selena, who closed the office door, shaking her head.

"Greetings, Mr. President, as my friends would say," Nikki replied. "You're on speaker with a group of Omnians, whom we once called Harakens. Colonel Morris and I are aboard the passenger liner *Rêveur* that once brought Alex Racine to our space."

"President Munford?" Nikki asked, after a few seconds of silence.

"Uh, yes, greetings," Elbert finally responded. "Whom do I have the pleasure of addressing?"

"I'm Envoy Olawale Wombo, President. Alex Racine has sent me on an urgent mission to your system."

"Our Olawale Wombo?" Elbert asked.

"The same, and yet, no longer the same," Olawale replied.

"What's your mission Envoy Wombo?" Elbert asked.

Olawale repeated his story. Nikki and Patrice clarified many points for Elbert, who often lost the thread of the conversation due to his inexperience with the Harakens when they visited Sol.

When Olawale finished his explanation, Elbert said, "I see we have two options, Governor Fowler. We can ask the Omnians to wait until we have the representatives' approval, or we can allow them to execute their operation and then explain afterwards."

"The former would take too long, Mr. President," Nikki replied. "I don't believe Envoy Wombo is prepared to wait a month or two, while this is debated with a possible end result of no permission." Olawale shook his head and Nikki added, "Make that definitely not prepared to wait."

"Governor, Colonel, I don't know two other people who've had more contact with the Harakens than you did. I would welcome your advice on this matter."

"There are four Earthers, now known as Omnians, who are sitting beside us, Mr. President," Nikki replied. "None of them were treated well by United Earth. They had every right to leave us to our troubles, but they came back."

"President Munford," Patrice said. "When the Harakens were at Idona, everything they said they were going to do they did, although sometimes we didn't understand what they said. You can believe them when they say there is a dangerous alien probe out there."

"According to Esteban —" Nikki said.

"Who?" Elbert interrupted.

"The SADE who is handling the computational analysis for the envoy," Nikki explained. "According to him, the probe will create an immense explosion, which should eliminate all doubt as to its alien nature."

Silence followed Nikki's statements. Olawale crooked his head at Nikki, who held up a hand, asking for patience.

An implant would be so useful in these circumstances, Nikki thought.

"I'm inclined to give the envoy permission, but I think this would go better in the aftermath if there were military witnesses from our side," Elbert said, after a lengthy pause to think.

"Esteban, possible observers?" Edmas asked.

The SADE checked the controller's recent telemetry data and reported, "A trio of medium-sized warships is a half-day out from the probe's orbital approach, Ser."

"That would be Commodore Binghamton's squadron," Patrice said.

"The commodore's lead ship is on my contact list, Esteban," Nikki said. She was quickly falling back into the comfortable habit that she'd adopted with the Harakens, which was to request everything. Odds were, they would be fulfilled one way or the other. This was despite her thoughts that the requests were ridiculously impossible.

Esteban culled the data from Nikki's reader and added the contact to the controller's list, activating a call.

"Lieutenant Fordham here, identify yourself, please," Tim requested. For him, it was the start of another boring rotation as the bridge duty officer. The comm board had failed to display a ship or station code, which surprised him.

"Lieutenant Fordham, this is President Munford —"

"Yeah, try again, buddy," Tim interrupted. "You'll have to do better than that."

Patrice covered her grin. As the commander of a wide swath of the rim's militia complement, she knew most of the naval officers, senior and junior, who patrolled her territory. Tim Fordham was a good kid, but young.

"Lieutenant Fordham, Colonel Morris here. Surely you recognize my voice."

There was an audible gulp on the conference comm. "Colonel, please tell me that I didn't just insult the president."

"Sorry, son, but you did," Elbert commented.

"There goes my career," Tim said softly.

"Maybe in the previous administration, Lieutenant," Elbert said, "but not in this one. Go wake your commodore and captain, and see if you don't have better luck explaining this call to them than we did."

While everyone waited, Elbert asked Patrice and Nikki, "Was this what it was like for you two, every now and then, with the Harakens?" Elbert asked.

"Oh, no," Patrice and Nikki chorused, then laughed.

"This is what it was like about every couple of hours, Mr. President," Nikki explained. "I've missed them," she added for the room's benefit, and the Omnians tipped their heads to her compliment.

"President Munford?" asked a sleep-deprived voice over the console speaker.

"Speaking. Whom am I addressing?" Elbert requested.

"Commodore Binghamton, Sir," came the suddenly galvanized reply. "Where are you, Mr. President?"

"On Earth, Commodore. Sorry to disturb you at your late hour, but I have a job for you. Please listen to Envoy Wombo."

The commodore, captain, lieutenant, and bridge crew listened raptly to Olawale's introduction, his story of the probe, and the necessity of destroying it.

"President Munford, what will be our duties during this operation?" Binghamton asked.

"You, Sir, are my observer. I'm giving the Omnians permission to destroy this thing. Immediately afterwards, turn over command to your senior captain, and take a fast packet to Earth. Bring detailed information with you to corroborate the Omnians' data. Expect to spend quite a few hours in front of the representatives and, afterwards, a few select governors and cabinet members."

"Understood, Mr. President."

"One more thing, Commodore. The Omnians are in charge of the operation, but if Governor Fowler gives you an order, obey it, as if it came from your admiral."

"Yes, Sir. Should I inform Admiral Thalis?"

"No, Commodore, I don't need the rumor mill working before I inform the cabinet and the representatives," Elbert replied. "Envoy Wombo, this is in your hands, but, before you go, let me say thank you on behalf of the people of Sol for not forgetting us."

"You're welcome, Mr. President," Olawale replied. He signaled Esteban, who dropped Elbert's connection.

"We'll need to know where we're going, Envoy Wombo," Binghamton said.

"Sir," Tim said, pointing to a monitor. It displayed a graphic of the squadron and the *Rêveur*'s positions relative to the far belt and the probe. Positions were marked with coordinates that the Earther Navy could interpret.

"What's our timing?" Binghamton asked.

The graphics display updated with an overlay that marked the new positions and the times based on the Earther's ship clocks.

Esteban had activated the table's holo-vid so that the room's occupants could see what the commodore and his officers were watching, except the holo-vid was projecting a three-dimensional image.

"Ask and you shall receive," Nikki commented softly.

"We'll be in touch, Commodore, when the ships are in position," Olawale said, and Esteban ended the link. Turning to Patrice and Nikki, Olawale said, "We've nearly another full day to sail. Make yourselves comfortable."

Esteban watched the two Earthers focus on him, with smiles on their faces.

"Sers?" Esteban queried.

"You owe us a story, Esteban," Patrice said, standing and extending a hand. She was surprised at the gentleness exhibited by the SADE when he gripped hers.

Nikki slid next to Esteban's other side and linked an arm in his.

"Olawale, we're borrowing Esteban for a while," Patrice called out, as the threesome left the suite arm in arm.

"Don't hurt him. I need him," Olawale replied, chuckling at the absurdity of his request.

"This should be interesting," Jodlyne remarked.

"Yes, I can well imagine the impact Esteban's story will have on our guests," Olawale commented, staring at the cabin door that had closed behind the threesome. "They enjoyed interacting with the Haraken SADEs, while they were on Idona."

"Now, they'll learn of the SADEs' unfortunate history," Francis said.

"And the events that freed them," Edmas added.

The Omnians glanced at one another, recognizing they shared an intimate secret that they would keep forever. It had never been revealed to any of them, but, as people in Alex's close orbit, they had divined the truth.

-21-
The Promise

<We're in position, Sers,> Esteban sent.

Shortly, the Omnians and Earthers assembled on the *Rêveur*'s bridge.

"No change?" Olawale asked Esteban.

"None, Ser, as expected."

"I was hopeful," Olawale replied.

Esteban eyed Olawale.

"It's a human thing, Esteban. Hoping against all odds that something will change if you want it bad enough."

"I'm aware of the concept, Ser. I wouldn't have thought that you, as a man of science, would participate in a process that, at its core, is illogical."

Patrice raised an eyebrow enough to catch Nikki's attention. The two women had been discussing the dangers that an alien probe represented to their system's future safety. It occurred to them that they should request support from the Omnians. The odd exchange, between a SADE and someone who essentially was an Earther transplant, gave them an inkling of the challenges that awaited them.

"We have greater concerns, Sers," Esteban announced. "Observe."

The holo-vid lit, displaying images of two probes.

"Here," Esteban said, highlighting one probe, "is the one found at Haraken. The other lies beyond us in Sol's outer belt. What do you see?"

"They aren't the same. I mean, you can see that the same race made them, but this one," Edmas said, highlighting the Sol probe, "appears to be more sophisticated, a later version."

"Precisely, Ser," Esteban said, with a touch of pride in his business partner. "Now, observe again."

The display changed to view the Sol probe, which nestled in a small field of asteroids.

"I will accelerate the event, which took place during the course of two days," Esteban explained.

"Did that probe steer away from that rock?" Jodlyne asked, when the sequence ended.

"That would be the only possible explanation, Ser," Esteban replied.

"Black space," Edmas commented, which earned him a nudge in the ribs from Jodlyne.

Patrice smiled. It'd had been many years since she'd heard that expression. "I take it something is wrong," she said.

"We have several problems," Olawale replied. "We want to catch the probe in as uncongested an area as possible, no mining sites and few rocks, which could be ejected like missiles from the blast. Now, we have a probe that can play hide and seek. For all we know, it's more maneuverable than our tool, the banisher."

"That rules out one of our destroyer's missiles," Patrice added.

"Are you sure the probe will detonate?" Nikki asked.

"The Méridiens used a salvo of rocks that eventually broke the probes into pieces, without detonating them," Francis explained. "But every probe that has been captured by a banisher or investigated has detonated."

At the mention of the Méridiens, Patrice and Nikki glanced at Esteban, who appeared to be undisturbed by the mention of his former masters.

"What's the plan then?" Patrice asked. When the Omnians' glances bounced from one to the other, she moaned, "Oh, great, the more technologically sophisticated and advanced civilization doesn't have an answer for removing our alien probe without creating potential collateral damage."

"Not yet, Ser," Esteban replied. "But, as a human, you should never give up hope." Then he smiled congenially at Patrice, who smacked his shoulder. She shook off the sting, while the others laughed at Esteban's twist on Olawale's comment.

"What about what the Haraken carriers did at Idona?" Nikki asked, staring at the holo-vid display. "Can this ship do that?"

Esteban raced through the controller's historical data on the carriers' defense of the station and reviewed Alex's technique that his people and SADEs implemented. He spooled images onto the holo-vid of one of the carriers racing forward and twisting to release a load of tethered asteroids.

"We have that capability," Francis said. "We'd have to clear the bays of travelers and banishers, but we could grasp two good-sized rocks. Esteban would be capable of executing the maneuver."

"But would the technique work against this probe?" Edmas asked.

"Maybe not on the first go," Jodlyne said, "but what if we set up a chase pattern?"

The Earthers were left out of the conversation, which took place among Esteban, Edmas, Jodlyne, and Francis, but they were able to follow the scenario, which was displayed on the holo-vid.

Esteban placed a timeline along the probe's route, as the team formed their plan. The *Rêveur* would shoot ahead of the probe and pull out a collection of dense asteroids, piling them up at the proposed attack point. Then Esteban would set the timing release of each set of rocks by the passenger liner.

"Won't the probe move out of the way of what you're throwing? You can only load two rocks and throw one at a time," Nikki asked.

"That's the concept of a chase attack," Jodlyne explained. "You don't expect results from the first step. You anticipate success by the final action or you repeat the process until you get the results you want," Jodlyne explained.

When Nikki frowned, Esteban elaborated. "We expect the probe to evade, but it will probably do so by backing away and using other asteroids to hide behind, always moving farther out in the belt. If fortune holds, we might strike an asteroid near it to damage the probe, preventing it from maneuvering."

"And if not?" Patrice asked.

"You continue launching rocks until you can break it into pieces or it self-destructs with minimal collateral impact," Jodlyne said.

"One way or the other, we will continue to pressure the probe," Francis summarized. "We might even chase it beyond the belt. If we do, we can launch the banisher at it. Our tool will be able to attain a tremendous velocity before contact, and the probe will not have anywhere to hide or time to evade."

Patrice updated Commodore Binghamton on the new plan, while Francis accelerated the *Rêveur* toward the first point Esteban had indicated. Meanwhile, the SADE was examining asteroids to choose similar types and sizes that the action required.

This time the rock-launching process would be much more difficult. The Harakens had the support of the belt miners, who harvested, prepped, and positioned the asteroids for the carriers.

It took several days before the plan was ready. The travelers and banishers waited beside the stockpile of asteroid missiles. A rock was held firmly in the grip of each bay's tethering beams. Esteban's kernel was fully engaged with the ship's controller. He'd automated every sequence he could, so that he had only to cue the next action.

When the countdown ended, Esteban signaled the controller, which launched the ship forward and, soon after, it swung to port to release one rock and swiveled to starboard to release the other. Esteban's triggering of a reload sequence had the controller reversing the ship's course so the crews could latch on to two more asteroids.

Esteban, the liner, and the crew, busied themselves during the next hours, launching wave after wave of rocks at the probe. When their pile of rocks was exhausted, Esteban signaled the end of the exercise to everyone. Jerry commed the other pilots to return to the ship, and Esteban recovered the two banishers after the travelers landed aboard.

"Now we wait?" Nikki asked.

"Now we wait," Esteban agreed.

"Why don't we use the time to gather another pile of rocks?" Patrice asked.

"An experiment requires you to observe the reactions to your actions," Jodlyne replied.

"Meaning, you think this might not work," Patrice pressed. When Jodlyne shrugged her shoulders, Patrice remarked, "Seems to me I've seen that response before. I didn't think much of it then, either."

Jodlyne smiled pleasantly at Patrice, who couldn't have known what Olawale had sent to his fellow Omnians, which was, <This is their system, and they're frightened by what we've said and shown them. Be patient with them.>

* * *

<It's time,> Esteban sent.

By the ship's clock, it was the middle of the night, and the Omnians hurried from their beds.

When the signal to the Earther women's readers failed to wake them, Esteban knocked politely at their cabin door, but that also failed to get a response. The SADE signaled the cabin door's release and silently crossed the small salon to the sleeping quarters. He knocked firmly and finally got an answer, notifying the women that they were needed on the bridge.

"Shades of the military academy," Patrice groused, bleary-eyed and barely awake, when she gained the bridge. Soon Nikki and Patrice were brought caf by a server, who Patrice wanted to gratefully kiss.

Francis had the holo-vid active and trained on the probe. The angle was wide enough to see the last moments of the rush of each rock at the Nua'll device.

"Slippery little thing, isn't it?" Patrice noted, after the probe slid aside from the initial onslaught of asteroids.

"More advanced software than we've seen previously," Esteban commented.

As time dragged on, individuals sat on the deck to watch, while Olawale and Francis enjoyed the comfort of the command chairs. Naturally, Esteban had locked his avatar and was analyzing the trajectory of each rock, local impacts, and the probe's reaction.

With only six more rocks to go, the probe moved behind an asteroid, which the liner's next rock struck, causing the displacement of the probe by the asteroid it hid behind. The fifth to last rock missed the probe, but it was in the open. That necessitated the probe dodge both numbers four and three of the countdown.

Then, without warning, vid cams were blinded by a massive explosion, the blast destroying and launching belt debris in all directions.

"Captain," Esteban said with urgency.

<Jerry, launch all ships. You have some cleanup work to do. Crew chiefs, ready the launch of all travelers,> Francis sent.

"What just happened?" Patrice asked, on her feet and staring at the holo-vid, which had regained the image of the belt. There was an enormous cleared area.

"We're launching our fighters to destroy the rocks, which have been thrown inward," Francis explained.

"Understood, Captain. My question was meant to ask for an explanation about what happened to the probe, besides exploding, I mean. We didn't hit it," Patrice riposted.

"Good question," Olawale said, glancing toward Esteban.

"Different probe, newer version, better programming," Edmas replied instead, enumerating the different factors they faced.

"Ser has the essence of it," Esteban agreed. "I would surmise the probe's detection programs recognized a pattern in the rocks that were approaching. It might have even connected their onslaught to our ship, as the instigating party. In which case, the application might have concluded that it had been discovered, which led to the detonation."

"The commodore," Nikki said, holding up her reader to Esteban.

"Captain Desgardes here," was heard over the *Rêveur*'s bridge speakers, after the SADE placed the call.

"Thus concludes the Omnian demonstration of the dangers of alien probes, Captain," Nikki quipped.

"And an eye-opening demonstration it was, Governor," Commodore Binghamton replied. "Are the odd ships that launched from your liner the Omnian fighters?"

"Travelers they're called, Commodore," Nikki replied.

"Please tell me you're doing everything possible to procure us the means of having these travelers for ourselves, Governor. It's rumored that the colonel and you are favorites of Alex Racine."

"Negotiations are ongoing, Commodore," Nikki replied, staring intently at Olawale. "By the way, you're free to begin your trip to Earth."

"One question for our friends, if they're listening, Governor?"

"They are, Commodore. Go ahead."

"Initially, you requested a clearance radius of 16 million kilometers, but then you doubled that. Our instrumentation registered the wave's destructive reach attained 21 million. Why the radius change, not that I minded being moved beyond what turned out to be the danger zone?"

"To paraphrase an Omnian captain, Darius Gaumata, who exhibits a healthy respect for the unknown, I chose to apply an extra portion of insurance, when I recognized that this probe was quite possibly a newer model," Esteban explained.

"Hmm," the commodore muttered, dwelling on the explanation. "I think I like this Omnian captain. He's my kind of officer, careful and smart. And my cap is off to you, Esteban, for your successful efforts. Governor, I'll be making my report to the president and putting in a good word for your friends. Binghamton out."

"I estimate the traveler pilots will be busy for 5.6 days, Ser," Esteban said, directing his comment at Olawale.

"We can take our guests to Idona Station and return for our travelers," Francis suggested.

"How about your pilots? Won't they need to rest during the next six days?" Nikki asked with concern.

"They'll have it, Governor," Esteban replied. "I'm programming their controllers so that the operations of prioritizing targets, closing on an asteroid, and destroying it are automated. The pilots can sleep and eat whenever they choose."

"Now I know the commodore would really want some of these," Patrice said, laughing.

"Well, we have a few days ride to Idona," Nikki said. "However, I'm now wide awake. This seems like the opportune time, Olawale, to have a quiet chat. Just the three of us, Patrice, you, and me."

"I'm at your disposal, Governor," Olawale said politely, and waved the women toward the bridge accessway.

Settling into the comfortable chairs in Olawale's salon, Nikki opened the discussion.

"Olawale, you, more than anyone else, know what the people of Sol have been through. The interminably long decades of deprivation and incarceration under United Earth nearly brought us to the brink of ruin. But we've changed, thanks to Alex Racine and his people, and there's no going back for us."

"Is your government still called United Earth?" Olawale asked.

"No," Nikki replied firmly. "When the new constitution was ratified by the elected representatives and governors, it was done so under the banner of Sol Enclave."

"But, and you'll appreciate this Olawale, people refer to the constitution as the Idona Accord," Patrice said, grinning.

"Olawale, we can't thank you enough for remembering your home world and returning to check on us," Nikki said. "The stories of the spheres are frightening, but knowing the probes are present across so many systems is absolutely terrifying."

"What does Alex think?" Patrice asked. Her eyes locked onto Olawale's, demanding a forthright answer.

"Alex and Julien believe the probes indicate that an ancient and widespread civilization is seeking ever more space and has been working at expanding its territory far longer than humans have been traveling to the stars."

Nikki and Patrice regarded each other. Words weren't necessary. They'd already discussed what they intended to ask Olawale. Now, what they'd thought might be a request had been suddenly transformed into an appeal.

"We need your help, Olawale," Nikki said. "Or, more precisely, we need the Omnians help. Sol is getting back on its feet, but it will take us a while before we reach the stage where we could protect ourselves from a sphere."

"Yes, we have heavy warships with firepower," Patrice added. "But they haven't the capability to intercept a sphere, and they fire missiles. It doesn't sound as if these would be effective against the sphere or its defenses."

Olawale silently shook his head.

"But, according to Esteban, Edmas, and Jodlyne, your people have increased their military power specifically to take on these Nua'll spheres," Nikki said.

The mention of his companion's names in conjunction with the information about Omnia Ships, which might better have been kept private, told Olawale how much his comrades wanted to help the people of Sol, who were valiantly trying to put an ugly past behind them.

"Do you think Alex will be successful against this second sphere?" Patrice asked.

"I'm worried, like most people are, Patrice, but, then again, it's Alex," Olawale said, lifting his hands to indicate that was all he could offer.

Patrice and Nikki nodded thoughtfully. Some animals, such as cats, were reputed to have multiple lives. Both women were considering the possibility that Alex was an amalgam of many cats.

"I can tell you," Olawale said, "that Alex requested a report on the progress that was being made for the people of Sol by your government. In that regard, I found the conversation with your president refreshing, and the fact that you two hold senior positions is illuminating."

"I knew there was a reason I wore my best dress to our first dinner," Nikki rejoined.

"And, it was most becoming," Olawale replied, a twinkle in his eye.

"I swear there's some of that Omnian advanced technology in you, Olawale," Nikki replied, laughing. "At times, you act like a man half your age."

When Olawale winked, Patrice groaned. "That's not fair, Olawale. We need that medical support as much as you. Can't you share?"

"I'm sorry. It's not possible, but, if you'd like to immigrate to Omnia, I'm sure you'd find life exciting."

"Probably more exciting than we can handle," Nikki admitted.

"You never know," Olawale replied, leaning back in his chair, an expansive air about him.

"Back to business," Nikki said. "Would Omnia be willing to help us?"

Olawale reviewed his conversation with Alex, who had left it to him as to what he could say. "I would like this conversation to be shared only with your most senior people," Olawale replied. "I can tell you that you're not requesting aid from the Omnian government but from Omnia Ships."

"One company?" Patrice asked.

"One man, Alex, who holds the majority of shares. The warships that Omnia Ships has built and are chasing the second sphere have come about because of some incredible technological innovations. How Omnia came into being, including Omnia Ships, is a long story. But, the upshot is this: Alex was setting up agreements with his ex-home world, Haraken; another single system, New Terra; and the multicolony civilization called the Confederation —"

"All human?" Patrice asked.

"Yes," Olawale replied. "When I left Omnia, these governments were considering a contract with Omnia Ships that allowed them access to our warship and scout ship technology, which they could construct, in exchange for supplying Alex with half their contingent to fight with the Omnians."

"And Alex thinks he will need that great a force," Patrice said, sitting forward on the edge of her chair.

"Seems so," Olawale replied.

"Would Alex consider offering Sol the same agreement?" Nikki asked.

"It's not that simple, Nikki. Your technology is far behind that of these other worlds."

"But we're another system of humans, Olawale," Patrice persisted. "We need protection, and we can help Alex. You know we won't shirk from a fight, alien or not."

"I have no doubt of the courage of you two," Olawale said, shifting to the edge of his chair. His big hands were clasped tightly together. He desperately wanted to help the people of his original home world, but he couldn't forget the many who had been sacrificed under the crushing boots of United Earth. To give Sol advanced technology, only to see the government backslide and use it against the populace would be unacceptable. Worse, it would scar Alex to think he'd done that.

Nikki hand signaled Patrice out of sight of Olawale. It asked her to wait and give Olawale time to think.

"I will promise you this," Olawale said, after a few minutes of silence. "My report to Alex will be favorable. That might lead to something, or he might want to visit and see the changes for himself. Either way, don't expect immediate results."

"What if that sphere visits us in the meantime?" Patrice asked.

"Highly unlikely, and you don't have to take my word for that," Olawale said, raising his hands to fend off Patrice's objections. "It's the consideration of the SADEs that this second sphere is investigating systems on the other side of our worlds."

"Meaning it will go through your worlds before us," Patrice surmised.

"That's exactly what I mean," Olawale replied.

"Enough said," Nikki said, rising. "We'll take you at your word, Olawale, and we hope to see Alex and you in the near future."

The women said good night and left Olawale to spend several hours considering what he would say to Alex.

* * *

When the *Rêveur* drew near Idona, Patrice arranged for a small militia shuttle to transfer Nikki and her to the station. After the Idona vessel landed aboard the liner's bay, the Omnians saw their guests off. It was a bittersweet moment — old friends separating again amid a cloud of uncertainty.

The last in line for goodbyes was Esteban.

"Thank you, Esteban," Nikki said, hugging the SADE.

"I'm happy that you've been freed, Esteban," Patrice said, when she embraced him, delivering a kiss to his cheek.

When the shuttle hatch closed behind its passengers, Esteban commented, "I rather like Earthers."

Olawale laughed and clapped him on the shoulder. "You liked being hugged and kissed."

"It was a pleasant experience," Esteban replied.

Francis returned to the site of the probe's detonation to collect the travelers, which had completed their destruction of the larger asteroids. The remaining rocks, much smaller in size, would burn up when they entered the atmosphere of any populated planets or the defense networks would remove them.

The Omnians settled in for the trip home, all of them wondering how their fleet was fairing.

-22-
Found and Lost

The squadron had transited seven times following their exit from the Worlds of Light. Each time the scout ships had searched and managed to pick up the sphere's trail, and the fleet had followed. Telemetry was analyzed to determine the approximate length of time that the systems' prime worlds had remained fallow since they were ravaged. The answers supplied by those estimations allowed the Omnians to count down the decades, as they closed on the Nua'll ship.

By the SADEs' calculation, there was a high probability that the last system entered might have contained the sphere. Now, the odds had reached nearly 100 percent that the Nua'll vessel would be found in any one of the systems the scout ships were presently searching.

"We're getting close, Alex," Tatia said, her voice earnest.

"Very close," Alex agreed, before turning in for a night's sleep. Unfortunately for Alex, sleep never came.

"My love," Renée murmured, half-awake in the early hours of the morning, "as much as I want you in our bed, I prefer you either paying attention to me or asleep. You've been doing neither. Go speak with Julien and resolve whatever is troubling you."

Renée rolled to her other side, away from Alex, and he slipped out of bed, pinging Julien.

<Can't sleep?> Julien asked.

<I'd like to chat,> Alex replied. <The grand park would be a nice spot, if we had one.>

<I miss the city-ship too ... for more than one reason.>

<I'm sorry to have separated you from your partner, my friend.>

<There will be time for us, Alex.>

The difference in lifespans between humans and SADEs reared its ugly head, and Alex grunted in reply.

The two friends met on the warship's bridge. A second lieutenant offered his command chair, but Alex waved him off. He sat with his back against the rear bulkhead, and Julien sat beside him.

The lieutenant never heard a word of Alex and Julien's conversation. The pair communicated entirely via implant and comm. They might have conducted this exchange from their respective places, without meeting. It just wasn't the way the two friends preferred to chat.

<What if we're not being clever or cagey enough about this sphere?> Alex asked.

<In what manner, Alex?> Julien sent in reply.

<Everything we've recently discovered about the Nua'll indicates that, historically, we've been fortunate. I don't mean about what happened in the Confederation but since then. At Libre, it appeared to be a single ship that we destroyed. The discovery of a second sphere didn't seem to be that intimidating, but the discovery of a probe in every system that we've investigated has me thinking that we're not prepared to compete at a high enough level.>

<You're considering that we've only begun to discover the extent of the Nua'll reach and their technological power,> Julien commented.

<Yes, that too, but specifically, I'm thinking about this sphere we're chasing.>

<How so, Alex?>

<We have this squadron of Tridents, bays full of fighters, and advance scout ships to prevent us from dividing our forces. Yes, everyone's a little nervous about a fight, but there's an attitude in the fleet that the Nua'll vessel is out of options, especially with only one remaining bullet ship.>

<You believe that we're being overly optimistic, expecting to win the upcoming fight.>

<If it is a straight-up fight, I think we can handle it. But, what if it isn't?>

<Explain,> Julien requested.

<Let's say you're in command of this sphere. What are you seeing ... collecting your information, day after day, annual after annual?>

Julien leaned his head against the bulkhead, imitating Alex. It was something that humans and SADEs close to the pair noticed about them. They were slowly adopting the habits of each other. The words *the other twins* were often mentioned in close circles when referring to them.

<I would receive continual input from my probes,> Julien sent. <They would be communicating information about the systems that I could prosecute, the opportunities on the prime planets, the civilizations present, the shipping in system, and the extent of the defenses. Under the circumstances of carrying a single bullet ship, I would choose the systems less guarded, as I would be on the defensive. Which means, I would be monitoring my probe broadcast intensely —>

Julien halted his summary and his head snapped off the bulkhead, as he sent, <And I would know that I'm losing probe signals in particular areas of the galaxy.>

<Especially in a trail behind you, growing ever closer to you,> Alex finished.

While the pair sat with their thoughts about what it meant to be hunting an adversary that might know it's being chased, Julien sent, <We're about to discover how well the enemy is aware of us, Alex. Linn's scout ship, the *Minimum Risk*, has reported it's located the sphere.>

* * *

Julien directed the squadron toward the new destination, and the fleet controllers dutifully executed their directives. Simultaneously, he notified the five other scout ships of the discovery and the rendezvous coordinates.

The energy and attitudes of the fleet's personnel changed, especially aboard the New Terran warships, where the arguments and fights ceased overnight. Boredom was replaced by anticipation. Frustration gave way to focused intention.

Tatia reviewed the attack scenarios with her senior officers, depending on the final disposition of their adversary. The *Minimum Risk* had reported the sphere was underway within the system. With the scout ship's orders to collect minimal telemetry and withdraw far beyond the system, there was no way the fleet could know whether the sphere was entering or exiting the system.

The fleet imitated the *Minimum Risk* and transited into a position far outside the target system. They waited for the lengthy time period that telemetry required to update at such a great distance.

When the data was received, Tatia eyed Alex and said, "I don't get it. The fourth planet outward should have been the sphere's target planet. It's the optimal body, if you want to consider that ice ball a resource. What's the ship doing parked near that gas giant with its hundreds of moons?" Tatia said.

"Waiting for us, I presume," Alex replied.

"And you were going to tell me this, when?" Tatia asked, rounding on Alex, irritation in her eyes.

"It was a theory that Julien and I were discussing last night. My question for you, Admiral, is this: Does your plan of attack change depending on where the sphere is stationed?"

"No, but —"

"And does it matter that the sphere might have suspected we were closing in on it versus seeing us coming for days, while we crossed space on our approach?" Alex pressed on.

"No," Tatia admitted.

"That's why I chose not to complicate your tactics with my musings."

"Still, it would have been nice to have been included," Tatia said, unwilling to give ground on the idea that she'd been left out of the loop. Julien wasn't spared either. He received a glower from her.

More than two weeks later, the last of the scout ships arrived. The six, tiny ships were scattered to positions that ringed the system and lay outside the orbit of the outermost planet. The vessels had no offensive capability but were tasked with determining the sphere's flight vector, if it ran for it.

Alex and Julien's consensus was that if the sphere chose to evade a fight, then the possibilities were good it would select a course that wouldn't launch it toward another probe. The fleet had depended on the sphere's single-minded pursuit of one probe signal after another. If it abandoned that routine, the Omnians would have little possibility of following it.

While the scout ships took up their positions, Reiko set her forces in motion. Eight Tridents spread out, six taking up positions around the ecliptic and one Trident each approaching the sphere from above and below the ecliptic.

Every individual, human and SADE, was glued to the fleet's telemetry feeds. Confusing to all was that while the fleet spread out, the sphere never moved.

"It's waiting and watching," Z said.

"We're showing our cards," Alex added, "and it's making judgments about the size and capability of our forces."

"It can strategize all it wants. The fact of the matter is that it has limited options … run now or run after it sends that single bullet ship out to fight and we destroy it," Tatia said with determination.

When the fleet was ready, Tatia looked at Reiko, "It's your fight, Commodore."

Reiko triggered the Tridents' controllers to execute the battle plan. Depending on their positions, the Tridents were launched in a delayed pattern toward their adversary, the farthest away from the sphere started first, and the others followed so that the eight warships would close on the enemy vessel together.

The crews' exhilaration gave way to the realities of space travel, even for highly developed technological societies. Officers changed bridge duty shifts. Crews ate, slept, and, when on duty, checked and rechecked their readiness. And still, the sphere didn't move.

"Maybe the poor thing ran out of power," Miranda quipped, at one point.

"Or maybe it managed to complete the other three bullet ships it's been building," Z commented.

Reiko looked between Z and Miranda, finally staring at Julien.

"If you're waiting for my comment, Commodore, I have none. I await the outcome of this fight," Julien replied.

"Now that's the kind of emotional support I appreciate," Reiko retorted, giving Z and Miranda a less-than-appreciative glance.

There had been a short discussion between Tatia, Reiko, and Svetlana about holding the OS *Liberator* back, allowing the other seven Tridents to be at the forefront of the attack. However, Alex heard, and he quickly truncated that discussion.

"Admiral, you haven't enough Tridents to effectively surround the sphere as it is," Alex said. "Holding this ship back will allow it wider avenues of escape. Worse, if you keep the other seven Tridents in the same dispositions, but we stay back, then the sphere might opt to come in our direction, throwing the bullet ship out in front of it to run interference. No, Admiral, stick with your original battle plan."

Despite the greatly increased strength and effective range of the Tridents' beams, the warships were hours away from beginning the attack, when the sphere made its move. The greatest avenues of escape were above and below the ecliptic, and the Nua'll sphere chose below.

Admiral Tripping's flagship, the NT *Geoffrey Orlan*, was on the ecliptic. Alphons Jagielski's Trident, the NT *Arthur McMorris*, was approaching the sphere from above, and the NT *Lem Ulam*, Bart Fillister's Trident, was in the path of the escaping sphere.

The sphere accelerated and twisted in half, as had the Libran sphere, exposing its four large ports, evenly placed around the circumference. Soon afterwards, the sphere's remaining bullet ship exited and sped ahead.

"Don't let that bullet ship get past you, Captain Fillister," Tripping ordered. "We can trap the sphere between us, if it's defenseless."

"Negative, Admiral Tripping, that's not one of the scenarios," Reiko said, isolating her comm to his ship. She was annoyed that she couldn't direct her comments to the admiral via implant.

Captain Morney watched the blood rise along the admiral's neck. As it was, Tripping chafed under Tachenko's command, believing he should have independent operational control over New Terran warships. But to be corrected by an Omnian commodore, during a fight, might have been too much. Morney worried that the admiral was about to commit a major blunder. But, slowly, Tripping regained control and ordered Captain Fillister to allow the bullet ship and sphere to pass unmolested.

As soon as the Nua'll ship was out of danger, it collected its defensive vessel and sped off into the dark, with the *Vivian's Mirror* hot on its vector.

Tripping retired to his cabin and contacted Tatia.

"That was a farce, Admiral Tachenko," Tripping declared heatedly.

"Commodore Shimada's call was warranted, Admiral," Tatia replied. "At best, the *Lem Ulam* would have destroyed the bullet ship at the cost of its own survival."

"And then we would have had the sphere at our mercy," Tripping replied.

"That's conjecture on your part, Admiral, but Omnians are not in the habit of trading our ships one for one with the enemy. We value our humans and SADEs too much to see their lives spent in that manner. When we have an overwhelming opportunity to take the sphere and its bullet ship down, we'll attack, but not before then. Do I make myself clear?" Tatia worked to control her temper, but her patience with Tripping was wearing thin.

When Tripping didn't reply, the metal rang in Tatia's voice, as she said, "I require an answer, Admiral."

"You're understood, Admiral Tachenko. But let me add that I can't wait for the time to arrive when I'm freed from operating under the Omnians' foolish manner of conducting a fight with humankind's enemy. At this rate, we will never defeat the sphere. And who knows how many more are out there?"

Tatia ended the comm and carefully stored the conversation with the hundreds of others she, her officers, and SADEs had collected.

Alex, who had been privy to the conversation, studied Tatia's worried face.

"What am I supposed to tell Reiko to do, Alex, if Tripping risks his ships and ours in the next confrontation with the sphere by contradicting her orders?"

"What I think you're asking, Tatia, is whether you should give Reiko permission to withhold our forces from supporting the New Terran ships, if Tripping endangers his Tridents contrary to her commands."

"When you put it that way, it sounds rather cowardly," Tatia replied.

"How do you think it will sound to Reiko and your captains?"

"Much the same way," Tatia admitted.

"Tripping has his override box?" Alex asked. He'd heard from Tatia of the admiral's request that in times of crisis, he should be allowed to divorce his Tridents from the conflict. To accommodate him, Z was requested to design a program for the NT warships that allowed Admiral Tripping two functions. He could cut off the *Liberator*'s controller interface with his ships, and he could shut down his ships' communication with the flagship.

"Yes, the admiral has it," Tatia replied.

"I imagine Z designed the interface so that the SADEs can't interfere with it."

"Unfortunately, Z did exactly what he was asked to do ... create an impregnable procedure. Makes me think I shouldn't have been so specific," Tatia said, frustrated with her decision in hindsight.

"I think we'll have to wait and see what happens, Tatia. Right now, I'm interested to see if we will get another shot at the sphere."

Alex and Tatia exited the admiral's cabin and returned to the bridge. Reports were inbound from the squadron and the scout ships, as to the vector the sphere was on when it exited.

"What do you have, Julien?" Alex asked, as he passed through the bridge accessway, noticing a small group had formed around the ship's holo-vid, studying the telemetry data.

"*Vivian's Mirror* was able to align itself directly behind the sphere for several moments before it exited this system's space, giving us a highly accurate fix on its vector."

"Any alignments with probes?" Alex asked.

"None," Julien replied. The SADEs had mapped the probes in the area when the warships had entered the system.

"None?" Reiko asked, disappointed that the one opportunity to capture or destroy the sphere might have slipped through their hands.

"Unfortunately, not, Commodore," Julien replied, "but there is an opportunity."

"Give us good news, Julien," Tatia encouraged.

"The sphere's vector aligns well with a blue white star."

"Which doesn't have a probe signal?" Svetlana asked. "I'm with the commodore on this. How is that possible? Every system we've investigated has had a probe. Why wouldn't this star have one?"

"Possibly due to the inevitabilities of space," Z replied. "It's logical that there would be accidents that would damage the probes, or there could have been a component failure that prevented this probe from communicating. In the latter case, it might be there but be silent."

"What's important to note is that this star doesn't produce a Nua'll signal, for whatever reason," Julien said, looking at Alex. The two of them relived the conversation the night they sat together at the rear of the bridge, discussing the Nua'll sphere's possible moves, when its enemy caught up with it.

"We've surmised the Nua'll have determined they're being followed," Alex said quietly, "which means there's a good chance we'll only get one more shot at them. They've jumped to a star without a probe. If we miss them there, it's highly likely they'll transit to open space and continue to move until they're sure they've lost us."

"It's inevitable the dastardly dear ones will communicate to other spheres about the big, bad aliens who hunt them and how they're using the probe signals against their ships," Miranda offered.

"Which should lead them to augment their probe programs or change tactics entirely," Z surmised.

"They might have already communicated the message that Miranda has suggested," Svetlana said.

"Hopefully, they haven't yet," Alex said, "but you can be sure that eventually they will."

"If you're correct, Alex," Reiko started to say, before she caught the expressions on the faces around her. "Okay, let me rephrase that," she said, which garnered a few snickers, "using your hypothesis, Alex, it would be smart not to transit right behind the sphere. We'd find it in open space and lose it. Perhaps, we should wait and give the Nua'll time to relax, if they can do that, and investigate the system. That would, at least, give us a chance to trap it in a gravity field."

"I agree, Commodore," Alex replied. "Julien?"

Julien briefly consulted with Z and Miranda. Afterwards, he smiled and said, "I'm suggesting four days, Z is arguing for ten, and Miranda believes that trying to understand the aliens' level of concern over whether they might be followed and what they might do next is a futile exercise."

"Consensus not so easily reached," Renée quipped. She'd been quiet, while others struggled to determine a new strategy. "We started destroying probes about two-thirds of a year ago, and we've been eliminating them behind us, as we followed the sphere. If Alex is right," she said, grinning at her tease, "why did these technologically advanced aliens take so long to change their habit? I can tell you in two words … the Confederation."

"Interesting insight," Alex said, nodding his head in agreement.

"Translation?" Tatia asked.

"We've surmised by the extent of probe distribution that we're dealing with an ancient civilization," Renée replied. "I offer the Confederation as an example of a highly developed civilization that has enjoyed seven millenniums of unimpeded growth. Of course, you'll note how elastic it is in adopting new ways."

Renée's comment generated murmurs and grumbles from the ex-Independents and SADEs, who'd all suffered under the Confederation.

"If the Nua'll are a much, much older race, they'll be holding on dearly to their methods, which have worked for them for who knows how long," Renée said.

"We'll wait four days, Admiral," Alex said, accepting Renée's logic. "Then we follow."

* * *

"Admiral, a moment of your time, if you please?" Reiko asked, after the evening meal ended. In one more day, the fleet would exit the system and transit to follow the sphere.

"Admiral, you're being too careful with our forces. Either we want that sphere, or we don't," Reiko said, once the door slid closed on Tatia's cabin.

"I think we can dispense with the titles, Reiko. What are you proposing?"

"Following Alex's logic, we'll have only one more shot, if that, at the sphere. More important, if it hasn't broadcast what it might have discovered about our activities, I think it's crucial that we do whatever is necessary to destroy it or, at least, prevent it from communicating."

"I don't disagree with your reasoning, Reiko, but I'm still waiting for your proposal."

"With our present strategy, Tatia, the sphere has too much room to slip past our squadron. If we want to prevent that, we have to commit the fighter squadron."

"Our travelers are no match for the bullet ship, whether they encounter it one on one or even four or five to one."

"I don't disagree, Tatia. Our fighters will have to swamp the bullet ship, and we can expect losses. But, if we eliminate the sphere's last defensive ship, it will be forced to flee."

"And how does risking our people in a close fight with the bullet ship help us trap the sphere?"

"Did you notice the distance that was kept between the sphere and the bullet ship the last time we encountered it compared to the vids from the Ollassa system?"

Tatia pulled the files from the ship's controller and ran a comparison for herself.

"In the Worlds of Light, the sphere allowed the two ships to extend several times farther out than when it had a single defender in the last system," Tatia commented. "The Nua'll are getting nervous about their protection. They're keeping it close."

"Agreed ... close enough for us to make use of that," Reiko replied.

Tatia thought through what Reiko was proposing and replied, "You're thinking that when our travelers eliminate the bullet ship, there will be a large arc of exit denied the sphere because of the fighter group's close proximity."

"In a manner. Look at this," Reiko replied. She activated the table's holo-vid and ran a simulation. "Julien helped me create this program using accurate figures."

Tatia watched the squadron close in on the sphere. Naturally, it chose the path of least resistance, with its bullet ship leading the way.

"What am I missing, Reiko? This scenario doesn't work."

"No, it doesn't, Tatia, because it employs the same approach with the squadron that we were anticipating using, and it doesn't give us an opportunity to independently attack the bullet ship or the sphere. But, what if we did this?" Reiko asked, and sent a second simulation to the holo-vid.

The squadron came at the sphere from above and below the ecliptic, dominating much of the escape opportunity. Left open were the paths across the ecliptic.

Reiko froze the simulation, adding, "Where we discover the sphere within the system will depend on how we structure our attack. We'll need detailed advanced telemetry."

"You want the scout ships to secure the telemetry and return to the squadron."

"I want one scout ship to transit far outside the system, gather the data, and then return."

"That amount of delay runs the risk of delivering outdated telemetry to us, Reiko."

"It can't be helped, Tatia. We can't afford to scare the Nua'll away. And, even if the sphere's position has shifted within the system, this scenario," Reiko said, pointing to the holo-vid display, "should easily adapt to the new sphere's position after the squadron arrives in system."

"What's the rest of the plan, Reiko?"

"Watch this final scenario, Tatia. In this one, we've scouted the system and determined the best vectors for attack and ambush."

The latest display showed the squadron entering far outside the system's space. The entire fighter group exited the Tridents, their velocity imparted by the warships. Then the Tridents executed a double transit to position themselves above and below the ecliptic, trapping the sphere between them.

Tatia froze the simulation and rotated the advantage point. "Ah, clever girl," she said, when she noted that the fighters were grouped tightly together and heading directly toward a gas giant, which screened them from the sphere.

"That's our ambush, Tatia. We drive the Nua'll toward a massive outer planet. The alien sphere will put the bullet ship out front, which our fighters can attack. In the meantime, our squadron will be accelerating to close the distance from behind. By the time the sphere decides to shift course, the Tridents should have closing velocity. Then it will be up to Alex to decide whether to use our velocity to make a single attack pass with our beams or to decelerate and see if the Nua'll will surrender."

Tatia laughed briefly and harshly. "Just how are we supposed to determine if the Nua'll are surrendering?"

"I fight the warships, Tatia. I leave decisions like that to Alex."

"With that, I agree, Reiko. I like your strategy, but we'll have to talk this over with Alex."

"He won't like the plan, Tatia."

"That's true, Commodore," Tatia replied, returning to her commander's role, "but I'll be interested to see how you sell it to him."

Reiko eyed her admiral, who was her complete opposite in stature — broad and blonde to her tiny and brunette. "You're too kind, Admiral."

"That's what everyone tells me," Tatia replied, with a wink.

-23-
Last Chance

Vivian's Mirror transited to the blue white star where the Nua'll ship had headed. The scout ship had orders from Tatia how to proceed, but Killian decided to amend them.

<And the reason for the new coordinates?> Trium sent to Killian and Bethley.

<Alex,> Killian replied.

<And that truncated reply is supposed to explain the change?> Bethley asked, a little piqued.

<Alex wants a confrontation with this sphere. Only one scout ship was chosen to investigate to minimize our appearance outside the system, and we were chosen,> Killian replied.

<A longer response, but no less clear,> Bethley replied.

<You're asking us to think about why Dassata chose us,> Trium reasoned.

<Or is it more a matter of our lead member unable to follow orders?> Bethley riposted.

<In a manner, yes,> Killian replied. <Alex and I have had many conversations, concerning the differences between humans and SADEs. What I've learned to emulate about humans is the concept of initiative, and I have concluded that Alex expects me to exercise mine.>

<We've arrived below the ecliptic, and you've selected a steep inward angle,> Trium sent, analyzing the transit data and the new vector. <This will bring us much closer in system than Admiral Tachenko allowed.>

Bethley quickly extrapolated where the vector would take the *Vivian's Mirror* and its possible appearance to the Nua'll. <We will intersect that heavy outer planet, pass through its field of moons, and be accelerated by its gravity above the ecliptic.>

<We should appear as simply another celestial body passing through the system,> Trium reasoned, <providing the Nua'll sphere doesn't take a close look at our shape.>

<In my calculations,> Killian sent, <I perceived less risk to being seen by the Nua'll if we appear as a rock coasting through the system, as opposed to standing stationary outside of it and waiting for our telemetry to update. In this way, we spend less time out here, come closer to the sphere, and collect more detailed telemetry.>

<A bold idea,> Trium replied.

<And a good one,> Bethley allowed, <if it works,> she added.

Many days later and far above the ecliptic, the *Vivian's Mirror* passed behind a small cluster of asteroids, which blocked the sphere's view of them. The SADEs took advantage of the screening to transit to the fleet's position.

<Alex, Admiral, we found the sphere,> Killian sent.

<Well done, the three of you,> Alex sent in reply.

<Is it my imagination or does Killian sound excited?> Tatia sent privately to Alex.

<They've been successful, Tatia. Why shouldn't Killian be happy?> Alex replied.

The Alex effect, Tatia thought, thinking of his influence on the SADEs.

Killian transmitted the scout ship's telemetry to the flagship, and the warship's controller relayed copies to all ships.

Immediately, Julien spooled the telemetry onto the *Liberator's* holo-vid, utilizing time compression for viewing.

"That approach definitely wasn't following my instructions," Tatia said, watching the scout ship enter space below the ecliptic and swing close to a giant planet, before curving above the ecliptic.

"True, Admiral," Alex replied, "but it was extremely innovative."

"The sphere was stationary during the entire time of the scout ship's passage," Julien noted. "It's holding a position near the sixth planet outward, a cold, barren rock."

"I think you have all the information you need, Admiral. Set your strategy in motion," Alex requested.

Tatia ordered the fleet to sail. They would be using Reiko's plan. Tatia busied herself with the SADEs, determining the final details — primary transit coordinates, fighter launches, and secondary transit coordinates.

Tripping was ecstatic when he reviewed the attack positions. His warships were still above the ecliptic, but, in this case, that meant they wouldn't play ancillary roles. They would be part of the attacking force. He fingered the tiny control device in his pocket. *This time the sphere doesn't escape, no matter what you say, Admiral,* Tripping thought.

The fleet transited to the first set of coordinates, which placed the ships far past the outermost planet's orbit. The Tridents accelerated inward, and the captains ordered the launch of their fighters. The travelers were sent forward, sailing silently toward the massive outer planet, at which they were aimed.

As soon as the fighters cleared the bays, the squadron executed two quick transits. The first movements sent four Tridents above the ecliptic and four below. The second transits placed the warships in positions to trap the sphere between them.

Each group of warships was in a square formation. Two were positioned directly above or below the sphere and the other two of each group were slightly inward. Their formations left the outward vectors across the ecliptic as the most favorable paths for the Nua'll.

Franz brought his fighter group to a stationary position near the outermost planet. He was guided by Z, who would coordinate the fighter group's ambush with the sphere and the bullet ship's movement.

Reiko focused intently on the holo-vid, which displayed the relative positions of the squadron, the sphere, and the waiting fighters. Her plan was to manipulate the battle formation, and the SADEs would emulate her actions via the ships' controllers.

"Drop the inward Tridents straight toward the ecliptic," Reiko ordered the SADEs. She wanted the Nua'll to realize that she was denying them movement in more than a hemisphere of direction across the ecliptic.

The SADEs executed the order and adjusted Reiko's display to match the warships' changing positions.

Reiko waited for a half hour before she said, "Now the forward pairs. Angle them outward at 10 degrees," and the SADEs complied. Reiko was working at appearing calm. Success would depend on how well she had designed the strategy. *Move,* she thought, trying to will the sphere to abandon its position next to the rocky planet.

The inward four Tridents had covered more than 20 percent of the distance to the sphere, when the Nua'll ship left the planet's orbit. It appeared to move slowly outward, but its acceleration soon became evident.

"Angle the outward Tridents to remain on intersection vectors with the sphere. Keep the inward Tridents at 5 degrees behind it," Reiko ordered.

<What's Reiko doing?> Renée asked Tatia privately.

<To direct the sphere, Reiko has to continue to deny the ship inward opportunities, in addition to escape above and below the ecliptic. That's why she's not aiming the inward Tridents directly at the sphere,> Tatia replied.

The early tension gave way to wariness, and that slowly gave way to routine operations. It would be a long chase.

Aboard the fighters, the pilots enjoyed a small meal, communicated within the group, and whiled away the time. Franz kept in touch with Ellie, who was annoyed about her assignment. Her ship, the *Redemption,* was above the ecliptic and paired in the inward position with Alphons' ship, the *Arthur McMorris.*

<At least my partner in this operation is the sane one of the New Terran captains,> Ellie complained to Franz.

<I thought Captain Fillister was the affable sort,> Franz sent in reply.

<He is, but he's likely to cave to Tripping's orders even if they contradict Reiko's,> Ellie replied.

<So how did you draw this assignment, Ellie?>

<I met with Tatia and Reiko to ask that very same question, Franz. Reiko said she didn't trust Admiral Tripping. They wanted me in this part of the formation because, of all the OS captains, I was the most experienced fighter pilot. Tatia said that it might be my skill that prevents the sphere from slipping upward past the three NT warships.>

<Why not split the New Terran forces between the two Trident groups?> Franz asked.

<Tatia told me that Admiral Tripping demanded his forces remain together.>

<What did you say to that argument?>

<I had my orders, Franz. What could I say? But I left those two with a final thought.>

<Which was?>

<I wished them luck.>

<What for?>

<I told them if anything happened to me because of this babysitting assignment with the New Terrans, then they would have to deal with Étienne.> Ellie listened to Franz's deep, heavy-worlder laughter, and it made her smile.

Aboard every Trident and fighter, the leaders, officers, and crews bided their time, ensuring that they were rested when the final conflict came. The Omnians depended on the rotating bridge crews and SADEs for any warning. The New Terrans attempted some semblance of normalcy, but nerves were wound too tightly to ensure that food digested well, or sleep was uninterrupted.

The singular exception to these efforts was Admiral Tripping. He sat in the *Geoffrey Orlan*'s bridge command chair, focused on the holo-vid display, and watched the distance to the sphere close. All the while, he wished for the sphere to make an about-face and make a run inward or toward his forces. And, while he waited, he fingered his controller device. Crew brought Tripping meals and hot caf, and, after a time, the admiral dozed for a half hour at a time, while the bridge crew kept watch.

Franz had checked his controller's feed nearly hourly, which mirrored the *Liberator*'s telemetry data, as did most every other fighter pilot, until he realized his foolishness. After that, he chatted on and off with Ellie to keep up her spirits. He desperately wanted to talk with Reiko, but he chose not to take her focus away from the upcoming fight.

Days later, Franz was asleep when Miranda pinged him. <Nap time is over, dear,> she sent. He discovered that Miranda had communicated to the entire fighter group. The pilots were hustling to take care of last-minute business. Then they hurried to their seats and donned their helmets.

Franz had divided his forces into four wings. They would swing out around the planet like a four-fingered claw, denying the sphere an exit along all vectors around the huge body. Unlike Ellie's situation, the New Terran fighters were spread among the four wings.

A quick check by Franz of his controller's relay from the *Liberator* confirmed that the sphere was heading slightly spinward of the planet, where the fighter group hid. Franz surmised the Nua'll were probably expecting to use the planet to accelerate out of the system. The sphere had yet to release its bullet ship. *Then again,* Franz thought, *you don't see any reason to yet.*

<Group leader to all pilots,> Franz sent. <Once we sling around this planet, things will happen quickly. Your controllers have been programmed with the scenarios, which I will execute. If this becomes a fight with the bullet ship, let the controllers do the work. They have the speed to intercept, fire, and evade. You don't.>

Franz had trained his pilots thoroughly in this concept, but there were a good many Omnians and every New Terran who had yet to be in a battle. Most of the experienced fighter pilots were either at Haraken or captaining a warship.

<Commanders, form up your wings,> Franz sent.

Thirty-two fighters, who had clustered tightly together to present a minimum silhouette behind the planet, divided into four wings of eight. Franz had assigned a commander to his wing, so he could concentrate on the fight, if it came to that.

Alex stood at the back of the *Liberator*'s bridge, leaning against the bulkhead. Renée stood beside him, and they were flanked by Étienne and

Alain. The four of them felt as ancillary as wheels on a starship, but there was no other place that they preferred to be.

A thought niggled at Alex's mind, and he sought to grasp it. It had something to do with his conversation with Julien that took place in this exact spot. It occurred to him that he might have only formed the thought but never expressed it. He replayed the exchange, which he'd saved. One of Julien's comments prompted him to wonder about the suspected age of the Nua'll civilization.

How do you maintain a society for eons? Alex asked himself. *It must require unswerving devotion to the society, and no sacrifice would be too great,* he thought.

Alex received Miranda's heads-up that the fighter squadron was in play, and he glanced at the holo-vid display. Reiko had placed the flagship in the forward pair of Tridents, which bored in on the sphere from below the ecliptic. Alex noted, as did the other senior officers, that the sphere chose to dive below the system, on the last encounter, and he approved of Reiko's decision. Their ship would share the fate of the fleet, if the sphere proved to be a more dangerous adversary than anyone surmised.

Z's calculations of the sphere's acceleration and the distance to the waiting fighters ran in a constant routine, updating at every tick of time. When the optimal moment arrived, Z signaled the controllers of the fighter group, and thirty-two ships accelerated on curved trajectories around the planet.

Reiko saw the fighters emerge from around the planet and accelerate toward the sphere. *Fight hard and come back safe to me, dear heart,* she thought, sending her love to Franz.

* * *

Franz's implant was filled with SADE communications. Embedded in his group leader application, which was developed by Z, were the attack scenarios. A list, with an attached visual display, enabled Franz to coordinate the group or the individual wings, with a thought. However, once the battle was engaged, it would be up to every pilot to play his or her role.

As opposed to Z's application, Miranda's messages were real time. She kept him informed, as the general strategy unfolded. This allowed Franz to focus on the upcoming confrontation but be able to understand his part in the evolving conflict.

Z had selected the first maneuver in Franz's implant, which launched the fighters on their journey around the planet. To maximize the appearance of a blocking force, the maneuver spread the fighters out and limited their approach velocity. The idea was to give the Nua'll time to observe the fighters and realize their dilemma. No one knew what the Nua'll would choose to do, but the fighters were following Alex's request.

<The sphere is rapidly decelerating, Franz,> Miranda warned. There were a few moments of delay before Miranda added, <Its halves are rotating … a bay is opening … you have your adversary, Franz. Good fortune.>

Franz's telemetry showed the sphere curving away from his two wings. He initiated one of Z's scenarios to direct the other two wings, which had circled the planet from the other side, to chase the sphere inward.

<Time to earn our credits, pilots,> Franz announced. <I'm selecting an attack pattern to maximize our velocity and minimize our pass time. You'll be released to individual control once your fighters are launched in the pattern. Let me repeat: Allow your controller to guide you once you're released.>

The Nua'll bullet ship maintained a relatively slow velocity on its approach. It was the more powerful vessel with a stronger beam than an individual traveler. The lesser velocity would extend the engagement time and allow the bullet ship to make use of its heavier weaponry. It would have the opportunity to eliminate four or five of the Omnian fighters with a single blast of its beam.

But Z's pattern hadn't sent the travelers straight at the bullet ship. Being a SADE and a collector of mathematical oddities, Z had borrowed Cordelia's patterning of Dagger Libran-X missiles from the early days.

His program sent the fighters in an evolving spiral pattern. Initially, the fighters flared out, the ships' agility aiding the maneuver, then they were brought spiraling together onto the target.

The bullet ship shifted its vector and managed to fire once before the travelers shot past. Two fighters were struck, and both were demolished. The other fourteen fighters scored beam strikes on the bullet ship, completely disabling its aft-mounted engines.

<Franz, the bullet ship is without drive power,> Miranda sent. <Order your group to stay away from the bow, in case the beam weaponry is still active. Otherwise, you can ignore it. And, I'm sorry for the loss of your two pilots.>

Franz had watched the icons of two of his fighters shift from green to red in his heads-up display. They were both Omnian pilots from the *Judgment*, Lucia Bellardo's Trident. Miranda's comment told him there would be no opportunity to recover the pilots.

<Group Leader Cohen, reform your wall,> Reiko ordered. <We have the sphere turning inward. Your new assignment is to act as a blocking force. Maintain your spread. Do not attack, unless ordered.>

<Trident captains, we're decelerating,> Reiko sent. <SADEs, I want to keep the Tridents spread and ready to shift locations relative to the sphere's movement. You have control in that regard.>

Julien, Z, and Miranda calculated the new trajectories that were required to augment Reiko's directive and signaled the warships' controllers.

Tripping sat in his command chair and stewed. Decelerating the squadron, at this time, wouldn't have been his call — attack would have been. He eyed the holo-vid display, which indicated that the squadron would reach zero velocity within two to three hours.

"Alex, the sphere is decelerating. I project it will soon come to a halt," Julien said quietly.

<Worst-case scenario, Admiral. It's decision time,> Reiko sent to Tatia.

Alex's mind was in turmoil. A single thought kept circling through his mind. *No sacrifice is too great.* For all intents and purposes, the sphere was at their mercy, but those who thought that way about their adversaries were deluding themselves. An enemy always had a final resort.

<Admiral Tripping, your ships are out of position,> Ellie sent over the fleet comm channel.

<Admiral Tripping,> Reiko called.

"Commodore, the flagship's signals are not being received by the New Terran Trident controllers," Z explained.

"The admiral has activated his device," Tatia added heatedly.

The flagship's bridge personnel listened to Ellie attempting to get Admiral Tripping's attention. She utilized her fleet channel so that the senior commanders could hear any communication she received from Tripping, but he was silent.

Captains Jagielski and Fillister were isolated from fleet command. They thought Admiral Tripping was relaying Commodore Shimada's directives. It was their assumption that the admiral had been authorized to take independent control of their warships. Only Captain Jonathan Morney knew the truth. He looked at his sleep-deprived admiral, who was staring at the holo-vid, the small, controller device in his hand.

"New Terran Tridents, attack," Tripping ordered his captains, after cutting their controllers free and silencing the *Liberator*'s comm channel. However, Tripping didn't expect an Omnian captain, one assigned to the upper ecliptic with his forces, to attempt communication with him. It was a scenario he hadn't considered, and it infuriated him the more insistent she became.

"Is Captain Thompson speaking to my ships?" Tripping asked, his teeth grinding.

Morney glanced at his comm officer, who pointed to a signal icon on his board.

"Captain Thompson is on the fleet channel, Admiral. All ships can hear her," Morney replied.

"Shut her down, Captain," Tripping ordered in a brittle voice. "I don't want her talking to my ships."

Morney glanced again at his comm officer, whose pained expression confirmed there was no way to accommodate the admiral's request.

Morney made a slashing motion across his throat with his hand and pointed to the admiral. The comm officer nodded, and ended Ellie's voice in mid-sentence.

"Ah, that's better," Tripping said into the quiet.

Ellie saw her link to the *Geoffrey Orlan* drop off. Oddly enough, the other two NT warships were still connected to her.

"Captain Jagielski, what has Tripping ordered you to do?" Ellie said over her bridge comm. When she didn't receive a reply, she tried again. "Alphons, talk to me. What's happening?"

"We have independent control of our Tridents, Captain, and we're under orders from Admiral Tripping to attack the sphere," Alphons reluctantly replied.

"Alphons, if you break our blockade, you'll offer the sphere an escape route, and the admiral can't be sure that the sphere has no defenses. Your three ships might not have enough firepower."

"I have no contradictory orders, Captain," Alphons replied.

"Captain Jagielski," Alphons heard. "This is Commodore Shimada. I'm relaying my signal through Captain Thompson's ship. You're ordered to cease your approach to the sphere and return to formation."

Ellie winced at the hard tone Reiko had taken. She felt she had been reaching Alphons, but his reply indicated that Reiko had turned him away.

"Commodore, this is something that Admiral Tripping and your superior should resolve. It's not right, nor fair, to place the captains in the middle of an authority fight between commanders."

"Captain Jagielski —" Reiko said, but her words didn't travel beyond the *Redemption*'s controller.

<Commodore, Captain Jagielski cut the link, and he's not answering my comms,> Ellie sent.

<And I thought the sphere coming to a stationary position was a worst-case scenario,> Reiko complained privately to Tatia.

Alex found himself the focus of attention on the *Liberator*'s bridge. The ugly *what if* question Tatia had asked was suddenly a real situation. Tripping had taken command of his warships. Now the question was whether the Omnians stood back and watched or whether they would commit to supporting the New Terrans, regardless of the misguided judgment of their commander.

"Alex, we need a decision," Tatia said. "Do we follow the New Terrans or not?"

"There are hundreds of good people aboard those ships, Admiral, led by one idiot," Alex growled out.

"The sphere's accelerating," Julien announced. "It's heading toward the New Terran ships."

Reiko froze. She was ticks away from ordering Ellie to reform the square with Tripping's Tridents. Instead, she asked quietly, "Why is it headed for our ships?"

Sacrifice, Alex thought, and the word echoed through his mind.

<Abort the attack, Commodore. Maximum distance from the sphere,> Alex ordered, his thought thundering through Reiko's mind.

Reiko relayed the message with an urgency she had rarely felt. Whether it was the power of Alex's sending that rocked her mind or the intense fear that accompanied his thought, she couldn't tell.

The SADEs signaled the controllers of the five Omnian ships and the fighters. Courses were reversed, and power applied at maximum to put as much distance between them and the sphere as they could. On everyone's mind was the question: What had happened? It was hoped there would be time later to learn the answer.

<SADEs, link me to the New Terran ships,> Alex sent.

Julien, Z, nor Miranda questioned Alex's request or sought to remind him of Admiral Tripping's cut-out device. They divided the ships, Z taking the admiral's flagship and attempting to find a way around his own creation.

Julien and Miranda managed to connect to Jagielski and Fillister's Tridents and linked Alex.

<We've temporarily usurped comm control, Alex, for these two ships, but they could shut us down manually, at any time,> Julien sent. <Send your message, Alex. It will be heard on their bridge speakers.>

"Aboard the Tridents *Arthur McMorris* and *Lem Ulam*, this is Alex Racine. Listen carefully. Your lives depend on what I'm about to say. As sure as I breathe, I'm convinced the Nua'll aboard that sphere have decided that they will no longer attempt to evade our forces, nor will they surrender. That sphere is headed toward you for one reason and one reason only. The Nua'll are determined to have their enemy join them in death. Veer off now and apply maximum acceleration."

<Z,> Alex sent.

<Not yet,> Z replied.

Jagielski's bridge crew eyed him. They'd heard Alex's message, and their faces reflected their anxiety.

"Comms, get me the *Lem Ulam*," Alphons ordered.

"Captain Fillister here," Bart replied.

"You heard?" Alphons asked.

"Loud and clear," Bart replied. "I'm not fluent in the law in these cases. Is Admiral Tripping in charge of our ships or not?"

"Our oaths were to the New Terran constitution," Alphons replied. "But Admiral Tripping signed an agreement with Omnia Ships to operate under Admiral Tachenko's orders. And her boss is the majority shareholder of Omnia Ships, who just told us to abort the attack."

"Putting aside the question of legality," Bart replied, "I'm thinking about Alex Racine's warning. You know the rumors about him, right?"

"Which one of the few hundred are you talking about?" Alphons joked, which seemed out of place under the circumstances.

"Okay, forget that ... what if he's right?"

"Then we're sailing two ships, hundreds of crew, and our sorry butts to join the galaxy's collection of space dust."

"I'm serious, Alphons," Bart replied, throwing aside formality.

"I know, Bart, that's why I called you. I think it's high time to think of our people. We've been warned by the man who has been right about aliens more times than I can count, and our admiral is disobeying the rightful orders of his senior officer. I'm for abandoning this foolhardy attack, as ordered by Alex Racine."

"Agreed, I'm reversing course," Bart replied.

"Make for a rendezvous with Captain Thompson," Alphons said.

"Alex, Captains Jagielski and Fillister are reversing course. Vectors will intersect the *Redemption*," Julien announced.

"Two ships saved," Tatia said in a soft exhale of breath.

<Z,> Alex sent.

<With regrets, Alex, I would be the first to tell you if I were successful,> Z sent with more than a little exasperation.

If asked, Z would have declared that it was a SADE's duty to create programs with a superior form. Privately, he was proud of his creations. But, in this case, he was disgusted with himself. He felt if he'd operated more like a human, he would have left a back door for unseen events like this. Instead, he'd ensured the program was sealed against intrusion by humans or SADEs.

"Captain, our sister ships are retreating," the *Geoffrey Orlan*'s navigator reported to Morney.

"What?" the admiral yelled, jumping up from his command chair. He stumbled, his legs weak from spending too much time sitting, despite the efforts of the chair's nanites to relieve the pressure in his lower body. Morney had extended a hand to help him, but Tripping angrily shook it off, after catching his balance.

Tripping glanced at the navigator's board and looked over his shoulder at the holo-vid. "Cowards," he muttered under his breath. Then he gathered himself, squared his shoulders, and announced in a loud voice, "Then the glory will be ours when we destroy this sphere, and two captains will face a Board of Inquiry when we return to New Terra."

Rounding on Morney, Tripping, said, "Are our beams ready to fire?"

"Yes, Admiral," Morney replied. "Safeties were released after the ship entered the system's space."

"Captain, I hope you will give me the honor of ordering the first beam salvo," Tripping requested.

"Of course, Sir," Morney replied. He had hooked his career to Tripping, despite the admonitions of the other two captains. They had repeatedly warned him about the admiral's dangerous habit of grandstanding. But, it was his thought that the squadron would be doing nothing more than playing war games. *How wrong you were,* Morney thought.

"Weapons, targeting," Tripping called out, standing with his hands locked behind his back. He'd seen some ancient vids of heroic captains of space and sea standing on their ships' bridges in that pose and had always admired it.

"Locked on the sphere, Admiral," the weapons officer replied.

"Time to firing?" Tripping asked.

"Four point six minutes, Sir."

"Excellent, stand by," Tripping ordered.

The time counted down. The bridge crew were breathing shallowly. Fear made their movements small and slow, and sweat formed on brows.

A part of Morney's brain was screaming at him to confine the admiral to quarters and retreat his Trident, as fast as he could.

"Inside our weapons effective range, Sir," the weapons officer said. There was a hint of sadness in her voice.

"Fire," Admiral Tripping ordered, personal affirmation strong in his voice.

That was the admiral's final word. The weapons officer tapped her board to release the tremendous amount of energy held in the ship's power crystals at the same time the sphere detonated. Hundreds of millions of metric tons of hot metal and gas from the enemy ship expanded in every direction.

The *Geoffrey Orlan*'s beams managed to eliminate a few thousand tons of the dangerous mixture. But behind those vaporized quantities came a massive amount of metal debris that sliced the Trident into pieces. The warship's power crystals were destroyed, and they released their energy. In the first moment, Tripping's ship was torn apart. Then, in the next tick, it too was an expanding ball of metal, hot gases, and organic matter.

"The sphere and the *Geoffrey Orlan* are gone," Julien reported.

"The Trident fired its beams," Miranda added.

Alex snapped his head around to lock eyes with Miranda.

"Checking, Alex," Miranda said, interpreting the reason for Alex's anxiousness.

"Negative, Alex," Miranda replied. "Telemetry data shows that the sphere's detonation and the Trident's firing of its beams were simultaneous."

"The Nua'll committed suicide," Svetlana said, turning to stare at Alex.

"It was a sacrifice, not suicide," Alex said quietly. "The Nua'll were intent on taking some of their enemy with them. That's who we face," he added in a stronger voice and gazed around at the bridge personnel, one at a time, to drive home his point.

<I think the two of you need a new name for Alex,> Renée sent to the twins, as she left the rear bulkhead to join Alex. <Madman doesn't seem appropriate anymore.>

Étienne and Alain glanced at each other in surprise. As far as they knew, madman was their private name for Alex. That Ser knew their secret was a complete surprise to them.

New Terra

Moments after the sphere detonated, taking the NT *Geoffrey Orlan* with it, the fleet recorded a second, significant detonation. The bullet ship had self-destructed.

A search was conducted at the sites where the warship and the two fighters were lost. All three ships were utterly destroyed. There was nothing left to recover.

The fleet rejoined, but there was a small problem. They'd lost a Trident, which had accommodated four fighters. Lucia's *Judgment*, having lost two ships, picked up two of the NT travelers.

Z determined there would be room to squeeze a third fighter in each bay of a Trident, if all ancillary material were removed. Svetlana ordered her crew chiefs to strip the *Liberator*'s bays. Afterward, the two remaining traveler controllers received virtual maps of the flagship's bays and slowly eased the ships aboard to tuck next to the other two fighters.

"Well done, Z," Svetlana complimented the SADE, when the bay doors closed. "We actually have centimeters to spare."

The fleet began the long transit home. By the time they would make Omnia, they would have been gone for ten long months.

Alex spoke with Reiko after the conflict. He'd noticed she was withdrawn. It wasn't the reaction he would have expected from her after a successful prosecution of her strategy.

"I lost a ship full of good people," Reiko had replied, when Alex heard what was bothering her.

"And eliminated a sphere," Alex had replied. "And here's another way of looking at it, Reiko. Now that we know how the Nua'll act when they're cornered, who's to say that if it wasn't for Admiral Tripping's foolhardy charge that more of our ships wouldn't have been lured closer. We might have lost most or all of the squadron."

The first evening after the encounter with the sphere, meals aboard every ship were subdued, more so aboard the New Terran Tridents. While many were relieved to be alive, survivor's guilt was running rampant and arguments or recrimination occasionally broke out.

"Admiral, I'll be traveling to New Terra with Captains Jagielski and Fillister. I can imagine the assorted receptions those two will receive when the full story gets out," Alex said, as he sipped on his cup of thé.

"They did what was ordered of them," Reiko said tersely.

"I don't disagree with you, Commodore, but that's our viewpoint, and Alphons and Bart aren't Omnians," Alex replied.

"Alex, what ship do you want to take to New Terra?" Tatia asked, working on the last of her meal. Despite the unsettled emotions of the evening, she fell back on her old TSF habits. In this case, it was to eat when you got the opportunity, as you never knew when the next meal will come your way.

"I want to give the fleet a break. The *Rêveur* will have returned by now," Alex replied.

"You can't have my half," Renée said quietly but with determination. She was seated across from Alex, and the two stared evenly at each other. The silence extended, and the table of individuals began glancing at one another.

"Well, I can't take half a ship, can I?" Alex finally said. "What do you suggest, Ser?"

"I suggest, from now on, that you, Ser, ride in the most powerful ship you can find. And, I don't care if they only have room on the deck to provide you a place to sleep. Your life has great meaning to me, but it has greater importance to the future of humankind, and you *will* be protected, whether you like it or not."

At Renée's conclusion, those at the table grabbed empty cups and pounded them or clapped and whistled, raising a huge ruckus that drew the attention of everyone in the meal room.

"I bow to my lady's wishes," Alex said gallantly and pursed his lips at Renée.

"You promise?" Renée asked. She was overwhelmed by the power of Alex's emotions that flooded through her mind via her implant. Renée's eyes closed, her head tilted back, and a warm smile formed on her face. "He promises," she whispered.

"Alex, you wouldn't be available to teach my partner how to do that, would you?" Tatia asked, which drew chuckles from the table.

"I noticed you clapping earlier, Captain, at the loss of my passenger liner," Alex said to Svetlana. "However, you and your crew will have to forgo your vacation time. I'll be taking the *Liberator* to New Terra."

"Well, at least I get my ship back," Svetlana quipped, eyeing Reiko.

"Not quite, Captain," Tatia replied, with a grin. "I'll be going with Alex."

The table burst out in laughter at Svetlana's crestfallen expression.

The head table's emotional release slowly spread throughout the room, and appetites regained a little of their former strength.

* * *

When the fleet transited into Omnia's space, four of the OS Tridents headed inward. The New Terran warships, in the company of the OS *Liberator,* made their final transit to Oistos, the New Terran star.

Alex took the opportunity to talk again with Alphons and Bart. He understood survivor's guilt, but the two men couldn't shake their feelings that they had committed a serious breach of naval protocol by refusing to follow their admiral's order.

Seated at his cabin's undersized desk, Alex linked to the *Liberator's* controller and established private connections with the two captains, who sat at their cabin tables with their comm consoles.

<Captains,> Alex sent, <I would like you to reconsider your decision to present yourself for review before I have an opportunity to speak to New Terra's leaders and senior naval officers. Once the public learns of

the loss of the *Geoffrey Orlan*, there will be a huge outcry from the families, which might sway the Board of Inquiry's opinion.>

"Alex, we appreciate your support. But this is something that Alphons and I feel we need to do," Bart said.

"I echo Bart's sentiments, Alex. You've been incredibly generous in your support, and while you're convinced of our innocence, we aren't," Alphons added.

<While I can't accept your choice to assume this guilt, I understand where it comes from,> Alex sent. <Losing friends, especially shipmates, is a terrible burden. But, know this, I don't intend to let this rest. Good night, Sers.>

"What do you think he meant about not letting it rest?" Bart asked, after Alex closed his link.

"You want me to tell you what Alex Racine is thinking, at any one moment?" Alphons asked. "I don't think anyone, but Julien, would know the answer to that question."

When the three Tridents transited into Oistos space, the populace buzzed with the news, spread quickly by the media. Two of the NT ships had been gone for more than a year, and the flagship for much of that time. It was only after an enterprising reporter pinged each ship and received IDs of one OS and two NT warships that the public's mood shifted. Questions were posed by media personalities about the absence of the admiral and his flagship, ranging from simple ones about where the ship might be to dark ones that supposed dire things had happened to them.

"Word's out, Alex, about the ship IDs," Maria Gonzalez said, without preliminaries, when she connected to Alex.

Alex was crammed behind his cabin desk, wearing a short robe, which was absorbing the last of the refresher's moisture. His console was set to voice comm, while Renée worked at drying his hair.

"Hmm," Alex replied, his voice muffled by the towel.

"Am I interrupting something, Alex?" Maria asked.

"Nothing I can't finish later," Renée replied.

"Youth ... it must be nice," Maria said. "I need to ask you, Alex. Where's Tripping's flagship?"

"Spreading out in little pieces across a cold system, many, many light-years from here, Maria, I'm sad to say," Alex replied.

"Please tell me that the admiral was a hero, and he died with his crew defending humankind," Maria said hopefully.

Alex leaned back in his chair, wrapping the towel around his neck, and Renée perched on the desktop. While Alex was trying to think of a way to answer Maria's question, Renée said, "He can't, Maria."

"I knew it," Maria replied hotly. "What happened?"

"That story will take time to tell, Maria. I'm more concerned about the guilt-ridden survivors, namely Captains Jagielski and Fillister," Alex said.

"Survivor's guilt is a heavy burden," Maria replied. "No one knows that better than you, Alex."

"Well, in this case, Maria, it's complicated by the circumstances of Tripping's demise," Alex replied. "He cut off comms with our flagship and ordered an attack, contrary to the battle commander's orders. I convinced Captains Jagielski and Fillister to abandon the attack. Now, they feel that they might have been dishonorable."

"How did the flagship meet its end?" Maria asked.

"The sphere self-destructed," Alex replied.

"Incredible," Maria said. "But, surely, that couldn't have been foreseen by anyone."

"Sorry to disabuse you of that notion, Maria," Renée replied. "But, I'll allow you one guess."

"What, Alex, did the sphere slip you a note saying, 'we don't surrender under any circumstances'?"

"Something like that," Alex replied, uncomfortable with the turn in the conversation.

Renée slipped off the desk to stand behind him, and she stroked her fingers through Alex's short, thick, still-moist hair.

"The way I see it, Maria," Alex said, "Tripping broke his agreement with us, issued an illegal order, managed to destroy his ship, unnecessarily, and attempted to take the other two Tridents with him. Now, his remaining captains think they should tell all and throw themselves on the mercy of the Navy's Board of Inquiry."

"And you don't agree with their intentions?" Maria asked.

"Muscle flexion on the jaw is about 60 percent, Maria," Renée said.

"I take that as an intense disagreement with the captains," Maria replied. "Well, then I don't need to ask why your flagship is here, do I, Alex? Speaking of traveling accommodations, why a warship?"

"Because I won't let him travel in a passenger liner anymore, Maria," Renée said forcefully. "It's Alex that's putting together the scope of what we face. Our adversaries don't consist of a couple of spheres. The Nua'll appear to be an old and advanced civilization that is intent on expansion. From now on, Alex travels aboard the most powerful ship we have, wherever he goes."

Maria had rarely heard mettle ringing in Renée's voice. She couldn't imagine what had transpired in the past year, but, if Renée was thinking like this, it couldn't be good.

"What do you hope to accomplish here, Alex?" This was the question Maria was afraid to ask but knew she must.

"Maria, these two captains are fine, honorable men, who believe they're unworthy of their positions because of some improper New Terran naval officer training. Unlawful orders from superiors must not only be rejected, training should reinforce regulations that allow subordinate officers to remove from command senior officers who issue those types of orders."

Maria had her answer, without Alex responding directly to her question. This was a matter of justice for him. Without a fair resolution, as Alex perceived it, the agreement to share technology and construct warships for defense and offense would be placed in jeopardy. Adding to this was the specter of a massive alien empire somewhere out in the deep dark. All this spelled incredible complications for New Terra's fledgling, space-capable, society.

"Will you see me when you make orbit, Alex?" Maria asked, hoping to have a face-to-face meeting with Alex to moderate his approach to New Terra's leaders.

"Certainly, Maria, if you're standing next to Harold Grumley at the time. He'll be my first stop," Alex replied.

"Good night, Alex, Renée," Maria replied, closing the comm link.

* * *

The three Tridents made orbit over New Terra. The two NT pilots offloaded their travelers from the flagship and made for the planet's fighter training base. Skeleton crews rendezvoused with the two NT warships to relieve the entire ships' complements, who had been missing their families and friends.

Alex winced as Julien reported to him the mass exodus of NT personnel aboard the warships' travelers.

<There goes control over the story,> Alex sent to Julien.

<I can imagine the number of versions that will be spread, Alex, with humans' penchant to elaborate and omit details.>

<That number would equal the total number of crew, except for two captains, who will be painfully honest,> Alex replied.

<It's being reported that the Board of Inquiry is set to convene in two days. The Tridents' controllers are being accessed, as we speak.>

<They aren't wasting any time,> Alex sent.

<The public is demanding to know what happened to their loved ones, and important personages are angry at the loss of their favored one, Admiral Anthony Tripping.>

<Meet you in the bay, Julien,> Alex replied. He lifted Renée up, kissed her soundly, and announced, "I go to do battle with the power denizens of New Terra."

"Don't forget your lance, Sir Racine," Renée replied. They were bantering about one of her favorite vids, a strange tale of men on horses, dressed in metal, and engaged in heroic deeds.

Franz readied a traveler for his passengers, Alex, Julien, Tatia, and the twins.

"Returning to New Terra feels stranger every time we arrive," Tatia commented to Alex, who sat across from her. "Seeing my parents becomes a little more surreal. I love them, but I know them less and less."

"I wonder what I'll feel when I see my parents and sister again," Alex replied.

"Cordelia and I have wondered the same thing about our youngest children," Julien added. "Humans have this habit of evolving in unforeseen directions in incredibly short periods of time."

The three sat quietly after that exchange. Franz dropped through the atmosphere and chose to land the traveler on the front grounds of Government House, the president's residence.

"This ought to be interesting," Tatia said, with a smirk, as she eyed the twins, who were wearing their shoulder-mounted stun guns and energy packs. It was a new standard that everyone around Alex insisted on, not that he approved, but he'd given up objecting to the small things. In his opinion, there were much more important things to worry about.

Tatia had forewarned the president's security about the escorts who would accompany Alex, but they were unprepared for the formidable weapons staring at them. The senior security officer asked the group to halt, while he examined the stun guns.

Alain used the opportunity to have his left shoulder weapon track the man, as he walked from the front of him to the side. It so unnerved the officer that he waved the group forward without another word.

<Behave,> Tatia sent to Alain, her partner, who flashed a grin at her. <Incorrigible,> she responded. <You two used to be so modest and introverted.>

<It's the Alex effect,> Alain shot back.

Inside Government House, an aide greeted Alex and asked the group to wait while they were announced.

Alex flashed back to his first visit to Government House with Renée de Guirnon at his side. At the time, he was intrigued by her, but they weren't partners yet.

Maria had arrived prior to the Omnians to brief the president, but Harold hadn't allowed her the opportunity before he launched into describing the situation, as he saw it. Maria listened patiently to Harold, as he droned on. She kept her eye on the chronometer, knowing Alex and company would be precisely on time. With a diminishing window to make her case, Maria interrupted the president.

"Harold, let me stress a few things to you before Alex arrives. He won't take into account your protestations of political pressure. And he certainly won't be concerned about how the captains are treated with regard to the effect it will have on your reelection chances. Alex Racine will be expecting just treatment for Captains Jagielski and Fillister. In his opinion, they made the right call. They followed the lawful orders of the battle commander, Commodore Shimada, and rightfully ignored the unlawful orders of Admiral Tripping."

"But, Maria, Tripping has a great many supporters, and they view him as a hero. They believe he must have sacrificed his life and ship to eliminate a dangerous enemy."

"What sacrifice are you talking about, Harold? Didn't you read Alex and Tatia's reports? The sphere blew up in an attempt to take as many of the squadron's ships with it as it could. Tripping's single salvo of beam shots didn't do anything except destroy a few tons of space junk that were hurtling at his ship."

"That's not the way it's being portrayed in certain circles," Harold protested.

"Well, Harold, I can tell you that you're about to get an education in a different way of looking at things," Maria said, just as an aide tapped at the conference room door.

"Mr. President, your pardon, but your guests have landed," the aide said.

"Ah, thank you, we have time yet," Harold said, glancing toward Maria.

"Um, Mr. President, to be more precise, your guests are here. Their traveler landed on the front grounds," the aide clarified.

Harold blinked at his aide, processing the idea that his guests would fly directly to Government House. It certainly wasn't protocol and perhaps even a little rude.

For her part, Maria was smiling and thinking, *Get ready, Harold, here come the Omnians.*

The aide, who had greeted Alex, hurried back to his guests, who were waiting in the rotunda next to the statue of Lem Ulam, the last captain of the New Terran colony ship before it was abandoned.

"This way, Mr. Racine," the aide said, indicating the direction with an arm and eyeing the shoulder-mounted weapons on the twins. "President Grumley and Envoy Gonzalez are waiting for you in the main conference room."

Knowing where to go, Alex's strides quickly outpaced that of the aide, who hurried to keep up with the group.

Omnians, the aide thought, with a certain amount of deprecation. He was used to much more decorum from visitors to the august residence.

"President Grumley, thank you for seeing us on such short notice," Alex said, entering the conference room, without waiting to be announced.

"You're welcome, Alex," Harold said, rising and shaking Alex's hand.

"Maria," Alex said warmly, embracing her.

"Good to throw my arms around you again, youngster," Maria replied.

Harold watched Maria's greeting of Alex and Tatia, with interest. The strength of their relationships was evident. But, what surprised him was the hug that Maria extended to Julien. It was as affectionate as those given to Alex and Tatia, and the SADE's expression indicated he appreciated it.

As Harold's three guests took seats at the conference table, he glanced toward the twins, who took up positions, one in the room's far corner and the other near the door.

"Extraordinary statement," Grumley said, regarding the weapons, which had unnerved his security forces and required an override from him.

"Yes," Tatia agreed, glancing at Alain, who stood by the doorway. When she had first seen them mounted on Alain, she had quipped, "I want a pair. Do you have them in extra-large?"

Turning to the president, Tatia said, "It's come to the attention of Omnians that this particular individual," motioning to Alex, "might be more important to us than we thought. But don't tell him that," which earned her a grin from Alex.

"I always thought so," Maria added, smiling at Tatia.

"Yes, well, to business, Alex," Harold said, "How can I help you?"

Alex eyed the president. It wasn't the opening he had hoped for. The president seemed determined to be coy. "Julien," Alex said.

The SADE placed a small holo-vid on the table and spooled off an enormous file he had compiled. It contained the events at system FYM-552, where the sphere was destroyed. As opposed to their summary reports, Harold and Maria heard and witnessed the action and communication in a series of integrated clips. The presentation was long but riveting, including right up to the last moment, when Alex urged the two New Terran captains to abandon the attack.

When Julien shut down the holo-vid, Maria eyed her ex-TSF major. Tatia knew what was on Maria's mind, and she tipped her head toward Alex to indicate that he had indeed perceived the sphere's action before it happened.

"Extraordinary and most convincing," Harold said, sitting back in the chair to consider his options. The presentation, in and of itself, if released to the public, would damn Tripping in the court of public opinion. Worse, it would create an outcry that could blow back on the government for promoting an obviously unqualified man to command New Terra's Tridents. It struck Harold that Maria's advice was right on the mark.

"What would satisfy you, Alex?" Harold asked, sitting forward and clasping his hands together on the table.

Maria recognized Harold's gesture, as the one he exhibited when he sought to mollify a complainant, and she breathed a quiet sigh of relief.

"You mean besides preferring to prosecute a dead man for incompetence, failing to follow orders, endangering his squadron, and killing everyone aboard his ship," Alex replied sternly, enumerating the points on his fingertips.

Harold gulped back his incredulity. He'd hoped he'd concealed his reaction from his guests, but a scan of their faces revealed he hadn't. This wasn't the dialog's opening he had expected. The one thing that restored his emotional balance was the twinkle he caught in Maria's eyes. She immensely enjoyed Alex's opening salvo.

"You can probably do little for me," Alex continued. "The public has undoubtedly formed their opinions, and, unfortunately, I don't foresee the captains adequately defending themselves. The Board of Inquiry is moving quickly, too quickly in my opinion, and I intend to be present at the inquiry to ensure the captains' stories are effectively presented."

"Alex, you do realize that you'll be relegated to the position of spectator?" Harold asked. He expected protestations, but Alex stared calmly at him, the hint of a lopsided smile on his face. Harold glanced at the admiral, looking for support, but she regarded him evenly, as if there were nothing more to be said. The discussion had been so disconcerting that it crossed Harold's mind to wonder if he had been negotiating with humans.

"In the future, President Grumley," Alex said, leaning his forearms on the table, "the New Terran commanders who sail with us must be vetted by our senior officers and will be promoted from your captains. No more jumped-up admirals."

"Alex, that's something I don't have control over," Harold protested.

"Then you can tell those who do handle the appointments that New Terra risks abrogating our agreement by refusing to abide by this demand," Alex replied, as he stood.

In one movement, the Omnians swept from the room, Alain first, Alex next, followed by Tatia and Julien, and Étienne last.

"They move like … like an integrated machine," Harold said, staring open-mouthed at the door. "And I didn't call for an aide to escort them out," he muttered.

To Harold's discomfort, Maria was laughing.

"Might I remind you, Maria, you're laughing at your president," Harold said, a little miffed.

"Then fire me, Harold, if you can't take it," Maria shot back, assuming a stern visage. "I tried to tell you, and all you could do is explain your political situation, as if I've never held the presidency. What I've done that you've never done is work with Alex and the Méridiens, then the Harakens, and now the Omnians. I understand them, but I seem to have to continually teach the individuals who hold this office about their natures."

"Alex Racine wouldn't break the accord; he needs us too much," Harold said defiantly, trying to regain ground with Maria.

"Don't you believe it," Maria replied hotly. "Alex would drop us in a heartbeat if we refused his requests. What you've failed to understand, Harold, is that Tripping's actions not only jeopardized our ships, he risked the lives of everyone in that squadron, and Alex won't stand for that. And, one more thing, the Confederation is now on board with Alex. In a tremendous societal course change for them, they're building warships, and they can launch a hundred for every one of ours. Alex doesn't need us; we need him."

* * *

Two days after making New Terra's orbit, Captains Jagielski and Fillister sat together at a small table, facing five naval officers, who represented the Board of Inquiry.

"Before we begin, the Board must deal with a most unusual request," Commodore Don Jacobsen, the Board's presiding officer, said. "Mr. Alex Racine, please approach."

Alex chose to stand beside the captains rather than take the position the commodore had indicated.

"Mr. Racine, the Board has received your request that you be allowed to be a witness for the captains," Jacobsen announced. "This is a Board of Inquiry. We're convened to hear the captains' personal descriptions of the events surrounding the loss of the NT *Geoffrey Orlan* and ask them questions regarding their testimonies. This isn't a trial, requiring witnesses. If we think that the captains have committed acts contrary to New Terra's naval code of conduct, we'll recommend that they're held over for trial, at which time, your witness statements may be admitted."

"I understand your procedures, Commodore Jacobsen," Alex replied. "I'm present to ensure that the captains accurately relate the events that occurred at FYM-552."

"Do you believe that Captains Jagielski and Fillister won't be truthful regarding their statements to this Board, Mr. Racine?"

"Commodore, I believe they will relay the facts accurately. I'm here to ensure the Board has the proper perspective surrounding those facts."

"Well, Mr. Racine, I regret to inform you that the only individual who may address the board, under those circumstances, is their senior officer, who, regretfully, is no longer with us."

"And that's why I'm here, Commodore," Alex replied. "You've already misunderstood the conditions at FYM-552. The senior commander, during the conflict, wasn't Admiral Tripping. It was Admiral Tachenko."

"Then, under those conditions, Mr. Racine, the Board would accept Admiral Tachenko's testimony."

"And I'm her senior," Alex replied, with a smile.

There were several asides between the commodore and the captains, who sat to the presiding officer's left and right.

"It's our understanding, Mr. Racine, that you hold no naval rank. Isn't that correct?" Jacobsen asked.

"Essentially, I'm the fleet's ultimate authority, Sers, especially as it relates to these captains, who operated in concert with my Trident squadron."

"Please clarify that statement, Sir," the senior officer said.

"The OS Tridents are owned by Omnia Ships, the stipends of officers and crew are paid by Omnia Ships, and I'm the majority shareholder of Omnia Ships."

"Are you asking us to believe that you've raised and are operating a private Navy?" a Board captain asked.

"I'm not asking you, Ser, I'm telling you what's true."

At that moment, the doors of the Board of Inquiry opened. Harold Grumley and Maria Gonzalez walked through, approached the front spectator row, and took seats. Two of the president's staffers had saved seats for them in a gallery otherwise packed with family members, supporters, detractors, reporters, and naval officers.

"President Grumley, the Board appreciates your attendance but hopes that you recognize that you have no official capacity during this inquiry," Jacobsen said.

"I do, Commodore," Harold replied.

"However, your timing is most apropos, Mr. President," Jacobsen said. "Would you please clarify for the Board the circumstances under which New Terra has entered into the agreement to build Tridents?"

"Certainly, Commodore," Harold replied. "The accord was signed with Omnia Ships, specifically with Alex Racine."

"Not with the Omnian government?" a captain asked.

Maria stood to be recognized.

"Envoy Maria Gonzalez, the Board would welcome any clarifications you might offer," Jacobsen said, a frown marking his forehead.

"Alex Racine owns the majority shares in Omnia Ships," Maria replied. "The faux shell that is used to build Omnian ships and our Tridents was invented by his people and donated to him. Mr. Racine has assembled an incredible group of humans, SADEs, and physical assets. New Terra is benefitting from his generous sharing of technology that just might prove to be what saves humankind from the advance of the Nua'll."

"Thank you for that clarification, Envoy Gonzalez, as incredible as it sounds," Jacobsen intoned, unnerved to have learned that his government was contracting with a private company for the vaunted warship technology. Jacobsen conferred with his other Board members until four heads were nodding in agreement.

"Mr. Racine, the Board recognizes your right to speak as the captains' superior. Sergeant, a chair for Mr. Racine," Jacobsen ordered.

"Here you are, Sir," a female sergeant said. She had Tatia's build and smoothly hauled a comfortable chair for him, unlike the ones the Trident captains sat on.

Alex accepted the chair and returned the sergeant's generous smile with one of his own.

Jacobsen began with Alphons and requested his recall of the events. Alex listened intently to the recitation. In his implants were the key points of the encounter, compiled by Julien. Each point was detailed with coordinates, time, individuals, and linked to the relevant communications. For the most part, Alphons' recall was fairly accurate.

When it was Bart's turn, he missed a few important details but managed to deliver a solid account of the events. At the end of their stories, each captain announced his regret in not following the admiral's lead, believing if he had, he might have changed the outcome and saved the *Geoffrey Orlan*.

The Board's commodore and captains questioned the details of the stories for two hours.

<It's a shame the Board doesn't have the account from Tripping's ship,> Tatia lamented privately to Julien. <Then again, they wouldn't have a full record of his ship's final moments anyway. Not with the man cutting off comms with the flagship.>

<It does seem rather foolish not to make use of technology, which they possess,> Julien replied. <They merely have to request our records of the event, much more detailed than human recollection, excepting yours, of course, Admiral.>

Tatia smirked at Julien, who smiled benevolently at her, as if he had only dared speak the truth.

"Mr. Racine, do you have anything you would like to add to clarify these accounts?" Jacobsen asked.

"Please don't play that holo-vid," Harold whispered so quietly that only Maria heard him.

Alex stood and said, "These are two fine captains, who made the right judgment that day, despite their survivor guilt. If they had followed Admiral Tripping, New Terra would have lost two more captains, two more crews, and two more warships."

"This is your opinion, Mr. Racine?" a Board captain asked.

"Negative, Ser. I have produced detailed telemetry of the event for President Grumley and Envoy Gonzalez. For reasons of my own, I prefer not to share the information with this Board, but those two individuals will attest to what they witnessed in my presentation. The Nua'll sphere drove at a portion of our squadron and deliberately self-detonated to take as much of the fleet with it as it could. The Admiral's ship was in the direct path of that explosion. These two captains reversed course and saved their people."

"Mr. Racine, that doesn't answer the fundamental question of why Captains Jagielski and Fillister chose not to follow their admiral," Jacobsen said.

"And that's why I stand before this Board, Commodore. What the captains haven't told you is that I ordered Captains Jagielski and Fillister to abandon the attack and reverse course at all speed."

"And why would you do that?" a Board captain asked. "Three ships had a better chance of defeating the sphere than one. These men couldn't have known the sphere would self-destruct."

"I knew," Alex said quietly, but with a voice that carried clearly throughout the room. It created a buzz throughout the audience, which required Jacobsen to call for order or he would clear the room.

"How could you know, Mr. Racine?" Jacobsen asked.

"Analysis of information gleaned during the past two-plus decades, Sers," Alex replied." While you enjoyed a period of peace, others of us fought the first Nua'll sphere. While you slept, we built warships. While you wondered about what lay beyond your star, we visited there, discovered intelligent life, and the presence of a massive enemy. And, while you traded for our technology, we hunted a second sphere for nearly a year. After a while, you come to understand your enemy, Sers, maybe better than you know yourself. The Nua'll will sacrifice themselves for their society. That's how their civilization has achieved its age and expanse. You'd do well to mark my words. If you don't seek them out, then, one day, they'll come for you."

Rather than sit down, Alex spun and marched out of the room, his people flowing in his wake.

-25-
The Dream

Following the NT captains' testimonies, the Board reviewed their Tridents' controller records. Three days later, their findings were announced. No charges were preferred against Captains Jagielski and Fillister, but the Board recommended they be removed from their command positions. It was obvious to the two men that their naval careers had been truncated. They would serve out their enlistment terms in administrative positions and then, more than likely, quietly retire.

"All that training time wasted," Tatia grumbled to Alex, when they heard the pronouncements.

"Who says?" Alex asked.

"Well, New Terra has two Tridents to add to the two they have in trials and no experienced battle captains to command either one of the four," Tatia replied. "From what I hear, they're planning to jump fighter captains into these positions."

"You mean like we did?" Alex asked, grinning at Tatia.

"Yes, we did, and look how long we spent training them. Could we have that much time to do it all over again, dear leader?" Tatia asked, her voice sweet and encouraging.

"Cute," Alex commented. "I don't know how long we have, but the sooner we seek out the Nua'll, the less time they'll have to find us. But, returning to the subject at hand, I'm not interested in what New Terra does with its Tridents. Those are ships, and we're going to have plenty of them. What we need, my dear admiral, are trained individuals," Alex said.

"Oh, I love the way you think, Alex," Tatia said, grinning broadly at him. "When and where?"

"No time like the present. I think we should invite Alphons and Bart to a meeting at Government House."

"Excellent," Tatia replied, sending a signal to Julien, the twins, and Franz.

Soon, the group was planet bound, with Franz at the helm of their traveler. Franz eyed his landing coordinates, checked his telemetry, and refrained from asking for clarification. Julien had supplied the data. He mentally shrugged and dropped through the clouds to descend over a suburban area. The coordinates pinpointed the middle of a road in front of a modest house, and Franz set the fighter down, impeding traffic.

Before the traveler's hatch opened, Alphons, his wife, and son came out of the house.

When the hatch dropped, Tatia decided not to descend and start a prolonged conversation. Instead, she yelled from the hatch opening, "Captain, you're late for a meeting. Get a move on."

Alphons hurriedly kissed his wife, while his son ran inside and grabbed his father's uniform jacket. Alphons hugged his son, grabbed his jacket, and ran to the traveler.

"Apologies, Admiral, I didn't receive your message," Alphons said, as he gained the fighter's deck. "My comm account might have been restricted."

"Hardly, Captain. You can't miss a message that was never sent. Take a seat, please."

When Alex indicated a seat beside Julien, Alphons sat down and greeted each of them. He waited for an explanation, but the SADE and human quietly ignored him.

Tatia decided to stay at the hatch for the next stop, which Franz indicated was nearby. Instead of a house, Franz discovered his coordinates placed him at the third-floor level of an upscale apartment building.

When the hatch opened, it caught Tatia by surprise. She was looking across 10 meters of space to a balcony.

<A little warning, next time, Group Leader,> Tatia admonished via implant.

<Apologies, Admiral, this type of pickup isn't in my training experience,> Franz sent in reply.

Although Franz sounded sincere, Tatia was sure that he was laughing.

The apartment's balcony door slid open, and Bart poked his head out. "Admiral?" he queried.

"Get dressed, Bart, you have a meeting to attend at Government House. Downstairs, quick time."

Franz landed, and soon Bart came running out of the apartment, shrugging into his jacket.

As Franz lifted, he could see the astonished faces of pedestrians and hover-car drivers, as they watched his traveler lift. Only the more adventuresome grav car riders had dared overfly his ship, while it was parked on the roadway. Most took an alternate route.

"What's up, Admiral?" Bart asked, as his feet hit the traveler's deck.

"Patience, Captain," Tatia replied. "Take a seat."

<Julien, Grumley,> Alex sent.

<I'm informed the president is in residence but is occupied, at the moment,> Julien replied, after checking on Harold's status.

<Inform the president's chief of staff that we are inbound and wish some of the man's time,> Alex sent.

There was no vocal conversation during the flight to Government House. Alphons and Bart exchanged glances of query, but neither seemed to have an idea as to what was happening.

Once again, Franz landed at Government House. The Omnians and New Terran captains were met on the front steps by the president's chief of staff.

"Mr. Racine, the president begs your indulgence," the chief of staff said, by way of a greeting. "He's anticipated the reason you're here and informs me that he'll be with you shortly. If you care to wait in the first floor's main conference room, Sir?"

Alex and the others waited quietly for a half hour before Harold hurried through the door.

"Apologies, Alex, friends, but let me announce my news before we begin. I've this very moment concluded successful negotiations to appoint a person to a new cabinet post, the Minister of Defense.

<I can't wait to hear what simpleton took this position,> Tatia complained to Alex.

<Put on a happy face, Tatia. We need to work with whoever has been appointed,> Alex replied.

Harold briefly touched his ear comm. "Hah, I'm pleased to present my new Minister of Defense," Harold said with a sweep of his arm, as Maria Gonzalez walked through the door.

"Into the dark together, my friends," Maria replied, a huge grin on her face.

"Yes," Tatia exclaimed, clapping her hands together and rushing to congratulate Maria.

After Tatia, Alex folded Maria in his arms, the two of them holding on to each other.

"And there's no better compliment than that," Maria whispered in Alex's ear, before she released him.

Julien hugged Maria, and then he turned to Harold, and said, "Mr. President, may I congratulate you on the wisdom of your choice?"

"I'm learning, Julien," Harold admitted.

Maria glanced at Alain, who stood near her. His head was bent and a hand on his heart. Across the room, Étienne held the same position.

Maria straightened and solemnly bowed. "Escorts, you honor me," she said, before lifting her head, pleased to see the grins on the crèche-mates' faces.

"Well, everyone, take a seat," Harold said, beaming. "I'm pleased to see you approve of my choice for the new ministerial post." He couldn't have been happier. From what appeared to be a politically unwinnable set of circumstances, he'd managed to solve multiple problems with a single solution.

"Alex, before we talk, I'd prefer to address the captains," Maria said. It wasn't necessary to ask Alex's permission to speak to her own people, but that was her style. For her efforts, she received a gracious nod from Alex.

"Captains," Maria said, and Alphons and Bart jumped to attention. "I have a question to address to each of you, regarding your fitness to serve."

"Yes, Minister," the captains chorused.

"I'm concerned about the difference between your views of the final events at FYM-552 and those of the Omnians, and, I should tell you, I trust their opinions far more than the two of yours. My question to each of you is this: Did you or didn't you do right by your crews? Fillister, I'll start with you."

"I saved my crew and ship, Minister Gonzalez, and I don't regret that. I don't understand why Admiral Tripping put us in that untenable situation. But, it made me realize one thing. While I love these ships, the Tridents, I'm not cut out to be a war captain."

"Admiral Tachenko, how would you rate Captain Fillister?"

"Superior," Tatia replied, staring quietly at Bart, who nodded his acceptance of the compliment.

"Hmm," replied Maria, taking time to consider Tatia's answer. Then her eyes speared Captain Jagielski.

It occurred to Alphons that the minister's civilian clothes were a disguise. Underneath them, she was entirely an ex-TSF general.

"Let's try the same question on you, Captain Jagielski," Maria said.

"Permission to speak plainly, Minister," Alphons replied.

"Among this group," Maria replied, sweeping her arm around the room, "that will always be the case."

"The appointment of Admiral Tripping was a terrible mistake. He wasn't qualified on a Trident, and he wasn't qualified to command a warship squadron. If I had the choice of serving under his kind again or jockeying a desk, please point out my admin chair."

"Well, Captain, I can set your mind at ease on that point," Harold interjected. "The Omnians have made it clear that, in the future, any of our naval officers who sail with them and are to hold a rank higher than captain must meet their approval."

"Most appropriate, Alex, Admiral," Alphons replied, and Bart tipped his head twice to add his approval.

"Continue, Captain Jagielski," Maria ordered.

"Do I regret not following Admiral Tripping? No, not really. I lament the loss of the New Terrans, many of them friends, who were aboard his ship. I keep wondering what I could have done differently."

"That's the terrible price of command, Captain," Maria replied. "If you had the opportunity to sail with the Omnians again, would you take it?"

Alphons looked hopefully at Tatia and Alex, but he couldn't read anything in their expressions, neither encouragement nor dismissal.

"If they allowed it, I'd serve," Alphons said firmly.

"And whose orders would you ultimately follow, Captain?" Maria asked.

"Those would be the orders of my squadron commander, as long as they didn't contradict the fleet's Omnian commander," Alphons replied.

Maria glanced at Alex, who said, "An acceptable answer."

"Captains," Maria said, "I have the authority to ignore the Board's recommendations that you be removed from command and given administrative positions. Those who haven't been in a fight have no idea what it takes to survive one. Captain Fillister, I appreciate your honest appraisal. How would you feel about training newly appointed Trident captains?"

"Could you be more specific, Minister?" Bart requested.

"At this time, we're turning a Trident out every three to four months. I need someone to bring new captains quickly up to speed on these ships and teach them basic squadron maneuvers in the Omnian style. That includes command methodology, SADE communications, ship controllers, and all."

"I'm your man, Minister," Bart exclaimed.

"I appreciate the offer, Captain, but you're a little young for me," Maria quipped, smiling.

Bart blushed and attempted to stammer a response, but Maria held up a hand to forestall him. "With what the Omnians are discovering, the future promises to be a hard road," Maria added. "Don't lose your sense of humor, Captain."

"Yes, Ma'am," Bart replied, returning Maria's smile.

"And, as for you, Captain Jagielski, I'm returning you to duty, as the captain of the *Arthur McMorris*. That ship, for its namesake, needs the best we have to offer."

"Thank you, Minister," Alphons replied, his shoulders straightening.

"Don't thank me yet, Captain," Maria replied. "You're going to be a busy man. You have two weeks to evaluate the group of potential captain appointees with Captain Fillister and send me your recommendations for the three available Tridents."

"Two weeks, yes, Ma'am," Alphons affirmed.

"When those captains are in place, you'll be promoted to senior captain, which the Omnians have already approved," Maria said.

Alphons looked across the table at Alex and Tatia. They were grinning now, and he couldn't help the smile that spread across his face.

"Now, mind what I say, Captains. Vet these people carefully. We're not looking for people who are good at sailing ships around the system and keeping their crews happy. We're looking for individuals who aren't afraid to join the fight that the Omnians tell us is coming. Understand me?"

"Yes, Minister," Alphons and Bart replied.

"Your orders will be in your readers this afternoon. One last item, Captains, New Terra's Trident defense force is a new entity that reports to me. It's separate from all existing naval operations. Dismissed," Maria said.

When the captains left the room, the leaders regarded one another.

"A long road," Tatia said, echoing Maria's words.

* * *

Alex asked Svetlana to apologize to the crew, but he needed some time with Maria Gonzalez, now that she'd been appointed Minister of Defense.

<Excellent decision. There's hope for New Terra yet, Alex,> Svetlana had sent in reply, when she heard the news.

Alex and Renée, along with others, were hosted at Maria's home.

"You can walk in the forest again, Renée," Maria said, when Alex and his people arrived. "That nest of biters is gone."

"Gone where?" Renée asked with concern.

"Permanently gone," Maria replied, laughing and throwing an arm around the slender Omnian, who she considered a daughter, as they walked into the house.

After an exceptional midday meal on which every human complimented Maria, she said, "Now, I know this group, with your capabilities, has detected Oliver in my house, but I have a surprise for you. Julien, would you request Oliver's presence?>

Oliver joined the group at the table, and Alex took note of where the SADE stood. It was close to Maria, perhaps a little protective of her.

"While Oliver and I worked together, we grew attached to each other. When his contract with our government ended, he was loath to return to the Confederation, and I was sorry to see him leave. So, we struck a bargain," Maria explained.

"I have this domicile," Oliver said, indicating the house with a wave of his arm, "a place from which to work and the company of a friend."

"Are you happy?" Alex asked, testing Oliver's progress.

There was the slightest of pauses before Oliver replied, "I am content, Ser."

"A good place to be," Julien commented.

"Oliver, my guests were raving about the food. I thought you would like to know," Maria said.

"You cooked the food, Oliver?" Renée asked.

"In a manner of speaking, Ser. Maria obtained a set of dispensers, food stocks, and recipes for me from Haraken. However, I've been experimenting with native materials and creating new recipes."

"Haraken-style dispensers have established a foothold in the food industry here," Maria explained. "But, what's propelling much of the new explosion is Oliver's recipe books. He's become extremely popular and is earning a substantial number of credits from sales," Maria said proudly.

"Is that what you want to be, Oliver, a chef?"

"It's an interesting pastime, Ser. However, my priorities will now shift to supporting the minister in her new duties. That's what will make me … more content," Oliver replied, directing his gaze toward Alex.

<Julien, commercial opportunity, the recipes, and food stock,> Alex sent.

<Negotiations are underway, Alex,> Julien replied. <I believe that Trixie would appreciate signing these contracts to support Omnia's development.>

<That makes me think, Julien. When these New Terran forces descend on Omnia —>

<We will need accommodations and supplies on planet, especially food recipes that remind them of home,> Julien finished for Alex.

<Well said, but you need to hand this off to someone else to manage, Julien.>

<Agreed,> Julien sent in reply.

* * *

Renée gazed at her hands. They were powerful. She held them away from her and saw her arms bulged with muscles. She was bewildered but not frightened. It was the familiarity of the limbs that prevented her fear, which might have awakened her from the dream. The realization intruded that what she was observing were Alex's arms and hands, and she chuckled. *I'm huge,* she thought.

There was no sense of place, which confused Renée. She swiveled her head and saw nothing but emptiness. *I'm floating in space,* she thought. Tiny distant lights appeared. The more she stared at them, the more she saw ... thousands, tens of thousands, hundreds of thousands ... the harder she looked, the more lights appeared.

In this enormous span of space, the lights blinked. They didn't blink as one, but individually. Each light pulsed with regularity but with an odd rhythm that didn't resemble the twinkling of a star. That's when Renée felt her body move, slowly at first, then faster and faster. She sped through the blackness, the lights streaming past her in a blur.

Then Renée abruptly stopped. There was no sense of deceleration. One moment, the distances between the blinking lights were crossed in mere ticks of time, as she zipped through the dark, and the next moment, she floated in place again, with no forward direction.

But something had changed. The tiny lights were to her left, right, above, below, and behind her. But they weren't in front of her. Everywhere that Renée looked, the lights continued their incessant beating, but forward of her was pure blackness, no lights, nothing. She felt a sense of foreboding, anticipating that in front of her was an abyss that endangered her or that it was the deep dark that had sought her out.

An intense desire for preservation intruded on Renée's subconscious, and she was shocked awake. Sitting up in bed, she gazed at Alex, whose eyes and limbs were twitching. Her anxiety subsided, replaced with sympathy. She realized her dream was that of her partner. It was a consequence of the frequent and intimate bonding of their implants.

Well, my love, if I must endure your dark dreams to enjoy what we have in bed, then it's well worth it, Renée thought. She reached over and gently shook Alex until he mumbled, "Are you okay?"

"I'm fine, my love, or I was until I shared your dream," Renée replied.

Alex groaned. "Apologies," he said.

Renée laughed softly and leaned over to kiss his cheek, letting her lips linger. "Well, if nothing else, my love, yours are so much more interesting than mine."

"Should I ask?" Alex inquired.

It fascinated both of them that Alex's implants didn't record what his subconscious created and Renée's didn't record what she received, even though the only way the dreams were transmitted was via an implant-to-implant connection. To add to the mystery, no one else received Alex's broadcasts, despite the intensity of some of his dreams.

"It was an odd one," Renée explained, sitting up. "I was you ... in your body, I mean."

"Massive weight gain," Alex mumbled.

"Hush," Renée replied, lightly thwacking his arm with her fingers. "I, we, were floating in space with stars all around us, except they weren't like regular stars."

"Why not?"

"Well, they didn't twinkle. They pulsed, with these strange rhythms."

"All in sync?"

"No, each light had its own rhythm."

"Hmm," Alex grunted.

"Then we started speeding past the lights."

"Lights or stars?" Alex asked.

"How do I know? It wasn't my dream," Renée replied, tartly.

"True. Go ahead."

"Anyway, we sped through the dark, the lights flashing past us. I got the feeling that we crossed a huge distance of space, and, then, all of a sudden, we came to a stop. And here's where it got strange."

"You're in my body, floating in space, and surrounded by oddly pulsing stars, and that isn't weird?" Alex asked.

"You'll pay later for interrupting my story, Ser," Renée warned.

"Apologies, my delectable partner, please continue," Alex replied in a conciliatory manner, while working to maintain a straight face.

"After speeding through the dark, we stopped, instantly stopped," Renée continued. "The lights were around much of us but not in front. It was like we were embedded in the middle of a vast wall. Beside and behind us were lights but in front of us, nothing. The universe was divided into lights and no lights. The dark that was ahead of me scared me so much that I woke up."

"Apologies, again, my love," Alex said, pulling Renée to him. He hated that he wasn't in control of this aspect of his implants, worse, that it impinged on Renée's sleep.

"Listen to me, Alex," Renée said, pushing away and taking Alex's face in her hands. "There was something different about this dream. Normally, they're a chaotic collection of imagery, which I can usually ignore, but this one was clear. Most important, it was coherent. It told a story."

Renée's eyes intently held Alex's. He might have dismissed her tale of the dream, except that she wasn't willing to take it so lightly.

"A regular or rhythmic pulsing," Alex repeated.

"Yes," Renée replied, pleased that Alex was focusing on the dream.

"And we came to a place where space was separated into pulsing and nonpulsing stars."

"Lights," Renée corrected, but it didn't appear that Alex heard her. She heard him groan, a deep, strong sound that was usually reserved for a self-deprecating moment when someone realizes his stupidity. Before Renée could ask, Alex grabbed her face with both hands and kissed her, deep and warm. He leapt out of bed and ran toward the bedroom's door. "Clothes, my love," Renée yelled out in time.

<Julien, front porch, if you please,> Alex sent, while he quickly dressed.

Julien politely ended his conversation with Oliver, sending, <Excuse me, Oliver, Alex requires some conversation.>

<At this hour?> Oliver asked.

<Something has disturbed his sleep,> Julien replied.

<I'm curious to learn more, Julien. May I join you?>

The request gave Julien a moment of pause. He didn't want to disturb the camaraderie of his late-night conversations with Alex, but he considered the request from his friend's perspective. Alex would be generous.

<We'll meet on the porch, Oliver,> Julien sent.

As Alex came through the front door, he saw both SADEs and glanced quickly at Julien.

<Oliver requested the opportunity to listen, Alex,> Julien sent privately.

"Welcome, Oliver," Alex said. "You may observe, but this conversation will take place solely between Julien and me, unless you're invited."

"Understood, Alex," Oliver replied. "Thank you for allowing me to witness the exchange."

"One other point, Oliver, this data is to be permanently secured. Only you may ever have access to it."

"Also understood, Ser," Oliver replied, setting the parameters on the data folder where the conversation would be stored.

Alex leaned back in a comfortable porch chair and stared out at the night. He'd always enjoyed the woods, the sights, the smells, and the animals. They were such a contrast to space, where he'd spent most of his life. When he was ready, he recited the dream sequence to Julien, as Renée related it to him.

Oliver was transfixed by the idea that Alex could dream, and Renée could receive the dream. This was an aspect of human implant exchange that he couldn't have imagined and that fascinated him.

"I find the aspect of rhythmic pulsing a key indicator," Julien said, when Alex finished.

"Me too. I'm thinking probes," Alex replied.

"That was my thought," Julien replied. "It seems your subconscious is indicating that we should map the probe signals that we've discovered over the star positions. Then, we could add the vectors of the spheres' travels. This plotting might indicate the path of the Nua'll expansion."

"There is the possibility that we come up with blank areas. In those areas, the probes might be too faint to read or were destroyed by natural accidents. Then again, maybe the Nua'll chose not to expand in those particular directions," Alex postulated.

"I would think those options would have limited probabilities, based on the data we've collected so far," Julien replied.

"Hmm, so you've not considered the idea that there are races out there that the Nua'll fear or a group of intelligent species who are cooperating and destroying probes, as they enter their territories. All these would be ancient races that would have been in conflict with the Nua'll before humankind walked upright."

Julien focused on Alex, while he reordered several indices, expanding the possibilities, as Alex had suggested. He had dwelt on the data surrounding the Nua'll, building schema about the species, their technology, their habits, and their probable actions. What he hadn't done was step back and imagine the universe that the Nua'll inhabited and postulate who else might be out there.

"My question, Julien, is: Do we have sufficient, sophisticated, and powerful enough telemetry capabilities in our warships to map that far out in front of us to detect the probes to the degree we've been discussing?"

"No, Alex, we would need the help of —"

"Willem," Alex and Julien said simultaneously, and laughed.

"But is he out and about aboard the *Sojourn*?" Alex asked.

"I will inquire into his location," Julien replied. "If he is journeying aboard the explorer ship, we can visit the observatory and inquire of the senior astronomer."

"Who has the post?" Alex asked.

"A SADE by the name of Jupiter."

"Jupiter, as in the name of the colorful planet orbiting Sol?"

"The same, Alex. When Theodosius discovered Trixie dropped her original ID of Lenora to adopt a new name, he decided to do likewise."

"Jupiter … good choice," Alex replied, grinning.

"Haraken first or Omnia, Alex?" Julien asked.

"The *Liberator*'s crew needs a rest. We'll head for Omnia and pick up —" Alex was halted in mid-sentence by Julien's head-on stare. He revised what he was going to say, which would have been to name the *Rêveur* and ended the sentence with, "a different Trident for the trip to Haraken."

Julien nodded his approval, and Alex stood up and yawned. He lightly tapped Julien on the shoulder, as he said, "Good night to both of you," and ambled off to bed.

Oliver was aching to ask questions of Julien, but the data parameters on the conversation restricted him from doing so. That the human had envisioned the existence of scenarios that suggested the Nua'll weren't the greatest threat to this portion of the galaxy made him realize how much he hadn't been open to greater possibilities. He too spent a considerable amount of time reordering his kernel, shifting hierarchy, rewriting algorithms, and calculating new probabilities. Oliver was determined to expand his thought processes to be the best assistant to the new Minister of Defense that he could possibly be.

-26-
The *Freedom*

Alex spent the following day in conference with Maria, discussing New Terra's warship construction progress, the number of ships that could be added to the Omnians' fleet, and many more details.

Oliver noted that Alex shared with Maria his intention to use the Haraken observation platform to review the extensive telemetry data collected during the past two decades. Alex appeared to be determined to see if the data yielded insight into the Nua'll probes placements and, by extension, the location of the race. Of note to the SADE was that Alex didn't share how he had come by the concept. It confirmed to Oliver that the information was reserved for the human's partner and his SADE friend, and Oliver felt privileged to possess the knowledge.

By late evening, the Omnians said their goodbyes to Maria and Oliver and returned to the *Liberator*. Tatia and Alain said farewell to her parents. Crew members kissed and hugged family and friends, as the ship's travelers scooped them up. In the morning's early hours, the third duty shift was sailing the Trident out of the system, headed for Omnia.

When the *Liberator* transited into Omnian space, there were palpable sighs of relief from the humans, starting with Tatia and continuing to the youngest crew member. It was a year since the warship had left Omnia in search of the Nua'll sphere. Although they hadn't fired a shot, the chase and final encounter were no less frightening.

The *Judgment*, Lucia Bellardo's Trident, had conducted star services for the two pilots lost at FYM-552, while Alex was at New Terra. With no remains to recover, small crystal cases were prepared, which enclosed their uniforms and personal items. Reiko had performed the remembrance ceremony and the cases were launched at Celus.

Omnian comm systems were overloaded with the exchange of communications between the *Liberator*'s crew and a host of other individuals. Julien and Cordelia occupied much of the *Liberator*'s extensive capabilities, and the SADEs frequently curtailed their exchanges to return more bandwidth to others in need.

Alex did receive a curious comm from Mickey.

<Congratulations, Alex, on your successful hunt of the second sphere,> Mickey sent via the *Freedom*'s comm. <Blew itself up, did it? Kind of tells us a lot about the Nua'll. But, I have to say, Alex, I had no idea I was being left behind for a year ... a whole year,> Mickey complained.

<Mickey, you wouldn't have enjoyed it,> Renée replied, joining the conversation, when Alex mouthed "Mickey" to her. The return to Omnia had given the couple some respite from the daily pressures, and they had been enjoying some peace and quiet in their cramped cabin. <For certain, Pia wouldn't have enjoyed the time, Mickey. This is a warship. Alex and I can hardly fit on this cabin's bed.>

<I'm happy to hear you say that, Renée,> Mickey replied, which caused the couple to frown at each other. <It's common knowledge that the forces our partner worlds are building are as much for offense as they are for defense, which means the combined fleet might be gone from Omnia, next time, for longer than a year.>

<And?> Alex prompted.

<Well, I've taken it upon myself to consider your and Renée's well-being, your creature comforts, so to speak. People such as you need space, a place to operate, a place to think, a place where —>

<Mickey, the point,> Alex prompted.

<I'm saying that you have all that aboard the *Freedom*,> Mickey replied.

<The city-ship can't protect itself, Mickey, and we can't devote six or eight Tridents to covering a ship that huge,> Alex argued.

<What if the ship could protect itself?> Mickey asked.

<What have you been doing, Mickey?> Renée asked, her question suffused with humor.

<I had the senior captain's permission,> Mickey said defensively. <Tell you what, Alex, this is better as a demonstration than a conversation. Here are the coordinates where, if you position the *Liberator*, I can show you.>

<Mickey, this crew needs downtime,> Alex replied.

<It won't take long, Alex, and I'd like the feedback of your senior officers.>

The mention of Tatia and Reiko had Alex considering that Mickey's idea wasn't cursory, so he agreed to give the engineer the time he requested.

Three days later, the *Liberator* was positioned where Mickey requested, and Alex and company were crowded around the warship's bridge holo-vid.

Mickey signaled Julien, and the SADE narrowed the warship's holo-vid view of the city-ship to a single bay.

"That's not an engineering bay," Alex commented, reviewing the enormous ship's plans in his implant, which he'd spooled from the Trident's controller.

"Indeed, not," Julien agreed.

<Ready?> Mickey sent.

<Proceed, Mickey,> Alex replied.

The holo-vid displayed the opening of one of the city-ship's pair of bay doors, and the group saw the focusing lenses of two beam weapons.

<These weapons are independently mounted. They have their own controllers and receive priority direction from the ship's controller, but they can target and fire without oversight, if necessary,> Mickey announced proudly.

<Okay, Mickey, give us the full presentation. I'll reserve my questions for now,> Alex replied.

<First, you and your fine commanders will want to know about the power. Isn't that right, Svetlana?> Mickey asked.

<You know me well, engineer,> Svetlana replied.

<Together, a pair of beams have 82 percent of the capacity of a Trident's twin outrigger hulls.>

<Wait, Mickey, I know I said I'd hold my questions, but how is that possible?> Alex asked.

<Oh, how foolish of me, Alex, I forgot to tell you about the new discovery created in our engineering lab. After all, you were gone for an entire year.>

The senior commanders chuckled at Mickey's characterization of being deserted by Alex.

<My congratulations on your new invention, Mickey,> Alex sent to mollify the engineer. <What was created?>

<When we designed these beauties to fit in a bay, Alex, the SADEs determined the power output was insufficient to provide protection in a battle scenario. Naturally, we had to design a more compact, power-crystal package.>

<You what?> Tatia interjected.

<Yes, Admiral, the specifications for the charge required —>

<Stop, Mickey, repeat in my language the part where you say your crystals are more compact,> Tatia sent.

<Admiral, our new, crystal-growth process compacts the layers, making them denser. It enables us to get about a 60 percent increase in power charge per kilo. They also charge a bit faster.>

<Black space, Mickey,> Alex muttered.

<Amazing isn't it, Alex? See, you need me and my team,> Mickey added, underlining his message about not being left behind again.

<Mickey, can these new crystals be retroactively installed in our Tridents?> Reiko asked.

<Assuredly, Commodore. Trixie has already created facilities to produce the new crystals. She's been turning some out for the squadron, and we can add this information to the agreements with the other worlds.>

<Back up, Mickey,> Alex said. <I need to understand the *who* behind these machinations.>

<Well, Alex, the discovery was made in the engineering lab with Edmas, Jodlyne, and a few SADEs. Every individual was employed by me. That makes the invention an Omnia Ships property,> Mickey sent.

<The facility to manufacture the new crystals and the subsequent production was done with my funds,> Cordelia sent. <If Omnia Ships decides to endorse this, you would need to reimburse me, Alex.>

<Consider yourself reimbursed, Captain Cordelia. Smart decision on your part. Where are we in the production cycle?> Alex asked.

<Ready to upgrade all Tridents, Alex,> Mickey sent in reply.

<Have your engineering team start with the *Redemption*, Mickey,> Alex ordered.

Tatia glanced at Alex, wondering about his choice of Ellie's ship.

<Well, now that we have the subject of crystals out of the way, let me continue with my demonstration,> Mickey sent, feeling in his element. <Jodlyne, if you would, please. Display our armament.>

The beam weapons slid from the bay on rails, extending their barrel lengths outside the ship. While the audience watched, the barrels moved independently, covering significant arcs, left, right, down, and up.

<Alex, with beam placements in every other bay on the ship's circumference, I can give the *Freedom* a 15-degree overlap along this central line. There is limited coverage directly above and below, but this isn't a sitting orbital station. The vessel can be underway, and Captain Cordelia can rotate the ship to allow coverage where needed, especially from something as large as a sphere or some bullet ships.>

<If my calculations are correct, Mickey,> Z sent, <in your scenario, you'll have the firepower equivalent of fourteen Tridents.>

<Close enough, Z,> Mickey replied, entirely enthused.

<Suddenly, my ship feels inadequate,> Svetlana sent, gazing at the twin beam weapons twisting in space in the holo-vid display.

<Alex,> Cordelia sent, <the concept of outfitting the *Freedom* with weapons was given a great deal of thought by humans and SADEs. You'll pardon my directness, Alex, but it's shortsighted of you to travel as a passenger on a warship. This applies to other critical individuals, whose safety should be paramount. Julien has shared with me your thoughts about whom we face, and it's obvious that alternate long-term considerations must be made.>

<I agree with Cordelia,> Tatia added. <Nothing personal, Alex, but I don't want the five of you on this ship,> she added, pointing to Alex, Renée, Julien, Z, and Miranda. <This is a warship, not a spectator platform.>

<And here I thought we were friends, dear,> Miranda said, pursing her lips in discontent.

<Stop it, you flirt,> Tatia laughed. <You know what I mean. I would dearly like the critical personnel off this flagship.>

<Careful, Admiral,> Alex said, <you might find yourself aboard the *Freedom*.>

<I would be content with that decision,> Alain sent privately to Tatia.

<Alex, the fleet will need supplies and possibly repairs,> Mickey added. <The Tridents aren't designed to carry what they need for an extended trip, especially if it involves one or more significant fights. The fleet lost a Trident and struggled to reacquire the spare travelers. Think of the tremendous number of empty bays available to us that encircle the *Freedom*.>

<I've heard all of you,> Alex said, ending the discussion. <Mickey, take care of the Tridents. Julien, update our partners with the data on the new crystals. Remind them that this technology is exclusive to the parameters we've laid out. Captain Cordelia, I'll review the engineering proposal for the *Freedom* with the senior commanders, and we'll have an answer for you soon. Mickey, thank you for an enlightening presentation,> Alex said, closing his comm.

Within hours, Alex convened a meeting aboard the *Freedom*. Crew had transferred Renée and his meager belongings from the *Liberator* to the couple's suite of rooms in the city-ship, and Renée was rejoicing. Her greatest gripe about the warship's tiny cabin was that Alex and she couldn't fit in the refresher at the same time.

Alex's eleven guests, Tatia, Reiko, Julien, Cordelia, Z, Miranda, and the five Trident captains, were scattered around the main salon, having been called to discuss the arming of the *Freedom* and whether the city-ship should accompany the fleet.

"Thoughts?" Alex asked, when the humans were comfortably settled with cups of thé.

"The longer the hunt for the second sphere lasted, the more the senior commanders and I discussed the concept of a long-range expedition, Alex," Tatia replied. "Mickey's absolutely right that the fleet needs ongoing support."

"It was a standard operating procedure for a fleet headed by a capital ship to be accompanied by freighters," Reiko said. "Unfortunately, we can't protect a group of freighters, not knowing what we'll be facing. But an armed city-ship could be an excellent support."

"Alex, consider extrapolating this discussion from supplying our five Tridents to those who will join us," Z said. "We might number fifty warships in our expeditionary force."

"We've been discussing supplies," Julien added, "but there is an argument to be made for ancillary personnel, not least of whom are the engineering team, who are proving to be indispensable."

"On that note, Alex," Cordelia said, "you might not be aware that Mickey employs 216 humans and SADEs, who work in three of this ship's bays. The list of projects that are underway are staggering. If we wish to have access to what they create, then they'll need to be near the fleet. In addition, they'll require supplies and raw material to continue their work."

"Dear man, I have a thought for your consideration," Miranda said. "What if we don't engage the Nua'll in a single, massive battle? What if this race, faced with an extensive display of military might and an enormous city-ship, chooses a protracted engagement or, perhaps, to negotiate? And consider this: These alternative actions will most probably take place an incredibly long distance from Omnia, our support base."

Renée, who had been keeping cups filled, poured one more for Alex, and sat beside him on the couch. "And here's my thought," she said. "We lost a ship and its crew due to the actions of one man. Through a conversation I had with Captain Jagielski at New Terra, I learned that he felt the admiral slowly became fixated on the idea that we, Omnians, were set on preventing him from achieving his goal of proving he could make a valuable contribution to New Terra's defense."

"That's interesting," Alex said, glancing toward Tatia, whose narrowed eyes indicated it was news to her.

"If we had the *Freedom*," Renée continued, "there'd be a place for officers and crew to relax. More important, our admiral would have the opportunity to have face-to-face time with her senior commanders. I'm sure that Tatia would have been able to detect Admiral Tripping's growing eccentricity."

Alex drained his cup of thé and regarded the group, who stared expectantly at him. The Trident captains had been silent, but he imagined Tatia and Reiko had expressed their opinions. The only key adviser who had said nothing was Julien. Alex lifted a single eyebrow in the SADE's direction.

<No matter the decision, Alex,> Julien sent, <it will create risk. Either we'll imperil the warships without support, or we'll endanger a city-ship full of noncombatants. However, one of these scenarios will assume a greater element of risk.>

<It's back to asking noncombatants to place themselves in harm's ways,> Alex sent in reply.

<And when have they ever failed to volunteer?> Julien riposted.

"It appears that you have a new project, Admiral," Alex said. "Have your senior people ensure that Mickey's efforts give the city-ship the most coverage possible. Mickey does elegant work, but I'm thinking robust is better."

"That's our preference too," Tatia replied.

"My crystal friends," Alex said, "you have your work cut out for you. Take note of Z's statements. What do five warships need in an extended period of engagement? What about twenty-five? Fifty? Cordelia, it's your ship. Handle the processes for recruitment and supplies, as we scale up."

"What's our timeline, Alex?" Cordelia asked.

"New Terra is close to sending two or three Tridents in another two months. Haraken should double or triple that number, in the same amount of time. They have the proper construction capabilities and the trained naval people. I don't know what to expect from the Confederation. They have the greater capacity to build ships, but they don't have a clue how to obtain trained personnel. My hope is that they sent their personnel to the Haraken naval academy.

"What about fighters and pilots for the *Freedom*, Alex?" Reiko asked. She twisted slightly in her seat and met Alex's stare.

"The arguments were clear and persuasive to turn the *Freedom* into an armed supply ship, Reiko," Alex said. "If we think of the city-ship in this manner, we'll probably fail all those aboard. As of this moment, you should think of the *Freedom* as a warship, and make your decisions on that basis."

"Understood, Alex," Reiko replied, nodding her head in agreement.

The group, except for Julien, Cordelia, and Tatia, who Alex invited to remain, exited the suite.

"Tatia, I need to send a clear message about the change in the *Freedom*'s status," Alex said.

"Agreed," Tatia replied. She stared thoughtfully at Cordelia, who peered back at her with interest.

Tatia imagined a new fleet organization. The massive city-ship would be on its own, often far from the squadrons and would require independent operational control. In addition, the vessel would be in charge of its own defenses. That would include Mickey's rail-capable beam weapons and a hefty squadron of travelers. The fighters would need their own wing commander, maybe even a group leader.

"I think Commodore Cordelia would be a good place to start," Tatia announced.

Cordelia glanced at Alex, who was smiling and replied, "Couldn't have said it better."

"Admiral," Cordelia said, snapping a salute at Tatia, who smiled and returned the honor.

"You might need to rethink the commodore's title, in the near future, Admiral," Alex said. "There's the question of what supply ships Haraken and the Confederation might send to accompany their warships. Our new commodore will need to have command over the support fleet."

"Agreed, Alex. If that happens, it'll be time to bump our new commodore again," Tatia replied.

Tatia shook hands with Cordelia. "Welcome aboard, Commodore," she said before leaving.

Renée hugged Cordelia and congratulated her, and Alex walked Julien and Cordelia to the suite's cabin door.

Cordelia halted in the doorway and turned to Alex. "From box to commodore in two decades. Thank you for freeing us," she said, pausing to gently kiss Alex's cheek.

* * *

Alex took the remainder of the day off, switching comm calls between Julien, Cordelia, and anyone else he considered appropriate to handle his queries. Later, Renée and he went to stroll in the ship's central garden, watch the fish in the ponds, and enjoy a couple of reality vids from Cordelia's display.

Long ago, Cordelia upgraded her reality vid suite to include bio ID recognition for key personnel. When Alex and Renée walked through the door, they weren't offered the menu from which to select a routine. Instead, lights dimmed, music played, and the couple was whisked away to a mysterious land of incredible landscapes and fantastical beasts that inhabited their scenery.

When the routine ended, Alex and Renée wandered out of the suite in a daze.

"That was incredible," Renée said, hanging on to Alex's arm for support.

"Didn't see that one coming," Alex said. "I think this calls for a drink."

Success, Cordelia thought, reviewing the cam vid taken at the suite's entrance, when she saw the couple's expressions. It had taken an extraordinary amount of computing time to research the concepts, configure the terrain, and design and animate the beasts. She had been determined to present Alex and Renée with an incredible memory. Unbeknownst to her, that vid routine would become one of the most popular pieces of entertainment for as long as the city-ship sailed.

Alex and Renée entered a small café on the other side of the grand park. They enjoyed a drink and decided to order a meal rather than join others for evening meal. After a night of entertainment and relaxation, the first thing Renée asked Alex to do, when they regained their suite, was to accompany her into the refresher. It was over an hour before they climbed out, exhausted and happy.

* * *

The following morning, Alex met with Olawale and Francis. Julien and Renée sat with Alex and listened with rapt attention to the story of their journey through Sol.

"An elected government with a constitution that they call the Idona Accord," Alex said, shaking his head in amazement, when the ex-Earthers finished their story.

"I loved hearing how well our friends, Patrice and Nikki, are doing," Renée added. "A colonel and a rim governor."

"Interesting details, concerning the probe," Julien commented.

"Esteban thought you might find the telemetry data fascinating," Francis said.

"It was the engineering team who believed the probe to be a later version than ours. In their opinions, design, maneuverability, and decision making pointed to a superior model," Olawale said.

"Let's put the probe and its destruction aside for a moment, Sers," Alex said. "I'm more interested in your summations about Sol."

"Astonishing changes," Francis commented. "I wouldn't have thought it possible."

"You clearly started a societal revolution, Alex. I think the greatest trigger was the economic turnaround of Idona Station," Olawale said.

"Not to mention that rebels and militia were working hand-in-hand with stationers," Francis added.

"Sorry to interrupt the conversation, Sers, but is the gemstone dedication still there at Idona?" Renée asked.

"I'm sorry to say, it isn't," Olawale said, his hand to his face, shielding his reaction.

"No?" Renée asked indignantly. "I loved that tribute."

Olawale unveiled his face, displaying a grin. "It was moved to Earth, Renée. It sits in the main rotunda of the building where the Assembly Representatives work and meet. According to Nikki, every representative must pass it on the way in or out of the building."

"You risk my wrath, Ser," Renée said, grinning, while pointing an accusing finger at Olawale.

"Protect me, my leader, from this vengeful woman," Olawale said, appealing to Alex and holding up his hands in terror.

"You're on your own there, Olawale," Alex said, laughing. "Back to business, Sers. What's your final opinion on Sol?"

Olawale and Francis glanced at each other in confusion.

"If you haven't guessed, Sers, Alex is requesting your decisions on whether Sol has achieved a level of democracy that warrants extending our technology to them," Julien said.

"If we don't help the Earthers and we lose to the Nua'll, Sol's present level of technology would doom them when the sphere arrived in system," Alex explained.

"What technology are you suggesting, Alex?" Olawale asked, with concern.

"Access to our medical nanites, crystal technology, comm probes, and traveler design without beam access. That sort of thing," Alex replied.

"But no weaponry?" Olawale asked.

"No, definitely not," Alex replied. "The technology I'm talking about will disrupt Sol's industrial base, much as it did New Terra's, when Méridien technology was introduced. But better to do it now, while the Earthers are rebuilding rather than later."

"I would concur with that," Julien added.

"Should I assume that you want us to go back, Alex?" Olawale asked.

"Unless you have something better to do," Alex said offhand.

"Who knew what I was getting myself into when my friends and I abandoned our explorer ship," Olawale said, chuckling.

"A fascinating life," Francis said, grinning at him. "I'm ready, Alex. How do we outfit this trip?"

"I'm thinking you'll need a Trident escort. I want the Sol government to have a vision of technology's future," Alex replied.

"Won't that infuriate them?" Olawale asked. "Seeing what's possible but not having access to it?"

"What do you think, Sers?" Alex asked. He waited while the two men exchanged thoughts. It took them a while before they came to a conclusion.

"No," Francis replied. "It will push them harder to employ their technology evenly across new industries and in support of their population. They'll want to impress you so that you extend the next level of technology to them."

"That was as Alex and I thought," Julien said.

"You already decided all this?" Olawale said, glancing from Julien to Alex and back.

Renée was laughing quietly, while Julien said, "It was one of our considerations."

"You'll need Edmas, Jodlyne, and Esteban," Alex mused. "They'll be familiar individuals, and you'll need SADEs, engineers, techs, and supplies. Julien will provide Esteban and the SADEs with a list of allowed items. The *Rêveur* and Trident's controllers will contain the design specifications and manuals that the Earthers will need."

"What?" Francis asked, noticing Julien was grinning.

"We'll be breaking out the GEN machines, once again," Julien explained.

"The what?" Olawale asked.

Renée delivered a fresh cup of thé to Francis and took a stance behind Julien's chair, placing her hands on his shoulders. "What seems like a lifetime ago," she said, "Julien and I made the momentous decision to lift up New Terra's technology in order for them to manufacture the material necessary to repair the *Rêveur*, which was damaged by the attack of a dark traveler. From his box on the bridge, Julien communicated with engineers on planet to build a series of machines, with three increasingly complex levels. The final stage was able to produce many of the items we needed. They were dubbed the GEN machines, and Alex and I have carried sets of them around with us ever since."

"You never know when they might come in handy," Alex added.

"Ellie's ship has been upgraded with the new crystals, Alex," Tatia said, during an evening meal. "Any reason that you're selecting her Trident?"

"A couple," Alex replied, attacking a fresh serving dish with gusto.

"Would you care to be less enigmatic?" Tatia asked, reaching for a handful of rolls.

"Yumi Tanaka, for one. She can visit with her parents, while I'm there," Alex replied.

"Any others?" Tatia asked, pausing to catch Alex's eyes.

"An evaluation," Alex replied.

Tatia regarded Alex a moment longer and resumed consuming her meal. She ruminated on the sort of evaluation that Alex might be considering. It wouldn't be testing Ellie's capabilities as a Trident captain. She was outstanding, in that regard. It occurred to her that Alex had the same concerns she did. If a fleet, many times the size of their squadron, was formed, Tatia would want to assign groups of the new warships to operate under her Trident captains.

Those thoughts brought up the question of what officer levels would accompany the new warships. Only New Terra had been told that Tatia must approve their senior commanders. And, in that regard, she wouldn't worry about Haraken, who would put their captains through a rigorous selection process before they were elevated. However, the Confederation's senior officers would be question marks.

"I'll be interested to hear your evaluation, when you return," Tatia said, mopping up a serving dish with the remains of a roll.

While Alex finished his meal, he signaled Ellie to prepare the *Redemption* for launch to Haraken the following morning. <Have crew

pick up our baggage at 20 hours, this evening, Captain,> he sent. <We'll transfer aboard in the morning.>

The next morning, Alex wasted no time boarding the warship with Renée and Julien. Alex had ordered the twins to remain behind, so they could spend time with their partners. "We're headed for Haraken," Alex told them, "not the deep dark."

When the three Omnians walked through the *Redemption*'s corridors, they found it alive with the hustle and bustle of crew. Alex had mentioned to Ellie that a full crew wouldn't be necessary. Obviously, she had ignored his suggestion, or her senior commander had. Nonetheless, he decided to keep his thoughts to himself.

"The captain's on the bridge, Ser," a New Terran-built lieutenant said to Alex, as he led them forward once they attained the main deck. "You have the ship's guest quarters. Your baggage is already there."

Each Trident had a more-than-comfortable suite, designed to accommodate a squadron's commodore or visiting admiral. The rooms weren't as expansive as the couple's suite aboard the *Freedom*, but they were luxurious compared to the small cabin they had inhabited for nearly a year on the *Liberator*.

Once Alex and Renée were shown to their cabin, the lieutenant asked Julien, "We have a choice of accommodations for you to consider, Ser. I can show them to you now, if you wish."

"Don't worry about me, Lieutenant," Julien replied. "I can always find a closet or supply room, if I need some privacy."

When the youthful lieutenant's mouth hung open for several moments, Julien took pity on him, patting his shoulder, and saying, "I'll be fine, Lieutenant. I don't tend to sleep much."

The lieutenant exited in a bewildered state, and Renée said to him, "Julien, you're incorrigible. That young man doesn't know whether you're teasing or not."

"I thought to give him an interesting story to tell his crewmates. Somewhere along the line, someone will disabuse him of the notion that I sleep in a closet."

Alex raised an eyebrow at Julien, making a note to talk to him later. His friend was usually gracious and understanding with humans.

The flight to Haraken was uneventful, and, as the warship transited into Hellébore space, Julien issued several messages.

"I'm sorry to say, Alex and Renée, the *Sojourn* is on assignment, and Teague and Ginny are aboard."

"Oh, I'm disappointed that we'll miss them," Renée said.

"President Lechaux is looking forward to your landing, Alex, and will clear her schedule for an extended meeting, if you so desire," Julien added. "On another note, there's a new orbital station dedicated to ship construction. It sits outward of Haraken, short of the inner belt.

"Size?" Alex asked.

"The configuration indicates three large bays and two small ones."

"Recently built to fulfill the agreement," Alex postulated.

"Undoubtedly," Julien agreed.

"Tridents in the system?" Alex asked.

"Underway," Julien replied, indicating he was tallying the Tridents, while reviewing the telemetry data on all ships in the Hellébore system. "Nine in system, Alex, and possibly more under construction."

"Nine," Alex echoed in surprise. "That's a good thing," he added, but he didn't sound enthused.

"A more robust economy and greater population," Julien commented.

"Alex, Omnia started from scratch," Renée said, intuiting the reason for Alex's reaction. "And the Dischnya weren't much help constructing our platform."

Alex chuckled lightly, his mind conjuring an image of Dischnya warriors in environment suits, assembling the station's girders in place.

Three days later, Alex's traveler set down in front of the home that the Swei Swee had built for Renée and him many years ago. Its blue, green, and white luminescent walls appeared as if they were laid yesterday.

"I never thought I would miss those colors," Renée said, as Alex's father, mother, and sister charged out of the house.

After hugs and kisses all around, the group moved into the house.

"Where are Julien and Cordelia's children?" Renée asked.

"At university, all of them," Katie said, laughing. "They live on campus. It saves them commuting time."

"Look what you miss, you three, while you're out saving our worlds," Christie said glibly. She meant it as a tease, but instantly saw that her jibe had struck at the emotions of the threesome. "I'm sorry. That was a terrible thing to say. I'm jealous of the exciting lives you're leading."

"Christie, those exciting lives you think we're leading have periods of pure terror, which sometimes fall to levels of quiet desperation," Renée replied quietly.

"Yes, well, Alex," Duggan said, attempting to change the subject, "tell us which of the reports we've received are true. The only common theme is that you located and destroyed a second sphere."

"Which goes to show you that you often can't believe what you hear," Alex replied.

"We cornered the sphere, Duggan, and it blew itself up and took one of the New Terran Tridents with it," Renée said.

The family members murmured their surprise. The thought of the Nua'll sacrificing themselves and their monstrous sphere rather than being captured seemed unnatural.

"So why are you here, Alex, and for how long?" Katie said, with interest.

"Researching a theory," Alex replied.

"Alex shares his dreams with me," Renée explained, which had the family members' mouths dropping open. "It's true," she added, shrugging her shoulders, as if to excuse the oddity. "Anyway, he dreamed of a strange division of lights and no lights in space, and I sent him to Julien."

"Alex shared his dream, or rather he shared Renée's report of his dream with me," Julien continued, picking up the narrative. "We believe that he's struck upon an idea of how to pinpoint where the Nua'll territory might begin. We're here to check on his concept via the observatory's accumulated telemetry data."

"Is it my imagination," Christie asked her parents, "or has my usually less-than-voluble brother become more taciturn lately?"

"Hush, Christie," Duggan said, eyeing his son. "What aren't you telling us, Alex?"

Alex stared at his father. Somewhere in the intervening years, after he'd left the Oistos system, he'd become his father's keeper, along with the rest of humankind, without realizing it. It made him feel much older than his years.

Duggan glanced at Julien and then Renée, who ducked her head.

"Oh, black space," Duggan whispered, worried about the reason his son was reticent to speak.

"This isn't about a single sphere, is it?" Christie asked. "Something about the probes has frightened all of you."

"We're finding them in every system, operational or not, Sers," Julien explained. "One was destroyed by our people at Sol."

"You sent a ship to Sol?" Katie asked.

"Olawale and Francis returned with Edmas, Jodlyne, and Esteban, their SADE partner," Renée explained. "And they were pleased to report there's been an incredible burgeoning of democracy that replaced United Earth."

"A probe in every system," Duggan murmured, dropping his head to think. "That takes a long time. It takes a commitment to the future, which means an ancient civilization," Duggan said, looking up at his son.

Alex met his father's eyes and sadly nodded in agreement.

Katie and Christie gripped each other's hand.

"That's what all the new contracts are about," Christie said. "We know Haraken has signed a deal with Omnia. Word is, so has New Terra."

"And the Confederation of all places," Renée added, shaking her head at the incredulity of it.

"One correction, Christie," Julien interjected. "These agreements aren't with Omnia. They're with Omnia Ships."

"That's you, isn't it, Alex?" Katie asked.

"Yes," Alex admitted.

"All these warships from every local human world will be under your control?" Duggan asked.

"Indirectly," Alex replied, "but the fighting, if it comes to that, will fall to the senior naval commanders."

"But where they go and whether or not they fight will be your decision," Duggan pursued.

Alex nodded, and Duggan looked at his son with sympathy. When Alex was young, Duggan imagined a future for his son punctuated with successes, a family, and, most of all, peace. He never envisioned and never would have wished for one that saw his son carrying such incredible responsibilities on his shoulders.

Silence descended on the family group until Katie jumped up and said, "Well, I think thé and a small repast is in order." While the humans ate, the conversation turned to small talk about the children, their studies, and Christie's career.

Alex and Renée turned in early for their morning meeting with Terese. Duggan, Katie, and Christie took the opportunity to learn the details of the past year from Julien. His stories became the stuff of their nightmares, when they slept.

After midnight, Julien left the house and walked to the family's gazebo. He stood looking over the ocean waves racing toward the beach below. Their white crests were highlighted by Haraken's moons. From his kernel, he spooled memories of the family's time on Haraken. He relived his emergence into an avatar, his growing liaison with Cordelia, the encounters with the Earthers, the adoption of the Idona orphans, the birth of Teague, and many more. He smiled at the pleasant depth of memories that had been accumulated in a few short years compared to his age.

But, Julien's smile was soon lost. The future looked dark to him. There was an ancient and powerful race allied against humans and SADEs, who appeared as youngsters to the entities they faced. *Are we capable of being clever enough, my friend?* Julien thought, addressing Alex. *I believe the Nua'll won't allow us a single misstep.*

In the morning, the parents and sister awoke to find Alex, Renée, and Julien gone, their traveler having silently arrived and departed not long after dawn. Alex had risen early, made his way down to the beach, and spoken with the new First. He had a polite and extended conversation with the Swei Swee leader, but, when Alex left, he felt unsatisfied. His friend, who had fought with him at Libre and convinced the hives to transfer to Haraken, was gone.

"I wanted to apologize to everyone, again, for my foolish comment," Christie lamented to her mother and father over morning meal.

"They know you didn't mean it," Katie said, patting her daughter's hand.

"They're scared," Duggan said, staring into his large mug of thé, "and that should terrify every human and SADE."

"Then we'll just have to hope that the spirit of Alexander continues to ride with our son," Katie said, trying to lift everyone's mood.

"I think Alex will be better served by the likes of Julien, Z, Miranda, his senior commanders, the rest of the SADEs, and the thousands who believe in what he's trying to do," Christie said fervently.

"I'll echo that," Duggan replied.

* * *

The *Liberator*'s traveler dropped swiftly onto the manicured front landscape of the naval academy's administration building, disgorging its passengers, before lifting quickly to return to the warship.

President Terese and Admiral Sheila Reynard came down the steps of the building to greet them. It was a warm reunion for old friends. Alex and Renée joked with the two Haraken women about the elevated positions they presently occupied.

"I think I preferred the medical profession," Terese quipped.

"You're working at saving lives, Terese," Alex teased. "It's just in a wholesale manner, rather than one at a time."

"Don't listen to Terese," Sheila said. "She loves being in charge. Always wanted to be the one giving orders."

"That's the way I remember it," Alex agreed.

"Enough about me," Terese said. "Inside, everyone, where it's cooler."

"Julien counts nine Tridents," Alex said, as they walked.

"Accurate, as usual," Sheila said, hooking her arm into Julien's. "And three are under construction."

"When do you think you'll need your share, Alex?" Terese asked.

"I'll have to tell you later, Terese. We have some research to conduct," Alex replied. "How is the Méridien training proceeding?"

"What Méridien training?" Sheila asked, as the doors of the admin building slid aside, and the blast of cool air hit them. "The Council's envoy arrived and announced they were constructing new facilities and could we send them the plans to copy our academy. Furthermore, they wanted some top administrators and trainers."

Alex stopped dead in his tracks.

"Alex, we gave them everything they needed, and that's the last we heard from them. That was about a year ago," Sheila said, lifting her hands palm up, as if to ask what else could she do.

Alex stared at Julien, and the three women could imagine the fierce exchange between the blood and crystal brothers.

"Where is the Confederation's naval academy?" Alex asked.

"According to our SADEs, it's at Bellamonde," Terese replied.

"Orbital platforms, which are producing their Tridents, are also there," Julien added, a moment later.

The group adjourned to a comfortable, private room reserved for senior commanders, and the Omnians updated the Harakens on the events of the past year — all of them.

When Alex finished, he regarded Sheila, "What do you see as your role in the upcoming expedition, Sheila?"

"To my regret, Alex, I've been directed to remain at Haraken. Depending on the number of Tridents we're able to send your way, there will probably be a commodore or two."

"Anyone we know?" Alex asked.

"Edouard Manet and Miko Tanaka are shortlisted with three others," Sheila replied, and Alex placed a hand over his eyes, a small groan escaping his lips.

"That's the way of it, Alex," Terese said, with her usual firm, bedside manner. "If the danger is as great as you surmise, we'll need our best on this expedition."

"There's always the possibility of negotiations," Sheila said encouragingly, looking at Julien.

"Learning a new alien language sounds intriguing, Admiral, until you realize that the only reason your enemies are coming to the negotiation table is that they want to take you with them when they detonate," Julien replied, a sour expression twisting his lips.

"If Edouard and Miko have the commodore positions, does this mean you plan to retire the *No Retreat* and the *Last Stand*?" Alex asked.

"Unless you can use the carriers in your expedition, Alex," Sheila replied. "They're obsolete. They've served their purpose."

"Let me think on that," Alex said. "How much would you want for them?"

Terese laughed. "Thinking of one-credit deals, are you, Alex?"

"It's a good price, but I can afford more now," Alex replied. "They might have a better use than sitting idle somewhere in your system. By the way, I understand the *Sojourn* is out on an exploration of its own."

"Yes, sorry you missed them, Alex," Terese said.

"They due back soon?" Alex asked.

"They should be entering their target system in a few days. Why?" Sheila asked, with rising concern.

"You might want to load a sting ship with a banisher from our Trident. Odds are there will be a probe in that system, and you don't want it reporting on your explorer ship's investigations, which it inevitably will do."

A small gasp escaped Renée's lips, and Terese's pale skin turned even whiter. Sheila stood up and turned away to focus on her implant, issuing the orders that would send a sting ship, with a knowledgeable SADE and an Omnian banisher, on its way.

The group continued to talk through the morning, a midday meal, and into half of the afternoon before they exhausted the exchange of critical information. At which time, Alex ordered their traveler. It was a quick goodbye on the steps of the admin building, and the Omnians were away, headed toward the observation orbital platform.

"Why do I think that each time I see that threesome that it might be the last time?" Terese lamented, watching the traveler lift.

Sheila glanced at her friend. Hellébore's light shone through Terese's red hair, amplifying its fiery nature. "Because every time it has a good chance of being true," Sheila said, and the two women stared at each other, hoping against the odds that it wouldn't come true this time.

* * *

Alex, Renée, and Julien exited the traveler in the observation platform's bay. The orbital station was built to conduct a search for new home planets for the Harakens. Its first director was the SADE, Willem, who now co-commanded the explorer ship, *Sojourn*, with Captain Asu Azasdau.

A SADE met the threesome, as they exited the airlock. He had midnight-black skin, littered with tiny colored dots, ranging from blue white to yellow to red. His synth-skin resembled the nighttime stars against the deep dark. Jupiter was a SADE who had plied the depths of space for more than century, guiding a freighter. It was his love of space that had kept him sane.

The freighter's captains were a succession of individuals, who rarely communicated with Jupiter. But that was fine with him. He had little time for humans. His fascination with the origination and transformation of stars and galaxies through the eons claimed his every free moment. Jupiter spent his enormous capabilities collecting every scrap of information he could locate on the evolution of stars, their deaths, and the creation of new systems through accretion.

Several times throughout the decades, Jupiter requested upgrades to his memory crystal. He was fortunate that his captains failed to ask the reason for the requests and simply approved them. With each increase, he was able to delve into more and more of the intricacies of the movement of galaxies and the interplay of gravitational forces, including those that affected a system's celestial bodies.

"Alex, Renée, Julien, I'm honored. I'm called Jupiter," the SADE announced, giving the Omnians a Méridien Leader's salute, dipping his head, and placing a hand on his chest where a human heart would beat.

The threesome dipped their heads in acceptance. Each of them had received Jupiter's original ID, which was Theodosius.

<Good name change,> Renée sent to Alex and Julien.

Alex described to Jupiter in detail the type of search he required, and the SADE stood politely, recording every word.

"How long will it take you to prepare your equipment and scan for what I'm requesting?" Alex asked.

"Ser, we've collected telemetry data for two decades," Jupiter explained. "Every increment of that data has been stored in this observatory's crystal banks. As we updated the scanning equipment with improved sensitivity and strength, we expanded the data storage to accommodate the greater volume of information we were accumulating. With respect, Ser, we possess all the data you require. It only requires that I program a query to search for the particular signal that Julien has just passed me, and I will have your answer. May I show you?"

"Yes, please, Jupiter. On the holo-vid, if you would?" Alex requested, and Julien and he grinned at each other.

The Omnians turned to observe the enormous holo-vid that Jupiter initiated. The SADE's eyes briefly fluttered with the extent of the data flooding from the memory banks through his kernel, even though the query had reduced the stored data by orders of magnitude.

The holo-vid lit with a massive number of dots of light.

"These are your probes, Ser," Jupiter announced. "I'm highlighting only the star systems that contain one of these alien devices."

"If you won't say it, Alex, I will," Renée whispered. "Black space."

"I must admit, Ser, under few circumstances would I have postulated that number," Jupiter said, staring at the display.

Julien augmented the holo-vid with bright dots of yellow light. "The worlds of Haraken, Omnia, and New Terra," he said. Next, he inserted a red point, adding, "Ollassa."

Finally, Julien drew a simple blue line and then a much more complex one. "Alex, the straight line is the approach path of the first sphere toward the Confederation system. The multi-jointed line represents the path along which we chased the second sphere."

"Fortune favored you, Sers, that you survived the insidious nature of your foe," Jupiter said.

Alex knew the SADE would have the truth of what happened at the final system, where the second sphere was cornered.

"Kind of you to say, Jupiter," Alex replied, laying a firm hand on the SADE's shoulder.

Julien's added touches allowed Alex to orient himself within the display. He stepped close to the holo-vid, recalling Renée's story of his dream, and eyed the short, blue line. The first sphere had arrived in the Hellébore system to scour Haraken, when it was known as the Cetus colony. Alex reversed the course and flew through the display.

Jupiter watched Alex drive past thousands of stars, where the probes lurked. His data query had retrieved them based on their unique broadcast signal. The probe-laced stars whirled past in a dizzying display, too fast for most humans to comprehend or measure, but the SADEs were tracking the distance that Alex traveled.

Suddenly, the lights winked out, and Alex reversed his course until he positioned the view where the final display of lights was found. "The wall," Alex marveled.

"That's an enormous wall, Alex," Julien said. His kernel was involved in analyzing the width and breadth of the space that the data displayed.

"Jupiter, what are these faint points of light?" Alex asked, peering closely at the display. The ones he highlighted in the display were found in the dark area, where they stood out. "Is the data displaying probes, and, if so, why are they so faint?"

"One moment, Alex," Jupiter replied. The SADE entered a fugue state, while he searched the data points for more detailed telemetry.

"Alex, I can tell you that these curious data points are found in the dark and the light areas. Those in the bright area aren't easily observable for human eyes among the points of light. However, to your question, my original query displayed data points that matched Julien's parameters within 95 percent accuracy. The items that you're indicating are near matches, which fall outside that accuracy. They were included because of relevance."

"Jupiter, what's the breakdown of the numbers of these nearly relevant points between the two areas?" Alex asked.

"I can confirm twenty-three within the area dominated by the probes, and another thirteen probable in the dark area, Ser."

Alex looked at Julien for his thoughts. The SADE replied, "The probes have a singular broadcast frequency or process, and these others are another form of communication similar to the probes."

"Spheres?" Alex asked.

"Possibly," Julien replied.

"Julien, share with Jupiter the signal from the Libran sphere."

"What have I received?" Jupiter asked Julien, since the SADE couldn't interpret the data.

"This is the first sphere's broadcast signal sent before it detonated," Julien replied. "We've been unable to decipher it or even separate the encoded data from the type of carrier signal. Do not attempt to break it down. Allow a root comparison to the telemetry data collected."

Jupiter ran a comparison exclusively against the thirty-six, anomalous, data points that the query had produced.

"Julien's broadcast signal is a 98 percent match, Ser, to all thirty-six points," Jupiter replied.

Alex slapped his hands together, creating a great boom, and he hugged a surprised Jupiter.

"Excellent work," Julien said, by way of explaining Alex's reaction.

"Might I inquire precisely what I've displayed that has you so elated, Ser?" Jupiter asked. "I request this because it would seem to me that we've potentially identified the location of the Nua'll civilization, and, if the vast area of space where no probe signals exist is any indication, it's enormous. In addition, I appear to have identified for you a significant number of the aliens' spheres both within the Nua'll territory and without."

"To quote Admiral Tachenko," Alex replied grinning, "when you begin to know your opponent is when you begin to defeat them."

<I presume you have these data points and the telemetry details, Julien,> Alex sent.

<You think too much of my capabilities, Alex. There is more data here than three times my entire memory crystal capacity. I've directed the information to the *Liberator*'s memory banks. The upload will be completed soon,> Julien sent in reply.

"Jupiter, you've been invaluable. I'll inform President Terese and Willem of your much-appreciated assistance," Alex said, shaking the SADE's hand.

"I don't believe I've done anything that any other SADE couldn't have done for you on this platform, Alex, but if you're feeling generous, I would ask a favor," Jupiter replied.

"Ask away," Alex replied.

"A second explorer ship is undergoing its trials. I would like to be considered the SADE to co-command it on its maiden voyage."

"I'll pass along your request, Jupiter, and I wish you good fortune," Alex said.

Jupiter beamed — literally. Light glowed from underneath his synth-skin, and it passed through the tiny dots in his midnight skin, making the stars shine.

Mock Fight

Yumi Tanaka enjoyed a full day with her parents, but Edouard and Miko were anxious to talk to Ellie. The parents asked Ellie to join them for dinner on the second evening. The Haraken captains wanted the latest updates from her, regarding the chase and cornering of the sphere. In addition, they were interested in spending some precious hours with an old friend, someone who had been part of Alex's workings since he arrived at the Libran colony.

For her part, Ellie was enjoying the dinner and company. Compared to the frugal quarters aboard a Trident, she was dining in a carrier's salon that was luxuriously appointed.

"What do you think are your chances for the commodore positions?" Ellie asked Miko and Edouard.

"Probably excellent," Miko replied. "We have pull with the admiral."

Ellie laughed at the characterization of a fellow Dagger pilot, who had risen through the ranks with them. Her laughter died, when she caught Yumi's wince, and Ellie glanced at Edouard.

"Our daughter believes that she should be the only one of the family to endanger her life," Edouard commented, leaning over to kiss Yumi's temple. "Parents should stay out of harm's way."

Yumi scowled but made no comment.

"It's normal to want to protect our loved ones," Ellie said, to ease Yumi's discomfort, "especially when they insist on doing a job they're qualified to handle."

The family knew Ellie was referring to her partner, Étienne, who protected Alex and Renée. There was often no more dangerous place to be than standing next to Alex Racine.

"But what about your carriers?" Yumi asked plaintively.

"They're outmoded, daughter," Edouard replied. "If we continue to act as their captains, we'll be passed over for promotion. This is our opportunity, and we must take it. We have long lives yet to be enjoyed."

"Yumi, we could be building these forces for no reason. The Nua'll might face us and decide to negotiate," Miko said. She looked at Ellie for support on this point, but Ellie returned her plea with a stoic expression.

Edouard was about to ask Ellie if she would like another drink, but the Trident captain held up a hand to signal an incoming comm.

"We have to cut our gathering short," Ellie said to Edouard, Miko, and Yumi. "Alex is requesting we launch soonest."

"Where are you headed?" Edouard asked.

"Presumably, we're returning to Haraken," Ellie replied.

"Has Alex said so?" Miko asked.

"No, which is why I'm waiting for confirmation," Ellie replied. "We came here to investigate something that Alex seems to be chasing. What, I'm not sure, but he visited the observatory platform this evening."

Edouard and Miko exchanged glances, wondering what the future held for them and their daughter if Alex was on the hunt, once again.

Ellie sent a recall to the crew via the *Liberator*'s controller. She ordered her traveler pilots to collect them from the planet and the local stations, as quickly as possible. Ellie and Yumi had dined aboard the *Last Stand*, which enabled them to get a lift from a carrier traveler to return to their warship.

Hours later, Ellie announced to Alex that they were ready to depart. It was the early morning hours, but Alex and Julien had joined Ellie and Yumi on the bridge until the third watch, who was standing by, began the remainder of their shift.

"Where to, Alex?" Ellie asked, assuming nothing.

"Bellamonde, Captain."

Yumi glanced questioningly at Ellie, who ignored her, saying, "Report our exit from orbit, pilot, and thread us through traffic. When you're clear, take a course for an efficient exit from Hellébore in Bellamonde's direction and have the controller calculate our transit. After that you can retire."

While Yumi worked, Ellie said to Alex, "I hear that they might abandon the carriers."

"Heard that too," Alex replied. "I'm trying to figure out if we can use them to support the *Freedom* and any freighters the other worlds supply."

"Alex, even if we can't use the carriers, they're carrying a tremendous number of travelers."

"Black space, how could I have missed that?" Alex said with heat.

Ellie chuckled at the intensity of Alex's statement. "Could be you've had a little too much on your mind lately. I don't know ... like the Nua'll."

Alex glanced at Julien, who protested, "Just because I have a fabulous processing ability and an enormous data repository doesn't mean that I haven't been preoccupied either."

"Good suggestion, Captain," Alex replied, appending a note about the travelers to the one concerning the carriers that was stored in his ever-full implants. "President Terese and I might strike a deal to have Haraken lend us the fighters to house in the Freedom's spare bays, or we could purchase the travelers outright. Come to think of it, neither of those ideas would do us any good without the pilots. Let me think on that."

Alex eyed Julien, and the SADE replied, "I have managed to make a note of the need for that discussion in case your human implants fail to remind you."

Alex laughed and wished everyone a good night.

* * *

"The OS *Liberator* has entered the Bellamonde system, Ser," the captain of the House liner said to Katrina Pasko.

Katrina glanced with concern at her partner, Gino Diamanté.

"Captain, can you determine the principals who might be aboard?" Gino asked.

"Negative, Council Leader. As I understand warship protocols, the Omnian Trident won't allow an open comm with its ship's controller. I can request the names of the principals from the controller, but it will be the prerogative of the captain to grant my request. Is there a difficulty, Ser?" the captain asked.

"You're new aboard, Captain," Katrina said, "but I'll remind you that this liner is the *Resplendent*, which once housed the SADE Allora."

"And I can think of only one reason an Omnian warship has entered the Bellamonde system," Gino added.

"Alex Racine has come to inspect our efforts," the captain supplied.

"Precisely, Captain," Gino replied.

At that same moment, Julien was updating Alex, Renée, and Ellie. "Telemetry indicates the Méridien footprint on Bellamonde is minimal."

"Has the planet recovered enough to start a new colony?" Renée asked.

"It doesn't appear to be a colony, as yet, Ser," Julien replied. "The only evident constructions on planet are the naval academy and its support facilities," Julien replied. "Also, I detect three orbital stations around Bellamonde. None of them appear as sophisticated, passenger-transfer platforms. They're dedicated to ship construction."

"Captain, we've been pinged by twenty-seven Confederation Tridents requesting more data than our ship ID," Yumi said.

Ellie waited for Alex's permission to respond, but he was staring into space, and Yumi glanced from her captain to Alex, wishing to understand the reason for the delay.

"Julien, ship positions," Alex requested.

The holo-vid sprang to life. "Blue dot, us; red dot, Bellamonde; yellow dots, enemy Tridents," Julien said, smiling, anticipating Alex's idea.

"Vectors on the enemy ships, Captain," Alex requested, eliciting a predatory grin from Ellie.

Yumi, who was not on board with the concept, nonetheless, dutifully added trajectory lines to the Confederation warships.

"If we make straight for Bellamonde, Alex, we'll pass behind these three Tridents within 13.8 hours," Ellie said, adding a translucent sphere around them.

"Perfect, Captain. I'll leave you and your pilot to design your sneak attack. When you have a shot lined up on any one of the warships, you're to ping them with a message that indicates you've fired. Understood?"

"What are my rules of engagement, Captain?" Yumi asked, fascinated how quickly Julien and Ellie had caught on to Alex's idea.

Ellie looked at Alex, who said, "Lieutenant Tanaka, you're to attack, create havoc, and score hits, but you're to survive the encounter. Captain, warn me before you attack."

"Understood, Ser," Ellie replied, straightening her stance.

When Alex and Julien left the bridge, Yumi said to Ellie, "It appears we're testing the Méridiens' training. This should be interesting."

No, my young pilot, Ellie thought, *Alex's testing the Méridiens and us.*

* * *

Senior Captain Descartes was whiling away the time, indulging in one of his favorite pastimes, calculating potential conflicts and the strategies to win them. To his delight, this afternoon had handed him a perfect opportunity to test his designs and his squadron's readiness. An Omnian warship was headed for Bellamonde and would pass to their rear.

<Captains,> Descartes sent, <we'll use the approaching Omnian Trident for a war-game exercise.>

<Shouldn't we seek permission from the commandant to engage in this type of operation?> Descartes' junior captain asked.

<What has Commandant Dorian repeatedly told us about testing our skills?> Descartes asked.

<That we must sharpen them now, while we have the opportunity, before we might truly need them,> the junior captain dutifully replied.

<And ask yourselves, Captains,> Descartes said, <who might be aboard this Omnian warship … a lone captain desiring to tour our facilities? The probabilities of that are too small to mention. No, it's a principal, perhaps Admiral Tachenko or maybe Alex Racine. This is an

opportunity to test our skills on a worthy adversary, or do you wish to wait until we face the Nua'll?>

The SADE, Descartes, was freed from his box two years ago and continued to serve aboard a House passenger liner during the following year of indenture. Secretly, he yearned to fly travelers, swirling them endlessly through space, swift and maneuverable.

When the agreement to produce Trident warships was introduced and approved by the Council, Descartes realized a better opportunity. At first, he sought to pilot a Trident, but when he discovered that a Haraken would be in charge of the naval training facilities, Descartes realized the possibility of an even greater goal. It would be possible for a SADE to captain a warship.

Sifting through his attack options, Descartes chose a three-pronged maneuver that suited his small squadron, and he signaled his intention to the other two captains.

<Don't shift your ship out of formation or otherwise signal our intentions to treat the Omnian ship as a combatant until I start the exercise,> Descartes sent.

* * *

Ellie was about to signal Alex and Julien that her attack run would soon begin, when she saw the pair walk through the bridge accessway. *Of course, you two were monitoring our position,* Ellie thought. Their close attention underlined her earlier thought. Alex and Julien were evaluating her, as much as they were the Méridiens.

Before the attack was initiated, Ellie reviewed Alex's engagement rules. He'd said to attack, create havoc, and score hits, but that they were to survive. It would be a difficult balance to strike, but it insisted on a real-world scenario versus a game strategy.

Ellie would leave the intricate fight maneuvers to Yumi, while she orchestrated the tactics. However, Ellie could envision an upcoming challenge with her youthful pilot. In the heat of battle, Yumi might choose to pursue and win, forgetting Alex's orders to survive. It would be her job to stay Yumi's hand, if necessary, at the crucial moment.

The *Redemption*'s holo-vid displayed the four warships. Ellie had marked the adversaries in colors. Every Omnian senior commander and captain had adopted Alex's preferences to use colors to identify entities rather than number designations in scenarios.

"Lieutenant, blue leader will probably be the first to move when we attack," Ellie said. "Be prepared to target red or orange for your first pass. If your attack is successful, your next maneuver will depend on their defensive pattern. Again, try for either the red or orange adversary. Blue leader will probably be the toughest target."

As the chronometer ticked down, Ellie briefly eyed Alex. Julien and he stood well back, watching the holo-vid display. It was as she thought. They would be silent observers.

"Now, Lieutenant," Ellie said quietly.

Yumi initiated the attack run she'd programmed into the controller. The Trident swung in a tight arc, chasing the Méridien squadron's rear.

Precious moments were lost to Descartes. The Omnian warship had the greater velocity and had swung to the attack before he'd initiated his maneuver. *So, we play, Captain,* Descartes thought, even as he signaled a new strategy to his captains.

Yumi witnessed the accuracy of her captain's prediction. Blue leader was the first to arc above the ecliptic, probably hoping to come behind her after the initial pass. Fractionally slower, red antagonist cut right and slightly below the ecliptic, which would complicate her attack. *For a recent trainee, blue leader is not acting like a newbie,* Yumi thought, as she signaled the controller.

The *Liberator*'s orange opponent failed to react quickly compared to the other two Confederation or CO warships, and that spelled its end. As the Méridien warship swung to the left and attempted to dip below the ecliptic, Yumi's Trident shot past it. The controller beeped twice, indicating it had scored two hits on the enemy.

<Captain Descartes,> the junior captain sent, <I've received a message from the Omnian Trident. It says, "You're dead. Fall off.">

<Do as ordered, Captain. Remain comm silent,> Descartes replied. When the Omnian moved first, he'd calculated that one ship was already lost and accurately identified which one it would be. He found it incredibly fascinating that the Omnian captain had the same idea that he had. *Or did the idea originate from a leader who is aboard?* Descartes thought, as his ship closed its arc above the ecliptic, completing its loop.

Having taken one Méridien ship out of the game but recognizing the blue leader's gambit, Yumi opted not to play. She stayed near the ecliptic, continued her swing inward and came parallel to her Trident's original course to Bellamonde.

Directly ahead and easily within reach for Yumi, before the enemy could gain her tail, was a dense line of asteroids. They weren't part of Bellamonde's twin asteroid belts, but there was enough rock to serve her purpose.

Shooting under the heavy pile of asteroids, each of them dwarfing Yumi's ship, she slewed the Trident around and retraced her course. In the time it took to accomplish that, the Méridien warships had arrived. They took up positions about 45 degrees apart on the opposite side of the asteroids and remained on the ecliptic.

Yumi grinned. It was what she'd hoped the enemy would do. They had stationed their ships too close to the asteroids, while she remained a good distance back. When she accelerated, arcing under the field of asteroids, the Méridiens lost precious time skewing away from her attack.

Yumi signaled her controller to target the red adversary, which she bore down on. The CO warship had belatedly tried to accelerate away from her, and Yumi scored two more strikes.

<I'm dead too,> Descartes received from his other captain. The SADE realized that it was only circumstance that had saved his ship. It easily could have been his Trident, which the Omnian captain targeted.

Quickly reorganizing the hierarchy of his strategy list, Descartes had an epiphany about the nature of battle. Not assigning blame to his commandant, he now understood that he'd taken much of his teachings too literally.

The Omnian warship had completed its arc and now shot above the ecliptic. He was traveling on it and away. Swinging his Trident into a hard arc, Descartes sought a head-on pass at the Omnian. The probabilities were good that the Omnian captain would best him, but Descartes had decided he would take the captain and her ship with him, if he could.

<Abort, Lieutenant. Break off the fight,> Ellie sent privately to Yumi, when she realized the Méridien's intention.

<I can take blue leader,> Yumi insisted with her thought. <I know what he's going to try.>

<Lieutenant, were my orders not clear?> Ellie sent, giving Yumi one last chance, before she would cut her off from the controller and possibly ruin Yumi's career.

Part of Yumi's mind yelled at her to object and find a way to convince Ellie that she could win the next pass. After all, it was only a game. But, Yumi had been raised by two warships captains. They had told her stories of how they'd often thought Alex wrong but chose to follow his orders anyway. Later, they'd discovered that he'd been right. It was those stories that made Yumi relent.

"Breaking off, Captain," Yumi announced firmly. She continued above the ecliptic, taking a broad arc to regain a course toward Bellamonde. She had the greater velocity on the Méridien warship, that wouldn't be able to catch her now.

<Senior Captain Descartes requesting permission to speak with the captain of the OS *Liberator*,> Ellie received, utterly surprised to discover that blue leader was a SADE. Quickly, she linked Yumi into the comm, noting that Alex and Julien were already listening.

<This is Captain Ellie Thompson,> Ellie sent.

<Yes, the distinguished Captain Thompson,> Descartes replied.

The SADE's enthusiasm was evident in his voice, and Alex glanced at Julien, grinning.

<I thank you, Captain, for the opportunity to learn from you,> Descartes sent.

<To give credit where it's due, Captain,> Ellie sent, <I constructed the strategy and targeting priorities, but my pilot, Lieutenant Yumi Tanaka, executed the attack.>

<My congratulations to the two of you, Captain. If I might, I have one question.>

<Please feel free to ask, Captain,> Ellie replied.

<You chose to abandon your attack after defeating two of my ships. Why didn't you accept my offer of a final pass with my Trident?>

<Orders, Captain,> Ellie replied, glancing toward Yumi to make her point. She was mildly pleased to see Yumi duck her head.

<Might I ask, Captain, who directed you?> Descartes asked.

<That would be me,> Alex replied, allowing the SADE to receive his bio ID.

<I'm honored you tested our readiness, Ser,> Descartes sent. <The maneuvers of your captain and pilot were inventive.>

<You did well by your squadron, Captain,> Alex replied.

<But two of my ships were lost, Ser.>

<My captain has perfected her skills throughout two decades,> Alex replied, <and my pilot completed Haraken naval academy with honors, flew travelers for three years, and piloted this Trident for nearly two years. And you?>

<I have three months of mock fighting, Ser,> Descartes replied.

<As I said, Captain, commendable,> Alex said.

<If I might, Captain Thompson, I would consider it a privilege to serve under you, should your seniors wisely choose to promote you. Good day, Sers. May the stars protect you,> Descartes sent before closing the comm link.

While the Méridien squadron reformed and the *Liberator* continued on to Bellamonde, two critical conversations took place.

<What was learned today?> Descartes asked his captains.

<The strategy lessons are only guidelines. In a fight, any and every technique must be considered to win,> the captain, whose ship Ellie had targeted as red adversary, replied.

<To hesitate is to die,> the junior captain replied. That he hadn't managed to do more than accelerate his ship before he was eliminated burned embarrassingly deep in him. Rather than shrink from it, it hardened his heart, and he vowed he wouldn't die so easily next time or any time after that.

The *Liberator*'s second watch, which had been standing by, took over from Ellie and first shift. As they left the bridge, Ellie sent, <A word, Lieutenant,> and led Yumi to the captain's cabin.

"I will give you the courtesy of hearing your reasoning for not immediately following my orders and then having the temerity to object to them, Lieutenant," Ellie said. She hadn't offered Yumi a seat and was standing with her hands clasped behind her in a parade-rest stance, realizing that she was imitating Tatia.

"I believed that I could take the Méridien, Captain. I sought to convince you of that."

"What did you believe blue leader intended to do, Lieutenant?"

"I wasn't sure, Captain. I just knew that I could outmaneuver his ship."

"And if he intended to sacrifice his ship, Lieutenant?"

Yumi felt as if she had been slapped. "But this was a game, Captain."

"It's never a game, Lieutenant. Think about what the sphere did when it was cornered. You had demonstrated superior skills to blue leader, who lost two-thirds of his squadron to you. It would have been an easy decision for him to make. He sacrifices his ship and takes you with him, thereby removing a deadly enemy in the process."

"I understand, Captain. You have my deepest apologies. Do you wish my resignation?"

"Not this time, Lieutenant, but never again hesitate to follow my orders. This was your one and only free pass. Think on this, Lieutenant. Next time, there might not be an opportunity for remonstration or resignation. Your hesitation to follow my orders might get all of us killed. And, in the future, Lieutenant, I would dearly appreciate it if you weren't foolish enough to disregard Alex Racine's orders, the last of which was that we were to survive. For failing to follow his directives, he might wish to remove both of us from his ship, and I've worked too hard to get here. Dismissed."

* * *

Robert Dorian, Bellamonde's naval academy commandant, finished the telemetry replay on his holo-vid for the Trident senior strategist.

"Unorthodox techniques, to say the least," Pietro Luchelli commented.

"Nonetheless, highly effective," Robert replied. "Two of our ships destroyed and not a single score against the enemy."

"It was a slightly unfair game, Robert," Pietro said, attempting to defend his senior captain.

"You're going to suggest that Descartes couldn't have anticipated his squadron would be attacked from the rear, despite the fact he was planning to ambush the Omnian warship."

"It was one of our own, a Trident, I mean," Pietro objected.

Robert laughed, his New Terran chest turning it into a rumble. "You're miffed that Descartes' quarry turned out to be a predator in disguise."

"Speaking of which, Robert, why would an Omnian captain want to test our squadron?"

"And what makes you think the captain chose to do that? I'll lay you odds, Pietro, that Alex Racine is aboard that warship, and he's the one who chose to check on the quality of our training."

"Well, we came up lacking," Pietro grumbled.

"Nonsense, I'd have expected the Omnian warship to have defeated the entire squadron."

When Robert received Alex's message that he was inbound and would like some time, he sent a quick, *I told you so*, message to Pietro. Robert met his guests in front of the administration building, as Alex, Renée, Ellie, and Julien descended from their traveler.

Alex and Robert greeted each other, as the old friends they were, slapping and pounding each other on the back as they hugged. Robert was equally enthusiastic with Renée and Ellie, careful to limit the strength of his embraces, and he gave Julien a double hand clasp.

"Well, what do you think?" Robert said, spreading his arms wide to indicate the academy, as he led them into the administration building.

"When we flew overhead, we got a quick peek at the massive size of this complex. Half of the grounds is covered in buildings, and traveler squadrons occupy every meter of open space," Alex commented.

"I'm reminded of the Confederation's size, and how quickly things can be built if the Council's will is focused on it," Ellie said, although her tone didn't necessarily say she was commending the Méridiens.

"Your naval academy looks to be about the only structure on the planet, Robert," Renée commented.

"It is. The SIF worked out a deal with the Council. They have been granted the right to design the repopulation of the planet. They've chosen to optimize the land. A maximum of 40 percent will be dedicated to settlement, once they've completed the restoration of flora and fauna. When the SIF's grand design is complete, the Council will open this place up to colonists, who must follow the SIF's guidelines for building and infrastructure."

Before Alex could reply, he spotted two heavy-worlders walking toward him, wearing huge grins.

"Stan, Eli," Alex shouted, clapping his hands. There was another round of hugs and backslapping, as Alex greeted his two old crew chiefs, Stanley Peterson and Eli Roth, from the *Rêveur*'s early days.

"Commanders, I see," Alex said, noting the men's insignias.

Stan picked up Renée, who laughed, while she was twirled around and handed off to Eli.

When Ellie saw Stan eye her, she said, "A little more decorum for a warship captain, please."

"Sure, Captain," Stan replied and hoisted her up, as he had Renée.

Ellie relented and joined in the men's infectious humor, as they handed her from one to the other. Her lithe Méridien build, which was the same as Renée, was no weight for the two New Terrans, who were near Alex's size. More important, these were old friends, and they'd gone through much together and survived.

Stan stared at Julien and waved a hand in dismissal, "You're too heavy, and I'm too old," he said. Then he lunged at Julien and grabbed him in a tight hug, and Eli joined them. The two men couldn't apply enough pressure to bother Julien, but they tried their best, and the smile on Julien's face said he enjoyed the enthusiastic greeting.

As the two commanders walked off, chatting about their encounter, Alex returned to the questions on his mind.

"An interesting arrangement between the SIF and the Council," Alex said. "Who has jurisdiction over the academy, the stations above, and the ship fleets, Robert?"

"That's a funny story, Alex," Robert said, ushering his guests into his plush office. "The Leaders argued for half a month over which House should be granted the rights to this new opportunity. But, they couldn't get past the sticking point, which was that half of the warships, loaded with fighters, would be sent to join your fleet. No Leader wanted the liability. In the end, they decided that the Council would have jurisdiction, which meant the potential ship loss would be shared. Essentially, that makes Council Leader Diamanté my boss."

The mention of Gino had Julien urgently sending a private message. <Robert, I noticed Katrina Pasko's passenger liner in our telemetry data,>

<They're hiding the *Resplendent* in orbit on the other side of Bellamonde. If Alex doesn't know that's the ship that Gino and Katrina brought, I wouldn't tell him,> Robert sent in reply.

<I haven't, and I don't intend to,> Julien replied.

"Robert, I notice that you have as many SADE IDs present as human bio IDs," Julien commented.

"That we do," Robert replied proudly.

"All in training for fighter and warship duty?" Alex asked.

"Yes and no. There are those who are here to help run this place, but most are in training for one ship position or another. And, it's a real competition for the fighter, captain, and senior officer positions," Robert replied.

"Who's winning?" Ellie asked.

"I'd have to say no one," Robert replied, the enthusiasm draining out of him. "It's not like at Libre, Alex. The people there were ..."

"Motivated," Ellie supplied.

"I was going to say driven," Robert added. "The individuals here want to learn and they're working hard, but, to most of them, these are games. They're enjoying the opportunity to play with their strategies. Even your discovery of a second sphere hasn't dimmed their eagerness to excel, but they lack that desperate edge that I know they need to stay alive."

"What you're saying, Robert, is that we can't let the Méridiens have their own squadrons. They'd be fodder for the spheres," Ellie commented.

"That's exactly right," Robert replied. "I don't want to tell you your business, Alex, and I don't know how it will settle with the commanders of the disparate fleets you're trying to cobble together, but the Omnians, with their training and experience are the best you have. They've got to command the other squadrons."

"We had a taste of the Méridiens' skills, when we entered the system," Alex replied.

"I watched the telemetry on that skirmish," Robert said. "It'll become the training lesson for the next few days, dissecting what went wrong for our ships. I heard from Descartes that your pilot is Yumi Tanaka. I wanted to congratulate her on her efforts. Brilliant. She didn't come down with you?"

"Not this time," Ellie said curtly.

"Oh," Robert replied. He didn't need to ask a clarifying question. He knew Ellie too well for that. There must have been a serious breach of conduct on Yumi's part to cost her a planetside trip to see the new academy.

"Robert, what's the promotion style that you're applying?"

"I insisted on a merit-based system, before I accepted the position, Alex, and Gino agreed. That gives the edge to the SADEs in the classroom, the simulators, and in routine operations, but humans have the upper hand when it comes to inventiveness. They intuit when to throw the enemy something unexpected. On average, the SADE captains win the games, but they can't win every time, which frustrates them. I know they spend unbelievable computation time trying to figure out why that is, but I have three senior captains, all Independents, who outwit the SADE squadron commanders three out of four times."

"What percentage of the humans are Independents?" Renée asked.

"The majority, which surprised me," Robert replied "I expected 100 percent but nearly one third are regular Méridiens, who've signed up for training in crew positions. Most of them come from the more mundane aspects of Confederation society. I think they just want something different for their lives. They're hard workers, and I'd like to see them promoted to pilots or bridge crew, but they refuse those jobs."

"Returning to the skirmish, Robert, how long before you think your warship captains will be ready to engage in a fight with a Nua'll sphere?" Ellie asked.

"My senior strategist believes another year, for those who are sailing now. I disagree, I'm afraid they might never be ready," Robert replied, holding out his hands in supplication to Alex.

The room was quiet, while Alex stood and paced at the back of the room, eventually pausing at a window to watch the activity below.

"What you need are worthy opponents, Robert, who will deliver defeat after defeat to your captains, until they either learn or quit and go home," Alex said. "Julien send a message to Admiral Tachenko. Her fleet will have had two months of rest by the time they receive it. Tell her to load up the fleet and make for Bellamonde. She's to stay here and compete with the Méridiens until Gino or Robert scream at her to go home."

"Done," Julien remarked.

"Which gives me another idea," Alex mused. "Julien, tell Admiral Reynard —"

Alex halted, when Julien cocked an eyebrow at him, and he rephrased his message. "Let's try … please ask Admiral Reynard if she wouldn't consider either taking her Tridents to New Terra or inviting them to Haraken for mock fights."

"A polite request has been sent," Julien replied, arching his eyebrow higher, and Renée tried to smother her snicker but failed.

Conversation about Bellamonde's recovery, which interested Renée, and the naval academy training continued, as lunch was served in a private dining hall reserved for the occasion. After they were seated, but before the food was served, Gino and Katrina were ushered into the room.

"Good, we're not too late for a meal," Gino enthused. "Please don't get up. We'll join you, if we may."

Gino and Katrina went quickly around the table, touching shoulders, shaking hands, and exchanging kisses with Renée.

<Julien, who knows the *Resplendent* is here?> Gino sent.

<I've only spoken to the commandant about your liner, Ser. If others know, they haven't mentioned it to me,> Julien sent in reply.

"Might I suggest that in this private meal among friends that we dispense with titles," Gino suggested.

"Excellent idea, Gino," Ellie piped up. "According to Robert, there are Independents here. Does that mean that the Confederation has dispensed with incarcerating them, and, if so, why are they labeled that way in the first place?"

Gino froze in the middle of picking up a glass of water. "Straight to the matter, Captain," Gino replied.

"Please, it's Ellie, Gino," Ellie said, as sweetly as she could manage, under the circumstances.

As Council Leader, Gino was not accustomed to being braced so abruptly by a mere captain, and it was on the tip of his tongue to respond forcefully. However, he found Omnian eyes quietly watching him, while they awaited his answer. Most important, Alex, who sat across from him, waited.

"We're taking measured steps, Ellie, but we're making progress," Gino said, carefully curtailing his anger.

"To answer your question in more detail, Ellie," Katrina said. "Méridiens are still identified as Independents. However, Alex's penchant for spiriting them away after they've been incarcerated has led the Council to do away with that."

It was obvious to the table that Katrina was speaking of the fallout that must have occurred at the Council meeting that followed the discovery of the loss of the Daelon Independents. To ensure there was no confusion as to where the moon base full of Méridiens went, Alex had left the Council a terse message.

"So where are they being kept now?" Ellie pressed.

"Many of them are here, Ellie," Gino said, adding a smile to encourage the captain to allow the matter to rest.

"Are they here voluntarily, and what about the rest of them?" Ellie continued. In her implant, she heard from Alex, <Steady, Captain.>

"Ellie, I've been assured that the Independents are here of their own choices," Robert said.

"But I wish to know what sort of choice they faced," Ellie persisted.

"Ellie, the situation is in limbo," Katrina said. "The Independents are under what you would consider House arrest. Their duties are curtailed to work and home. If they chose active duty here, they are relieved of duty to their House and assigned the category of naval personnel."

"What happens to their status if they wish to leave the military someday? Let's say, they've participated in the defeat of a number of Nua'll spheres, which might have threatened the Confederation," Renée asked.

"We haven't figured that out yet, Ser," Gino admitted. "At this point, if they left the academy or military service, they'd be returned to their House and would resume their status as Independents," Gino said, deflated by the turn in the conversation.

Gino was proud of what the Council had accomplished by its quick action to undertake the Confederation's defense. It was his hope that this aspect of naval personnel recruitment would never have come to light. But, it was never that way around Alex and company. They always wanted the undecorated truth.

Gino glanced at Robert, whose lips were twisted in a grimace. He understood the man's distaste for what he'd heard. The commandant hadn't been lied to, but he hadn't been told the entire story either.

A pall settled over the conversation, as Robert signaled the servers, who'd been waiting, that they could finally deliver the food.

Alex was another individual who wasn't happy with the turn in the conversation. He had important issues to discuss with Gino, but he'd been intrigued to learn about the Independents too. *You should have suspected the answers to the questions weren't going to be palatable,* Alex mentally admonished.

<Gino,> Alex sent, <have you a cheerful piece of news about the Independents?>

<I can say that the numbers, who are declared as Independents, continue to drop every year. People are more willing to accept variations in behavior. The Leaders aren't happy with the change in attitudes, but they're incapable of stopping it,> Gino replied.

Around the table, Gino and Katrina noticed an easing of tension and a resumption of casual conversation.

<Sharing private conversations, Alex, are we?> Gino sent, recognizing what Alex had done by linking to his fellow Omnians to share his comments.

<You know how it is, Gino. I didn't tell you a lie; I simply failed to tell you everything,> Alex replied.

The heat and power that Gino received with Alex's thought underlined his misstep. He'd not been forthright from the beginning and that included the Haraken commandant. Now, he'd have to work to repair the Omnians' confidence in him, if that was something that could be fixed.

After a fairly quiet meal, Alex asked for a private conversation with Gino, Katrina, and Robert.

"Robert informs me, Gino, that you have the ultimate responsibility for the development of the academy, the ships, and the readiness of these Méridiens to fight," Alex said. "I can tell you that Robert and I believe that these individuals aren't ready. Worse, we believe the vast majority of your fighter pilots, Trident captains, and senior commanders might never be ready."

Gino started to respond, but Alex held up a hand.

"I've taken the liberty of arranging something to help," Alex added. "I've ordered Admiral Tachenko to sail the Omnian fleet here. The fleet will challenge your fighter pilots and Trident captains in ways they couldn't imagine."

Gino breathed a sigh of relief. Despite the rocky start to the day, the more important aspect of what he was trying to accomplish was in good hands if the Omnians were going to help. He'd been unable to convince the Council to allow Confederation naval training to take place at Haraken, where it would have been more rigorous. It wasn't that Robert was doing a bad job. The problem was the training environment at Bellamonde. It was devoid of competition.

"We deeply appreciate the support, Alex," Katrina replied.

"Don't thank me yet," Alex replied. "Tatia has orders to push the competitive nature of the games, and she'll offer advice to Robert that will change the officer training programs. You might receive a great many complaints and lose a good many individuals. Be prepared to accept that. We aren't looking for numbers in this expedition. We're in need of highly trained and motivated pilots, captains, and commanders."

"Understood, Alex," Gino replied. "I will ensure the Council takes these changes in stride."

"Then, I'll wish the three of you good day," Alex said. "I have somewhere to be. By the way, Katrina, you can order the *Resplendent* to come around to this side of the planet. The liner means nothing to me. It's an empty hunk of metal that once housed a vibrant, young entity, but she's gone now."

Alex hated making the strong comments, but he was intent on never letting the Leaders discover they'd been duped.

-30-
The Wall

Everyone trooped to the bridge at Alex's invitation, after their traveler landed aboard the *Liberator.*

"Are we ready to launch, Captain?" Alex asked, when all appeared ready with the bridge crew.

"We're ready, Alex," Ellie replied.

"Julien," Alex said.

The holo-vid displayed an enormous map of stars with a yellow dot and a blue dot at opposite ends of the image.

Alex linked to the controller and requested a comm link to every crew member. When the links were established, Alex mirrored the holo-vid display to everyone.

<I take it we're not headed back to Omnia, Alex,> Ellie sent over the communal link.

<We aren't, Captain,> Alex replied. <We have one more trip to make.>

<Could you orient me, Alex?> Yumi requested, gazing into the holo-vid display. <The controller is reporting a negative response when I query if the yellow dot is Bellamonde.>

<That's because this display originates from Julien, not the ship's controller, Lieutenant,> Alex sent. <The yellow dot encompasses the worlds of the Confederation, Haraken, Omnia, and New Terra.>

There were audible gasps from the bridge crew when they realized the amount of space displayed by the holo-vid.

<And we're headed for the location indicated by the blue dot,> Ellie surmised.

<We are, Captain,> Alex replied. <Julien will need to set the transits for the controller. According to the SADE, Jupiter, who's our

information source, a direct transit isn't possible to our final destination.>

<Is there an estimation of travel time?> Yumi asked.

<It will be approximately 6.23 months,> Julien sent.

Silence accompanied Julien's remark. To travel for half a year to another star was many times farther than any human starship had journeyed.

<And why are we going there, Alex?> Ellie asked. Although she was curious as to their destination, she would have gone anywhere Alex ordered, without question. She asked for her crew. There were many who would be anxious to know, although she had an inkling of the answer.

<According to our research at Haraken's observatory platform, this might be the edge of Nua'll civilization. We're going to go knock on the hatch and see who answers,> Alex replied.

<Without the fleet?> Ellie asked.

<This is merely a courteous visit, Captain. We're saying hello to our neighbors and letting them know that we're aware of their territory. As the trip will be lengthy, I'm putting Julien, Renée, and you in charge of entertainment. Don't disappoint me, Sers. I'm expecting a happy crew by the time we reach our destination,> Alex sent and ended his link.

Julien left the conference comm up, allowing the crew to study the holo-vid display. He added three lines of varying length and vector changes to indicate the transits from Bellamonde to their destination.

"Julien, you have control of the ship," Ellie allowed.

"Captain, Lieutenant," Julien said, sending information to the controller and links to Ellie and Yumi. It was his hope that by acting in this manner, the captain and pilot wouldn't feel that he'd usurped their operations. "The first coordinate set will direct you toward this system's exit. The second set locates your first transit destination. Travel time will be about two months for this first leg of the journey. After we set out, a chronometer will count down the travel time, until we arrive."

* * *

The *Liberator*'s crew took the opportunity provided by the four days it took to clear the Bellamonde system to send copious messages to family and friends. Each transmission added the note that the warship would be on a mission with Alex for a year or more and to not bother replying.

Alex knew Julien would have communicated the warship's journey to Cordelia, but he felt it incumbent on himself to officially notify Cordelia, Tatia, Terese, Grumley, Maria, and Gino.

As the entertainment committee, Renée and Ellie immediately instituted the implant games. Once again, it became Julien's job to referee and balance the teams to keep the competition fair. However, the women were aware that the games would occupy the crew for only so long before they would tire of them.

Ellie was the first to score a new opportunity. The warship's exercise space could only accommodate about thirty people at a time. If the central mats were in use, it forced the other exercisers to the room's periphery. This morning, Ellie was waiting for the shift change, which was regulated on the hour, and would signal the few individuals on the mats to clear off.

"What is that, Chalmers?" Ellie asked the crewman, who had been teaching several other New Terrans, when the hourly notice chimed.

Chalmers was breathing heavily and sweat poured down his broad, bare chest.

"It's an ancient sport called Greco-Roman wrestling, Captain," Chalmers replied.

"It looks like an exhausting sport," Ellie replied. "What's the object?"

"Two opponents grapple, work to off balance each other, and throw the opponent to the mat," Chalmers replied.

"And this is done without tunics," Ellie said, eyeing the mass of muscle exhibited by the four New Terrans.

"The ancient Greeks practiced it naked, as they did most of their sports," one of Chalmers' practitioners replied.

"Well, Sers, I admire your restraint in not giving into authenticity," Ellie said, which made the New Terrans grin. "Excuse us, Sers, I'd like to speak with Chalmers in private," Ellie added.

When the others had departed, Ellie said, "You seem to have no difficulty defeating your shipmates."

"I've practiced the sport for more than twelve years, Captain, and I'm a little heavier than these three. That makes the competition unfair."

"What you're telling me is that you would need either a bigger opponent or a more skilled one or both to make it a challenge for you."

"Sure, Captain, I'd love to have that. If you'll tell me who might be interested, I'll go talk to them."

"Let me sound them out first, Chalmers. I'll keep you posted."

"Understood, Captain," Chalmers replied, before grabbing his towel and heading back to his cabin.

Ellie discovered that the few crew members who had waited with her for the change of the hour had most of the exercise space to themselves. While she'd been talking to Chalmers, the place had emptied out. As was her habit, she kept an implant record of her senses that recycled every quarter hour. The habit enabled her to replay a conversation or something she might have witnessed. If after reviewing the sequence, it proved critical, she could permanently store it.

Recalling the latest loop, Ellie noticed the vast majority of individuals exercising around the room's edges were women. Ellie examined the female crew members' faces closely. Most were pretending to exert themselves, while they kept a close eye on the wrestlers.

After Ellie's round of exercise, she cornered Renée. "You need to sacrifice your partner for the good of crew morale," Ellie announced, with a grin.

"I'm all for morale boosting, Ellie, but I've invested too many years training this New Terran to give him up easily. You'll need to convince me of your idea's worthiness."

Ellie shared with Renée the wrestling segment she'd stored.

"And you want Alex to take up this sport?" Renée asked, her brow furrowing in confusion.

"Wait, there's more," Ellie replied.

Renée viewed Ellie's recording of the female crew members, who had been watching the Greco-Roman wrestling. "Captain, I'm surprised at you. You're asking my partner, the Omnians de facto leader, to parade around shirtless for the edification of female crew?"

"I think some of the men would watch too," Ellie protested lamely, taken aback by Renée's response.

"Okay," Renée said in a mild voice. "When and where?"

"You had me worried there, Ser," Ellie replied, exhaling in relief. "Tomorrow at 10 hours."

"The entertainment committee has to stick together, Ellie. No sacrifice is too great," Renée replied, heading to her cabin and whistling a tune from a musical vid.

Renée's conversation with Alex was terse, to say the least. "You put Julien, Ellie, and me in charge of entertainment, Alex, and I'm drafting you to help. At 10 hours tomorrow, you're learning Greco-Roman wrestling from Chalmers. Good fortune, my love," she said, and stripped to enjoy the cabin's refresher.

Alex immediately queried the controller for details on the sport. Chalmers had collected a series of documentaries that explained the history and the techniques of the ancient game. As opposed to the training regiments of Tatia and the twins, whose swift movements Alex could never imitate, this sport fascinated him. He spent several hours that evening, programming some of the movements into his implant.

Also that evening, Ellie and Renée quietly mentioned the next day's Greco-Roman training to a few crew members and let gossip do the rest. By the time Alex arrived, the exercise space was crowded, standing room only.

"I take it we're the central characters in this scene, Chalmers," Alex commented.

"I believe we are, Sir. Do you need to warm up first?" Chalmers asked.

"Negative. I'm ready," Alex replied.

Chalmers slipped off his deck shoes and pulled his tunic over his head. That's when Alex noticed the three participants sitting at the other end of the mats were shoeless and bare-chested too.

<My love, you're a devious woman,> Alex sent, <and will be roundly punished this evening.>

<Ah, so many promises and so little time,> Renée replied.

Alex heard her throaty laugh, as she closed the link. He slipped off his shoes and pulled his tunic over his head, to the applause of the onlookers.

Chalmers, who was ready to help Alex learn the sport, thought different, as he eyed the mass of muscles across the man's neck, shoulders, chest, and arms. <If you don't mind me asking, Sir: What did you do before you became captain of your own ship?> Chalmers sent.

<Collected junked space metal with my father for years. Weightless in space, but the pieces got heavy on the ground,> Alex replied.

<No mechanical assist?> Chalmers asked.

Alex replied to Chalmers' question by holding his arms out to the sides, bunching his fists, and tightening his muscles.

<Understood,> Chalmers replied. He walked Alex through the basics, surprised that the man had many of the elemental moves.

"You've done this before, Sir?" Chalmers asked, after having to use one of his more complex moves to throw Alex. Even then, it took most of his strength.

"Studied last night and did some implant programming," Alex replied, climbing up from the mat. He took the opportunity to reorganize some of his programmed techniques and link a few of them to offensive tactics.

Alex's answer drove it home to Chalmers, whom he faced. Not just a heavier opponent, but a man who'd been setting up his implants to analyze every movement Chalmers demonstrated. In addition, Chalmers realized his opponent was busy building strategies around what he was experiencing.

The hour chimed softly, but no one moved. Even several newcomers to the space, who were ready to take to the mats, signaled they could wait.

"Some more tries?" Chalmers asked.

"I'm willing," Alex replied, taking a moment to walk to the edge of the mats to dry his hands. Conveniently, a towel was handed to him by a female crew member, who accompanied it with a bright smile.

Three more bouts later, which Chalmers won, he signaled to Alex that he was done.

"Tomorrow?" Alex asked, feeling he was beginning to close in on the techniques he would need to employ.

"We only have three sessions a week, Sir," Chalmers replied.

"I could arrange more, if you'd like," Alex replied.

Instead of accepting, Chalmers offered Alex explanations about crew duties, drills, and other thin excuses. He knew he'd need to give the nanites time to repair his body. *Like grabbing metal,* Chalmers thought.

Alex's tunic was offered him by the same female crew member. "Do you need toweling off, Ser?" the Méridien-built, brown-eyed, brunette asked. "I'm offering my services."

"Kind of you, Melissa," Alex said, accessing her bio ID. "But this human is categorized as look, but don't touch. Partner's orders," Alex replied, grinning.

Three times a week, Alex attended the Greco-Roman training regiments. It soon became necessary for the foursome to alternate challenging Alex. In the beginning, they managed to wear him down by the end of the hour. By the eighth week, Alex's programming allowed him to quickly analyze the moves of his opponents and anticipate their tactics. This enabled him to effectively counter their styles. The four men would troop forward, one at a time, and, within moments, each one would be on the mat.

Thereafter, Alex attended only a single session each week to give the men some competition. He had considered the idea of backing off and allowing the other participants to win, now and then, but that didn't sit well with him.

The good news for the entertainment committee was that, while many of the crew were enjoying the wrestling demonstrations, Renée had discovered another opportunity. She had been seated with Alex, enjoying a vid on the cabin's monitor, when an idea struck her that would keep the crew occupied.

In a long message, which Renée embedded on the controller, sending a link to everyone, she explained her idea. However, she was disappointed in the weak response. Just four brave individuals replied that they would try it.

A week later, following evening meal, Renée announced the game. "As I offered, you'll see four contestants this evening. Each has chosen a character from a vid. They will perform a short imitation, and then you'll see a segment of their character from the vid. At the end of all four presentations, you'll choose the winner. Julien, of course, will tally the votes."

"What do they win, Ser?" a male crew member asked.

"The winner has a choice. He or she may sit at the head table for the day's meals and ask any question of anyone or the winner may sit at the head table for a week to listen and learn."

Murmurs went through the meal room. The prize hadn't been announced beforehand. What was thought to be a frivolous demonstration had been turned into a game worth playing.

The night's contestants did their best, but they provided more humor for the audience than skill. Still, Yumi, who had a fair singing voice, managed a close approximation of an actress in a musical vid and won the prize.

"And your choice, Lieutenant?" Renée asked, after congratulating Yumi.

"Must the members of the head table answer my questions?" Yumi asked.

"Fully," Renée replied, eyeing the individuals at the table in question.

"I'll take the one-day option," Yumi replied and received the audience's applause.

<This trip might have become time dilated,> Ellie sent to those around the table. <I think it's going to feel like a lot longer journey than it'll actually take.>

During the next day and much to the head table's relief, Yumi's questions were quite innocent. It was a lesson for the senior people. Younger crew members were anxious to learn from them. What the leaders had come to accept as common knowledge was actually experience accumulated throughout the years.

After the first evening's barely passable performances, crew members became energized to compete and win the opportunity to sit at the head table. The competition was launched at full power.

Inventiveness was at the forefront of the crews' efforts. Both clothing fabricators were in great demand, as crew set about creating costumes, recut from worn uniforms and then colored.

Hitherto unknown talents were uncovered, singing voices, musical instruments, and the odd but entertaining skill.

Nearly two months into the competition, the audience was stunned when a broad-chested New Terran crew chief appeared in a flowing gown and a handmade hat, complete with fine wire molding that imitated feathers. When he opened his mouth, he sang a tune in a wonderful falsetto voice. After the chief finished, the crew saw the actress, whom he had imitated. They broke out with whistles and stamping, standing to deliver their applause for the flawless performance.

The crew chief had the gumption to curtsy to his audience, although it wasn't the most graceful of motions. Awarded the evening's prize, he selected the right to listen to the head table's conversations for a week.

When it became known that crew members were banding together to support someone they thought could win, Renée added a second competition. She allowed two or more crew members to compete for the prize, and those groups alternated with the single performances.

The contests were the hit of the journey and were still ongoing, when every human felt the exit from the third and final leg of the journey.

<Don't stop the activities,> Alex sent to his entertainment committee. <I don't know how long we'll be here.>

<A word, please, Alex,> Ellie replied, when Julien brought the warship to a stationary position. Julien followed Ellie, as she met with Alex and Renée in their cabin.

"Early telemetry indicates that we're sitting outside a dead system," Ellie said to Alex, but glancing toward Julien.

"That's accurate, Captain," Julien said.

"Now what?" Ellie asked, waving off Renée, who was indicating the thé brewer.

<Located, Alex,> Julien sent privately.

"There's a probe in this system, Ellie," Alex said. "It's probably been here forever or at least a few eons. It's had nothing to report simply because this system was devoid of significant life forms or activity. You're about to correct that. I want you to cruise this system. Check out some middle planets. Fly a few travelers to investigate them ... that sort of thing."

"Then what?" Ellie asked.

"Then launch a banisher and destroy the probe," Alex said.

"It's active?" Ellie asked, glancing toward the SADE.

"Yes, Captain, it's transmitting," Julien replied.

"If I understand your strategy, Alex, isn't this like waving a flag at an enormous predator and saying, 'Hello, look at us. We're timid herbivores. Come eat us'?"

"I like the imagery, Captain," Alex replied, chuckling. "I don't intend to engage whoever comes out to meet us after we've destroyed their probe. I'm merely interested in seeing who shows up and how long it takes them to arrive. There's a great deal that we can learn by letting the Nua'll show their hand first."

Ellie left the meeting feeling unsettled. She instructed the second shift pilot to pick a central orbiting planet and make for it.

"Any one in particular, Captain?" the pilot asked.

"Your choice, Lieutenant. Surprise me," Ellie replied. Afterwards, she unpacked her present from Commandant Dorian.

When Ellie had a private moment with Robert on Bellamonde, she asked, "Do you have the original evasion and escape routines that were embedded in the Daggers?"

"Those routines have long since been upgraded to work with the travelers and Tridents, Ellie. Why would you want them?" Robert had replied.

"I have the feeling, Robert, that I'll need them for my ship."

"You want to treat your warship as if it's fleeing from a superior force?"

"That's exactly right, Robert. There's the distinct possibility that I might not be able to offer an offense of any sort. Purely evade and retreat in the face of the enemy."

"Is that where you're going, Ellie? Someplace dangerous and alone?"

"If I'm reading Alex right, and he hasn't disclosed this to me, I think we're about to do something incredibly risky."

<Julien, I need you,> Ellie sent, as she marched toward the bridge.

<Coming, Captain,> Julien replied, pinging the controller for Ellie's location.

* * *

Ellie outlined her request to Julien, left the details in the SADE's hands, and crawled into bed. It was late in the evening, but sleep was slow to come. When it did, it was full of strange dreams. In most of them, she was seeking Étienne, as events sought to overtake her, but her partner kept slipping away from her.

After a few hours of tossing and turning, Ellie rose and spent a prolonged time in the refresher, until even she got a warning of shut off unless she reactivated it. Immediately after morning meal, Ellie joined Yumi on the bridge.

"Lieutenant, I want you to study some routines that Julien worked up for me," Ellie said, sending a link to Yumi. "Study them carefully. Select the ones that best suit a maximum opportunity for us to evade without any celestial bodies around us."

"Captain, I don't understand," Yumi replied. "Are there adversaries in this system? I looked at the telemetry after I woke up. It appears quiet."

"That's right, Lieutenant. There's nothing to interest us here but an active probe. We're going to make like explorers and traipse around this system before we eliminate that probe. Then we're going to park out there in the dark and see who comes in response to our knocking, according to Alex."

"Who do you think will come, Captain?"

"I have no idea, Lieutenant. Maybe no one, maybe a sphere, maybe the entire Nua'll space fleet. If I've learned anything from Admiral Tachenko, it's don't expect a good outcome from your actions. Anticipate the worst you can imagine, and then prepare for something twice as bad as that."

"I'll get on these routines, Captain" Yumi replied, her eyes wide.

"You do that, Lieutenant. Your skills might be the difference between us becoming space junk and returning to Omnia."

Ellie had proved she was one of the best fighter pilots. But where she had spent years training to become that good, Yumi had proved early on that she was a natural, effortlessly wringing the most out of a Trident's maneuverability. Ellie thought there might be only one person, make that one entity, who could best her pilot, and that would be a SADE, one who had previously piloted a starship and worked with the Omnian squadron.

The *Liberator* toured the dead system, stopping to orbit several planets and launch the travelers to investigate moons and asteroid belts.

It might have been exceptionally boring, except everyone knew what Alex was planning to do and tension was elevated.

After twenty-one days of playing explorer ship, the third rotation pilot came on duty and waited several hours until the travelers were aboard. Then a course was laid and activated. It drove the warship toward the outermost planet, where the probe hid among a collection of moons.

Days later, Yumi halted the Trident at a distance many times farther than what was normally reserved for destroying a probe.

"Alex, the banisher can't get a clear shot at the probe. It's embedded among the moons," Ellie said. "If the probe detonates, the explosion is liable to create a significant disruption in that gas giant."

"More than likely, it will, Captain," Alex replied.

With that being the extent of Alex's answer, Ellie sent, <Chief, launch a banisher.> She waited, watching the controller confirm what she heard from the crew chief, as a bay was cleared, decompressed, doors opened, and the banisher launched.

"No use waiting around for a day or so, Captain," Alex said, adding, "Julien, final destination, if you please."

The SADE sent a curving vector path and a set of coordinates to the controller. Then he sent links to Ellie and Yumi before messaging both of them. <Captain, Lieutenant, here's the course I recommend. It will keep us far away from that gas giant, while we head for a stationary point outside the system.>

The *Liberator* had passed the outer planet's orbit, when telemetry registered a massive explosion.

"The probe detonated on contact," Julien said, during the evening meal.

"Was that expected?" Sherilyn, a traveler pilot, asked. She was the most recent winner of the single's performance and had elected to ask questions for the day.

"This probe, so close to the Nua'll territory, was considered to be an early model," Julien replied. "Therefore, no evasion techniques were expected, but it was highly probable that it would detonate when the banisher's clamshell claws closed on it."

"Won't the probe's detonation cause a surface eruption on the gas giant?" Sherilyn asked, eyeing Alex.

"Yes," Alex replied.

"This means that we've communicated our presence in several ways," Sherilyn mused. "We've sailed around the system, which the probe communicated. Then the probe's broadcast was abruptly ended, when our banisher destroyed it. Finally, this planet's expulsion of a huge hot mass will create an extraordinary signal flare that you're expecting the Nua'll not to miss."

When Alex shrugged his shoulders in response, Sherilyn nodded her head thoughtfully. She was intrigued by the strategy's boldness.

The following day, Ellie began running emergency drills, including fast launches of the travelers. The pilots recognized that they wouldn't have a significant gravitational field for their shells to intercept. They would exit the warship with the charge they carried, which meant the four fighters were expected to be a blocking force that would allow the Trident to escape.

In addition, Ellie had Julien create hundreds of scenarios of attacking forces. These enabled the traveler pilots and Yumi to practice various simulated evasion and escape tactics. The better the pilots got, the more Ellie had Julien increase the attackers' numbers and velocity advantage. Eventually, she expanded the attackers' degrees of approach until the escape avenues were minimal and required coordination with the travelers to open a route for the warship.

The entertainment and exercise routines ground to a halt and were curtailed as part of the ship's daily life. The entire crew was on edge, waiting for the arrival of whoever was coming.

However, the intensity could only be maintained for so long. Eventually, the anxiousness slid into boredom, as the days rolled by. Besides, the incessant number of ship drills and tactical simulations on escape scenarios by the bridge crews were leaving too many crew members exhausted and able to do no more than fall into their bunks after rotation.

* * *

One late evening, thirty-five days after the *Liberator* had taken up its stationary position outside the system, Alex located Julien. The two wandered down to the ship's bay level. At this hour, the corridor was deserted. Alex slid down to the deck and Julien joined him.

"You've not been yourself lately, Julien," Alex said. "Not much repartee between you and me, and you've exhibited a lack of patience with the young ones. What's on your mind?"

Julien raced through a nearly innumerable list of potential answers, and then he halted all kernel response activity. *When did I start conditioning my replies to Alex?* the SADE asked himself.

"The data we're collecting on the Nua'll indicate they're more formidable and dangerous than we could have perceived," Julien replied.

"We've been seeing this coming for a while, Julien. Why the change in your attitude now?"

Julien reached back through his memories from the moment of his inception to the present and considered the reasons for his algorithms' priorities.

"When all you perceive is an endless repeat of your days, there's not much to hold dear for the future," Julien replied. "Without hope, dreams dwindle and die."

"And now?" Alex asked, realizing Julien was referring to the period before he was freed from his box.

"Year after year, for more than two decades, my future has grown richer. For all the processing power I possess, I couldn't have imagined the life I have today, and I owe its start to you."

"I thank you for that thought, Julien, but you've given me as much as I've given you."

"I would deem it impossible to compare our lives, Alex. They are what they are. What's important is our future, and I sense that it grows short for both of us. Humans and SADEs represent a small population. The probabilities are high that we won't be able to compete against the likes of an ancient and vast alien civilization."

"Who says we have to compete?" Alex replied. "You, my friend, are holding on to the moment too tightly. That has to restrict your thinking."

"What are your intentions, if not to compete, Alex?"

"Julien, how great would you estimate the Nua'll territory to be?"

"If I were to extrapolate from the wall's curvature and form a virtual sphere, it would encompass thousands of stars, possibly more than ten thousand."

"And how many races do you think the Nua'll subsumed during their expansion?" Alex asked.

"That would be impossible to calculate, Alex, but, certainly, numerous intelligent species were either coopted or destroyed."

"And how many races do you think came knocking on their hatch?"

Julien had to smile at the question. "The probabilities are that it's only one, led by a foolish human."

"And what do you think this ancient race will think of a species that doesn't exhibit fear at the sight of them, has destroyed two of their spheres, and not only located their hidden probes, but destroyed them?"

"A civilization this old would have a well-established order, and we would be disturbing it."

"One last question, my friend. What do you think is the ultimate purpose of the probes?"

"Ah, an easy one," Julien replied. "The Nua'll have taken the long view. They're keeping an eye on worlds with developing species, and they're sending out spheres to remove any races that have attained or are capable of attaining space travel. The Confederation encompassed the first human worlds to attract their attention, and, most likely, our starships were death sentences for our colonies."

"Now, Julien, I want you to believe that you won't live to see Omnia again, so that your mind is clear of worry about the future. How would you put all this together?"

"The Nua'll have size and power on their side, but they'll have become accustomed to having their way. Everything and everyone has succumbed to their advance. We show up, disrupting their habits, their protocols, which will confound them. They'll want a closer examination."

Alex raised an eyebrow, as if to say, "Precisely."

Julien smiled in return. "We'll intimidate them with our single ship, sitting stationary at the edge of their territory, and they'll be asking themselves endless questions and debating possible actions before they decide what to do."

"We don't have a choice, Julien. We can't move our populations, and we can't wait until the spheres arrive en masse at our systems. Like you say, the Nua'll have the power. That means that we have to be clever and proactive."

Julien nodded in agreement, and said, "And if I'm to be of help, then I must accept that the future is unknown and be at ease with what I have attained."

"Just so," Alex replied.

Julien stood and extended a hand, easily helping Alex to his feet. "You will have my every ability, Alex. Of course, it will be difficult to follow you, as I lack the benefit of your formal jester training."

Julien's hand was locked on Alex's, when he froze. "We have company, Alex. Third watch is notifying the Captain. I suggest we attain the bridge."

* * *

By the time, Alex and Julien walked through the bridge passageway, Ellie was present, buttoning her jacket and smoothing her short hair. The holo-vid displayed several ships.

"The telemetry view is pushed in for a closeup, Alex," Ellie said. "They're a long way out and decelerating rapidly."

"Continuing their present rate of deceleration, Alex, these ships will come to a stop an estimated 20 million kilometers from us," Julien said.

"They're being cautious," Alex said, grinning at Julien.

Julien caught Ellie's quizzical expression, and he sent privately to her, <Moments ago, our fearless leader and I were speaking. We were supposing the reactions of the Nua'll to our provocation. It was the jester who proposed that we would confound an ancient race with our absurd stance.>

<Who was playing the part of the jester?> Ellie asked.

<It used to be me, Captain, but I admit to having recently abdicated my post. However, I've chosen to regain my title,> Julien sent.

A jacquard print cap, peaking in a small gold sphere, appeared and disappeared so quickly from Julien's head that Ellie wasn't sure what she saw until she replayed her visual recording.

<Welcome back, Julien,> Ellie sent.

"Julien, my guess is that we would be signaled or, perhaps, investigated in some manner," Alex mused.

"Undoubtedly," Julien replied.

"I'd like to capture the raw transmissions."

"Not recommended, Alex. Whatever we record will pass through our controller, and we have no idea of the enemy's signal capabilities. Conceivably, they could render our ship inoperable."

"What if we interrupted the signals directly after our comm receptors and delivered them to secondary memory crystals, thereby protecting our controller? It's not like we need to talk to our people or them," Alex said, pointing at the display.

Julien grinned at Alex. He signaled two engineers and three techs, launching them from their bunks with orders to collect various pieces of equipment and tools. Then he ran from the bridge at a speed that shocked Ellie. He planned to meet the engineering team near the warship's aft end where the main lines emerged from the comm equipment.

"That's quite the growing reception party," Ellie commented, nodding at the holo-vid.

Alex eyed the image. The ships were rapidly increasing in number and size.

"Captain, with Julien absorbed in my request, I want additional bridge crew woken up and searching our telemetry net. This main party is tucked much too tightly together out there. I believe they want us to think that's everyone that's coming, and I don't like that."

"Understood, Alex," Ellie replied tersely, waking most of the first watch, including Yumi.

No sooner had the new watch group arrived than other crew members hurried in carrying extra bridge chairs for them. Nanites in the seat bases were signaled, attaching them to the decking. Soon, another group arrived with pots of thé to refresh the third watch and waken the first.

On deck two of the Trident, techs were busy spreading a nanites paste to release a section of the bulkhead. This allowed the engineering team to access a tertiary memory bank, which was available to the controller, but had never been used.

Julien isolated the memory core from the controller. Then, when an engineer signaled Julien that they had access to the comm cabling, the SADE shut down the power to the comm station.

Immediately, the techs accessed a junction line and rerouted the main comm signal to a convertor box that they had brought with them. The device was needed to interface between the comm station and the memory bank. Finally, they connected the output of the convertor to the memory bank's input.

When Julien received a tech's acknowledgment that the crew were ready, he returned power to the comm station and requested the crew reseal the bulkhead cutout.

<Alex,> Julien sent, <the comm station is prepared to feed the memory crystals. Recognize that if we launch the travelers, they'll be unable to communicate with us.>

<Understood, Julien. The captain has played with scenarios that launch the travelers, but I have no intention of allowing them to exit this ship.>

"Captain," a bridge crew member called out, attracting Alex's attention away from Julien. "I have a large vessel on our horizon. The ship is located 90 degrees to port. It's about the same distance out as the main group."

"Captain, another ship. It's also on the horizontal plane but 90 degrees to starboard," a second crew member announced.

"Just the one ship in each location?" Ellie asked and received affirmatives.

During the next several hours, more of the enormous ships appeared, dividing the quadrants of space and surrounding the Trident warship.

"Captain, I don't get this," Yumi said, standing close to Ellie so that she could whisper. "The Nua'll can't be so foolish as to think they can cut off our escape by positioning single ships every 45 degrees of arc around us like this."

"That's because they aren't single ships, as you imagine them," Alex said, coming from behind Yumi.

"No?" Yumi queried.

"More than likely, Lieutenant, they're carriers," Ellie said.

<Julien,> Alex sent. <Any idea as to whether we're recording Nua'll comm or telemetry detection signals?>

<I've been monitoring the interface device, Alex ... purely in a passive mode,> Julien hurriedly sent to assure Alex. <I estimate that the memory crystals are about 19 percent full.>

<Already?> Alex responded.

<Our neighbors appear to be quite voluble or their transmission technology requires a much greater data density than ours.>

"Captain, the timing of our exit is now in your hands," Alex said. "One condition and one request. The condition is that you can't launch the fighters. The request is that you allow our memory core to record the Nua'll transmissions, as long as possible, without jeopardizing our opportunity for escape."

"Did I ever tell you, Alex, that your captains and senior commanders, including myself, are often particularly annoyed by your convoluted directives?"

"Seriously?" Alex asked, grinning at Ellie, who ignored him, as she tapped her third watch pilot on the shoulder.

"Yumi, take a seat. I want options for exit, and I want them fast. Plan for those capital ships dumping out some sort of fighters and spreading a wide net," Ellie ordered.

Alex linked to the controller to watch Yumi sort through her escape scenarios. It appeared she'd planned for enemy strategies Alex hadn't considered. *A brilliant mind,* he thought.

Yumi selected the few scenarios that responded to a wide arc of coverage by the Nua'll. She was about to speak to Ellie, but several crew members on telemetry watch interrupted her, as they sang out, "Fighters launched."

The holo-vid display lit up, detecting hundreds and hundreds of fighters dumping out of the enormous ships that sought to enclose them.

"One thousand, three hundred, fifteen fighters and counting," Julien announced.

"Time to go, Yumi," Ellie said quietly but with authority. "Don't be afraid to take a radical approach."

The one thing that Edouard and Miko constantly said about their daughter was that she had an uncanny means of seeing to the heart of a problem. Now, more than ever, Yumi wanted to call on that ability. Observing the three-quarter sphere of fighters that blocked their escape in Omnia's direction, Yumi selected a vector and accelerated the Trident at full power.

Ellie, Alex, and Julien observed their warship rush toward the central greeting party. They exchanged glances, and Alex cocked an eyebrow at Ellie.

"Interesting choice, Lieutenant," Ellie said. "Care to explain your tactic."

"Yes, Captain," Yumi replied, concentrating on her board display and her link with the controller. "I realized that the enemy assumed we would only choose to flee away from that massive fleet in front of us. That's why they didn't bother to completely surround us with fighters."

"The size and number of those ships in front of us would seem to indicate that they're not worried about a single ship charging them," Ellie commented.

"And I thought about that too, Captain," Yumi replied. "I took a few moments to review the arrival of the main party. What was interesting was that as the larger vessels arrived, they formed a hollow ball, which I thought was strange. Then the last ship arrived. I was surprised to see that it was a small sphere. Interestingly, Captain, that sphere stationed itself in the center of that formation. It's about 25 meters in diameter and doesn't appear to have any armament."

"Curious," Ellie commented.

"That's what I thought, Captain," Yumi replied, "which led me to wonder: Is that fleet in front of us designed to intimidate us or to protect those aboard the sphere."

"Those ships could be doing both, Lieutenant," Ellie purposed.

"I agree, Captain, but I decided a rearward exit had little chance of success. The number of fighters dumping out of those carriers limits our avenues of escape, and we have no idea of the armament they possess. Worse, we'd be targeting small ships, one by one, with our beams, while the vast majority of them would be targeting us from all directions."

"And we'd run the power crystals empty against a multitude of little targets and be swamped by the others," Ellie finished for Yumi.

"Exactly, Captain," Yumi replied. "A rearward exit wasn't a viable option. That left the front. I'm betting on those aboard that small sphere worrying that we're coming for them. And, maybe, just maybe, they're thinking that we're capable of doing the same thing as their sphere did when we cornered it."

"Meaning we don't have to fight our way through to that orb. We only have to get close and detonate our ship," Ellie supplied.

Yumi nodded, immersed in making a subtle course correction. The small sphere had shifted laterally inside its protective environment, possibly checking to see if the foreign warship was targeting it. Yumi's new vector kept the *Liberator* traveling straight at it.

Time ticked down, as the Trident raced forward. Nerves tightened further. A crew member, who was estimating the distance the warship had covered to the waiting fleet, said, "Thirty-five percent."

"Movement, Captain," Julien said quietly. "The ships in front of us are retreating. What's of note is that they're not breaking formation, and the sphere remains in the center of the protective shield."

"Excellent analysis, Lieutenant," Alex said. "It appears those ships were there primarily to protect the orb."

Telemetry detected the main party continuing to accelerate. They were in full retreat. Yumi waited until her warship had closed the distance to approximately 50 percent of the way. This ensured that the enemy retreat was well underway, and she'd cleared the fighters' partial sphere. Then Yumi arced the Trident up, taking a line between the main party and the carrier-fighter forces.

Yumi continued to drive the Trident at full power, monitoring the engines' statuses. She needn't have worried on that score. Nearly every bridge crew member, not occupied with monitoring telemetry for more enemy ships, was eyeing those readouts.

<We're well inside Nua'll territory,> Julien sent to Alex.

<And isn't it interesting that they weren't prepared for this eventuality, especially from a lone ship,> Alex sent in reply.

<Yumi was clever and proactive,> Julien commented, repeating the words Alex had spoken to him.

"Well done, everyone," Alex said, applauding the bridge crew and Julien. The holo-vid indicated that Yumi's continuing arc would eventually allow the *Liberator* to make a complete course reversal far overtop of the fighter shield. Better yet, none of the enemy ships were pursuing them.

Turning to Julien, Alex asked, "How did we do on the comm memory?"

"Nearly three-fifths full, Alex," Julien replied, smiling, and displaying his trademark fedora.

<My friend is back,> Alex sent to Julien, laying a hand on the SADE's shoulder before gently squeezing.

-32-
Return Home

When the *Liberator* exited into Omnian space, Alex chose to stay off the comm, while the crew taxed the warship's bandwidth with a mountain of messages and comm links.

After the *Liberator* had left the Nua'll fleet far behind, Julien and the engineering team had reversed their surgery on the comm station linkage. At one point, Julien had suggested to Alex that he investigate what the memory crystals had stored.

"Absolutely not," Alex had replied, horrified. "Didn't you tell me that the Nua'll could produce deviant signals, which would be a primary concern for the ship's controller?"

"Yes, but I'm much more sophisticated than a ship's controller," Julien had replied.

"Granted," Alex replied. "But that might not be enough."

"Your concern for me is touching," Julien said, with a lift of his eyebrows.

"It's no such thing," Alex replied offhand. "I'm concerned that we've come all this way to observe the Nua'll reaction to our presence and capture their broadcasts, and, if you go tinkering about with the information, we might lose it."

Julien had laughed at Alex's excuse and decided to leave well enough alone.

When Alex pinged the warship's comm bandwidth and found it at less than half capacity, he linked to the *Freedom*.

<Welcome back, Alex,> Cordelia replied.

<It's good to be back, Cordelia,> Alex sent. <Mickey, please.>

<Alex, the taunter of great civilizations, returns home triumphant,> Mickey announced.

<Amusing, Mickey,> Alex sent, his thought devoid of humor.

<And to what do I owe the honor of this comm?> Mickey replied, unfazed by Alex's reaction.

<How goes the work on the *Freedom*'s armament?>

<Oh, you mean the task that we completed seven months ago? Fine.>

<Good, then you're free and bored, Mickey, waiting for a new one. This one might challenge you.>

<Ah, good. At least you've come home bearing gifts.>

<Julien managed to deviate the comm station's reception of the Nua'll broadcast directly to memory crystal. At present, it's completely isolated, and I want it to remain that way. This is precious stuff, which needs analysis without risking ships or SADEs.>

<Now, that's a challenge. How much did you get?>

<It's the *Liberator*'s tertiary memory bank, and it's at 58.7 percent of capacity.>

<How much data was on it before you started recording, Alex?>

<It was empty, Mickey.>

<How long were you exposed to the Nua'll fleet? I heard it was brief, but you're saying you have a half full memory bank.>

<It was hours, Mickey, not days. Start your transfer-analysis design with your engineering team. I want complete isolation, backup copies, and techniques that protect the SADEs. There's no telling what the Nua'll were capable of sending us that could corrupt programming. Remember, this wasn't a conversation between us and them. This was a one-way broadcast at our ship by the Nua'll for hours.>

Alex dropped the secondary link to Mickey and retained it with the *Freedom*.

<Who's next, Alex?> Cordelia asked.

<You, Cordelia,> Alex replied. <Do you have any reports from Tatia, Terese, and Olawale?>

Cordelia had copious communications from the three individuals who Alex requested. The smallest group originated from Terese, and she summarized those for Alex, while she worked on the next group.

<President Terese sent her wish to Omnia for your safe journey. I've taken the liberty of informing her of your return.>

<Thank you, Cordelia.>

<New Terra accepted Admiral Reynard's first offer,> Cordelia continued. <The NT Tridents have been training at Haraken. Admiral Tachenko took the fleet to Bellamonde, as you requested. She reported that in the first quarter, 23 percent of the new recruits resigned. It has since dropped off to less than 7 percent in the latest quarter. Also, she reports a significant improvement in the tactical performance of the captains, and the Méridiens are developing a strong rapport with her senior commanders.>

<Good to hear, Cordelia.>

<Of interest to me was Admiral Tachenko's report of the crews' favorite downtime efforts, Alex. They're helping the SIF repopulate the flora and fauna of the planet. They've rigged the fighters to disperse seeds in the areas designated by the SADEs, and they manage the incubator pods that develop the new embryos. Once birthed, these faunas are introduced to the environment under controlled conditions.>

Alex mulled over that one. He could imagine the individuals, who participated in the SIF plan to restore Bellamonde to a healthy planet, experiencing emotionally cathartic events.

<And our friends at Sol?> Alex asked.

<There have been only three messages, Alex. Each was lengthy. Olawale recorded his thoughts on a daily basis. Then he sent them on a quarterly basis.>

Alex checked his calendar app. The length of time that the *Rêveur* had been gone from Omnia, minus the initial travel time, said that there should have been a fourth report. In fact, a fifth would be due within little more than a month.

<Yes, Alex. His last report is overdue. However, I can set your mind to rest. His diaries, if I may call them that, detail great progress with the Earthers, at all levels, government, military, and populace. If I can extrapolate from the rate and amount of entries, Olawale and his team became increasingly busy.>

<Understood, Cordelia. Thank you for your briefing. I'll send messages to all individuals.>

* * *

The *Liberator*'s crew was more than happy to decamp the warship and enjoy time off aboard the *Freedom*. Only a few individuals remained aboard, when Mickey and his team arrived. Julien led them to the temporary bulkhead access, which had been opened again.

"I recommend taking this convertor with you, Mickey," Julien said. "It handled the flow of the Nua'll broadcast without interruption."

"Why do you think that was?" Mickey asked.

"Simplicity, Mickey. There was little programming for the broadcast to corrupt, if that was the intention of the Nua'll. It merely relays signals at a rudimentary level."

Mickey grunted and indicated the device to a tech, who set to work removing it.

"Did you sample the stream, Julien?" Mickey asked.

"I was forbidden to touch the data," Julien replied.

Mickey lifted his head away from examining the tech's work to stare at Julien, several thoughts rushing through his mind. "That scared of its potency, was he?" Mickey asked.

Julien shrugged his shoulders in reply.

"It's difficult to put close friends in harm's way," Mickey murmured.

When Mickey signaled Miriam that she was free to begin the transfer, the SADE carefully attached leads to the memory bank from a secondary power supply that resided in a large shipping crate. The *Liberator*'s power supply was disconnected, and the memory bank was released from its containment facility. Carefully and slowly, Miriam transferred the crystals and their support parts to the crate. Two SADEs sealed it and carried it to the waiting traveler.

Miriam could have carried the crate herself, without much challenge. However, when the SADEs heard Mickey, who knew them well, repeat their instructions three times, they knew their operations must carry as close to zero risk as possible. They were taking all precautions to act accordingly.

The traveler transferring the crate made planetfall, landing at one of Mickey's engineering labs outside Omnia city. It was a fairly isolated building. More important, Mickey and his team had the space to prepare a special lab. It was protected against every transmission that they could conceive. Furthermore, there were no cable connections or power from the lab to the outer rooms. The work lab was entirely self-contained, as far as any signal transmission was concerned.

Mickey, the engineers, and the SADEs had chosen to construct a set of controllers that were prepared to review, sample, and analyze the data. The idea was to connect the first controller to a single crystal of the memory bank, with a cutout switch. The processed data would be held within the controller rather than be returned to the Trident's memory crystal.

A small operations device received a link from the controller to record the steps that the controller took. It was considered a backup, which few thought necessary.

When all was prepared, Miriam signaled Mickey, and the remainder of the team assembled outside the lab. A simple switch was employed to start the operations. Mickey triggered a timer and exited the space. When the timer ended, the switch closed and completed the connection between the controller and the warship's memory crystal. Soon, the team watched their first controller overheat and shut down, smoke pouring from its casing.

"Black space," Mickey whispered.

Miriam immediately sent an image to Julien. <This happened within 0.075 hours after the controller began sampling the Nua'll broadcast.>

"Set up the second controller," Mickey ordered the lab techs. "Miriam, please recover the ops download."

This time, Mickey had no need to warn the SADEs to be careful. The operation had taken on a sinister aura for every digital entity.

Little was learned from the analysis of the ops download. In order not to repeat the exact process, Mickey had the SADEs change out the warship's crystal to test another. The memory bank held ten crystals.

This time the controller lasted almost an eighth of an hour before it was ruined. And so the process went: pull the ops download, set up a new controller, trade out the Trident's crystal, and repeat.

After the third controller was smoked, the team immediately began making new ones. Initially, they'd only prepared ten.

After two days of testing and burning through forty-three controllers, Mickey called a halt to the operations. Facing Miriam and the other SADEs, he said, "I believe the way forward lies in the ops downloads. We've tested each of the *Liberator*'s crystals four or more times. My question is: Why did identically built controllers last different times before they overheated?"

A tech returned the latest crystal to be tested to the bank's cradle. He waited until the tiny convertor box from the Trident registered it was online. When the device signaled the crystal was operational, he noted the bank's capacity.

Warned against using implants within the testing lab, the tech hurried over and tapped Mickey on the shoulder. "Ser, the convertor box indicates the memory bank has lost nearly 2 percent of the data."

Mickey was about to say impossible, but, then again, he was dealing with alien technology.

Miriam said, "That explains the different controller burn times, Mickey. Conceivably, every time a crystal was reloaded, it had a little less data, and, with a shift in the data stream, we experienced a shift in the burn times."

Another SADE raised a finger to indicate he had a thought, but Mickey held up his hands. "Friends, let's vacate the lab to talk. I'd feel a great deal better if this lab was sealed, while we conversed."

"Now, please, Luther, continue," Mickey requested, when they were outside.

"It occurs to me that we're observing two different forms of data, Ser," Luther said. "The first form passes through the controller's circuitry without issue. Our device probably had relevant information stored for us before it was destroyed. The ops download indicates sampling and analysis was occurring. The second signal type is an ephemeral stream that's destructive.

"Are you suggesting that this other form sat in the crystal, inert as it were, until it had a target?" Mickey asked.

"Precisely," Luther replied.

Mickey had little reason not to pay attention to Luther. The SADE had worked for a Méridien House that was responsible for comm systems.

"There is another fact to consider, Mickey," Miriam said. "If we calculate the total amount of time the controllers were in operation and the rate at which they consumed data, the loss in crystal data is not equivalent. Not even close."

Mickey examined the calculations Miriam passed the team.

"This underscores Luther's reasoning. A virulent data form might be scattered throughout the broadcast. This is good news," Mickey said, clapping his hands in delight.

"We await your insight, Mickey," Miriam replied, placing her fists on her hips.

Mickey recognized Miriam's posture. She'd copied it from Pia, and it was equally effective for both females.

"Sorry," Mickey said contritely. "What we have to do is separate or filter the real broadcast from this virulent data."

"Okay, Mickey, how?" Miriam asked.

"Luther?" Mickey said, turning to the SADE with a hopeful look. It generated a round of chuckles, not the least of which was because Luther appeared as if he had been handed an explosive device to diffuse without a manual.

"This will require some thought, Mickey," Luther replied, which was newly freed SADE speak for "I need a few moments, while I enter a fugue and focus on my kernel's processing."

Humans took the opportunity to grab a bite and a cup of thé. They had missed the midday meal. In the meantime, the SADEs communed with Luther to offer their support.

When Mickey, the engineers, and the techs returned, the SADEs were nowhere in sight.

Mickey pinged Miriam and located her in the assembly lab, with the other SADEs. The humans discovered the SADEs furiously constructing a device, which was housed inside a large cabinet. Within an hour, the SADEs completed their devices and carted them to the testing lab.

The SADEs set about hooking up two controllers in tandem. The first controller was also connected to the cabinet, and the second controller was connected to a fresh memory crystal bank. Finally, a squat-looking box was attached to the cabinet's output.

"We're ready for the first warship crystal, Mickey," Luther announced.

"To quote, Miriam," Mickey replied and placed his fists on his hips.

Miriam laughed, not only at Mickey's antics but the confused expression on Luther's face.

"Luther educated us on comm-filtering techniques," Miriam explained, "it occurred to several of us that we are dealing with a malevolent entity, which seeks to destroy. Therefore, it was decided to emulate one of Alex's techniques."

"Which is what, in this case?" Mickey prompted.

"We will entice our adversary to make the first move and show its hand, Mickey. Whatever is buried throughout this broadcast data waits to attack sophisticated electronics. It's meant to cripple them," Miriam replied.

"Am I to understand that it's your plan to fool this dangerous stream into taking the path toward the cabinet?" Mickey asked. "What's to prevent the broadcast data that we need from going the same direction?"

"Digital gravity," Luther replied. "We've added a small interface at the front of the first controller. The broadcast data will pass through the interface and into the controller normally to be sampled and analyzed. Then it will be sent to the second controller to be stored in the new memory crystal. However, the interface at the front of the first controller will offer the destructive signal a route toward a much more tempting target. We're confident the malevolent data can't resist our offer."

"I feel like I'm listening to a director explain the concept for an ancient horror vid," Mickey replied. "There's a great deal of equipment in that cabinet, Luther. Once a bit of Nua'll treachery gets in there, it's going to create a significant fire and probably destroy most of the lab."

"Negative, Ser," Luther explained. "The cabinet is merely a delay device. It will add a significant amount of transmission time, while the destructive data flows through it."

"Then where's the bait?" Mickey asked.

"The temptation," Miriam replied, translating New Terran speak for Luther, "is in that small box, which is heavily fire protected."

"Curious," Mickey replied, examining the small enclosure. "What would interest this ugly data more than a controller?"

"Embedded in the interface of the first controller is a set of algorithms, Mickey, which indicates a SADE's kernel is on the other end of the link," Miriam explained.

"I'm confused," Mickey said. "How does an empty kernel attract this data stream?"

The SADEs grew quiet, and Mickey looked at Miriam for an answer.

"It wouldn't, Mickey. The kernel isn't empty. It contains a copy of my kernel."

Mickey blanched, and he glanced at the other humans, who were as uncomfortable with the concept as he was.

Miriam searched for a means of relieving the unease swirling through the humans' minds. "I'm detecting some jealousy from the humans in this room," Miriam said.

"What?" Mickey asked in surprise.

"You heard me," Miriam repeated. "You're jealous that the Nua'll corruption stream finds SADEs more desirable than mere humans."

First a tech snickered. Then a couple of engineers snorted, and, soon, humans and SADEs were laughing.

"Pretty good one, Miriam," Mickey said. "Let's find out how tempting you are."

"That aspect of my persona is not to be doubted, Mickey," Miriam replied, with a nice touch of hauteur. "What we must discover is how tempting I am to the Nua'll."

The engineering team wasn't required to run another forty-three tests, but Miriam did have to copy her kernel nineteen more times.

"Credit to Alex's foresight," Miriam said, when the team saw the malevolent signal's definitive preference for a SADE kernel over a controller. *And Alex protected you, Julien,* Miriam thought with pride for the status that SADEs held in Alex's world.

That only twenty tests were required to run through the memory crystals' entire data was credited to the copies of Miriam's kernel fending off the initial attacks. The SADEs reasoned that the kernel succumbed only after the attack of a multitude of virulent streams.

When the filtering process was complete, the team supposed that they had acquired a new memory bank of untainted broadcast data. The warship's crystal bank indicated a loss of nearly a fifth of its original data total.

"A clever integration of weaponized signal broadcasting," Luther said admiringly. "I must consider a means of protecting our ships before they next meet the Nua'll."

Luther found humans staring at him with expressions ranging from concern to horror.

"That's an excellent idea, Luther," Mickey said, laying a hand on the SADE's shoulder. "We mere mortals, would appreciate not being left to the mercy of the Nua'll, when the SADEs and our ship controllers became permanently inert."

"I will be diligent in my responsibilities, Ser," Luther replied with gravity, failing to recognize Mickey's humor.

"Okay," Mickey said, clapping his hands enthusiastically, "I want to test our cleaned data. Reconfigure the original setup. Let's pass the data from our second set of crystals through a new controller to a bank of clean crystals and hope we don't produce a burned controller."

In little more than an hour, the entire trove of broadcast data was cleared by a single controller without a mishap.

"The data should be safe now," Mickey announced. "But there's to be no sampling of the data. Instead, we'll need some linguistic specialists to program a controller to decode the Nua'll broadcast."

"We have linguistic experts?" Luther asked.

"We have the next best thing, Luther," Mickey replied. "We have the SADEs who deciphered the Swei Swee whistles and were some of the first to master the Dischnya language.

-33-
Master Race

Alex convened a meeting in a *Freedom* conference room with Renée, Ellie, Mickey, key SADEs, and Yumi, who was surprised to have been invited.

"Mickey, you have the floor," Alex said, to open the discussion.

Mickey walked everyone through what transpired in the Omnian lab. While it wasn't news to Renée or any SADE, Ellie and Yumi were particularly horrified by what had targeted their Trident.

"What about the next time we meet the Nua'll?" Ellie asked.

"Luther," Alex prompted.

"I haven't yet devised the exact method, Sers, but it will be similar to what was accomplished in the lab. We can't afford to change out equipment as it's destroyed. It must be a permanent solution that filters their destructive streams from their broadcast," Luther explained.

"Won't the Nua'll change up their processes when they discover they're ineffective?" Ellie asked.

"Undoubtedly, Captain. I have considered that, which makes the design process ever more difficult. I must create a solution for today and one that anticipates what the Nua'll might do in the future. I find the task … challenging, to say the least. That I have so many of my kind to assist me, makes me confident that we will be successful."

"I've every confidence that you will be, Luther," Alex said.

"Ser," Luther replied, nodding his head and touching hand to chest.

"Julien, you're next," Alex said.

Julien explained that the SADEs weren't able to decipher the broadcast in its entirety. They lacked sufficient references to translate the language, but he considered the portions they had gleaned were worth sharing.

"We discovered that the broadcast repeated its message in several hundred languages," Julien said.

"Several hundred," Yumi repeated in amazement.

"Gives you an idea of the number of races that the Nua'll might have conquered, Lieutenant," Alex said.

"We targeted one language in particular," Julien continued. "It had words that resembled Swei Swee terms. We, the SADEs, believe that this particular portion of the broadcast was in the Nua'll language. Our familiarity with the Swei Swee terms of the Nua'll, such as world, traveler, star hunter, and others enabled us to tease out portions of the broadcast."

"What did you understand, Julien?" Ellie asked.

"One moment, Captain. There is more to comprehend, regarding the origination of these signals," Julien said, as politely as possible. "What we wish to bring to this group's attention is that we're certain it was the Nua'll who were broadcasting to the *Liberator*. The carrier wave from the orb, at the wall, was the same technique used by the spheres and probes. However, in the case of our warship's comm station, obviously, the orb chose a method of transmission that it perceived we would be able to handle. How it determined that is a mystery to us."

"But it's one that I'm working on," Luther added. "The capture of the broadcast and the Trident's comm station logs are providing incredible insight into the Nua'll comm techniques."

"We understand the Nua'll broadcast was a ruse, while they bombarded our ship through their comm attack," Julien continued. "But they sought to present a real invitation in case their attack failed. They were covering their bet, so to speak," Julien said, tipping his head to Alex. "In their invitation's repetition, the Nua'll listed a series of proper names, which we understood to be the names of other races. And, here's the critical point, Sers, it's our belief that we were invited to speak with their masters, for lack of a better word, who these races serve."

"While you digest this idea," Alex said into the conversation that ensued from Julien's announcement, "I want to review the discussions I've had with several of you, but not with this group as a whole."

The table's holo-vid sprang to life, and the various ships that the Omnians met at the wall were displayed.

"Z, your turn," Alex said.

"Pilot Yumi noted that I should examine the arrival of the ships at the wall," Z said. "Several of us have analyzed the ships' propulsion methods and noted significant variations. These differences indicate a lack of a single, technologically homogenous population."

"Also evident are the tremendous ship design variations," Miranda added. "Someone should help the poor dears coordinate. It would have been much more intimidating for them to have arrived at the wall displaying unique ship functionality, while constructed on a similar design principle."

"It's our estimate that there were, at least, eleven unique races represented in the main fleet alone," Z said. "Surprisingly, the fighters didn't appear to resemble the carriers they exited."

"To sum it up," Alex said, clasping his hands in front of him. "The Nua'll, who we thought were intent on expansionism and wiping out any developing species, might be just lackeys, who, along with other races, work for even worse entities."

Yumi, who'd been ever more flummoxed as the information about the adversaries piled on, looked around the table. The concern of the faces of humans and SADEs reflected her own. "I know I'm speaking for myself," she said, "but I feel thoroughly intimidated. Defeating a sphere or two was one thing. Defeating a civilization composed of hundreds of races seems like a daunting task, if not impossible."

"Undoubtedly, Lieutenant," Alex replied. He sat with his arms crossed and one hand rubbing his chin, "if that was what you were trying to do."

"It isn't what we're going to do?" Yumi asked in confusion.

"Z, Miranda, how different would you say these ships were from one another?" Alex asked.

"Technology hasn't been shared, Alex," Z replied. "Propulsion gases indicate vast technological differences. It's evidence of species eons apart in technology."

"Armament displays and ports speak to a variety of weapons among the different ships," Miranda commented. "It's a theme that echoes our analysis of the propulsion mechanisms: the older the drive techniques, the older the weapons."

"And the small sphere or orb, as everyone calls it?" Alex asked.

"The most sophisticated of the ships, by far," Julien said.

"I didn't recognize any of these ships as having a design similar to the bullet ships that the spheres carried, did anyone else?" Alex asked, and received a series of negative responses.

"Does that make the eleven, which were represented in the main party, one greater?" Ellie asked.

"Not necessarily, Captain," Z replied. "It's conceivable the bullet ships are made by the master race for the Nua'll, who appear to operate as their envoys."

"And exterminators," Renée added, with disgust.

"I'd like to return to the lieutenant's question, Alex," Cordelia said. "She thought defeating such a massive civilization of many races to be impossible, and you intimated that wasn't your intent."

"What do you see, Commodore, when you observe multiple races, who've probably been cobbled together for millenniums, but they haven't received the benefits of shared technology?" Alex asked.

"I don't see benevolence," Cordelia replied.

"Just so," Alex agreed. "I think the situation creates a short-term and a long-term goal for us. For our immediate future, we must claim our territory and send a message to the Nua'll and their masters."

"The spheres, which are this side of the wall," Julien supplied.

"Exactly," Alex replied. "They're our targets and must be eliminated from this side of the wall."

"How many were there?" Ellie asked.

"Twenty-three, Captain," Julien replied.

"Alex, it would take a force of twelve or more Tridents, loaded with travelers, to adequately trap and take down each sphere," Ellie calculated. "Plus, we'd need to have competent commanders leading these fleets. We can't let the Méridiens or New Terrans encounter a sphere by themselves."

"That's not what I intend to do, Captain," Alex replied. "I intend to send our entire force against the nearest sphere. It would be an excellent opportunity for the fleet to practice maneuvers."

"And it would be extremely intimidating," Miranda added. "I can just imagine the last message that will be sent by the sphere before it detonates."

"Speaking of which," Renée interjected, "how can the fleet be protected from a sphere's tendency to take ships with it when it explodes?"

"That will be an opportunity for the *Freedom*, Ser," Cordelia said. "Our orbital platform has been splitting production in half between fulfilling traveler orders from other worlds and providing the city-ships with fighters. Z and Miranda have installed ancillary programs in every traveler, which will allow them to operate in concert, independent of the city-ship's controller or a pilot's directions. We use these unmanned fighters to eliminate the bullet ships. Once the sphere is defenseless, we'll send the travelers in to close the cordon. Two or more of these automated fighters will attack and tempt the sphere to detonate."

Alex marveled at the authority and flexibility that the SADEs had exhibited in his absence. His smile was wide and generous, as he gazed across the table at Cordelia. Then he turned his admiring expression on Z and Miranda.

<My dear man, if I was capable of blushing, that expression would have elicited mine,> Miranda sent.

"Could we automate every traveler so that the lives of pilots won't be risked?" Renée asked.

"Unfortunately not, Ser," Cordelia replied. "These methods will work in simple scenarios, where the travelers have a single target and a fairly simple purpose. In a full-scale operation, which would demand multiple maneuvers, there wouldn't be time to program and coordinate the fighters."

"Julien, if we were to prosecute the spheres, one at a time, how long would it take the fleet to sail to the present locations of these twenty-three spheres?" Yumi asked.

Julien blinked in the time it took him to calculate the distances between the stars where the spheres had been located, allowing for the shortest path to reach them. "I estimate the travel time to be about 14.5 years, Lieutenant," Julien replied.

Yumi's mouth fell open. Closing it, she said, "Plus time for in-system travel and the fights."

"Assuredly," Julien replied calmly. He understood Yumi's concern. To hunt and destroy the spheres that had been located, she would give up more than 8 percent of her expected lifespan — if she survived. SADEs would share the danger but wouldn't fret the time.

"Lieutenant," Alex said calmly, "you're envisaging events as all or nothing. Things are seldom that way. Imagine you're the Nua'll, who must answer to this master race. Your spheres are out among the stars, stamping out existing or potential spacefaring life forms. Recently, you've lost two spheres to some minor upstarts. It's worrying but containable. Now, if in the course of less than a year, you lose four or five more spheres, decisively. What would you do?"

"I would order the spheres to band together and travel as a squadron," Yumi said. Then, she corrected herself. "No, that wouldn't work, not with the size of the attacking fleet that the spheres would have reported before they detonated. No, I'd recall them." Yumi said. The smile on Alex's face told her that she'd reasoned correctly.

"That's how we'll claim our territory," Alex said, eyeing each member of the table.

"The probes, Alex," Julien said. "Terese said she was considering abandoning the Haraken carriers."

"And?" Alex asked.

"We use the carriers to eliminate the probes. Load them with banishers and a few travelers for protection," Julien replied.

Alex started to ask a question but stopped. Instead, he grinned and said, "Brilliant, Julien. Will it require new equipment on the bridge or merely programming for the controllers?"

"For the rest of us, Alex," Renée interjected.

"Julien, it's your idea. Go ahead," Alex offered.

"We automate the carriers," Julien explained, "adding functions for defense of the ship and offense against the probes with the banishers. In the event a carrier encounters significant forces, it abandons the system and moves on to the next one."

"What about reaction mass, emergency repairs, or running low on banishers or travelers?" Ellie asked.

"For the most part, Captain, these are all programmable events," Julien replied. "In regard to reaction mass, your concern is noted. The carrier has a great number of bays that won't be in use. We can add additional tanks there, and it might be prudent to set a date by which the carriers return to us for service."

"Essentially, we'd set up the carriers to eliminate the probes, system by system, without involving our warships or crews," Alex allowed. "And President Lechaux will love the idea of putting the carriers to such a valuable use, as opposed to scrapping the ships."

"After we've hunted the spheres and forced them to retreat to their territory, do we intend to return to the wall?" Ellie asked.

"Do what?" Yumi asked with trepidation.

"We certainly can't hope for détente," Alex replied. "Our grav drives weren't displayed to the ships at the wall, but probes have reported our ship movements in multiple worlds. The master race knows of our growing capabilities. I believe that an intelligent species that has lived for millenniums, maybe eons, under a mantra of expansionism, can't imagine existing any other way. If we pause and hope for peace, they'll be using the time to conceive of a means of eliminating us."

"Then what's our long-term goal?" Ellie asked.

"After we've sent the carriers to destroy the probes, eliminated a few spheres, and seen the spheres fleeing to the other side of the wall, we'll need to confront this civilization," Alex replied.

"And how are you proposing to do that?" Renée asked, worried that Alex was thinking of a horrendous fleet confrontation.

"Divide and conquer," Alex said enigmatically.

Julien smiled and nodded.

"It came from one of your vids, Renée," Alex said, in answer to the questioning look on his partner's face.

"What did?" Ellie asked.

"The answer to our dilemma lies in determining which races, represented by these ships," Alex replied, indicating the holo-vid display, "are the most vulnerable to persuasion."

"The probabilities are great," Z interjected, "that each of these species occupied its own territory prior to being absorbed by the master race. If we can identify the most recent group to be usurped, we'll probably find its territory at the edge of the master race's dominion. That would make access to those worlds less problematic."

"And, as the more recently absorbed species, the memory of domination would be fresher. This might make them more amenable to turning against their masters," Julien reasoned.

"Or they could play both sides against each other and expose us to retaliation by the masters," Ellie reasoned.

"That will certainly be part of the challenge," Alex admitted. "But, once we turn one group, it will be easier to turn another, especially with the intelligence about the master race that the first race should provide."

"How do we go about identifying which species is the most vulnerable?" Ellie asked.

"Like Luther's answer to the question of protecting our ships from the Nua'll broadcast, it's a work in progress," Alex replied and dismissed the meeting.

* * *

Alex and Renée had retired for the evening. They were sipping thé on a couch, cuddled together, and happy to be relaxing in their salon aboard the *Freedom*.

"Do you know what I like best about our suite?" Renée asked Alex.

"Hmm," Alex replied, as he took a swallow from his cup.

"Trident cabins, even the ones we had, weren't meant to be comfortable for two people, for as long as we were aboard, especially with one as large as you, my love."

"I did notice that we had a little more body contact than was usual for us."

"I did enjoy it for the first month or so, my love. But, after that, it felt as if I was experiencing incoming asteroids and their collisions."

"I wasn't gentle in our contacts?"

"Your deceleration was adequate, my love," Renée replied, kissing his temple. "But, if you haven't noticed, your Greco-Roman workouts have returned you to the hardness of when we first met, if not more so."

"Would you like me softer?" Alex asked, with a smirk.

"You know that's not the way I like you," Renée replied, with a tempting grin.

<Good evening, Alex and Renée,> the couple heard in their implants from Cordelia. <I hope I'm not interrupting anything.>

<Nothing that can't be continued, Cordelia,> Renée replied.

<I have two important messages addressed to both of you. One message is required to precede the other. And, before you ask, the senders of the first message requested that I withhold relaying their comm until you had an opportunity to relax. Good evening, Sers.>

A link was left in their implants, and Alex regarded Renée, who signaled her readiness, and he triggered the link.

<Alain and I fervently hope that your journey was safely concluded,> Étienne had sent. <In your absence, my crèche-mate and I have thought long and hard about our commitment to your personal safety.>

Alain added, <We believe our skills are inadequate in regard to ensuring your safety with the lives you lead, and we respectfully request to be released from your service. If you refuse, we'll honor our commitment.>

Then Étienne continued. <Please understand that it's not that we don't wish to see you protected. It's that Z and Miranda are more capable of personally defending you, especially with their avatar speed and weapons. We've chosen another way of being of service to you.>

Alain explained. <We've traveled with the fleet to Bellamonde and have enlisted in the naval training academy. We intend to become fighter pilots to defend the fleet and, therefore, the two of you.>

<We ask for your understanding, Sers,> Étienne finished.

Alex looked at Renée. Her hand was over her mouth and tears swam in her eyes. "You don't want them to go?" Alex asked.

"No, no," Renée cried. "I've been worried about them for years. Lately, there's been little need for their escort services, but I didn't want to hurt their feelings. They're proud men. It's wonderful that they've chosen a new direction for themselves. But fighter pilots? I could have wished for a safer occupation for them."

"You thought they would shift from trying to keep me alive, to say, working in the meal room?" Alex asked.

"No, I suppose not. They were bound to choose something dangerous, where their skills could be put to use," Renée replied and triggered the second link that appeared in her implant.

<I'm hopeful the wanderers have made it home safely,> Tatia had sent. <I'm sure that you'll have much to say when we meet, Alex, and you'll have had my general reports from Cordelia. This one is of a personal nature. I wasn't sure what to do about Étienne and Alain's requests. In the end, I decided to do what you would do, Alex. Let them choose their own paths.>

Alex and Renée heard Tatia pause and the rustling of bedclothes before she continued.

<To the twins' disappointment, I removed them from fighter training and put them through Trident training. They were too good to be wasted

in travelers. They graduated top of their class … together … odd thing that, but probably not when you consider they're twins and crèche-mates. This means, Alex and Renée, you'll be addressing the de Long captains when you next speak to them. What you won't believe will be watching this pair in action. With two Tridents, they consistently beat a squadron of three Méridiens. Against Omnian squadrons, they often accomplish a draw, which is to say, five Tridents out of action. I hope you'll be as proud of them as I am.>

Alex closed their comm links. He was mulling over Tatia's statements about the twins' combat skills, when Renée interjected her thoughts.

"I would have thought Tatia would be worried for them, especially for her partner, Alain. Then again, it's probably safer for them to be in Tridents than standing next to you, my love. I will miss them, as close companions," Renée said, climbing into Alex's lap.

Two more friends in harm's way, Alex thought, his anger rising against the Nua'll and their master race.

— Alex and friends will return in *Nua'll* —

Glossary

Celus-5 Swei Swee

Star Hunter First – Swei Swee name for Alex Racine
Wave Skimmer – Hive Leader, called the First

Dischnya

Dischnya – Intelligent species in Celus system
Homsaff – Heir to the Mawas Soma nest
Neffess – Nyslara's heir
Nyslara – Queen of Tawas Soma nest
Sawa – Celus-4, Dischnya home world
Sawa Messa – Celus-5, Dischnya's second world
Soma – Term for Dischnya
Wasat – Warrior commander

Dischnya Language

Dassata – Peacemaker
Ené – Pronunciation of Renée
Fanz – Pronunciation of Franz

Earthers

Binghamton – Destroyer commodore
Desgardes – Destroyer captain
Elbert Munford – President
Mel Dormer – Adjutant to Colonel Morris
Nikki Fowler – Rim governor
Patrice Morris – Militia colonel
Selena – President's aide
Thalis – Admiral
Tim Fordham – Destroyer bridge duty officer

Harakens

Asu Azasdau – Captain and co-commander of the *Sojourn* expeditions

Bibi Haraken – Matriarch of Haraken clan

Christie Racine – Alex's sister

Duggan Racine – Alex's father

Eli Roth – Bellamonde naval academy co-commander over crew training

Elizabeth – SADE

Ginny – Young ex-Earther and friend to Teague, Alex's son

Jason Haraken – Grandson of Bibi Haraken

Jupiter – SADE directing the observatory platform, original ID Theodosius

Katie Racine – Alex's mother

Keira – Security member of the *Sojourn*

Mutter – SADE and Hive Singer

Pietro Luchelli – Bellamonde naval academy senior strategist

Robert Dorian – Bellamonde naval academy commandant

Stanley Peterson – Bellamonde naval academy co-commander over crew training

Terese Lechaux – Newly elected president of Haraken

Tomas Monti – Partner of Terese Lechaux

Willem – SADE

Méridiens

Allora – SADE lost in transfer from her ship

Bartosz Rolek – House Leader

Confederation Council – Supreme ruling body of the Méridiens

Confederation Hall – Building that houses the Council Chambers

Council Chambers – Assembly location of the Leaders for deliberation

Darse Lemoyne – House Leader

Descartes – Trident senior captain and SADE

Domino – Risk assessment SADE

Emilio Torres – House Leader

Gino Diamanté – Council Leader, partner of Katrina Pasko

Independents – Confederation outcasts, originally exiled to Libre, rescued by Alex Racine

Katrina Pasko – House Leader, partner of Gino Diamanté

Lawrence Teressi – House Leader

Linton – Risk assessment SADE
Mahima Ganesh – Ex-Council Leader
Oliver – Leader Lemoyne's ex-House SADE
Pierce – Risk assessment SADE
Serge – Risk assessment SADE
Shannon Brixton – House Leader
Theodore – SADE with Gino Diamanté
Winston – SIF director, ex-Council SADE

New Terrans

Alphons Jagielski – Captain of the Trident, NT *Arthur McMorris*
Anthony W. Tripping – Admiral
Bart Fillister – Captain of the Trident, NT *Lem Ulam*
Darryl Jaya – Minister of Space Exploration
Don Jacobsen – Board of Inquiry presiding officer
Edouard Manet – Carrier captain
Harold Grumley – President
Jonathan Morney – Captain of the Trident, NT *Geoffrey Orlan*
Maria Gonzalez – Envoy, new Minister of Defense
Miko Tanaka – Carrier captain
Sheila Reynard – Admiral
Teague – Alex and Renée's son

Ollassa/Vinians

Citron Mandator – Accompanies Scarlet Mandator to the Life Giver
Golden Executor – Bridge operations
Flame Executor – Mesa Control crew
Frosted Tasker – Comms operator at Mesa Control
Indigo Executor – Mesa Control crew
Life Giver – A progenitor of the plant people
Melon Tasker – Bridge comms operator
Mist Monitor – Mesa Control crew
Olive Tasker – Crew member
Plum Executor – Bridge operations

Scarlet Mandator – Commander
Teal Monitor – Bridge navigator crew
Umber Interpreter – Interpreter with a Life Giver

Omnians

Alain de Long – Twin and crèche-mate to Étienne, partner of Tatia
    Tachenko
Alex Racine – Partner of Renée de Guirnon, Star Hunter First (Swei Swee
    name)
Benjamin Diaz – Known as Little Ben and Rainmaker, mining expert,
partner of Simone
Bethley – Scout SADE teamed with Killian
Cedric Broussard – Z's New Terran avatar
Chalmers – Crew member aboard the *Liberator*, Greco-Roman wrestling
    enthusiast
Claude Dupuis – Engineering tech, program manager for SADE avatars
Cordelia – SADE, partner of Julien, senior captain of the *Freedom*,
    promoted to commodore
Darius Gaumata – Captain of the Trident, OS *Prosecutor*
Edmas – Young engineer, works with Mickey Brandon, partner of Jodlyne
Ellie Thompson – Captain of the Trident, OS *Redemption*
Emile Billings – Biochemist
Esteban – SADE, works with Edmas and Jodlyne
Étienne de Long –Twin and crèche-mate to Alain, partner of Ellie
    Thompson
First – Leader of the Swei Swee hives
Flits – Single person grav-drive flyers
Francis Lumley – Captain of the *Rêveur*
Franz Cohen – Fighter group leader, partner of Reiko Shimada
Glenn – Ex-Independent, who managed Daelon bay control
Hector – SADE, captain of the city-ship, *Our People,* partner of Trixie
Hive Singer – A unique Swei Swee treasured by the People
Jerry – Traveler pilot at Sol
Jodlyne – Engineer, works with Mickey Brandon, partner of Edmas

Julien – SADE, partner of Cordelia
Killian – Plaid-skinned SADE, friend of Vivian, lead scout ship SADE
Linn – Scout ship SADE
Lucia Bellardo – Captain of the Trident, OS *Judgment*
Luther – SADE originally from a House constructing comms
Mickey Brandon – Engineer, partner of Pia Sabine
Miranda Leyton – SADE, partner of Z
Miriam – Engineering SADE
Myron McTavish – Commandant of the Dischnya military academy
Olawale Wombo – Ex-Earther, head of the Dischnya school
People – Manner in which the Swei Swee refer to their collective
Pia Sabine – Medical officer, partner of Mickey Brandon
Reiko Shimada – Commodore of the Trident squadron, partner of Franz Cohen
Renée de Guirnon – Partner of Alex Racine
SADE – Self-aware digital entity, artificial intelligence being
Sherilyn – *Liberator* traveler pilot
Simone – Partner of Ben Diaz
Svetlana Valenko – Captain of the OS *Liberator*
Swei Swee – Six-legged friendly alien
Tatia Tachenko – Admiral, ex-Terran Security Forces major, partner of Alain de Long
Trium – Scout SADE teamed with Killian
Trixie – Confederation SADE, original ID Lenora, partner of Hector
Vivian – Little girl, an Independent from Daelon
Yumi Tanaka – Pilot, lieutenant, of the OS *Redemption*
Z – SADE, partner of Miranda

Places, Things, and Enemies
Aigre – Fruit drink favored by the Méridiens
Banisher – Mickey's device for removing probes
Board of Inquiry – New Terra's naval review board
Central Exchange – Haraken financial system
Confederation – Collection of Méridien worlds

Dagger – Original New Terran fighter

Espero – Capital city of Haraken

GEN machines – Devices created by Julien to produce starship parts

Government House – New Terran president's residence

GravMania – Company of Edmas, Jodlyne, and Esteban

Idona Accord – Alternate name for the Sol constitution

Idona Station – Sol station at the crossroads to the far belt and inner worlds

Manels – Ollassa unit of distance

Mesa Control – Central space command located on the Ollassa home world

Nua'll – Aliens who imprisoned the Swei Swee

Omnia Ships – Business owned by Alex Racine and others

Prima – New Terra's capital city

Sadesville – Defunct enclave used by first SADEs to immigrate to Haraken

SIF – Strategic Investment Fund of the Confederation SADEs

Sky tower – Méridien residences kilometers tall and supported by anti-grav technology

Sol Enclave – New name for the Sol constitutional government

TSF – Terran Security Forces

United Earth – Previous government body ruling Sol

Planets, Colonies, Moons, and Stars

Arnos – Star of the planet Libre

Bellamonde – Site of the Méridien's naval academy

Celus – Star of the planet Omnia

Cetus – Star of the planet New Terra

Daelon – Moon orbiting sixth planet of an unnamed system, last colony of the Independents

FYM-552 – System where the second sphere was located

Haraken – New name of Cetus colony in Hellébore system, home of the Harakens

Hellébore – Star of the planet Cetus, renamed Haraken

Libre – Planet invaded by Nua'll, Alex Racine rescued Independents

Méridien – Home world of Confederation

New Terra – Home world of New Terrans, fourth planet outward of
    Oistos

Oistos – Star of the planet New Terra, Alex Racine's home world

Ollassa – Vinian home world, also called World of Light

Omnia – World settled by the Dischnya, Swei Swee, SADEs, and humans

Sawa – Celus fourth planet outward, Dischnya's home world

Sawa Messa – Celus fifth planet outward, Dischnya's second world

Sol – Star of the Earthers

Vinium – System named by Killian when his scout ship was captured

Worlds of Light – Planets of the Ollassa system

Ships and Stations

Freedom – Alex's primary city-ship

Il Piacere – House Diamanté passenger liner

Last Stand – Haraken carrier

Minimum Risk – Linn's scout ship

NT *Arthur McMorris* – Alphons Jagielski's Trident

NT *Geoffrey Orlan* – Jonathan Morney's Trident, Admiral Tripping's
    flagship

NT *Lem Ulam* – Bart Fillister's Trident

No Retreat – Haraken carrier

OS *Deliverance* – Deirdre Canaan's Trident

OS *Judgment* – Lucia Bellardo's Trident

OS *Liberator* – Svetlana Valenko's Trident, and the squadron flagship

OS *Prosecutor* – Darius Guamata's Trident

OS *Redemption* – Ellie Thompson's Trident

Our People – Second city-ship

Resplendent – House Pasko liner

Rêveur – Alex's passenger liner

Rover – New Terran passenger liner

Sardi-Tallen Orbital Platform – Omnia's premier ship construction station

Scout ships – Small vessels crewed by SADEs

Sojourn – Haraken explorer ship

Sting ship – First warship constructed by the Harakens

Tanaka – Haraken sting ship

Travelers – Shuttles and fighters

Trident – Omnian tri-hulled, beam-armed warship

Vivian – Killian's scout ship

Vivian's Mirror – Killian's replacement scout ship

My Books

The Silver Ships series is available in e-book, softcover print, and audiobook versions. Please visit my website, http://scottjucha.com, for publication locations. You may also register at my website to receive email notification about the publish dates of my novels.

If you've been enjoying these series, please consider posting reviews on Amazon and Goodreads, even short ones. Reviews attract other readers and help indie authors, such as me.

The Silver Ships Series
The Silver Ships
Libre
Méridien
Haraken
Sol
Espero
Allora
Celus-5
Omnia
Vinium
Nua'll (2018)

The Pyreans
Empaths
Messinants (2018)

The Author

I've been enamored with fiction novels since the age of thirteen and long been a fan of great storytellers. I've lived in several countries overseas and in many of the US states, including Illinois, where I met my wonderful wife. My careers have spanned a variety of industries in the visual and scientific fields of photography, biology, film/video, software, and information technology (IT).

My first attempt at a novel, which I've recently retitled *The Florentine*, was a crime drama centered on the modern-day surfacing of a 110-carat yellow diamond lost during the French Revolution. In 1980, in preparation for the book, I spent two wonderful weeks researching the Brazilian people, their language, and the religious customs of Candomblé. The day I returned from Rio de Janeiro, I had my first date with my wife-to-be, Peggy Giels.

In the past, I've outlined dozens of novels, but a busy career limited my efforts to complete any of them. In early 2014, I chose to devote my efforts to writing fulltime. My first novel, *The Silver Ships*, was released in February 2015. The series, with the release of *Vinium*, numbers ten.

The new series, Pyreans, relates the tale of a third Earth colony ship and gives readers an opportunity to follow new characters, who struggle to overcome the obstacles of a world tortured by geologic upheaval. Humans are divided into camps — downsiders, stationers, spacers, and the *Belle*'s inhabitants of empaths and the discarded.

My deep appreciation goes out to the many readers who embraced the Silver Ships and Pyrean series and their characters. Thank you!

Made in the USA
San Bernardino, CA
22 November 2017